Check
to rer
www.
www.b

EDGE OF BATTLE

DALE BROWN

EDGE OF BATTLE

HarperCollins*Publishers*

HarperCollins*Publishers*
77–85 Fulham Palace Road,
Hammersmith, London W6 8JB

www.harpercollins.co.uk

Published by HarperCollins*Publishers* 2007
1

First published in the USA by
HarperCollins 2007

A catalogue record for this book
is available from the British Library

ISBN-13 978 0 00 721731 0
ISBN-10 0 00 721431 6

Set in Granjon

Printed and bound in Great Britain by
Clays Ltd, St Ives plc

be
ed,
l,
rior

CAST OF CHARACTERS

MAJOR JASON RICHTER, U.S. Army, commander Task Force TALON

DR. ARIADNA VEGA, Ph.D., deputy commander Task Force TALON

CAPTAIN FRANK "FALCON" FALCONE, USAF, operations and intelligence officer Task Force TALON

FIRST LIEUTENANT JENNIFER MCCRACKEN, USMC, deputy commander for operations Task Force TALON

CID PILOTS

HARRY DODD, Sergeant First Class, U.S. Army, Task Force TALON

MIKE TESCH, formerly of the Drug Enforcement Administration, Task Force TALON

SAMUEL CONRAD, President of the United States

SERGEANT MAJOR RAYMOND JEFFERSON, U.S. Army, National Security Adviser

THOMAS F. KINSLY, Chief of Staff

GEORGE WENTWORTH, Attorney General

KELSEY DELAINE, director of Federal Bureau of Investigation

SPECIAL AGENT JANICE PERKINS, Kelsey DeLaine's assistant and bodyguard

CHRISTOPHER J. PARKER, Secretary of State

LEON POINDEXTER, U.S. ambassador to United Mexican States

ALEXANDER KALLIS, director of National Intelligence

RUSSELL COLLIER, Secretary of Defense

GENERAL GORDON JOELSON, USAF, commander U.S. Northern Command

JEFFREY F. LEMKE, Secretary of Homeland Security

JAMES A. ABERNATHY, director of U.S. Customs and Border Protection

ANNETTE J. CASS, U.S. Attorney, southern district of California

BRUNO WATTS, FBI deputy assistant director for counterterrorism; new FBI commander of Task Force TALON

ANGELICA PIERCE, Special Agent in Charge, FBI San Diego field office

OPERATION RAMPART PERSONNEL

BRIGADIER GENERAL RICARDO LOPEZ, national deputy director of the Army National Guard, commander of Operation Rampart

GEORGE TRUJILLO, deputy director of Customs and Border Protection, deputy commander of Operation Rampart

CAPTAIN BEN GRAY, USAR, Rampart One, Boulevard California

SERGEANT MAJOR, JEREMY NORMANDIN, USAR, Rampart One

BORDER PATROL AGENTS

PAUL PURDY

ALBERT SPINELLI

ROBERT "RAIDER" O'ROURKE, nationally syndicated radio talk-show personality in Henderson, Nevada

FAND KENT, producer, Bob O'Rourke's *The Bottom Line* radio talk show

GEORGIE WAYNE, sound engineer, Bob O'Rourke's *The Bottom Line* radio talk show

COMMANDER HERMAN GEITZ, American Watchdog Project

UNITED MEXICAN STATES GOVERNMENT OFFICIALS

MS. CARMEN MARAVILLOSO, President of the United Mexican States

FELIX DÍAZ, Minister of Internal Affairs, Director-General of the Political Police

JOSÉ ELVAREZ, deputy minister of the Ministry of Internal Affairs, director of operations of the Political Police and *Sombras* (Special Investigations Unit)

HECTOR SOTELO, Minister of Foreign Affairs

GENERAL ALBERTO ROJAS, Minister of National Defense

RAFAEL NAVARRO, Attorney General

ARMANDO OCHOA, deputy consul general, United Mexican States consulate, San Diego

MAJOR GERARDO AZUETA, border task force commander, Mexican Army

LIEUTENANT IGNACIO SALINAS, company commander, Mexican Army

MASTER SERGEANT JORGE CASTILLO, Mexican Army

ERNESTO FUERZA, "Comandante Veracruz," drug and human smuggler

YEGOR VIKTORVICH ZAKHAROV, former Russian oil company executive and oligarch, military leader of the Consortium terror group

SMUGGLERS
VICTOR FLORES
MARTÍN ALVAREZ
LUIZ VASQUEZ

WEAPONS

CONDOR, an unmanned airship, resembling a seagull or large bird, with a 120-foot wingspan; built of lightweight carbon-fiber skin and Mylar; ducted prop-fan engines; maximum endurance thirty-six hours; maximum altitude ten thousand feet aboveground; maximum speed ninety knots; maximum payload two thousand pounds, including cameras, UHB radar, or air-dropped CID units.

GUOS, a grenade-launched unmanned observation system; small man-launched drones capable of carrying satellite-uplinked images; can fly up to one thousand feet aboveground for up to two hours.

GULLWING, an unmanned reconnaissance aircraft (also known as a UAV), assembled and launched from a Humvee, endurance eight hours; maximum altitude five thousand feet AGL; mini-turbojet powered; retrieved by flying into a recovery net; carries a variety of sensors including low-light TV, UHB radar, and imaging infrared; capable of transmitting images and data by satellite; can be steered from ground stations or by commands from a CID squad.

MMWR, a millimeter wave radar, capable of detecting tiny amounts of metal from long distance and even underground.

SA-14, an improved version of the Russian SA-7 man-portable surface-to-air missile; 2.2-pound warhead, maximum target range 3.6 miles, maximum target altitude ten thousand feet.

TEC-9, nine-millimeter semiautomatic pistol.

VH-71, next-generation presidential transportation helicopter, called *Marine One* when the President is on board.

ACRONYMS, ABBREVIATIONS, AND TERMINOLOGY

AG—Attorney General

AGL—above ground level

AMO—Air and Marine Operations (Department of Homeland Security)

APC—armored personnel carrier

ARTCC—air route traffic control center

ATV—all-terrain vehicle

BDU—battle dress uniform

"bent" —device or system inoperable

BORSTAR—Border Patrol Search, Trauma, and Rescue

BORTAC—Border Patrol Tactical unit

CBP—U.S. Customs and Border Protection Service

CHP—California Highway Patrol

CID—Cybernetic Infantry Device

Council of Government—Mexican presidential advisers

DAICC—Domestic Air Interdiction Coordination Center

DCI—Director of Central Intelligence

DDICE—digital distant identification and collection equipment

DHS—U.S. Department of Homeland Security

DNI—Director of National Intelligence

DRO—U.S. Deportation and Recovery Operations Service

DSS—Diplomatic Security Service

ETA—estimated time of arrival

ETE—estimated time en route

FEBA—forward edge of the battle area

FLIR—forward-looking infrared

FM—farm to market

FOL—forward operating location

GSW—gunshot wound

GUOS—grenade-launched unmanned observation system

Humvee—high mobility wheeled vehicle

HUWB—high-powered ultra wideband radar

ICE—U.S. Immigration and Customs Enforcement

INS—Immigration and Naturalization Service, changed to USCIS (see USCIS)

klick—kilometer

LZ—landing zone

MANPADS—man-portable air defense system

MMWR—millimeter-wave radar

Mode C—radio signal that reports altitude to air traffic control radar

Mode 3—radio signal that reports aircraft identification information to air traffic control radar

MOU—memorandum of understanding

NIS—(pronounced "nice") nanotransponder identification system

NORTHCOM—U.S. Northern Command

NVG—night vision goggles

OAS—Organization of American States

OHV—off-highway vehicle

OTH-B—over the horizon-backscatter long-range radar

OTMs—other than Mexicans—illegal immigrants to the United States from countries all over the world who cannot easily be deported and, because of budget shortfalls and overcrowding in detention facilities, are often released from custody with nothing more than a notice to appear (see *permiso*) before a deportation judge. Over 60 percent of OTMs fail to appear for deportation hearings and are untraceable by immigration officials.

PDA—personal digital assistant (handheld computer/organizer)

permiso (colloquial term)—order to appear before a judge for a deportation hearing. Mostly issued to illegal immigrants from countries where deportation is difficult or expensive (see OTMs).

PLF—parachute landing fall

SAC—special agent in charge

SAM—surface-to-air missile

SOP—standard operating procedures

SOW—U.S. Air Force Special Operations Wing

SUV—sport utility vehicle

TA—technical area

TEMPER—tent, modular, personnel

TFR—temporary flight restriction

Top—unit first sergeant

TZD—technical zone delta

UAV—unmanned aerial vehicle

UN—United Nations

USCIS—United States Citizenship and Immigration Service (formerly INS)

UXO—unexploded ordnance

wilco—"will comply"

REAL-WORLD NEWS
EXCERPTS

Defense Advanced Research Projects Agency (www.darpa.mil), August 2000—Human Identification at a Distance: The HumanID program objective is to develop automated multimodal surveillance technology for identifying humans at a distance, thus allowing for early warning of possible terrorist attacks. Technologies will be developed for measuring (and collecting) biometric features that will identify an individual from a distance of more than 15 feet, operating twenty-four hours per day in all weather conditions. The resulting probability of detection should be 0.99; the probability of false alarm should be 0.01 given a database of up to a million known individuals.

HumanID will focus on four essential elements or components of technical research: technology development to solve HumanID tasks, database collection, independent evaluations, and scientific experiments to assess validity of these technologies. The program will provide tools for crucial aspects of countering asymmetric threats including automatic cataloging of repeat visitors, automated detection of known suspects, accelerated interdiction, and collection of forensic evidence when attacks do occur. If successful, HumanID will make security personnel more effective in identifying people who may have harmful intent, and will allow early warning to expedite interdiction.

MEXICO PROVIDES GUIDE TO ILLEGAL IMMIGRATION—FOX News, January 5, 2005—Los Angeles—Mexican immigrants hoping to cross the Mexico-U.S. border can use an illustrated guide to help them break U.S. immigration laws and live in the United States illegally.

The thirty-two-page booklet, free with popular comic books and advertised at bus stations and government offices south of the border, comes courtesy of the Mexican government.

... The book's main focus seems to be instructing people on how to cross the border safely. For example, it warns Mexicans that when crossing the border, "thick clothing increases your weight when wet and makes it difficult to swim or float" and "if you cross in the desert, try to walk when the heat is not as intense..."

... The guide also gives advice on how to live unobtrusively in the United States, advising illegals not to beat their wives or go to loud parties because either action may attract the attention of police.

INCREASING VIOLENCE ON THE U.S.-MEXICAN BORDER—Strategic Forecasting Inc., www.stratfor.com February 3, 2005—The U.S.-Mexican border in Arizona has seen an increase in illegal activity. In a recent change of tactics, smugglers have been using snipers, who shoot at U.S. Border Patrol agents, ostensibly to provide a diversion to cover illegal border crossings. While the agents go for cover, a shipment of drugs or possibly undocumented immigrants slips through in a sport utility vehicle...

THE UNITED STATES, MEXICO, AND CROSS-BORDER BLOODSHED—Copyright © 2005, Strategic Forecasting Inc.—... [Osiel Guillen] Cardenas, who runs the Juárez-based Gulf Cartel from prison, has resolved to take over the Tijuana-based Arellano Felix cartel. To that end, he has deployed his chief enforcers—"Los Zetas" —to Tijuana. Mexican government sources say Cardenas plans to wipe out the remnants of the Arellano Felix family and its top competitor, Ismael Zambada, in one bold move, thereby giving him control of the drug trade on Mexico's Pacific coast.

. . . *Los Zetas*—who have highly skilled military experts among them—can be expected to operate with a higher degree of precision than less-capable killers. One FBI official has referred to Los Zetas as "an impressive bunch of ruthless criminals." Los Zetas also use heavy weaponry—AK-47 and AR-15 assault rifles— meaning they often have more firepower than local police. Although their brazen methods have generated a high level of alarm among law enforcement officials, Los Zeta's tactical skill and meticulous planning will make it more difficult for law enforcement to detect, track and interdict them . . .

U.S. AUTHORITIES CHARGE 18 WITH RUSSIAN WEAPON-SMUGGLING PLOT—© 2005, The Associated Press, March 15, 2005—U.S. authorities have charged 18 people with weapons trafficking, including an alleged scheme to smuggle grenade launchers, shoulder-fired missiles and other Russian military weapons into the U.S.

The arrests resulted from a year-long wiretap investigation that used a confidential informant posing as an arms trafficker selling weapons to terrorists, the office of U.S. Attorney David N. Kelley said Tuesday.

Kelley said in a statement that the defendants also are charged in a criminal complaint with conspiring to traffic in machine guns and other assault weapons, and with selling eight such weapons during the investigation . . .

MEXICO PUBLIC ANNOUNCEMENT, April 26, 2005, U.S. Department of State— . . . Violent criminal activity fueled by a war between criminal organizations struggling for control of the lucrative narcotics trade continues along the U.S.-Mexico border. This has resulted in a wave of violence aimed primarily at members of drug trafficking organizations, criminal justice officials, and journalists. However, foreign visitors and residents, including Americans, have been among the victims of homicides and kidnappings in the border region.

A power vacuum within criminal organizations resulting from the imprisonment of several of their leaders along the Mexico-U.S. border continues to contribute to a deterioration of public safety in the region. In recent months, the worst violence has been centered in the city of Nuevo Laredo in the Mexican state of Tamaulipas, where more than 30 U.S. citizens have been kidnapped and/or murdered in the past eight months and public shootouts have occurred during daylight hours near frequented shopping areas and on streets leading to the international bridges. One of the shootouts spilled onto the Mexican side of the bridge itself. Four police officers have been killed in Nuevo Laredo since March. Mexico's police forces suffer from lack of funds and training, and the judicial system is weak, overworked, and inefficient. Criminals, armed with an impressive array of weapons, know there is little chance they will be caught and punished. In some cases, assailants have been wearing full or partial police uniforms and have used vehicles that resemble police vehicles, indicating some elements of the police might be involved . . .

INCREASING DANGER ON THE U.S.-MEXICAN BORDER, © 2005, STRATFOR, www.stratfor.com, June 14, 2005—Mexican President Vicente Fox ordered Mexican army troops and federal agents to detain all 700 officers of the Nuevo Laredo police force June 13 and assume policing duties in the town, just across the Rio Grande from Laredo, Texas. The move, which came in response to a breakdown of law and order in the city, will be extended to other border towns, authorities said. It is indicative of the serious deterioration in the security situation along the U.S.-Mexican border.

... Growing anti-U.S. sentiment in Mexico, stoked by election-year rhetoric and negative publicity over a group of American vigilantes that organized its own border patrol in Arizona, also contributes to a dangerous situation for Americans on the border. To further complicate the situation, the so-called Minutemen are soon to expand their activities from Arizona into New Mexico and Texas.

... With drug wars raging on both sides of the border—and law and order broken down in Nuevo Laredo to the point in which the army has been sent in—the U.S.-Mexican border has become a dangerous place.

CATCH AND RELEASE POLICY FREES ILLEGAL ALIENS TO MOVE FREELY ABOUT THE COUNTRY, © 2005, The Associated Press, July 4, 2005—
... Since the September 11, 2001, terrorist attacks, more than 118,000 foreign nationals who were caught after sneaking over the nation's borders have walked right out of custody with a *permiso* in hand.

They were from Honduras, El Salvador, Guatemala, Brazil. But also Afghanistan, Iran, Pakistan, the Philippines, and Yemen, among 35 countries of "special interest" because of alleged sponsorship or support of terrorism.

These are the so-called OTM, or "Other Than Mexican," migrants too far from their homelands to be shipped right back. More than 70,000 have hit U.S. streets just since this past October.

... The government has no place to put all the "OTMs" while they await deportation hearings, so they are released with a *permiso,* or notice to appear in immigration court. Over the years, thousands have failed to show up, disappearing, instead, among the estimated 10 million undocumented migrants now living in America.

... Front-line officers voice concern that so many who break the law to enter the country are systematically set free. "I absolutely believe that the next attack we have will come from somebody who has come across the border illegally," says Eugene Davis, retired deputy chief of the Border Patrol sector in Blaine, Washington. "To me, we have no more border security now than we had prior to September 11. Anybody who believes we're safer, they're living in Neverland."

STRATFOR: DAILY TERRORISM BRIEF—August 2, 2005, © 2005, Strategic Forecasting Inc.—CHAOS ON THE U.S.-MEXICAN BORDER: OPPORTUNITY FOR AL QAEDA?—U.S. authorities closed the U.S. Consulate in Nuevo Laredo, Mexico, on August 1—four days after intense firefights rocked the town of more than half a million people across the Rio Grande from Laredo, Texas . . .

. . . The chaos on the border is increasing concerns within the U.S. intelligence community that al Qaeda–linked groups or other terrorists could exploit the situation and cross operatives into the United States. Al Qaeda, investigators fear, could use well-established smuggling routes to bypass the enhanced scrutiny of passengers on air traffic "no-fly" lists. From an operational security perspective, terrorists could be wondering why they should run the risk of having their documents scrutinized by outbound immigration and inbound inspectors when they can bypass all of that at the U.S.-Mexican border . . .

SUV CARRYING ILLEGAL IMMIGRANTS, DRUGS CRASHES—San Diego, California, © 2005, The Associated Press, August 18, 2005—The driver of an SUV packed with suspected illegal immigrants and nearly 700 pounds of marijuana sped from police the wrong way on Interstate 8 before crashing head-on into a California Highway Patrol car, officials said. Authorities say the incident late Wednesday was part of a pattern by smugglers who try to evade border checkpoints by veering into oncoming traffic, often at night, sometimes with their headlights off. The SUV involved had been modified [with nondeflatable silicone-filled tires] to enable it to flee more easily . . .

ICE NABS THREE AT NUKE PLANT—INSIDE ICE: Volume 2, Issue 19—Blair, Nebraska— In the latest in a series of arrests involving illegal aliens at nuclear facilities, ICE [U.S. Immigration and Customs Enforcement] special agents arrested three illegal aliens in Blair September 15 when they attempted to enter the outer secure area of the Omaha Public Power District's Fort Calhoun Nuclear Station to perform contract work at the plant for the first time.

The three men, all citizens of Mexico, had been hired by an independent contractor to perform maintenance work at the nuclear facility. As they attempted to enter a secure area of the plant, the men presented identification documents that raised the suspicions of Omaha Public Power District employees. They contacted ICE special agents for assistance, who responded and arrested the men after determining that they were illegally present in the United States . . .

BORDER CROSSING DEATHS SET A 12-MONTH RECORD—By Richard Marosi, *L.A. Times* Staff Writer—October 1, 2005—A record 460 migrants died crossing the U.S.-Mexico border in the last year, a toll pushed higher by unusually hot temperatures and a shift of illegal migration routes through remote deserts.

The death total from October 1, 2004, through September 29, [2005,] surpassed the previous record of 383 deaths set in 2000, according to statistics compiled by the U.S. Border Patrol.

The dead were mostly Mexicans, many from the states of Mexico, Guanajuato and Veracruz, but also from the impoverished southern states of Oaxaca and Chiapas. Migrants continue to die in automobile accidents and from drownings while crossing waterways into California and Texas, but 261, or more than half the total, perished while crossing the Arizona deserts, the busiest illegal immigrant corridor along the nation's two-thousand-mile border with Mexico.

The migrants, herded across the border by smugglers, have been traversing increasingly desolate stretches of desert as the Border Patrol cuts off more accessible routes . . .

EDGE OF BATTLE

PROLOGUE

The youngest child in the group, an eleven-month-old girl, died
sometime before midnight, a victim of a rattlesnake bite the day
before, suffered when her mother set the baby down in the darkness near an unseen nest. The infant was buried in the desert of
southern California, just a few miles north of the border that they
had worked so hard to cross. Two other children, one a four-year-
old girl, the other an eleven-year-old boy, wept for their infant sib-
ling, but their bodies were too dehydrated from spending almost
two days in the desert to shed any tears.

It was all the same to Victor Flores, the seventeen-year-old *coyote,* or human smuggler, escorting the group of twelve migrants
across the southern California border. It was sad, of course, the
baby dying—he prayed with the others for the baby's safe deliver-
ance into heaven, hugged the mother, and wept with her. But one
less child meant one less cry in the night to alert the Border Patrol,
one less reason to slow down on their long trek across the desert—
and, of course, there were no refunds. It was five hundred dollars
a head, Federal Highway 2 in Mexico to Interstate 10 in the
United States of America—no refunds, cash on the table.

Besides, he thought ruefully, children had no business out here. He was seeing lots more mothers and their children these days on these trips across the border, not just the men. That was a frightening trend. Things were bad in Mexico, and probably had been forever, but typically the family stayed in Mexico, the father went to search for work, and he returned months later with cash; he stayed long enough to crank out another child or two, then departed again. The exodus of women and children from Mexico meant that things were only getting worse there.

Not that the economic, sociological, or political situation was looking any better in the United States these days, but it was a heck of a lot better than in Mexico.

The calendar said it was spring, but daytime temperatures had soared above ninety degrees Fahrenheit every day since the group was dropped off beside Federal Highway 2 about ten miles south of the border. They camped when Victor told them they needed to stop, crossed Interstate 8 on foot at night when Victor told them to—it was much easier to see oncoming cars at night than in the daytime, where heat shimmering off the pavement made even huge big rigs invisible until just a few hundred feet away—and stopped and made shelters with their spare clothing in dusty gullies and washes when Victor said it was time to hide. Flores had a sixth sense about danger and almost always managed to get his *pollos* (or "chickens," what the coyotes called their clientele) into hiding before the Border Patrol appeared—he even somehow managed to evade helicopters and underground sensors.

He knew his route well, so they traveled at night. That usually meant a more comfortable journey, but in the arid, cloudless air the desert released its sun-baked warmth quickly at night, and now the temperature was in the low forties. The *pollos* baked during the day and shivered at night. There was no way around it. It was a hard journey, but the work and the money at the end of the trail hopefully made the sacrifice worth it.

Victor's specialty was the El Centro Border Patrol region of eastern Imperial County, between Yuma, Arizona, and El Centro,

California—what the coyotes called the Moñtanas del Chocolate, or Chocolate Mountain region of southern California, an area of roughly two thousand square miles. He led a small group of migrants all the way north to Interstate 10 somewhere between Blythe and Indio, California. With decent weather and a cooperative group, Victor could escort a group of twelve along that route to his drop-off point in two days, sometimes less, with almost one hundred percent probability of success.

For an additional fee, he would take *pollos* as far as they desired—Los Angeles, Las Vegas, Sacramento, Reno, even Dallas, Texas, if they desired. But the real money was in the short trek across the deserts of southern California. Most migrants hooked up with friends or relatives quickly once they got to the farming communities of the Coachella or Imperial Valleys or along the interstate highways, and Victor's prices for travel beyond southern California were steep. It was safer traveling with him than trying to take the bus or trains, since the Border Patrol checked IDs of Hispanic-looking individuals frequently on those two conveyances. Victor charged mightily for the safety and convenience of longer-distance trips, but it was well worth it.

Victor never bragged about his skills at evading the authorities, but he never denied them either—it was good for business. But he was not gifted with any sort of extrasensory perception. He was successful because he was smart, patient, and didn't get greedy, unlike many of his friends who also worked the migrant underground railroads. Where other coyotes took twenty migrants in more conspicuous vans and rental trucks, Victor took a maximum of twelve in smaller vehicles; when others raced and took unnecessary risks to do the job in one or two days and were caught at least half the time, Victor was careful, took extra time, and made it 95 percent of the time.

Many thought he was good at his job because he was a *bebé del angel,* or "angel baby," born in the United States. Perhaps most folks wouldn't consider being born in an artichoke field in Riverside County near Thermal, California an angelic thing, but Victor had something that his friends didn't have—a *real* American birth certificate.

About ten miles north of the border, just before daybreak, Victor came upon his "nest," and after removing a few branches and rocks and a sand-covered canvas tarp, his pride and joy was revealed—a 1993 Chevy Suburban with four-wheel drive. Before doing anything else, he started inspecting the outside of the vehicle.

"*¿Qué usted está haciendo?* What are you doing?" one of the male *pollos* asked in Spanish, with a definite Eastern European accent. This guy was somewhat different than the others. Victor at first thought he was a *federale,* but he had paid cash and observed all of the security precautions without question or hesitation. He wore sunglasses all the time except when walking at night, so it was impossible to see his eyes. His hands were rough and his skin toughened by the sun, but he didn't carry himself like a farmworker.

Of course, more and more migrants using Victor's service were *not* farmworkers. This guy looked tough, like he was accustomed to fighting or violence, but at the same time he was not pushy or edgy—he seemed very much in control of himself, capable of springing into action but very content not to do so right now. An Army deserter, maybe, or some sort of fugitive from justice or prison escapee trying to sneak back into the United States. Victor vowed to keep an eye on him—but *he* was not his biggest concern now.

"*Comprobación primero,*" Victor replied. Very few of his clients ever spoke to him, which was probably best—this was business, pure and simple. He believed these were his people, even though he was an American, but he wasn't in this line of work to help his fellow Mexicans—he was doing this to make money. Besides, in this business, except for the question "How much to L.A.?" or "How much to the I-10?" the only other ones who ever asked questions were *federales.* "Checking first. Maybe the Border Patrol inspected or bugged my *yate,* or the *lobos* sabotaged it."

The man looked at the beat-up Suburban and chuckled when he heard Victor refer to it as his "yacht." *"Lobos?"*

"Los contrabandistas," Victor replied.

"But *you* are a smuggler," the man said.

Victor smiled a pearly white smile and corrected himself, *"Los contrabandistas malvados.* "The *evil* smugglers." I smuggle honest workers who want to do honest work, never drugs or weapons."

The man nodded, a half-humorous, half-skeptical expression on his face. "A man of principle, I see."

Principles? Victor had never thought of himself like that—he wasn't even sure what it meant. But if it meant *not* moving drugs or weapons across the border, he supposed he had some. He shrugged and went back to work, noticing that neither the man nor any of the other *pollos* offered to help him. Yep, just business. He was the driver; they were his passengers.

After not discovering any evidence of tampering, Victor uncovered a second hiding place and pulled out a canvas bag containing a battery and ignition components. He filled the battery with water from his water jugs, quickly reassembled the parts in his SUV, and fired it up; the *pollos* let out a little cheer when the big vehicle started amid a disturbingly large cloud of black smoke. With his clients' help, he eased the truck out of the depression, and they clambered aboard quickly and wordlessly, thankful they didn't have to walk for a while.

They followed dirt roads and trails for several miles, then crossed the Coachella Canal and entered Patton Valley. A large portion of the environmentally sensitive Glamis Dunes desert was closed to vehicles—and the off-highway vehicle enthusiasts, afraid of losing all their favorite driving sites, patrolled the off-limits areas just as well as the police and park rangers—so Victor was careful to avoid the off-limits areas that trapped so many other coyotes. He stayed on dirt roads and trails, being careful to keep moving and not pull off into a parking area because he didn't have a camping permit and anyone stopping in a camping area had to display a mirror hanger or be cited on the spot. He crossed Wash

Road north of Ogilby Camp Off-Highway Vehicle (OHV) Area, emerged onto Ted Kipf Road, and headed northwest toward the town of Glamis, occasionally pulling off into a hidden OHV trailering area and mixing in with the dune buggy riders when his senses told him patrols were nearby. His trusty "land yacht" did well in the sandy desert and low hills of Patton Valley.

A few *pollos* got out at Glamis, ahead of schedule, but it was entirely up to them. Glamis was near the fertile Coachella Valley farming region, and there was work around if you knew where to ask—but of course, there were plenty of Border Patrol agents hereabouts as well. Victor stopped long enough to gas up and let the two migrants out, then hurried back onto the road.

He took Highway 78 north around the southern end of the Chocolate Mountain Gunnery Range, then exited on Imperial Gables Road. A turn onto Lowe Road, past Main Street into the town of Imperial Gables, then a left onto a dirt road northbound, through fields of every imaginable kind of produce. They made several turnoffs and stops, sometimes prompted by a signal from a worker in the fields that the Border Patrol was nearby, but most times by Victor's sense of nearby trouble. After nearly twenty miles of negotiating the dirt farm roads, they emerged onto Wiley Well Road, and it was an easy cruise north to the intersection with Chuckwalla Valley Road, just south of Interstate 10, shortly after sunset.

Unlike Imperial Dunes and Sand Hills, this area was lush and green thanks to the series of irrigation canals that crisscrossed the area—right up to the areas beside the freeway that had no irrigation, where the earth immediately turned to its natural hard-baked sand. There was a closed fruit and vegetable stand, a self-serve gas station, and a large dirt open area with a few portable bathrooms where truckers could turn around and park for the night, awaiting another load. Victor did not pull into the turnaround area, but stayed just off Chuckwalla Valley Road near an irrigation control valve sticking out of the fields near the road, trying to make himself look like a repairman or farmer.

"Pull up there," the military-looking man said, pointing to the truck parking area. True to form, he was still wearing his sunglasses.

"No, señor. *Demasiado visible.*"

The man nodded toward the parking area. "They don't seem to think it's too conspicuous," he said. There were four produce trailers parked there, two tandem rigs, a beat-up old pickup that looked like it belonged to a ranch foreman . . .

. . . and a large brown and green panel truck with fat off-road tires that Victor recognized, and his warning alarms immediately started sounding.

"There is my ride," the man said. "It looks like *mis amigos* have already arrived. Take me over there."

"You can walk, sir," Victor said.

"*¿Nos asustan?*" the man asked, smiling derisively.

Victor said nothing. He didn't like being insulted, but getting in a customer's face was bad for business. He ignored the remark about his courage, took a clipboard, put on a straw cowboy hat, and went out beside the irrigation manifolds sticking out of the ground to make it look like he was taking water pressure readings. He carefully looked up and down Chuckwalla Valley Road and Interstate 10, then waved at his Suburban, and the rest of the migrants quickly jumped out. The mother of the dead baby girl gave him a hug as she stepped past him, and they all had satisfied albeit tired and worrisome expressions on their faces. Within seconds, they had disappeared into the fields.

It was a tough business, Victor thought. One out of every twenty *pollos* he dropped off near the interstate highway, mostly young children or older women, would be killed trying to cross it. Two out of this group of ten would be caught by the Border Police within a matter of days. They would be taken to a processing center in Yuma or El Centro; photographed, fingerprinted, ID'd if possible, and questioned. If they resisted or complained, they would be taken to the Border Patrol detention facility at El Centro, Yuma, or San Diego for booking on federal immigration violation charges. If they were smart, stayed cool, and said, "We are just here to work," they would be treated fairly well by the Americans. They would be fed, clothed if necessary, given a fast medical checkup, and within a few hours taken to the border crossing at Mexicali or Tecate and turned over to Mexican authorities with their possessions.

Their real troubles would begin then. If they or their families had money, they could pay their "bail" by bribing their way out of jail on the spot; if not, they would be taken to jail until they could raise "bail." Their clothes and all possessions would be taken away, they would be given prison rags to wear, and they would serve as virtual slaves for the *federales* in any number of menial, dangerous, or even criminal tasks—anything from road crews to prostitution to drug running to robbery, anything to raise the "bail" money and secure a release.

To Victor's dismay, the tough-looking man was still there beside the Suburban by the time Victor made sure his *pollos* were on their way. Victor said nothing as he walked around to get in, but the man asked, "Where do they go?"

"No sé," Victor replied. "To work, I suppose."

"Well, well, it's Victor Flores, late as usual," he heard. It was none other than Ernesto Fuerza, probably the most notorious and successful smuggler on the U.S.-Mexico border. Tall, young, good-looking, wearing a dark military-looking utility uniform without any badges or patches, black fatigue cap over a black-and-white patterned bandana, long hair and goatee, and well-cared-for military-style boots laced all the way up, Fuerza had successfully made a worldwide reputation for himself not as a criminal, but as an entrepreneur, satisfying the needs of Americans and Mexican immigrants alike . . .

. . . and also because Fuerza had no compunction whatsoever to abandon his *pollos* if the *federales* closed in on him. It was widely suspected that Fuerza had ditched one of his trucks filled with migrants in the middle of the desert and escaped—except the authorities never showed up until days later, to find over fifty migrants dead inside from heatstroke.

Fuerza nodded to the European. "I told you, it would have been better for you to come with me, Señor Zakharov. *Dovol'nyi Vy bezopasny, polkovnik.*"

"We speak only Spanish here, señor," the man named Zakharov said in Spanish. "See that you or your men do not forget again or I may have to cancel our contract." Fuerza lowered his eyes but offered no other apology. "Any difficulties, señor?" he asked in a low, menacing voice.

"Of course not. Everything according to plan, exactly as promised. It would be better if we departed right away."

Fuerza scowled at Victor. "He made us wait too long in this area, which could easily alert the Border Patrol."

"I thought you said this location was secure."

"We took precautions," Fuerza said. "But if young Flores here would learn to get his ass in gear and be on time, we wouldn't have any concerns at all. Next time, Señor Zakharov, you should come with me."

"It was operationally dangerous to all go in one vehicle," the man named Zakharov said. The little hairs on the back of Victor's neck began to stand up. This was no ordinary migrant-worker smuggling job, nor even a fugitive entry—these guys looked and acted as if they were on a mission. Something was amiss here, he decided, and the sooner he was gone from here, the better. He was extremely relieved when Zakharov said, "No matter. Let us be on our way." He reached behind him, and Victor thought the shit was going to hit then—but to his surprise, Zakharov pulled out a hundred-dollar bill from his pocket and handed it to Victor. "*Buen trabajo, señor*. 'Good job.' Perhaps we will meet again. I am sure this will buy your absolute silence." Victor managed a polite nod and accepted the money with a shaking hand.

"Buy yourself a life, Flores," Fuerza said as he spun on a heel and left with the two men. Victor got into his Suburban as fast as he could without looking like he was panicking.

Fuerza and the others had just crossed Wiley Well Road and were almost back at the panel truck when suddenly a white-and-green Border Patrol van pulled up and parked directly behind it, blue, red, and yellow lights flashing. Two Border Patrol agents got out of the van. The agent on the driver's side had a microphone to his lips and was aiming the vehicle's spotlight in the other hand; his partner had a large portable spotlight in one and his other was filled with plastic handcuffs. *"La atención, ésta es la frontera de Estados Unidos patrulla,"* the first agent's voice said over the vehicle's loudspeaker.

Victor was about to start up the Suburban and jam it into reverse, hoping to get away from the area, but the headlights and flashing lights of a second Border Patrol van suddenly appeared in his rearview mirror, blocking his exit. *"Ésta es la frontera patrulla!"* another voice said over the loudspeaker from the van behind him. *"¡Usted en el* Suburban*, puso su reparte la ventana, ahora!"*

Shit, Victor cursed at himself, this is unbelievable! He was about to get popped with Ernesto Fuerza, the biggest coyote in Mexico, and a mean-looking dude who looked like a big-time terrorist on a hair trigger. He stuck both hands out of his window. Spotlights began moving in his direction. Damn, it was all over. Victor looked in his side mirror and thought he saw a few of his *pollos* in the back of the Border Patrol van behind him. That was worse—they would finger him as their smuggler just to show cooperation with the authorities. He was screwed.

"You two, turn around, kneel down, hands behind your head," the first agent ordered in Spanish over the loudspeaker. Fuerza and Zakharov did as they were told. When they complied, the agent radioed, "You inside the truck, get away from the door and get down on your knees. *No resista.*" His partner stepped up to the truck, inspected the latch, found it unlocked, undogged it, and moved back to the van. "You inside the truck, lift open the door slowly. *Ponga sus manos en su cabeza y no salga del vehículo hasta ordenado para hacer tan.* Repeat, 'Put your hands on your head and do not exit the vehicle until ordered to do so.' "

The lift door to the truck began to slowly open, and both agents carefully directed their spotlights inside. As Victor watched, a familiar-looking Border Patrol agent swept his spotlight inside Victor's Suburban, opened the driver's door, grabbed Victor's left wrist, pulled it around outside the window frame, and then wrapped a plastic handcuff strap around both wrists, securing Victor to the door. "We meet again, eh, Victor?" U.S. Border Patrol agent Paul Purdy said in Spanish, "*La tercera vez es el encanto.* 'Stay put and relax,' okay, partner? We'll do the drivin' from now on."

"I have nothing to do with any of this, Agent Purdy," Victor said in perfect English. "I'm just here taking a nap. You know very well I'm an American. I've got ID."

"Save it for your arrest statement, Victor," Purdy said. Unlike many of the veteran Border Patrol agents in this sector, Purdy was tall, rather boyish, and friendly, with an old-fashioned "flat-top" haircut and a silver-gray mustache. He was somewhere in his mid- to late fifties, old for a field agent of today but probably rather typical of the breed from a generation earlier. "Two of your recent clients already gave you up. Now shut up and just relax, okay, amigo? You've probably been on the road a couple days—take it easy. Besides, you know I'll tell the prosecutors anythin' you tell me now, so if you're lyin' you'll be caught in a lie, and that'll make it worse for you." Purdy and the other agent from the second unit started walking toward Fuerza's truck, spotlights scanning every inch of the outside.

Victor could see just the very far left edge of the inside of the truck, but it was obvious that it was packed full with migrants. He could see a woman and two men with work clothes standing in the open door, and judging by the way they were being jostled from behind, it seemed like they were being pressed by many more *pollos* in there. "You persons standing in the door, get down on your knees slowly and put your hands on your head." The first agent put the public address microphone down and reached into the van for the radio mike, obviously requesting more vans to take all of the migrants away. Victor could hear the radio request from the van behind him and the dispatcher's response.

"Christ, looks like we got ourselves a long night ahead of us," Purdy said, reaching behind him for his bundle of nylon hand-cuffs stuffed into his utility belt. "We'd better . . ."

At that instant, all hell seemed to break loose right in front of him.

Several migrants, the ones standing in the open door, suddenly flew out of the van, landing headfirst on the hard-baked dirt. Men and women screamed, and spotlight beams darted in every direction. More screaming . . . and then heavy automatic gunfire erupted. It seemed as if dozens of yellow tracer lines zipped out from inside the truck, focusing on the two Border Patrol agents behind the vehicle.

"*Holy Christ!*" Purdy swore. Both men ducked almost to the ground as the automatic gunfire rang out, dropping their hand-cuffs and spotlights. "*Split up and take cover!*" He dashed off to the left; the other agent half-rolled, half-stumbled to the right. "*Code ninety-nine, code ninety-nine!*" Victor heard Paul Purdy's voice coming from the van's radio as he spoke on a portable transceiver. "Patrol One-Seven, *shots fired, shots fired,* Chuckwalla and Wiley Well Road, south of I-10, west of Blythe. Get someone out here, *now,* we're under heavy fire!"

Victor watched in absolute horror as at least ten men, dressed in black and carrying military-looking rifles, jumped out of the back of the truck. Two of them advanced on the first two Border Patrol agents and fired single shots into both of them from point-blank range. He could see that all of them were wearing black ski masks and gloves and combat boots. Several of them advanced toward Victor, rifles at the ready.

Suddenly there were several shots fired from the right from Purdy's partner. One of the attackers was hit, but he did not go down, and he swept the vegetation line with automatic gunfire.

"*Get out of there, Bob!*" Victor heard Purdy scream. "*Run!* They're wearing body armor! Get away! Hide in the fields! I called for backup! They'll be here in five minutes!"

"Cover me, Paul!" yelled the second agent.

"*No . . . !*" Just then a loud *bang!* and a blinding flash of light erupted in the fields, and Purdy's partner began rolling on the ground, arms covering his eyes and ears, screaming from the effects of the flash-bang grenade. Another attacker ran up and fired a three-round burst into the agent, immediately silencing his screams of pain.

At that instant, Purdy broke cover and ran for Victor, diving behind the Suburban's door just as a hail of bullets flew past. He skidded to a stop like a base runner sliding into third base, and in a flash he had a knife in his hands and had cut off Victor's plastic handcuffs. "Get going, Victor!" Purdy ordered, his sidearm in his hands.

"You . . . you saved me, Agent Purdy . . ."

"We're both going to be dead in ten seconds if you don't *move!*" Purdy shoved Flores behind him, fired three shots, then turned, picked up Victor by the back of his trousers, and hauled him up toward the Border Patrol van. He threw Victor behind the van, then opened the vehicle's doors. "*¡Usted adentro! ¡Salga! ¡Ahora salga!*" he shouted. The woman and the boy inside the van cowered in fear on the floor. "Victor! Help me get these people . . ."

His voice was cut off as bullets ripped into his back. Purdy gurgled, his mouth opened like a dying fish, his eyes rolled up inside his head, and he pitched forward and rolled into a dry ditch.

"*Vy proverjaete dlja bol'she veschestv?*" a voice shouted. Victor didn't understand a word—it was a language he had never heard before—European, he thought, but not German or French.

"*Sí,*" another voice responded in Spanish, much closer. "*¡Y hable español, usted idiota!* Now check that truck for any other surprises!" Shit, Victor swore, they were coming for *him*. He was behind the van, too scared to decide what to do. If he ran left he would have to cross the ditch, a road, and the freeway; if he ran right, he would have to jump over the irrigation pipe and a wide clearing before reaching the fields; if he ran back down the farm road, he'd be an easy target. He heard footsteps and the clicking and clattering of gun mechanisms as the attacker reloaded. One voice was getting very close.

"We've spent too much time here already!" a gunman shouted.

"*¡Cierre para arriba! ¡Me estoy apresurando!*" The gunman was *right beside him!* Victor heard the attacker searching the Border Patrol agent's body, probably removing weapons, ammunition, IDs, and radios; then the attacker opened the hood of the Suburban.

"*¿Es bueno ir?*"

"*No, es tiro.*"

"*¡Cabron!* I told you not to shoot the damned truck!"

"*¡Carajo!* I was under fire. I . . ." The gunmen stopped, and Victor heard the upraised rifle. "*¡Hey, hay alguien aquí!*"

This is it, Victor thought. He froze in place and closed his eyes tightly, moving his lips in a silent prayer, waiting for the heavy-caliber bullets to blow his brains into a million pieces. A few moments later, he heard two gunshots . . .

. . . but *he* wasn't shot. He heard a loud, anguished woman's scream, then two more gunshots. "*Dos pollos en la furgoneta. Ningún problema,*" the gunman shouted. A few more moments later, the gunmen were gone.

Victor stayed motionless until he heard no more vehicle sounds. When all was quiet, he rose and looked into the ditch beside the farm road. Paul Purdy was one of the few good guys on the U.S. Border Patrol—he really seemed to want to help the migrants, not just round them up. He went down into the ditch and saw the three large-caliber bullet holes in Purdy's back, and he was afraid to touch him anymore. The body was twitching and heaving grotesquely.

The Border Patrol was no match for these gunmen, Victor thought. Those bullet holes were massive—the exit wounds would be many times that size. Purdy was definitely a goner. The other agents would be here shortly; they would know what to do with Agent Purdy.

He stepped out of the ditch and looked inside the Border Patrol van. With horror he recognized the two dead migrants: the woman who had thanked him when she was dropped off after their safe journey, and her eleven-year-old son. He would have been old enough to identify the attackers to the authorities, so of course he had to be eliminated too.

That boy didn't deserve to die—all he did was accompany his mother to America in the search for work, searching for a better life. Victor was the one who deserved a bullet in the head. It was his fault, he thought bitterly, that all these people died at the hands of that murderous bastard Fuerza.

Unbidden, the child in Victor Flores finally reemerged, and he began to cry just as loudly and sorrowfully as he did when he was a child. He sank to his knees, emotionally and physically spent.

After several long moments of uncontrolled sobbing, his innate sense of danger rang loud and clear, and he jumped to his feet. The Border Patrol was on its way, he could feel it, and he took off running down the dirt road, parallel to the irrigation pipe. He knew enough not to try running through the fields, because the Border Patrol's infrared cameras could pick him out from a mile away. He ran about two hundred yards, then immediately turned left toward the freeway. In the pitch-black darkness, he made out a shallow culvert. It was small, but he managed to slip inside . . .

. . . moments before he heard sirens approaching, then saw the impossibly bright light from a helicopter-mounted spotlight. He scrambled deeper inside the culvert, clawing frantically at every rock, piece of garbage, and bit of soil he could to find room to wriggle in. Victor didn't have enough room to turn around to see if his feet and legs were all the way inside the opening—if they weren't, the Border Patrol agents would be on him within minutes, guided in by the helicopter's observer.

But he had made it. The sound of the helicopter moved away, as did the sirens. When he thought it was safe, he tried to snake his way backward, but he couldn't move. He had no choice but to go forward. After almost twenty minutes of crawling, he found himself on the other side of the culvert, on the north side of the eastbound lane of Interstate 10. He knew enough not to try to cross the highway—agents would be scanning the highway with night vision equipment. He also knew he could not stay there—the Border Patrol would be quickly setting up a perimeter around the murder scene.

He crawled on his belly in the sandy median between the east and west lanes of the interstate highway, praying that the sand and dirt that covered him from head to toe would allow him to blend in with the earth. A few minutes later he came across a culvert on the westbound lane, and he crawled in. This one was a bit larger, and he found it easy to crawl to the other side. He found another irrigation pipe and decided to follow it, pausing to hide behind a concrete support or valve whenever he heard any vehicles approaching. As his eyes adapted to the dark, he spotted several barns and other service buildings nearby in the fields, but he dared not try to enter any of them because he knew that's the first place the police would look for him.

After almost an hour of nearly continuous running, interspersed with frantic searches for hiding places, he came across a knoll and a service road that crossed the westbound lane of the interstate. His throat was completely dry, and he was becoming dizzy from dehydration and exertion. He saw several men sitting on the side of the service road, speaking Spanish and passing a large bottle of something in a paper bag back and forth between them. He would only stay for a second, he told himself—one sip of whatever they had, that was all. He started to stand up and raised his arms to flag them down . . .

. . . then instinctively dropped to the ground—just as a sheriff's patrol car, slowly and quietly cruising down the service road on the other side of the interstate, turned on its red flashing lights. "¡No muévase! ¡Este es la policía! ¡Levántese con su arriba las manos! ¡Tengo un K-9!" came the order from the car's loudspeaker.

Oh shit, a *dog!* Victor didn't hesitate. He crawled into the field to his right, took a few moments to find the deepest, smelliest open furrow he could, then began to scoop soil on top of himself. In moments he had completely covered himself in coarse, sandy loam, stinking of fresh fertilizer and decaying vegetation. If the men tried to run and they let the dog go, he was caught.

But the men didn't run. Victor could hear bits and pieces of conversation: it turned out all the men had identity cards and lived
nearby—they may have been illegals, but the Riverside County
Sheriff's Department rarely detained undocumented workers
who were minding their own business. If they tried to arrest even
a third of them, their jails would be full to bursting, Victor knew.
The questioning took some time, but the sheriff's deputy never let
his dog loose, and eventually the patrol car departed.

Not long afterward, Victor rose up from the putrid stench of
the furrow when he heard the workers leaving. He was shivering
from a combination of thirst, hunger, fear, and adrenaline. He
didn't want to, but he heard himself call out to the workers, "Hey,
amigos. *Espere, por favor.*"

Each of the men instantly produced a weapon—pocket knives,
a tire iron, a tine from a tractor-pulled rake, and an ax handle.
"*¿Quién es ello?*" one of them called out.

"My name is Victor, Victor Flores. I need help."

"Victor? *El coyote?*" another asked.

"*Sí.*"

"Victor! What's happening, my man?" The older man with the
tire iron ran over to him. "I am Jorge. You brought me and my
brothers across the border many times, my friend." He handed
Victor a bottle of warm malt liquor; Victor nearly puked on it, but
he gulped down a few mouthfuls. "What has happened to you?"

"We must get out of here, Jorge," one of the other workers said.
"The sheriff will be back."

"Shut up, Carlos. This man has helped me more than you ever
have." Jorge looked at Victor carefully and said, "They say there
was a shooting back there. Were you involved in that, Victor?"

"Let's get out of here, dammit!"

"Look, Jorge, help me," Victor said. "I was not involved in the
shooting, but the ones responsible will find me if I'm caught by
the police." He produced the hundred-dollar bill the one called
Zakharov had given him. "This is all I have, but it's yours if you
help me."

The one named Carlos licked his lips and made a step toward the money, sensing its value even in the darkness, but Jorge blocked his way. *"Vete a hacer punetas, puta avara!"* he swore. "Victor has helped me many times in the past—now I will help him." He turned to Victor and said, "We are waiting for a ride to a farm in Indian Wells, my friend. We can take you as far as that."

"Gracias, amigo," Victor said, holding out the money to him.

"Keep your money, Victor—you may need it later," Jorge said. "Just tell me you were not involved in a shooting."

"I saw what happened," Victor said. "A group of Ernesto Fuerza's *pollos* killed four Border Patrol agents and some migrants. I . . . I got away."

"¡Mi Díos!" one of the workers gasped. "Comandante Veracruz? He attacked *la Migra?*"

"Him and a *pollo,* a big guy."

"The fight for freedom and liberty from American repression must be underway!" the worker said happily. "Comandante Veracruz has been calling for the workers of the world to rise up and resist the American oppressors! He must have raised an army and the fight is beginning!"

"Shut up, you idiot," another worker said. To Jorge, he said, "You cannot let him travel with us—we will all be taken to prison or killed by the Border Patrol in retaliation if he is caught with us!"

"I said Victor will go with us, and he shall," Jorge said. He looked at Victor. "But Carlos is right, my friend—it is too dangerous for you to stay with us."

"I won't," Victor said. "Indian Wells would be fine. I can find my way from there."

About an hour later, a large produce truck stopped near the service road overpass, and the men piled in. No one spoke to Victor for the rest of the trip. When the truck stopped and everyone got out, no one at all said a word—they just walked off toward their destination, none of them expecting Victor to follow them. He didn't.

He watched the sunrise as he lay against a rock about two hundred meters away from Route 74 outside Indian Wells—secretly he hoped the rock hid a rattlesnake or some other desert predator that would just put him out of his misery. But thinking of suicide was sinful, an affront to Jesus the savior, and he immediately regretted those thoughts.

Instead, he thought about going home. He was born not far from here, and he had not been back in many months. Technically Thermal was not his real "home," since his parents were migrants from Mexico and he didn't have a real home, but he always considered the fertile, expansive Coachella Valley his home, and that's where he thought he should go. He knew he shouldn't risk it—he was an American citizen, so he assumed the government knew a lot about him, including his place of birth and the names and addresses of his closest living relatives, so that's where they were sure to look for him—but he was tired, bone-tired, and still more scared than he had ever felt in his entire life. He had to do something, or the fear would surely cause him to go out of his mind. After a few more minutes' consideration, he got up and started walking toward the sun rising over the Orocopia Mountains, toward home . . . and, hopefully, some rest.

The air was crisp, clean, and not yet hot; there was a gentle breeze blowing from the west that actually seemed to help him as he headed east. Yet the horrible, stupefying stench of death and guilt encircled his head like cigar smoke, and would, Victor was certain, remain with him for the rest of his life.

CHAPTER 1

"Don't talk to me about bigotry, xenophobia, or racism," Bob O'Rourke said even before the country-western bumper music faded completely away. "Don't you *dare* call this show and call me a racist. I'm mad enough to chew nails right now, my friends, and I might just lose my temper."

Fand Kent, Bob O'Rourke's producer and call screener on the top-rated nationally syndicated talk radio show *The Bottom Line,* smiled broadly as she turned the gain down on her headphones. If you looked up the term type-A personality in the dictionary, you might find Bob O'Rourke's picture there. He was *always* headstrong, dynamic, animated, energized—but he was even more so behind the microphone. During their one-hour production meeting before each show in Bob's office, he had the usual array of national newspapers stacked up on his desk and his ever-present tablet PC notebook ready to take electronic notes, but today when she walked in for the meeting there were just as many newspapers on the floor, and crumpled up and tossed toward the wastebasket.

Bob O'Rourke's loud, deep, rapid-fire voice with just a slight Texas twang in it was exactly opposite of his physical appearance, which Bob carefully worked to conceal (and which cost the jobs of a few other producers when they slipped up and released unflattering descriptions of their boss): he was five six and weighed one-forty soaking wet, with thin black hair, a thin neck, very light skin, despite living in a town with eleven months of sunshine a year, and rather delicate-looking features. He was so self-conscious of his physical stature that he wore a cowboy hat, boots, and sunglasses all the time, even in the studio, and had trained his voice to become deeper. Some might call it a "Napoleon complex," others might call it ego and vanity carried to the extreme. Fand Kent knew enough to keep her mouth shut whenever that subject was broached. You never knew when a rival producer or media reporter was nearby.

"If you ask me, my friends," O'Rourke went on, "this attack, this assault, this brutal *assassination* is every bit as serious and troubling as the terror attacks in San Francisco, Houston, and Washington in recent months. Don't give me that look, Fonda. Don't you *dare* roll your eyes at me! You know what I'm talking about!"

Fand was busy with the phones and her computers and hadn't even looked up at him, but it didn't matter—he constantly accused her of disagreeing with his comments and ideas, which were all part of the show. She was smart enough never to let him know her true opinions.

"I know, I know, it's not Fonda, it's 'Fand,' the Celtic goddess of truth, goodness, happiness, understanding, and Kumbaya, or some such nonsense that you were named after. To me, it sounds like 'Fonda,' another liberal tree-hugging 'everyone be happy let's all get along' character, so that's what I'm going to call you. I'm warning you, Fonda, the O'Rourke trap is open and you're one step away from getting chomped, young lady." Fand only shook her head and smiled as she went about her work.

"I am not talking about numbers of dead or injured, my friends," he went on to his worldwide radio audience. "I'm not talking about weapons of mass destruction. I am talking about the enormity of the attack, the audacity, the sheer brazenness of it.

You liberals think that an attack against the United States has to kill hundreds or thousands of persons, or law enforcement officers killed in the line of duty aren't to be considered victims of an 'attack.' Well, my friends, I don't.

"In case you don't know what I'm talking about here, in case you've been living under a rock or hugging a tree or counting snail darters in Lake Mead with your head underwater and your brains up your butt, I'll bring the ignoramuses in the audience up to speed," O'Rourke went on. "Yesterday evening, four United States Border Patrol agents were gunned down just off Interstate 10 between Blythe and Indio, California. No, wait, just hold on. 'Gunned down' is too soft, too gentle, too Fonda. Let's call it what it was: they were *slaughtered*. They were shot to death by automatic gunfire as they were making an immigration stop. These men were *executed*. And for what? For enforcing the immigration and border security laws of the United States of America, that's what.

"The assassins didn't stop there, my friends, oh no, not by a long shot. They killed a total of ten Mexican nationals, including a pregnant woman and an *eleven-year-old* boy. The killers then made off with a Border Patrol vehicle. Incredible. Simply incredible. Horrifying is more like it. This is the worst killing in the line of duty in the history of the Border Patrol."

As if he needed something to get him even more hopped up, O'Rourke took a handful of chocolate-covered espresso beans and popped them into his mouth before continuing: "So what's the status of the hunt for the killers? I called Mr. James Abernathy, director of U.S. Customs and Border Protection, the folks who run the Border Patrol. He said he could not comment because of the ongoing investigation. Same response from Attorney General Wentworth. Fair enough. I'm not going to aid and assist the terrorists by pushing the investigators into revealing any clues that might make the killers scatter.

"But I asked both gentlemen what's being done to secure our borders and prevent another attack like this from happening again, and do you know what they said? Mr. Abernathy's spokesperson said, 'We're doing everything possible.' Attorney General Wentworth's spokesman said, 'Everything legally authorized is being done, with all due respect for the rights of those involved in this activity.' *Excuse me?*"

O'Rourke hit a button and the recorded sound of a large steel trap snapping closed went out over the airwaves. "I sense fresh meat in the O'Rourke trap, my friends. " 'Everything possible?' My friends, do you realize that the four agents killed yesterday represented *one tenth* of all of the agents assigned to patrol the eastern Riverside County area of southern California? *Ten percent* of the agents assigned to ground patrol duties were killed *in one night*. Forty agents assigned to patrol about twenty-five hundred square miles of some of the busiest illegal migrant activity in the southwestern United States? That's one agent for roughly every fifty square miles. Imagine having two cops to patrol a city the size of Las Vegas. How many crooks do you think they're going to capture?

"Attorney General Wentworth's spokesman said that the government is going to respect the 'rights of those involved in this activity.' " The *snap!* of the steel trap closing sounded again. "Wrong! I believe Attorney General Wentworth's spokesman is referring to respecting the rights of illegal migrants, migrant smugglers, and maybe even the rights of murderers. Is he actually suggesting that we consider the rights of the trespassers and murderers versus the rights of endangered American citizens before deciding what we're going to do to combat these border incursions and attacks?

"As all my loyal listeners around the world know, I always have a copy of the Constitution of the United States right in front of me, and I refer to it often in questions like this. The Fourteenth Amendment to the Constitution says that all rights, liberties, and protections of the Constitution apply to citizens of the United States. It also says that no state can deny any person—including illegal aliens and murderers, I suppose—life, liberty, property, or access to the legal system without due process. My question to Attorney General Wentworth is: what further considerations are you bound to give illegals and murderers before deciding how to enforce the law? We have laws against murder and crossing the borders through other than regular border crossings; we have agencies legally set up to enforce those laws. No one is being denied anything. So why isn't the government acting to stop illegal immigration?

"The bottom line: this wishy-washy feel-good politically correct nonsense has got to *stop,* my friends, before we blindly allow more violence across our borders," Bob O'Rourke went on. "This namby-pamby mealy-mouth tap-dancing rhetoric regarding such a basic, fundamental, and important national policy such as controlling immigration, sovereignty, and security is a national outrage. An estimated one *million* persons illegally cross the borders of the United States every year. Estimates of the number of persons illegally in the United States at any given time range from ten to twelve million, and the number is increasing every year despite the attacks on Nine-Eleven and the recent Consortium terror attacks. The United States can put a man on the moon, read newspapers from twenty-one-thousand miles in space, and fly a plane across the country in two hours, but we can't stop poor uneducated Mexican peasants from strolling across the border?

"I say we can, my friends, and I say we do it *now,* before any more law enforcement officers get slaughtered. Those four men left behind wives, children, family, and friends, and our country owes it to them and owes it to all citizens to do something *right now* to stop this tidal wave of illegal immigration.

"As you all know, because I've been harping on it for months now, the effort to repeal the Posse Comitatus Act is stalled in Congress, and President Conrad seems unable or unwilling to push it. This is another outrage, and the President had better have the guts to take the hands of the wives, children, and mothers of those slain officers in his, look them in the eye, and promise he'll get the job done. What else will it take? Will more

officers and illegals have to die? Does another city have to be attacked before this President gets off his best intentions and puts
his political and personal reputation on the line to repeal Posse
Comitatus and protect the borders?

"All of my loyal listeners across this great country know my
plan, but in case you're tuning in for the first time or you're just a
bleeding-heart liberal illegal-hugger like Fonda, here it is, so *listen
up*. It's simple: bring every National Guardsman home from overseas and put him and her to work patrolling the nation's borders.
We've had experts on this show many times that say the U.S.-
Mexico border can be sealed off with fewer than ten percent of the
entire manpower of the Army and Air National Guard, or twenty
percent of the manpower of the Guard just in the south border
states of California, Arizona, New Mexico, Florida, and Texas.
The National Guard was originally established to protect, defend,
and secure the individual states and the United States, and only
secondarily to augment the regular forces. We already have a nationwide declaration of war against terrorism—the governors
don't need any more authority or repeal of Posse Comitatus to deploy Guard forces in their own states.

"But the active-duty military forces have the real equipment,
training, and manpower to make this work, so they need to be
brought in as soon as possible. Therefore, step two: Congress
should repeal the Posse Comitatus Act immediately, or at the very
least the President should suspend it while the country is in a state
of war, as we are now, and all of the strength and capabilities of
our military forces should be brought to bear to secure the borders.

"I've been in the Air Force command centers up at Beale Air
Force Base in California watching unmanned Global Hawk aircraft twenty thousand feet in the sky locating and tracking individuals from half a world away; I've seen infrared detectors spot
individuals hiding under trees or even in underground spider
holes; I've seen Joint STARS aircraft identifying and tracking
hundreds of vehicles by radar over thousands of square miles.
Guess how many Global Hawks we have patrolling Iraq and

Afghanistan right now? *Seven,* according to the public affairs folks at Beale Air Force Base. How many do we have patrolling anywhere in the U.S.? You guessed it—*none!* How many Joint STARS patrolling Iraq and Afghanistan? Six—that's all we have, my friends, leaving *none* to protect our own borders. We have less than twenty percent of the Air Force's fleet of smaller Predator unmanned reconnaissance aircraft patrolling our own borders.

"Technologically, I know we can do it—the question is, do we have the political will to do it? You will hear that illegal immigrants do work that Americans don't want to do." Again the sound of the trap snapping shut. "O'Rourke says 'hogwash'! Farm owners prefer immigrant labor because they're cheap, plentiful, work in absurdly deplorable conditions, and don't complain or cause trouble for fear of deportation. If farmworkers were paid an honest wage instead of a slave laborer's wage, more Americans would do those jobs, or the farm owners would modernize their equipment and procedures to make farming even more efficient and profitable. Any higher costs would just be passed along to consumers anyway, where the market would then dictate prices—but undoubtedly unemployment would go down in the meantime.

"You will hear that politicians don't like legislating against illegal immigrants because it will anger ethnic voters." *Snap!* "Again, O'Rourke says 'hogwash'! Legal immigrants and naturalized citizens oppose illegal immigration just as much as native-born citizens do because illegals are breaking the law—which hurts everyone—paints them with the same bigoted, racist, xenophobic brush as the illegals, and diminishes all the efforts they've made to come into this country legally."

O'Rourke paused for a few breaths, then went on: "I know a lot of you are advocating a guest worker program. Say *what?* A *what* worker program?" *Snap!* "Bullpies! I won't even *consider* a guest worker program until every last man and woman in this country who wants a job *has* a job, and that'll be a long, long time in coming, my friends. Don't you *dare* try to sugarcoat the issue by telling me that Mexicans do jobs that Americans won't do! Illegals have done those jobs because farmers and other employers would rather pay them a few pennies an hour rather than what a worker is legally entitled to. Pay an honest wage for an honest day's work and you won't need to hire slave labor to do the work.

"And don't you *dare* try to call it a guest worker program, as if the illegals will leave when we ask them to and won't come back unless we invite them. Calling someone a 'guest' implies that we *want* these people to enter our country. We can't have it both ways, my friends. We can't demand sovereign, secure borders, no risk of terror attacks, and no risk of skyrocketing costs associated with providing public services to illegals, and then ask for allowing undocumented, untraceable persons the right to legally enter the country and work. Trading security for comfort and convenience is not the answer.

"Step three is the stick: anyone found violating immigration laws risks detainment, not just deportment. Anyone caught without proper proof of citizenship is sent to a detainment facility to await administrative processing and deportment. These detention camps are minimum security, minimum amenity facilities—the persons detained are not there for rest and relaxation, but to await deportation, in which the length of time they are detained depends on the size of the facility, the number of judges assigned to work the cases, and the number of detainees. Multiple violators face federal jail time. Children born in a detainment facility are not considered U.S. citizens. If they must lose wages because they go to a detention camp every time they're caught without a guest worker permit, or if their offspring are denied citizenship, maybe they'll think twice before trying to sneak across the border.

"I see Fonda rolling her eyes at me already," O'Rourke said. This time, his little bit of radio theatrics was right on—she *was* rolling her eyes at him. Although Kent knew about today's topic and was ready for the onslaught of calls, even she looked at O'Rourke with a bit of trepidation. The phone lines were beginning to light up, and she knew that not everyone was going to want to talk with the host. The angry but radio-shy among them would scream at *her* instead, and she really hated that—it was her job, of course, but she still hated it. "I can hear the politicians in California calling me a racist and likening all this to Japanese internment camps in the 1940s. Folks, there's no doubt that those camps were born of mass hysteria and xenophobia—every man or woman after Pearl Harbor with sloped eyes was a Jap spy. That *was* racism, and that *was* wrong.

"Here's O'Rourke's bottom line: those found illegally entering the United States *are* criminals. At best they are trespassers, flouting our laws and taking money and services from legal citizens. At worst, they could be terrorists, murderers, rapists, and vandals. This is unacceptable. This madness has got to stop. Are you listening, Washington? Are you listening, President Conrad?"

O'Rourke looked up and saw Fand with her hands upraised in surrender, and a quick glance at the computer screen told him why: the switchboard was completely full. "All right, you people, I've ranted enough. The lines are jammed, so keep your comments short and sweet and let everyone have a chance to voice an opinion. America is once again under siege, not only by illegal immigrants but now by terrorists sneaking across the border *with* the illegals. We're talking about illegal immigration and what the Conrad administration must do about it *right now*. I'm Bob O'Rourke—welcome to *The Bottom Line*. Let's get it on—right after this commercial message. Stay right there."

The Oval Office, the White House,
Washington, D.C.
That same time

"That rat bastard!" the President of the United States, Samuel Conrad, thundered as he exited his private study adjacent to the Oval Office. "Who does that guy think he is? He doesn't know anything except what some hack reporter puts out over the wires. Somebody save me from the know-it-alls in the world."

The President's National Security Adviser, Sergeant Major Ray Jefferson, U.S. Army, had just walked into the Oval Office when the President finished his tirade. The President's Chief of Staff, Thomas F. Kinsly, was fixing the President a cup of coffee—decaf, Jefferson hoped—and he immediately made his way over to fix himself a cup. The White House had the best coffee in the world, Jefferson learned, but the Oval Office stuff seemed even better, and he never failed to grab a cup when he could.

Ray Jefferson took his coffee, stepped back behind the sofa in the little meeting area of the Oval Office—and almost seemed to disappear from sight. That was his favorite of all his many talents learned over almost three decades in the military: the ability to seem insignificant, blend into his surroundings, and look completely disarming. He was of just over average height, wiry, with short dark hair and blue eyes that seemed to reflect his mood at any given moment: they could be light and friendly one moment, dark and angry the next, but they were sharp and rarely missed anything. His ability to stand perfectly still, listen, and observe people and events around him had always served him well, and even more so now in his rough and tumble political role as the President of the United States' National Security Adviser.

Thomas Kinsly, the President's White House Chief of Staff, was everything Jefferson was not. Like the former Chief of Staff Victoria Collins, Kinsly was another one of the President's close friends; a successful fund-raiser, and political organizer and operative, he was an expert at networking and strategizing but had almost no experience working with entrenched Washington bureaucrats and politicians with their own agendas—even Ray Jefferson, a soldier since age seventeen, was more politically astute than Kinsly. He was younger than his predecessor, tall, dark, and good-looking, well spoken and affable with the media, but known as hard-charging and relentless with his staffers. Kinsly had made it clear early on that Jefferson was not, and probably would never be, a member of the inner circle.

Fine with him, Jefferson told himself early on. He didn't have to kiss ass to get access to the highest seats of power in the free world.

"There you are, Sergeant Major," the President said, finally noticing his National Security Adviser's presence even though he had been there for a while. Samuel Conrad was tall, gray-haired, and distinguished-looking—a photo-perfect figure of the chief executive. After graduating from Rutgers University with a degree in accounting and then Rutgers School of Law, almost his entire professional life had been in public service: two terms in the New Jersey legislature, two terms in the U.S. House of Representatives, two years in the White House Budget Office, four years as Undersecretary of the Treasury, two terms as the governor of New Jersey, two years in the White House Chief of Staff's office, and one term in the U.S. Senate before reaching the Oval Office. He was normally unflappable and in control—this was the first time in Jefferson's recollection that he ever saw the President in the Oval Office with so much as his tie loosened, let alone with a raised voice.

Jefferson didn't care much for politicians or bean counters, but he felt an obligation to this President as a way to make up for the death and destruction caused by Jefferson's old boss, the previous National Security Adviser to the President, who betrayed and almost killed the President and who was responsible for the deaths of thousands before he was finally stopped. Anything that got this President so angry had to be serious.

Jefferson waited to see if the President would explain what the shouting was about, but that was not yet forthcoming. "Any updates on the Border Patrol killings last night, Ray?" the President asked.

"Just what Director DeLaine sent over from the Bureau about an hour ago, sir," Ray replied. "No new leads. These guys were pros—I reject Secretary Lemke's theory that it was a turf war between smuggler gangs."

"Why?"

"Pistols and shotguns, maybe—but AK-47s put these guys several steps above the average smuggler," Jefferson replied. "Plus the evidence of body armor. These guys were professional soldiers."

"Your analysis, then?"

"Same as this morning's briefing, sir—it was an infiltration by a heavily armed and trained commando squad, similar to what we encountered with the Consortium," Jefferson replied. The energy monopoly–turned terrorist organization known as the Consortium, secretly led by now-deceased former National Security Adviser to the President of the United States, Robert Chamberlain, had been held responsible for the terror attacks in Houston, San Francisco, and Washington. Despite the efforts of hundreds of law enforcement agencies around the world, the organization was believed still in operation, now led by ex–Russian oil oligarch Yegor Viktorvich Zakharov. "Could even *be* another Consortium infiltration: Zakharov looking to even the score and sending in troops via a different, more established—and frankly, highly successful—route. I'd consider using human smugglers to bring my terrorist forces into the U.S. if I wanted to sneak in: chances are better than five-to-one I'd make it."

The President nodded, then picked up a briefing folder. "I read your recommendations about this 'Operation Rampart' project, Sergeant Major. Lots of tough love in here." He saw Jefferson's eyes narrow, and the piercing glare made him decidedly uncomfortable. "Something on your mind, Ray? Let's hear it."

"I'd appreciate it, sir, if you tell me flat out what you think of my plan," Jefferson said. " 'Tough love' doesn't tell me a thing."

"That's out of line, Jefferson," Kinsly snapped.

The President raised a hand toward his Chief of Staff, then tossed the folder back on his desk. "I've gotta learn to be more direct with you, Sergeant Major," he said. He motioned to the memo. "Let me get this straight, Ray: you want to put an entire Army *division* on the border?"

"I proposed forming a task force which would be about division-sized—about twenty thousand troops, including Army and Air Force aviation reconnaissance, logistics, and communications support assets, sir," Jefferson explained. "I recommend Reserves or National Guard units instead of active-duty forces, each working in their own home state—it might give them a little added incentive to do a better job."

"And you expect them to completely seal off the southern border?" Kinsly asked.

"It wouldn't be one hundred percent, Mr. Kinsly, but it would be a hell of a lot better than what we have now." He turned to the President. "Sir, the military as you know is legally prohibited from performing law enforcement duties, but they can *assist* law enforcement, and already do on a regular basis. Let's step up surveillance along the borders and see if the level of illegal border crossings is on the increase, then interdict some of these migrants and find out who they are—migrant workers, illegal immigrants, or in fact terrorists. That's the real question we're facing here, isn't it?"

"What do you mean, Ray?"

"I mean, if those Border Patrol agents were gunned down by a few stoned, desperate, or rambunctious migrant farmworkers with itchy trigger fingers, nothing more will be done about it," Jefferson said. "But if on the other hand it was some kind of terror group infiltrating through our southern borders, and they retaliated to prevent being discovered or captured, we should retaliate with everything we got.

"If you want to secure the borders and try to prevent what happened last night, sir, let's do it," Jefferson went on resolutely. "In my opinion the Border Patrol is not up to the task—in fact, the entire Customs and Border Protection Service is not equipped to secure the borders. They're a law enforcement unit, not a security one. I'm sure they've upgraded their weapons and tactics over the years, but in my mind they're still the guys on horseback and in pickup trucks cruising the desert looking for Chicanos sneaking into America. The military knows surveillance and reconnaissance the best—let them do their jobs."

"Putting the military in a law enforcement function is against the law, Sergeant Major."

"This tasking is not a violation of the Posse Comitatus Act," Jefferson responded. "I still believe we should be working to repeal Posse Comitatus, but in case it's not repealed this operation would not violate it. The military would serve a surveillance and interdiction role only, the same as they do with antidrug smuggling operations—the Border Patrol, Immigration and Customs Enforcement, FBI, customs, or state or local law enforcement would make the arrests and conduct the investigations. We can start immediately and have it completed in less than six months."

"*Six months?*"

"Secure a mostly open three-thousand-mile border of the United States from illegal entry by groups of persons or undeclared, unidentified vehicles? Yes, sir," Jefferson said. "It'll take manpower and technology, but most importantly it'll take strong backing by the federal, state, and local governments and support from the citizens. But it can be done. A combination of strategic and tactical reconnaissance and rapid-reaction forces strung out across the border, similar to what the Coast Guard and Customs Service do along American waters and ports."

"Sounds like you're going to war here, Sergeant," Kinsly said.

"It's 'Sergeant *Major,*' Mr. Kinsly, not 'Sergeant,' " Jefferson said, affixing a warning glare and voice inflection that were not so subtle as to be overlooked by the Chief of Staff. "Large numbers of unidentified, heavily armed gunmen coming across the border and killing Americans—it sounds like war to me too, sir." To the President he said, "If you want action, sir, this is what it'll take, in my best estimation. I can't guarantee a few terrorists or illegals won't slip through, but with proper backup and support from state and local agencies I think we can get the job done."

The President remained silent, which prompted Kinsly to press his arguments even more. "You want plain talk, Sergeant Major? I believe your plan would be a political disaster," Kinsly said, emphasizing the words "sergeant major" sarcastically enough to elicit another warning glare. "It would outrage Hispanics, liberal politicians, human and civil rights groups, the Mexican government, the governors of the border states, and probably several dozen other groups I haven't even thought of yet."

"I don't report to any of those people, sir—I report to the President of the United States, same as you," Jefferson said flatly. "The President requested my opinion on how to stop illegal immigration, not how to placate several dozen disparate political groups. That's someone else's job."

"You're wrong there, Sergeant Major—the political aspects of this office is *everyone's* job, just like the military decisions made in this office affect the political landscape," the President said. "Remember that."

"Yes, sir, I will." He scowled at Kinsly, who withered under his glare. "Anything else for me, sir?"

"I'm going to fly out to San Diego to attend the funerals of those Border Patrol agents killed last night," the President said somberly. "I'll meet with the directors of the Customs and Border Protection Service and the Immigration and Customs Enforcement Service afterward."

"I'd like to go along and hear those briefings too, sir."

"I thought you might. Approved."

"Thank you, sir," Jefferson said. "I'd like permission to bring along my own advisers as well."

"Of course; bring anyone you need. Submit their names to Tom for clearances. Who do you have in mind?" But before Jefferson could respond, the President's eyes widened, and he said, "Richter and Vega, I presume?"

"Implementing a major border security program with a division-sized task force will take time, sir," Jefferson said. "I thought it would be prudent to try a smaller task force first. Task Force TALON is already formed; it already has a security and antiterrorist mission and full authorization to gain assets from any active or reserve units necessary; and they're already located in the southwest." Task Force TALON was a joint military and FBI counterterrorist strike team led by Ray Jefferson before he became the National Security Adviser; now Major Jason Richter and Dr.

Ariadna Vega, formerly of the Army Research Lab, were in charge. "I want to bring in an officer from the National Guard Bureau to listen in too."

"I thought TALON was disbanded after the Chamberlain fiasco," Kinsly said.

"Negative, sir," Jefferson said. "TALON received additional funding from the Departments of Defense and Homeland Security under a secret emergency authorization. Since the Consortium attacks last year, TALON has grown to company size, about two hundred members. They have eight CID squads—sixteen CID units—plus one training and maintenance squad. They operate missions all over the world: they are still active in north and central Africa and Central Asia, hunting down Zakharov and other surviving members of the Consortium."

Kinsly nodded. "I have to admit TALON is the pride and joy of the nation after what they did in San Francisco and Washington," he said. "It'll be a much easier sell to have TALON involved than just saying we're militarizing the southern border." But he turned to the President with a serious expression. "But we *are* militarizing the border—or that's how it's going to be perceived in the world, Mr. President. The United States has always prided itself on having unarmed borders. This will erase almost a century of cooperation and coexistence between us and the Mexican government, and it's almost certain to raise criticism against us, charging bigotry, xenophobia, isolationism, even racism."

"Before Nine-Eleven, Kingman City, San Francisco, and now these killings near Blythe, I would never consider doing it," the President said. "Now, I have no choice—something has to be done, and right *now*." He looked at both Kinsly and Jefferson. "But I want fresh ideas on the illegal immigration problem, gents," he said. "I know what the Border Patrol wants: more money for more men and equipment. That's one solution, but I want *new* ideas, better solutions."

"I want to send Task Force TALON in ahead of our visit so they can give us a report after we hear from CBP and ICE, sir,"

Jefferson said. "That'll give them a complete perspective on the situation along the borders."

"That could be an invitation to disaster, Jefferson," Kinsly said. "We don't want any complaints from immigrant or human rights groups. Your task force can hunt down terrorists in the U.S., but they should be directed to keep their hands off any illegal immigrants they find. Let the Border Patrol and Immigration and Customs Enforcement do their jobs."

"Ray?" the President prompted.

"They can act as observers only, unless they find anyone they consider to be terrorists," Jefferson said. Kinsly's expression showed his distrust, but he said nothing, giving tacit approval.

"Thank you, Sergeant Major," the President said. "Anything else for me?"

"Yes, sir. May I ask what your outburst was about a few moments ago?"

The President smiled and nodded knowingly at Kinsly. "I tell you, Tom, that's why I hired this guy: he says what's on his mind."

"I prefer to think of it as 'curiosity killed the cat,' " Kinsly said drily.

"Did you happen to catch Bob O'Rourke's radio show this morning, Sergeant Major?"

"No, sir."

"But you're familiar with his show?"

"I've heard the name, sir, but I don't listen to talk radio or TV—in fact, I don't watch much TV or listen to the radio at all. Never have."

"Why is that?"

"I've got my own theories and ideas, sir, and they're based on information and sources I know are accurate," Jefferson replied. "Anything else is propaganda, disinformation, or entertainment."

"O'Rourke's radio show has ten million listeners a day on seven hundred stations around the world, plus satellite and shortwave— it's even streamed live on the Internet," Kinsly said. "He has an opinion column syndicated in a thousand newspapers around the world. He's one of the most popular and influential media types in the United States, probably the world."

Not surprisingly, none of that seemed to impress Jefferson in the least. "Bob O'Rourke and all those radio commentators say what they say to shock or outrage their listeners," he said. "I see no value in listening to him. If I want entertainment, I'll visit the senior enlisted club at Fort Myers on payday."

"Seems like a rather myopic and self-centered view of the world, Jefferson," Kinsly said haughtily. "You pick and choose what you want to listen to and make decisions based on a limited perspective. Perhaps you need to broaden your exposure a bit more."

"I serve as the National Security Adviser of the President of the United States, Mr. Kinsly," Jefferson said, his voice becoming deeper and, both Kinsly and Conrad recognized, more menacing. "I have access to sources and data that I never even dreamed existed, even when I was the former National Security Adviser's aide-de-camp. With the information at my fingertips now, why would I waste my time listening to a hack like Bob O'Rourke?"

"I listen to his show when I'm near a radio, Sergeant Major," the President said with a smile. "Do you think I'm wasting my time?"

"Yes, sir, I do."

Kinsly looked aghast, which quickly changed to rising anger. "Have a little respect for the office, Jefferson," he said.

But the President only laughed. "That's why I picked you for this job, Sergeant Major—I know you'll give me a straight answer every time."

"That's my job, sir."

"It may interest you to know that your proposal is almost precisely what O'Rourke talked about on his radio show this morning."

The President thought he detected a very slight uptick of a corner of Jefferson's mouth—which may or may not have been a *smile*. "Maybe this O'Rourke character has something on the ball after all."

"Was that a *joke,* Sergeant Major?" the President asked with mock surprise.

"I'm a military man, sir," Jefferson said, ignoring the sarcasm. "My perspective has always been and probably will always be from a military perspective"—he glared again at Kinsly before adding—". . . *not* a political or entertainment one. Border security and illegal migration began as a societal and cultural problem, grew into an economic problem, and has now exploded into a national security problem. I'm sure there's a political element in there too, but I don't feel I'm qualified to handle that."

The President raised a hand. "Message received loud and clear, Sergeant Major," he said. "I hired you for one simple reason: I want straight talk and honest answers. I have no doubt that if we stray into an area that you can't help me with, you'll say so and not try to bullshit me."

"Roger that, sir."

"Good." He nodded at the plan Jefferson had submitted and went on, "I'll staff your proposal and present it to the congressional leadership for feedback, but after what happened down there in Blythe I'm ready to implement your plan immediately. Get everyone ready to go and I'll give you the go-ahead as soon as possible."

"Yes, sir."

The President held up the order. "Have Secretary Lemke or his designee be in overall charge of the sergeant major's Operation Rampart program, but we'll put Task Force TALON in charge for now until the forces ramp up. Have Major Richter fly out with me to San Diego aboard *Air Force One* so we can talk, and afterward meet with the Border Patrol and other Homeland Security folks in southern California.

"Also, draft an executive order implementing Operation Rampart," the President went on. "We will begin construction of the border security apparatus in four phases: California, Arizona, New Mexico, and Texas. Request an emergency appropriation for the first four years of the California portion of the system, to begin construction of the forward operating bases and procurement of the unmanned aerial vehicles and support equipment immediately. The rest we'll have to put through the normal budget process. The order will include federalization of the National Guard and Reserves and mobilization of the necessary active-duty personnel and equipment per the plan." He turned to Jefferson. "Ray, whom do you recommend to oversee the operation?"

"Mr. President, I've nominated Brigadier General Ricardo Lopez, the national deputy director for the Army National Guard, for overall command of Rampart," Jefferson replied. "I've received nothing but glowing endorsements from the Pentagon on his nomination, and I recommend his appointment wholeheartedly. I would also like to nominate the deputy director of Customs and Border Protection, Special Agent George Trujillo, to be deputy commander of Rampart. I think this combination of a military commander and a Border Patrol deputy brings the right mix of experience and places the proper emphasis on the mission. General Lopez will report directly to me."

"Agreed," the President said. "I want to speak with both men as soon as possible. Set it up, Thomas."

"Yes, Mr. President," Kinsly responded.

He looked at Jefferson. "Ray, you said this was a cultural problem that escalated into an economic and then a national security problem. What do you mean?"

"Sir, the basic problem with illegal immigration is much more than Mexicans freely crossing the border looking for work," Jefferson replied. "It has to do with the perception—many Mexicans would say the 'reality'—that the United States went to war with Mexico and took their land as a result of the Mexican-American War. In essence, the western half of the United States really belongs to Mexico."

"Are you talking about the Texas Revolution, Jefferson," Kinsly interjected, "as in the battle of the Alamo?"

"No, sir. The Mexican-American War was from 1846 to 1848, *following* the War of Texas Independence," Jefferson replied. "The Mexican-American War was America's first conflict fought outside its own borders. We accused Mexico of invading and occupying the United States after the Texas Revolution and we went to war. We ended up with territory that makes up most of the states in the southwest United States—Texas, New Mexico, Arizona, Nevada, and California: the border states."

"So Mexico thinks those states still belong to Mexico? That's why they don't see anything wrong with crossing our borders like they do?"

"Some Mexicans do claim that the border states still belong to Mexico, sir—historically, insurrections and guerrilla attacks have taken place to try to capture or force a state to secede, such as the attacks by Pancho Villa in the early 1900s," Jefferson said. "Some firebrands in Mexico will never forget the American invasion of Veracruz by General Pershing during the punitive wars—it's a million times worse than what many Iraqis feel about America going to war to force 'regime change' there.

"But the point is that the region is culturally and historically Hispanic, and it will always be so," Jefferson went on. "The borders are artificial, arbitrary, and in most areas not even marked or in any way delineated—for many Mexicans there *is* no border, in every sense of the word. Most border towns look, sound, and feel more like Mexican towns than American. In addition, the Hispanic population is growing faster than the white population—Hispanics are no longer a minority in California, for example. Anti-immigrant activities will never be popular in that region."

"This is very entertaining, Jefferson, but this is the twenty-first century, and all of that is practically ancient history," Kinsly said. "Besides, if I'm not mistaken, we *paid* for the land we took in that war, did we not? We didn't steal it—we *bought* it."

"Most Mexican nationalists consider that blood money, sir—in any case, most of the money went back to the U.S. to pay war reparations," Jefferson said. "Part of the problem in dealing with illegal immigration is the cultural undercurrent running through this region—any government activities against Mexicans will be seen as an attack against Mexican culture and heritage, not just against illegal migrants or terrorists."

"I'm impressed, Sergeant Major," the President said. "You ex-hibit quite a detailed knowledge of the history and origins of the problems down there."

"Thank you, sir. I studied up on it as part of the planning process for Operation Rampart, and brushed up on it after learn-ing about the attacks on the Border Patrol agents last night."

"To *me,* you sound like that nutcase who makes those video-tapes that air every now and then . . . what's his name . . . ?"

"Veracruz. Comandante Veracruz," Jefferson said. "Named after the Battle of Veracruz, the largest and deadliest U.S. Army battle before the Civil War. It was also America's first amphibious invasion—twelve thousand soldiers landed on the beach in Vera-cruz, Mexico, in less than one day. Major General Winfield Scott had the city outnumbered four to one but Scott still refused to ne-gotiate terms of surrender. The Army blasted the city continu-ously for twelve days. It was a great victory for America but was considered a disgrace and humiliation to Mexico."

"It almost sounds like you're sympathetic to the Mexicans, Sergeant," Kinsly added.

Jefferson turned his whole body toward Kinsly and gave him a look that made little hairs on the back of the Chief of Staff's neck stand up; Kinsly tried to regain his composure but found his throat had turned completely dry in the blink of an eye. Jefferson's ex-pression was clear: you are my immediate supervisor, but if I don't get the simplest sign of respect due me, I'll rip your head off your pencil-thin neck and shit down your throat.

"Do *not,*" Jefferson began in a voice that was more like a growl, "confuse analysis with sympathy, *Mr.* Kinsly. It's essential to study the enemy personality, composition, terrain, logistics, and tactical situation in order to identify the enemy's center of gravity and compose a plan of action. Basic combat strategy." He took one step toward the Chief of Staff, impaling him with his eyes. "I'd be happy to meet in your office, one on one, *any time,* to discuss it fur-ther. *Sir.*"

The President found his own throat a little dry after watching

Jefferson putting Kinsly in his place, and he took a sip of coffee before speaking. "Now it's the 'enemy' we're talking about, Sergeant Major?" the President asked.

"It is if you tell me it is, sir, yes," Jefferson said. "As I said, I believe there's a military solution to the illegal immigration situation, and I'm prepared to implement it whenever I'm given the order. However, I'm pointing out the inherent difficulties created by the historical, anthropological, and cultural situation. We could very well win every battle and lose the war."

"Why?"

"This Veracruz guy is a known drug smuggler, sir, but he has enormous popularity all around the world for the Mexican cause. He represents a militant backlash to anti-immigration sentiment that's growing in the United States, fueled by guys like Bob O'Rourke. Veracruz could start an uprising among the migrants in America."

"An uprising? That's ridiculous," Kinsly said. "The Mexicans are here to work and earn money for themselves and their families, not revolt against America. Besides, who is this Veracruz guy? Is he a general? What army does he command?"

"His *audience* can turn into his *army* if we're not careful," Jefferson said. "Remember that there are an estimated ten million illegal immigrants in America today, at least a million more enter every year, and over a third of all the live births in the southwest U.S. are children of illegal immigrants. If even ten percent of them decide it's time to listen to 'Comandante Veracruz' and fight, he'd have an army twice as large as Mexico's itself. He shouldn't be underestimated."

CHAPTER 2

CAJON JUNCTION, CALIFORNIA
THE NEXT MORNING

Any business consultant would have told them what they already knew: it was the perfect place for an enterprise such as theirs. The area featured ready access to transportation outlets such as Interstate 15, the major freeway artery between Las Vegas and Los Angeles, which made transporting both raw materials and finished product quick, easy, and secure; it was on the edge of the Mojave Desert where land was cheap, but also at the edge of the San Bernardino National Forest so it didn't seem as if they were actually *in* the desert; and they had ready access to over ten million potential customers, without having to directly compete against the hundreds of other manufacturers scattered around the Los Angeles megalopolis.

Of course, their real market was Los Angeles, but they chose to locate in San Bernardino County instead—along with going up against the competition, they would have to go up against the infinitely better-funded and -organized Los Angeles County Sheriff's Department rather than the much smaller San Bernardino County Sheriff's Department. One had to balance customer service, marketing, and location of facilities with the competition factor, and their competition was not only the other manufacturers, but law enforcement.

This was Ernesto Fuerza's pride and joy—one of the largest and most successful methamphetamine labs in southern California. Mostly built on trucks and trailers for easy portability and concealment, the lab produced almost a hundred kilos a day of crystal meth, or "speed," worth almost a hundred thousand dollars; mixed with cheap fillers and sold on the street, the drug could be worth ten to twenty times that amount.

The best part was that it was far less expensive for Fuerza to manufacture meth in the United States than many of his competitors because he received the raw materials from Mexico rather than from the United States, where controls on the sale of the compounds needed to make meth were far less stringent. The same smuggling networks that allowed Ernesto Fuerza to bring hundreds of illegal immigrants a month to the United States also allowed him to import tons of epinephrine, hydrochloric acid, caustic soda, and chlorine gas to his southern California mobile labs for very little cost and almost total security.

Like any successful business owner, it was important for Fuerza to personally oversee his operation, let his employees see the boss regularly on the job site, take a look at the books, inspect the facilities and product, question his staff, and hand out punishment and rewards, and that's what Fuerza was doing that morning . . . when they received an unexpected visitor.

As always, the San Bernardino County Sheriff's Methamphetamine Interdiction Tactical Team swept in with black armored Humvees with lights and sirens on. Deputies on foot wearing black fatigues, ballistic helmets, and bulletproof vests led captured lookouts into the compound at gunpoint, and all of the lab workers were quickly rounded up, cuffed with nylon handcuffs, and secured in the middle of the compound. The deputies were especially rough on Fuerza himself, hog-tying, blindfolding, and gagging him and throwing him facedown in the dirt in front of his workers.

"Ernesto, you must be working your men too hard," said Sergeant Ed Nuñez, commander of the Methamphetamine Interdiction Tactical Team. "My men found your security guys fast asleep." He looked around at the trailers and trucks and shook his head. "Two tractor-trailers here instead of just one, Ernesto? You didn't tell me you are using two labs now. You broke the rules, Ernesto, and it's going to cost you. You're under arrest. Get him out of here." Fuerza was pulled up by his arms and dragged across the compound to Nuñez's Humvee. Just before being thrown into the backseat, Nuñez landed a fierce right cross on Fuerza's left jaw, causing the smuggler to spin around like a top and slam against the vehicle, with a noticeable spot of blood growing on the outside of the hood covering his head.

Once inside the vehicle, Nuñez removed his helmet, balaclava, and gloves and lit up a cigarette, leaving Fuerza in the backseat still bound and gagged. "I hope for your sake that one of those tractor-trailers is empty, Ernesto, because I'm going to have to confiscate one of them, and I'd hate for you to lose an entire mobile lab. That would be bad for both of our businesses." He took a deep drag, then removed the hood and gag, leaving the rest of the bindings intact. "What the fuck, Ernesto? We agreed you could keep operating as long as you tossed me a few kilos of product and a few rival smugglers every now and then, and as long as you didn't get too greedy and try to expand. What's the matter with you?"

"Listen to me, Nuñez," Fuerza said. Fuerza was tall, in his late thirties, with long dark hair secured with his signature black and white Middle Eastern–looking "chain-link" bandanna, a long goatee, sunglasses, and wiry features. He moved fluidly and silently—obviously a result of extensive military training. "I might have a deal going that will greatly expand my distribution. I am not trying to screw you, I swear—I am trying to make us both rich . . ."

"I told you before, 'Comandante,' that I don't want rich and powerful cookers and dealers in this county—I want everybody kept small time so they don't attract attention from the state or the feds," Nuñez said. "Money makes you cookers greedy and stupid, and that hurts everyone. Now you're going to surrender one of those trucks and a couple of your men to me."

Fuerza nodded, looking dejected and defeated. "*Talvez,*" he said. "Take the trailers then. Just don't take my delivery truck, okay? That is important to my business. And don't run no computer checks."

"That's not your call, Ernesto," Nuñez said, giving the Mexican a mischievous grin. "I'll need a contract tow company to take the trailers, and I don't want any outside eyes back-checking my report, so I'll take the delivery truck instead."

"Nuñez, I ask you, do not take my delivery truck, please . . ."

"Sorry, Fuerza. Maybe next time you'll play straight with me. Stay here until I have your men in the paddy wagon, and then I'll let you 'escape.' "

"You greedy bastard. I told you, I have a deal going that will make this lab setup look like a child's chemistry set. I could use your help."

"Tell me what this deal is about."

"I got me an army, Nuñez," Fuerza said. "I got me some good fighters, real pros. They . . ."

"More of your pansy Mexican stoners, 'Comandante'? No thanks."

"No, not the Rural Defense Corps—these guys are for real. No hassles for you at all. We will not stay in San Bernardino County—we just need safe passage for these guys when I bring them across."

"Pros, huh? Who are they?"

"You do not want to know who they are, Nuñez," Fuerza said. "They will take over security and enforcement for my network. All you and your guys need to do is let them through when I tell you they are coming."

Nuñez thought for a moment; then: "Okay, Ernesto. But I'm raising my fee to twenty thousand a week."

"*Twenty thousand?* You do less work for more money?"

"You think it's easy or cheap to explain to the bosses how over a million dollars' worth of Mexican crank gets discovered in Los Angeles, Riverside, and Imperial Counties every month, but not in San Bernardino County?" Nuñez asked angrily. "There's a lot more than just my team involved in this, Fuerza—everybody from the state narcotics control bureau to the DA to the fucking newspaper reporters have their hands out. It's going to cost you big to go big-time."

"I tell you, Nuñez, back off, and there will be plenty of money for all of us."

"Twenty thousand a week, starting now," Nuñez insisted. "Maybe that'll take care of this sudden urge to expand your operation. Take it, or I'll confiscate more than just the damned truck."

"Okay, okay, I will pay," Fuerza said. "But please, do not go near the delivery truck, and tell your deputies to stay off the computer."

"Stop whining about that truck, Ernesto," Nuñez said. "Be thankful I'm not impounding *everything* here and tossing your sorry stupid ass into jail. Now shut up and stay put until I come for you." Fuerza plopped back on the hard bench seat of the sheriff's department Humvee and waited.

It did not take long. Nuñez returned a few moments later: "What the hell is going on, Fuerza? We just ran the plates on your truck for wants and warrants, and the whole fucking world exploded on us! Were you involved in some sort of border incident down in Imperial County?"

"I do not know nothing about any border incident, Nuñez. I have been here for . . ."

"Bullshit, Fuerza. You're going down big-time, jerkoff. You should have told me what you're involved with when I first nabbed you. This whole area will be swarming with feds in an hour—the computer reported the tag check to every law enforcement agency on the damned planet. You'll be lucky if you just end up with life in a federal prison. It's out of my hands now, asshole."

He disappeared again, shouting, "Bag up any cash and product you see before the damned feds get here, boys. We're going to lose this crime scene in just a few minutes, and then we'll be sucking hind tit as usual. Search that truck good and . . ."

The gunfight lasted less than a minute. Fuerza heard and felt a few heavy-caliber bullets ricocheting off the Humvee, and he hunkered down on the floor until it was over, then sat up and shouted, *"Coronel, aquí."*

A few moments later, the door of the Humvee opened up, and Yegor Zakharov appeared, aiming a pistol inside the vehicle. He glared angrily at Fuerza. "You drove us to an ambush with the *police?*" Zakharov shouted. "I should kill your ass right now!"

"It was a shakedown, Colonel—that deputy is even more crooked and greedy than you," Fuerza said. He turned around, and Zakharov cut off the plastic handcuffs. "Usually a few thousand dollars and some lab equipment and empty chemical drums satisfies him, but he was looking for more this time."

"What happened to your security? Don't you have anyone guarding this damned place?"

"We can talk about that later, Colonel," Fuerza said. "Right now, I suggest we collect all the money, weapons, and product we can and get out of here before the *real* police arrive."

OVER SOUTHERN CALIFORNIA
THE NEXT DAY

The shadow flitted across the hard-baked sand in an instant, so quickly that no one really noticed it. Eyes seared by the sun, stinging from sand, salt, and sweat, it was not hard to understand. Most eyes were concentrating on the path ahead, not on the sky. A false step could result in a twisted ankle or nasty fall, and that would delay everyone. Besides, shadows from birds flying overhead were common—usually the birds were buzzards or California condors, large carrion birds looking for animals in distress below for their afternoon meal. Humans were not on their preferred menu, but if one fell and looked as if it was dead or incapacitated, they would circle overhead and wait patiently until it died all the same.

This time, however, the shadow overhead was not from a living animal, although even from close-up it resembled a very large Canada goose. It moved slowly, no more than ten to fifteen knots depending on the winds, flying just five hundred feet above ground. It had very long thin wings with ducted turboprop engines underneath, a long neck, a large bulbous body that was not as long as the wingspan, and a broad flat tail.

The group of fifteen Mexicans crossing the desert stopped for a water and pee break, and it was then that one of the men noticed the shadow, looked up, and saw the flying object overhead. "What is it?" the man asked.

"Shh! *¡Escuche!*" the coyote leader ordered. Now they could hear the faint, low, throaty sound of the device's small jet engine, and that made everyone in the group upset. "It is a reconnaissance aircraft, probably Border Patrol."

"They will catch us for sure!"

"Maybe," the leader said. He unslung his backpack and quickly pulled out a sawed-off twelve-gauge shotgun. "But they'll have one less eye in the sky to bother us the next time we cross." He found it child's play to track the spy plane because it was moving so slowly, and he squeezed off a shot.

"You fool! They will hear you!" one of the other coyotes complained.

"We are twenty miles from the nearest road and thirty miles to the nearest town—no one will hear this small rifle," the shooter said. He fired again, then reloaded.

"That little popgun isn't going to hit it from this distance, you idiot!" one of the *pollos* shouted. But just then the little aircraft turned sharply to the north and started to fly away.

"Not going to hit it, eh?" the coyote said happily. "Too bad it got away—I really wanted to see that thing come spinning out of the sky, like a wounded duck," he said gleefully. "Let's get moving. The more distance we can put between us and this spot, the . . ."

"¿Cuál es ése?" one of the pollos suddenly exclaimed. The coyote looked in the direction of the migrant's outstretched arm. There, at the top of a small rise about a hundred yards before them, was a . . . well, it was impossible to tell what it was. It resembled some sort of child's toy robot, with broad chest and shoulders, bulbous head, slim waist, and large metallic arms and legs, but it was about nine or ten feet tall. It had appeared out of nowhere—none of the sparse vegetation for miles around could have possibly hidden that thing.

One of the pollos unslung his backpack and reached inside it, but another stopped him. "No, don't," he whispered. "Don't you recognize it? I saw it on TV, back during the attacks on Houston and Washington. Usted no puede matarle." The first man took his hand out of the backpack but kept it close.

"Whatever it is, let's get away from it," the coyote said. But as they moved a little farther east to try to get around it, the robot thing moved with them—it made no move to walk toward them, but simply shadowed their movements. "It's moving with us, but it's not making any attempt to stop us. Maybe it doesn't belong to the Border Patrol?"

"¿Qué hacemos?" one of the migrants asked worriedly.

The coyote thought for a moment; then: "We split up," he said. "There's only one of it—it can't follow us all. Up ahead about three kilometers is a gully. Follow the gully toward those mountains until you come to a concrete alcantarilla. Stay out of sight until we meet up with you."

"What about our pickup?" one of the men asked. "You had better not call him off, asshole . . . !"

"We have a deal, dammit. Just do as I say. Now split up!" The pollos did as they were told, breaking up into two- and three-man teams and fanning out. The smuggler chambered a round in his rifle and approached the robot, shouting, "Hey, you! What are you? What do you want?"

"*No tire en el avión,*" the robot said in a machine-synthesized male voice.

That was bad—the spy plane was apparently beaming down its images to this contraption, because the robot knew that he had fired on it. "Fine, fine. I won't fire on your spy plane anymore, *prometo*. Now leave us alone."

"What is your name?" the robot asked in Spanish.

"Are you the police? Border Patrol?"

"No. But the Border Patrol is watching you. What is your name?"

"How do I know the Border Patrol is watching?" the coyote asked. "I don't have to tell you shit." He leveled the shotgun at the robot. "Now leave us alone, *ojete!*"

"That's Martín Alvarez," Senior Patrol Agent Albert Spinelli said, watching the video feed on a laptop computer broadcast via satellite from the Cybernetic Infantry Device unit on the scene. They were outdoors at a vacant area adjacent to Runway 27 Left at Gillespie Field near El Cajon, California, standing beside a Humvee with a small satellite dish on top. The entire area north of the parallel runways, including the runways themselves, had been closed off to all air traffic, and a small encampment had been set up with two Humvees, a satellite dish, and a large thirty-foot-long, ten-foot-high nylon net strung across Runway 27 Left to recover the Gullwing unmanned reconnaissance aircraft. "No surprise seeing him in this area." Spinelli definitely appeared uncomfortable at watching this group of illegals crossing the border near Campo, California, just east of the steel security fence that stretched ten miles either side of the Potrero-Tecate border crossing station.

"The bastard took a shot at my UAV," Dr. Ariadna Vega, deputy commander and chief engineer of Task Force TALON, a joint military–Federal Bureau of Investigation antiterrorist strike force, said in a surprised, worrisome voice. She too looked extremely uncomfortable watching this encounter, although for decidedly different reasons.

The Border Patrol agent looked at Vega suspiciously. "Alvarez is small time, usually nonviolent," Spinelli said. "First time I've ever heard of him using a weapon. He's usually too drunk or stoned to even walk straight, let alone shoot straight."

"There's something strange about those migrants," Ariadna remarked.

"What?"

"They look . . . I don't know, pretty well organized, like they're used to walking out in the middle of nowhere in the desert," Ari said.

"The migrant farmworkers are already pretty tough hombres to do the kind of work they do," Spinelli said. "A lot of the migrants have made this trip dozens of times, and you have to be tough to survive it." He looked at Vega again, trying to guess what was wrong with her expression. "Don't worry—after the shootings at Blythe, we'll be on guard for any violent characters."

"What are you going to do with them?"

"Our patrol will be there in twenty minutes," Spinelli replied. "We'll pick them up, drive them back here, and give them all a checkup. We have a group of volunteer nurses and paramedics and a volunteer doctor on call who'll help us out. Then they'll be processed. We'll identify them the best we can and weed out the criminals and the violent ones. Any wanted suspects are processed by the Departments of State and Justice for extradition. The Mexicans will be deported across the border; the OTMs—other than Mexicans—will be deported after a hearing. If they have any outstanding warrants, either in the U.S. or with any other Interpol reporting agencies, they'll be detained until they can be transferred to the proper authorities. We're seeing more and more of them with lengthy criminal records."

"The others will get deported?"

"Yep. They'll be bused across the border from San Diego to a Mexican processing center in Tijuana or Mexicali." He thought for a moment, then went on: "Alvarez, the guy with the shotgun, concerns me. Smugglers with guns are getting more and more common on the border, and we want to clamp down on that hard and fast. I think Alverez is wanted in Tamaulipas State on suspicion of killing a Mexican *federale*. I want him for questioning. Have your guy . . . robot . . . CID unit, whatever you call him, hold that man until our agents arrive."

"We can't," Ariadna said. "We're prohibited from making an arrest. We're out here to observe and report, nothing more."

"I can authorize him to pass along an order from me to stay where he is until my agents arrive," Spinelli said. "I'll be the agent in charge. You'll just . . ."

"We can't get involved, Agent Spinelli—that's final," Ariadna said resolutely. She touched the comm button: "CID One, you are authorized only to keep the subjects in sight and report their position and movement. You may not detain or interfere with them in any way. Is that clear? Acknowledge."

"Received and understood, Ari," U.S. Army Sergeant First Class Harry Dodd, piloting CID One, responded.

"That guy took a shot at your recon plane, Dr. Vega—you saw it, we all saw it," Spinelli said. "That's a federal violation for sure. Plus he's wanted in Mexico on a murder charge. You can't just let him go."

"Task Force TALON is not the Border Patrol, Agent Spinelli— we're not here to do your job for you," Ariadna said. "We're here simply on National Security Adviser Jefferson's suggestion."

"But . . ."

"As far as you're concerned, Agent Spinelli, we're nature lovers out here on a stroll to take pictures of the flora and fauna," she interrupted. "CID One, continue your assigned patrol."

"Roger." It was only a few minutes later when Dodd radioed back: "I'm picking up a vehicle approaching—a small Ford van, no license plates . . . subject Alvarez is waving it down. Looks like a rendezvous."

"You can't let him get away, Dr. Vega," Spinelli said. "Alvarez just walked across the border. That's illegal. You've got to stop him." But Ariadna said nothing.

"Ari? What should I do?"

"Continue your patrol, CID One," Ariadna replied. "Observe and report."

There was a slight pause; then: "O-kay, Ari. The first subject has made contact with the driver of the van . . . he's now waving at the other subjects . . . they're running toward the van. Looks like they're all going to get in."

"At least get up there and see who the driver is, Sergeant!" Spinelli exclaimed. Dodd trotted over to the van, but the driver and a man in the front passenger seat had their faces well hidden with hats and sunglasses. "The other guy has a gun!" Spinelli pointed out excitedly. "I saw a submachine gun in his lap! That's another federal violation! You can't let them get away!"

"Ari . . . ?"

"Continue to observe and report, Sergeant," Ariadna repeated stonily. Spinelli banged a hand on the console and muttered an expletive. Moments later they watched as the van sped away.

"Want me to follow it, Ari?" Dodd asked.

"Yes! Follow it!" Spinelli shouted. "We might be able to intercept him before he reaches the highway."

"Negative. Resume your patrol, Harry."

"What is with you, Vega?" Spinelli exploded as he watched the van speed away through the video datalink. "I thought you were here to help us! Instead, you just let a wanted criminal get away!"

"My orders are to send one CID unit and a Gullwing UAV out to this area, patrol for ten hours over varied terrain and operating conditions in both day and night, and report back to Major Richter and Sergeant Major Jefferson," Ariadna said curtly. "I don't much care what you thought."

Spinelli was ready to continue arguing with her, but instead he looked at her and nodded his head knowingly. "Oh, I get it now. What is it, Vega—afraid 'your people' are going to get persecuted by the big bad *federales?*"

Vega whirled around and pushed Spinelli hard in his chest with two hands. "Kiss my ass, Spinelli!" she shouted.

"I seem to have hit a nerve here, eh, Vega?" Spinelli smirked. "I run into that all the time. Most of the Border Patrol's recruits are Hispanic because it doesn't cost as much to teach them Spanish and they blend in with the border area population better. But the downside is that sometimes they don't want to catch the illegals as bad as others in the Border Patrol do. Some even have family members that are illegals, and they're afraid they're going to catch a relative or friend of a relative if they do their job well enough. They're good agents, but they let their heritage get in the way of their duty. They don't last very long in the service. After all, they're just wetbacks in uniform."

Ariadna's eyes blazed, and others in the room watching this interchange thought she was going to rush at him again. Instead, she hit the comm button on the console: "Harry, bring it in," she ordered. "The exercise is over." The Border Patrol supervisor smirked again. "And wipe that smile off your face before I do it for you, Spinelli."

"*Sí, señorita,*" Spinelli said. Ariadna glared at him but said nothing. It took only a few minutes for her to pack up her gear. "You come back when you're ready to do some *real* border security work, Doctor. Until then, the ghosts of the four Border Patrol agents who were killed the other day will thank you and your precious Mexican heritage to stay the hell out of our way."

MISSION VALLEY, CALIFORNIA
TWO DAYS LATER

The memorial service for the four slain Border Patrol agents was held at Qualcomm Stadium, just outside San Diego, where more than fifty thousand attendees witnessed one of the largest gatherings of law enforcement officers from around the world ever—

over three thousand men and women in uniform, some from as far away as South Africa, Australia, and Japan, assembled on the field to pay respects to the fallen agents. The caskets were brought into the stadium by simple wooden one-horse wagons, emblematic of the Border Patrol's frontier heritage, led by a company of one hundred bagpipers that filled the air with an awful yet stirring dirge.

The President of the United States, Samuel Conrad, stood at the podium before the four caskets and the thousands looking on. He took his prepared notes out of a breast pocket, looked at them briefly, then put them away. The audience was completely still— even the horses that drew the caissons seemed suddenly frozen in place.

"My staff prepared a eulogy in which I was going to talk about the dedication and professionalism of Border Agents Caufield, Tighe, Purdy, and Estaban," the President began, his voice cracking. "But I can't read it. I didn't know these men. My words might bring some comfort, coming from the President, but they'd be meaningless. These men were not my friends. They were public servants, guardians, protectors, law enforcement agents, and I am the President of the United States. Their bravery, professionalism, and dedication to duty have already been attested to by the men and women who knew them. I know that being a Border Patrol agent is a mostly lonely, difficult, and thankless job; unfortunately, it is also becoming a more dangerous one. They knew this, and still they went out into the deserts and did their duty. I thank these men and their families on behalf of our nation for their service, and I recognize that, ultimately, I am responsible for their deaths. I am their boss, their commander in chief in a sense, and I failed to adequately give them all the tools they needed to do their jobs.

"I know my words at this time and place probably don't mean much to you right now, but that's all I have to offer you, and I hope you'll accept them," the President went on, a tear rolling unbidden yet unchecked down his cheek. "I promise you that the deaths of these four fine men will not go unavenged. I promise I will act immediately to hunt down the killers and punish them. I further promise to do everything within my powers to make sure it doesn't happen again." With that, the President left the dais, shook hands and spoke a few words to each of the dead officer's family members, and departed the stadium with an angry, taunt-jawed expression. The President's aides and advisers had to scramble to keep up with him.

The President, Secretary of Homeland Security Jeffrey Lemke, and Customs and Border Protection Director James Abernathy were flown from the stadium by helicopter to March Air Reserve Base in Riverside, then traveled by motorcade to the Domestic Air Interdiction Coordination Center, the joint Federal Air Administration–Customs Service–Air Force radar surveillance facility. After meeting with the facility director and his staff and getting a brief tour of the facility, they were led into a secure con-ference room, where a number of persons were waiting for them to arrive.

The first to address the audience was National Security Adviser Sergeant Major Ray Jefferson, who was already on hand when the President arrived. "Welcome, Mr. President, to this border secu-rity operational briefing," he began. "This briefing is classified top secret, no foreign nationals, sensitive sources and methods in-volved, and the room is secure.

"This briefing concerns Operation Rampart. As directed by the President in Executive Order 07-23, Operation Rampart's mission is the integration of military, paramilitary, government, and civil patrol and law enforcement agencies to completely secure the southern borders of the United States from illegal intrusion.

"According to my staff, sir, based on arrests per sector, agents per sector, local law enforcement statistics, and patrol patterns in each sector, we estimate that approximately seven hundred and eighty thousand persons per year successfully cross the southern borders at other than legal points of entry," Jefferson went on. "Approximately one percent of those that cross the border are ar-rested. According to Customs and Border Protection statistics and reports, the number of illegal border crossings is rising approximately two percent a year. In addition, illegals are becoming more desperate and more violent because of the economic situation in their home countries and the sophistication of surveillance in more populated areas.

"Operation Rampart seeks to reduce the number of illegal border crossings by increasing surveillance, detection, and apprehension of illegal migrants through the use of more sophisticated surveillance technology and rapid reaction by high-speed aircraft and vehicles. In other words, sir, Operation Rampart will turn the borders of the United States into a true active military security zone that will prevent anyone from crossing the borders except at designated crossing points. It will also improve detection and apprehension of illegal aliens already in the country, improve the Department of Homeland Security's ability to protect and defend the United States from all manner of enemy or criminal activity, while at the same time offering opportunities for foreign workers to earn a decent wage and improve their way of life in this country."

"I've read your proposal, Sergeant Major Jefferson," Secretary of Homeland Security Jeffrey Lemke said. The former director of the Federal Bureau of Investigation was short and thin but tough-looking and serious. Following the shakeup in the Cabinet after the revelation that the former White House National Security Adviser Robert Chamberlain had financed and engineered several attacks against oil company facilities around the world, including a nuclear explosion near Houston, Texas, Lemke was going to resign along with many other government and Cabinet officials but was instead elevated to Secretary of Homeland Security. Lemke felt his distrust for Chamberlain was vindicated by his actions, and he had a natural skepticism of any projects or programs coming out of the National Security Adviser's office. "Although I'm intrigued by some aspects of it, my staff and bureau directors have serious reservations about the plan as a whole. This needs to be studied further." He glanced over at one of the other persons on the dais. "And the presence of Major Jason Richter of Task Force TALON is ominous to say the least. While we all applaud the major's heroic victories against the Consortium, I don't think border security is an area where TALON should get involved."

Jefferson turned to Richter, who stepped out to the lectern. He was dressed in pixilated desert battle dress uniform, including sand-gray boots, and a web belt with an empty pistol holster. Richter was tall and handsome, but seemed uncomfortably young, even for a major in the modern U.S. Army, especially standing beside Jefferson. His hair was dark and "high and tight," his uniform had only his name, rank, and "U.S. ARMY" tags, and he had a black beret tucked into his web belt. He stood rather uneasily, shuffling slightly from foot to foot, not nervous but as if fighting off surges of energy coursing through his body.

"First off, Mr. Secretary," Richter began, "I would like to extend my condolences to you and your department on behalf of TALON on your tragic loss at Blythe."

"Thank you, Major," Jeffrey Lemke said woodenly. "But frankly, this Operation Rampart and the way it's being cobbled together with such short notice is not making me feel much better; I'm also very concerned about Task Force TALON's involvement in this. But please continue."

"TALON is involved because I believe the Consortium is behind that attack against the Border Patrol agents at Blythe, sir."

"I wasn't briefed on that," Lemke said.

"It's my opinion only, sir," Jason said. "But we have had three incidents in less than a week with migrants carrying automatic weapons, something they rarely if ever did before the Consortium attacks. According to FBI Director DeLaine, most of the other known terror, insurgency, and supremacy groups in the U.S. went to ground during the Consortium attacks and have not really resurfaced following the Washington confrontation because of stepped-up security—yet more and more migrants are traveling with heavy weaponry. I think Yegor Zakharov is orchestrating these cross-border incidents, possibly to bring fighters and weapons into the U.S. to carry out more attacks. He's a wounded animal, and those are the most dangerous."

"I tend to agree with the major's assessment, Mr. President, which is why I recommended putting Task Force TALON on the borders as part of Operation Rampart," Jefferson interjected. "We can pull Task Force TALON units away from border security duties quickly if needed elsewhere. The CID units' big advantage, along with their firepower and versatility, is their mobility and deployability."

The Secretary of Homeland Security was immensely skeptical and made no attempt to hide his doubt; this only encouraged the Chief of Staff's objections: "We can't raise the 'Consortium' and 'Zakharov' warning flags every time there's a shooting in America," Kinsly said perturbedly. "Congress will start to lose patience if we cry wolf every few weeks."

"Then we'll say that TALON is the best choice because they're already formed up and can be swung into action fast," Jefferson said. "We can have four teams ready to go in twenty-four hours, even before the first patrol base is fully constructed."

Lemke shrugged noncommittally. "The other problem I have is this budget," he went on, shaking his head in disbelief. "I believe your numbers are gross underestimates. And if you add in administrative and judicial costs, you're looking at an initial outlay of between six and eight billion dollars to start, and four to five billion dollars a year to maintain it. And that's *before* Congress starts tacking on it's own pet projects to the appropriation bill. I would expect the initial cost of this program to be close to ten billion dollars this year alone and fifty to sixty billion dollars over the next ten years to maintain. That's more than the *entire* Bureau of Customs and Border Protection budget! How in the world am I supposed to sell this program to Congress and the American people, Mr. President?"

"Remind them of the four dead agents that are being buried today, Mr. Lemke," Jefferson responded.

"Excuse me, Mr. Jefferson, but I'm not going to use the dead to

justify this—I have too much respect for those men and their families," Lemke said bitterly. He turned to President Conrad. "Mr.
President, we absolutely *cannot* put robots on the U.S.-Mexico border—folks will think we're creating some sort of sci-fi prison
around the United States! I recognize the invaluable service Major
Richter and his team has performed battling terrorists, but using
these multimillion-dollar robots to catch migrant farmworkers
seems like trying to use a main battle tank to stomp out cock-
roaches!"

"Secretary Lemke, the equation is simple," Richter said. "The
Bureau of Customs and Border Protection, which is in charge of
securing the borders, is completely understaffed and overwhelmed. I estimate it would take at least five thousand new
agents on the U.S.-Mexico border alone to even begin to get illegal
immigration under control. We can't afford that. You have just
two alternatives: use five thousand National Guard troops—or use
Task Force TALON."

"You think your robots can do the work of *five thousand* National Guard troops, Major?"

"Combined with advanced surveillance assets—I know they
can, sir," Jason replied. "They can do it better, faster, and cheaper.
All I need is the go-ahead and the political support of the administration and I'll have the U.S.-Mexico border completely secure in
twelve months."

"A three-thousand-mile border—*completely* secure in just
twelve months?" Lemke retorted. "That's impossible, even with a
hundred of your robots."

"I can do it, sir," Jason said confidently. "You've seen the capabilities of the Cybernetic Infantry Device units in the battle with
the Consortium. They're even more capable now. This is the type
of mission best suited for them."

"I asked the staff to come up with innovative and original ideas
for border security, and this certainly fits the bill," the President
said. To Richter, he asked, "How many of these CID units do you
have available, Major?"

"Ten, Mr. President," Jason replied. "I want to use eight for this mission, at least two per base, with two set aside for training, as a spare, and for other contingencies. Our emergency budget and engineering resources should give us another sixteen units on-line by the end of the year."

"The cost of which hasn't been factored into this budget," Lemke said. "This is beginning to get out of control here, Jefferson. You need to rethink this proposal a lot more before presenting it to the Cabinet for approval, and certainly get the congressional leadership involved in the planning."

There was a strained silence after that; then, the President motioned to Jefferson. "Sergeant Major, continue the briefing, please."

"A preliminary security evaluation was recently concluded by Major Jason Richter, and he is here to present his findings. Major Richter?"

"Mr. President, Task Force TALON has studied the deployment of the U.S. Border Patrol over the past two days in both day and night operations, and we've toured several Border Patrol sector operations centers and observed their operations," he said. "The current border control system uses a combination of ground and air patrols that deploy out of sector patrol locations, intelligence data collected by Border Patrol agents, twenty-foot-high steel fences erected within fifteen to twenty miles either side of the twenty-five legal border crossing points along the U.S.-Mexico border's legal crossing points, and underground vibration sensors for the majority of all other areas. Approximately thirty percent of the border has some sort of electronic surveillance or a physical barrier. Of the remaining seventy percent of the border, however, my task force considers surveillance and security nonexistent."

"I hope the Border Patrol gets an opportunity to respond, sir," James Abernathy, director of the Bureau of Customs and Border Protection, interjected pointedly.

"Don't worry, Jim, you'll get a chance," Secretary of Homeland Security Lemke said. Under his breath, some of the audience heard him mutter, "I hope."

"The fences are generally considered effective when properly maintained," Richter went on, "but it has resulted in driving most illegal border crossings out into isolated, uninhabited regions beyond the fences. In most of these areas there is no fence of any kind marking the border; where private lands are adjacent to the border, there is usually just a typical barbed-wire cattle fence, which is easily crossed or cut down. Illegal migrants regularly do a lot of damage to private and public property in their efforts to make it into the United States.

"The vibration sensors are generally considered effective in detecting movement. When motion is detected, Border Patrol surveillance officers make a best guess on the number of persons detected by the sensors and report this to the on-duty sector duty officer. He then checks the deployment of his sector patrol units. Based on unit availability and the number reported by the sensor operator and other factors such as weather, intelligence data on wanted persons traveling in a certain manner or area, distance to travel, and availability of support units and detention facilities, he or she makes the decision whether or not to deploy patrol units."

"The bottom line: you can generally see them, but you don't or can't always go get them," the President summarized.

"The major's analysis barely scratches the surface of the situation, Mr. President," Abernathy said bitterly. "He can't possibly make a fair evaluation after only observing our men and women in action for two days."

"Understood," the President said. "Continue, Major Richter."

"It appears to my task force that the problem with border security is mostly due to a lack of resources," Jason went on. "Simply put, there are simply not enough patrol agents or sensors in the field to cover such a long border. The terrain and climate are two major factors. Most of the border is not well patrolled because it is simply too rugged, too barren, too far from usable roads, or too difficult to operate in for any length of time. Weather conditions are usually extreme: hot, cold, windy, dry, and everything in between, factors that hamper effective patrol operations but won't deter a determined smuggler or migrant from attempting the crossing." Jason was happy to see that Abernathy was nodding slightly in agreement. "That concludes my briefing, sir."

"Thank you, Major Richter," Jefferson said as he returned to the lectern. "Mr. President, Operation Rampart will achieve its mission objective by utilizing reaction teams composed of unmanned tactical surveillance aircraft with specialized sensors to detect, locate, and track any person or vehicle crossing the borders, combined with fast-reaction ground and air units positioned in numerous locations along the border to stop the intruder and make an arrest. Instead of being deployed from headquarters areas to the border, these reaction teams will be located *on* the border. Each surveillance base will be spaced approximately ten miles apart, depending on terrain."

"How many bases are you proposing, Ray?" the President asked.

"Approximately fifty bases, sir," Jefferson replied.

"*Fifty bases?*" Lemke asked, astonished. "You want to build fifty air bases along the border?"

"Yes, sir," Jefferson replied. "They are not full-up air bases— they are small bare-base airfields with detention and support facilities. Each surveillance base houses a reaction team composed of an air flight, composed of two long-endurance surveillance airships, three utility helicopters, and field maintenance facilities; a security flight, composed of perimeter, facility, prisoner, and personnel security officers; and a support flight, which takes care of lodging, meals, physical plant, power, water, detention, transportation, and common areas." Jefferson changed Powerpoint slides on the screen before the audience. "Each base would have about fifty personnel, which are deployed from active, Reserve, or National Guard military bases for a week at a time, once per month. They would . . ."

"*Twenty-five-hundred troops a week?*" Lemke exclaimed. "Do we *have* that many troops?"

"The Army National Guard and Army Reserves have a total of

seven hundred and fifty thousand personnel," Jefferson responded. "Of these, about three hundred thousand are infantry, light mechanized, air cavalry, security, and intelligence-trained, appropriate for this mission. If we use just ten to fifteen thousand of them and rotate them to the Border Patrol mission once a month, we can fulfill the manning requirements. The advantage is that these citizen soldiers will be deployed right here, in the United States, close to home. That is a tremendous cost savings and morale booster. It may also be possible to augment some of these forces with volunteers." He turned to the President and added, "It's a substantial mission to undertake, sir, there's no question. It might mean fewer infantry, support, logistics, and intelligence forces available to augment the active-duty force . . ."

"Assuming you use each unit just one monthly rotation per year, that means over one hundred thousand troops per year," Chief of Staff Kinsly pointed out. That's over a *third* of all Guard and Reserve units assigned just to border security!" He turned to the President and went on: "That's major, sir. That'll send an awfully in-your-face message to the Mexican government, to the Hispanic population, and to civil rights and immigration rights groups."

"I want to hear about the plan first, Tom," the President said irritably, "before I hear about potential political problems. One headache at a time, please."

"I see men and equipment for surveillance and detention," Secretary of Homeland Security Lemke pointed out, "but nothing for actually *stopping* anyone from crossing the border. Seems to me you're not solving the problem here, Sergeant Major—we can see them, but we can't stop them. Your ten thousand troops per month are only there to support the surveillance stuff—how many more will you need for patrol and apprehension? Or are you just going to rely on the Border Patrol?"

"We can always increase the size of the Border Patrol," Jefferson responded, "but I have another suggestion: using CID units."

"Why am I not surprised?" Kinsly moaned.

Jefferson turned to Jason Richter, who stepped back to the lectern: "The CID units have the right capabilities for this mission, sir," he said. "They're fast, have better rough terrain capability than Humvees, they can carry a lot of heavy equipment, and they can perform other missions such as search and rescue, medevac, armed intervention . . ."

"What about your other task force missions, Major?" Jeffrey Lemke asked. "Won't this slow down your pursuit of the rest of the Consortium? And what exactly will these CID units do?"

"They receive surveillance data from the unmanned aircraft or from ground sensors on anyone observed to cross the border and respond to the location to investigate," Jefferson said. "If it encounters any illegal migrants, they can detain them until Border Patrol officers arrive to make an arrest."

"Let's get to the bottom line, Sergeant Major," the President interjected. "What's this plan going to cost?"

"Personnel costs are approximately one hundred thousand dollars per month per base, or one hundred twenty million dollars per year. Total manpower required is approximately twenty-five hundred soldiers rotated among the facilities every week, or a total manpower commitment of ten thousand troops per month, or one billion dollars per year. Cost to operate the ground vehicles is eighty million dollars per year; cost to operate the helicopters and UAVs is approximately eight hundred million dollars per year. We estimate we will have approximately twenty-five thousand detainees in custody in our facilities; they will cost another billion dollars a year to feed, house, and provide support for them. This brings the total cost of this program to approximately three billion dollars a year, plus approximately a billion dollars to build the bases themselves."

Lemke looked at the briefing slides projected onto the screen before him. "What about these detention facilities, Mr. Jefferson? Assuming your reaction teams work as advertised, what do you propose to do with the detainees you capture?"

"They will be held in detention facilities at each surveillance base until processed, sir," Jefferson replied. "Each base will have facilities to house two hundred and fifty detainees. We anticipate that detainees will be held a minimum of thirty days until their identities, political status, and criminal records are checked; repeat offenders will be detained for longer periods of time, or transferred to other federal facilities."

"You're going to *arrest* them, Jefferson?" Lemke asked. "Women, children, old men—*arrest* them just for trying to cross the border, make a better life for themselves, and do work that others won't do?"

"No, Mr. Secretary—we're going to arrest them because they broke the law," Jefferson said. "I did check, sir, and the United States still does have a law against crossing the borders outside of legal border crossing points or ports of entry. It does *not* mention any extenuating circumstances. There is no age limit, medical qualification, or lawful purpose for doing so except for political asylum: it is still illegal."

"Don't get smart with me, Jefferson!" Lemke snapped. "I'm very well aware of the law—I'm the one chosen to enforce it, not you."

"And I'm very well aware of my duties, Mr. Secretary," Jefferson shot back. "There is a national security issue here, especially apparent after the murders of the four Border Patrol agents near Blythe."

"If the attackers were wearing uniforms and helmets," the President interjected, "it seems to me there would be no question in anyone's mind that the United States was under attack and that there was a national security deficiency here. Why is there a question now, Jeffrey—because the illegal migrants are old, young, or female?"

"To me, sir, it's a question of whether someone committing an illegal border crossing is entitled to due process," Lemke said after an uncomfortable pause, unaccustomed to being queried directly by the President of the United States. "It is assumed, and I think everyone here will agree, that putting the military on the borders by definition means that we're taking away due process . . ."

"And I would disagree, Mr. Secretary," Jefferson interjected. "The military has for many years assisted law enforcement, and it would be no different here. The Bureau of Customs and Border Protection would still be one of the lead agencies involved in Operation Rampart; the military would be in a major support role."

Lemke held up Jefferson's presentation outline. "I think the question of who is in charge would be a subject of considerable debate, Sergeant Major Jefferson, since you propose putting a military officer in charge of the operation," he said. He dropped the outline back on the table and shook his head as if very frustrated and confused. "So your task force finds and detains the migrants crossing the border and you put them in your detention facility. Are they allowed to be bailed out?"

"They are subject to normal criteria for release imposed by a federal judge," Jefferson replied. "As far as I'm aware, the prevailing criteria are government-issued identification, U.S. resident or resident alien status, a verified U.S. address, and no outstanding wants or warrants. Most illegal migrants would not fall under these criteria and would probably be held without bail or at a higher bond amount."

"So you're going to build a hundred of these Guantanamo Bay–like prison facilities right here in the U.S.?" Lemke asked incredulously. "Are they allowed to have legal representation, or do we just allow the International Red Cross to visit them?"

"Who's being sarcastic now, Secretary Lemke?" Jefferson asked. "I see no reason to withhold legal assistance or representation. They may prefer to waive their right to trial and accept detention rather than risk being held in detention for an unknown number of days until their case comes to trial."

"So it's like getting a speeding ticket, eh, Jefferson?" Lemke asked derisively. "Pull 'em over, throw 'em in a camp, and make 'em sign a confession? If they plead guilty they spend a couple weeks in a camp?"

"We feel the loss of income from being detained would provide some measure of deterrent for many migrants, yes, sir."

"When was the last time you visited a federal detention facility or even a medium-sized county jail, Sergeant Major?" Lemke asked. "You could have hundreds, perhaps thousands, staying there for months, including children—are you prepared to handle that?"

"Yes, sir."

"And then they spend a couple weeks in a camp—where, by the way, their living conditions might be markedly better than their conditions either in Mexico or on a farm—and then what? Your only option is to deport them, and everyone knows that becomes a simple revolving door—they'll try to make another border crossing as soon as they're able. You took away all those weeks of income, so they'll be even more hard-pressed to try a crossing again. You'll have to expend the time, energy, manpower, and money into recapturing the same immigrant over and over again."

"First of all, Secretary Lemke: the mere fact that this program will be difficult, expensive, and manpower-intensive shouldn't be the major disqualifying factor," Jefferson said. "Government's duty is to uphold the law and protect the citizens—as far as I'm aware, how much such duties cost has never been a criteria for whether or not it should be done."

"It's a criteria if Congress says it is, Sergeant Major," Lemke pointed out.

"Second: we have technology that may allow us to help in identification," Jefferson went on. "Major Richter?"

Jason stood up, then held up an oblong pill the size of a large vitamin tablet. "It's called NIS, pronounced 'nice'—nanotransponder identification system."

"Cute name—obviously trying to make it sound pleasant and peaceful," Lemke said, chuckling. He motioned to Richter, who brought the device over so Lemke could examine it. "What is it . . . a suppository?" The audience broke out in strained laughter. "Pardon me, Major, but I think getting rid of that won't be much of a problem."

"Not a suppository, sir—a system that implants thousands of

tiny microtransceivers throughout the body," Major Richter explained. "The transceivers are powered by the human body itself and emit an identification signal when interrogated by another transmitter, much the same as an aircraft transponder transmits the aircraft altitude when interrogated by air traffic control radar. The cells last for years and can't be shut down by the body's normal immunological system."

"You have *got* to be kidding me, Major Richter," Jeffrey Lemke said, looking at the tablet in amazement, then putting it down on the table in front of him as if worried that the little robotic cells could slip under his skin and invade *his* body. "You actually expect someone to *swallow* one of those things?"

"Yes, sir, I do," Jason said. "In fact, I already have."

"What . . . ?"

"Two days ago, when I was first briefed by Sergeant Major Jefferson that I'd be giving this briefing," Jason said. Ariadna Vega walked up, carrying a device that resembled a short baseball bat, and pressed a button. After a short wait, one of the overhead electronic screens presented a list of information. "Dr. Vega is demonstrating a prototype NIS scanner," Jason explained. "The scanner is sending out a coded digital interrogation signal, and the NIS devices respond with their individual code number. The NIS system can then call up information on the person."

"Why are there three lines of information on you, Major?"

"Because there are three persons within range of the scanner—approximate range is about two miles—with active NIS cells: myself, Dr. Vega, and Sergeant Major Jefferson."

"*You* actually *swallowed* one of those things, Jefferson?" Lemke asked incredulously.

"Of course I did," Jefferson said. "I wouldn't ask anyone to do anything I wouldn't be willing to do myself. It's perfectly harmless; the interrogation codes can be changed remotely in case the code is compromised; the NIS transmissions are encoded; and unless they're being interrogated, the NIS cells are completely dormant. The strength of the coded NIS reply signal is high enough to possibly cause cardiac arrhythmias if the interrogator is left on continuously for long periods of time, more than one or two hours. But activating the scanner for just a few seconds causes every NIS cell within a couple miles or so to respond, and their positions can be recorded and plotted immediately—there's no need to continuously broadcast an interrogation signal."

"How do you get rid of them?"

"The transmitters are quiet unless interrogated by a specific coded signal, so if the interrogator is shut off the cells are dormant," Jason replied. "The cells themselves are carried away by normal bodily functions at different rates depending on where they implant themselves and how active they are. The average age of a NIS cell itself is around ten years, but the body would probably flush out all of the cells within three to five years. They can probably be destroyed by certain chemicals or radiation, but the level of exposure necessary to kill every NIS cell would probably kill the person too."

"This . . . this is pretty unbelievable," Lemke said, shaking his head. "Why don't you just fingerprint and photograph the migrants when you capture them? Why use these nanotransponder things at all?"

"Fingerprinting someone doesn't do any good if they manage to sneak back into the country, or if we decide to implement a *bracero* guest worker program where legal migrant workers might intermingle with illegals," Jefferson replied. "The NIS system allows us to quickly and remotely scan large areas or large numbers of persons. The scanner can be mounted on an unmanned aircraft to scan large areas of land like farms and cities; they can be set up to work alongside metal detectors; or they can be used by enforcement personnel on vehicles or as hand wands."

"But if you don't take one of those tablets . . . ?"

"NIS is designed to facilitate identification, not to locate illegals, sir," Jason said. "If you were scanning a group of persons and someone didn't reply with an NIS signal, you would detain them and use other methods to try to obtain their identity. NIS has possible uses outside border security: it could be used for any sort of identification, such as at airports or high-security buildings. It might even have commercial purposes: the unique identification code broadcast by NIS can be tied into any number of databases that could allow individuals to securely pay for items without using credit cards, unlock doors without keys, provide access to confidential medical data without paper files—an almost unlimited number of applications."

"So the system identifies persons *legally* in the country, and then you must *assume* that everyone else is a suspect," Lemke said. "We're forced to take away the right of privacy of the innocent in order to help identify the possible lawbreaker? That's not how our society is supposed to work, Major Richter."

"It's done all the time, Mr. Secretary, especially in a free and open society such as ours," Jefferson said. "NIS is no different in concept than putting locks on doors or building fences around neighborhoods: it's an inconvenience for the innocent in order to protect them against the criminals."

" 'Giving up your freedom in order to ensure safety makes you neither free nor safe.' Benjamin Franklin," Lemke quoted. "Is that where we're headed now, Sergeant Major? Plant microscopic tattletales on innocent men, women, and children in order to weed out the undesirables—is that truly what we want to do?"

"Mr. Secretary, Task Force TALON is responding to my request for proposals on the issues of border security," the National Security Adviser said. "Our intention is not to address every legal, moral, or civil rights question that may arise—I don't believe we'd ever get anything accomplished if we canceled every project or innovation because it *might* have a civil rights issue.

"Launching unmanned aerial spy planes and deploying forty thousand troops to patrol the borders wouldn't be enough, even if they were one hundred percent effective—we need some way to locate illegal persons who are already in the United States, those who slip past our security, or those whose status changes while in the country," Jefferson went on. "Regular identification methods can't work because they are too easily forged and it assumes your subject comes before you willingly to submit his or her ID, if they even have any. Of course it would be better to use the NIS system in illegal persons, but that's unworkable: a guilty person doesn't stay guilty, and a guilty person may not cooperate with authorities, presenting the prospect of forcing a person to submit to the NIS system as part of release, probation, or parole."

"This is sounding more and more like 'Big Brother' by the moment," Lemke said. He turned to the President. "Sir, are you sure you want to travel down this path? Civil rights groups are going to scream bloody murder about this obtrusive electronic ID program."

"Jeffrey, we have been wrestling with these legal and moral questions ever since Nine-Eleven: whether the government can install more obtrusive security and identification systems on the law-abiding public in order to try to protect the public against deadly attacks," the President responded. "How much is too much? The people are entitled to life, liberty, and the pursuit of happiness; the government's responsibility is to do everything possible to ensure they get it. We put up with security, monitoring, and other restrictions to freedom now that would make the framers of the Constitution scream in agony."

"Then I suggest that you don't take the next step, sir—don't make the situation worse by throwing the military into it," Lemke said. "The Department of Homeland Security already uses thousands of National Guardsmen and Reservists for duties like searching cargo containers assisting both Immigration and Customs Enforcement and the Bureau of Customs and Border Protection; we've already absorbed the U.S. Coast Guard, which has primary responsibility for patrolling and safeguarding the coast and ports. We've always stopped short of putting the military on the borders because an open and free society shouldn't have to militarize its borders, especially with friendly neighbors . . ."

"Our neighbors may be friendly, Jeffrey," Jefferson said, "but they are not always cooperative. Illegal immigration and undocumented workers are of great benefit to countries like Mexico because they reduce the strain on services in Mexico and bring millions of U.S. dollars into the Mexican economy each year. The Mexican government has done a lot to make sure it is safe to travel back and forth across the borders illegally, if not outright promote illegal immigration."

The President turned to Director of Customs and Border Protection Abernathy. "Director Abernathy? Your thoughts."

"Operation Rampart alters the relationship between the United States and Mexico in a very drastic manner, Mr. President," Abernathy said. "Neighbors should do whatever's possible to cooperate with one another if a problem develops. Militarizing the border is counterproductive and is in my opinion a downright aggressive posture, along the lines of the East and West German border region during the Cold War. We have the technology to take surveillance, security, and identification to a whole new level of effectiveness—the question is, *should* we do it, even if it means putting yet another level of government intrusion on our lives?"

The President sat back in his seat and wearily rubbed his eyes. "Before Nine-Eleven, I would have said no—we should be doing everything possible to preserve freedom and privacy. I have always believed in smaller government; I believed some of the laws passed in the angry emotional aftermath of Nine-Eleven went too far. I always believed the guilty have the same rights as the innocent. But then there was Kingman City, San Francisco, Washington, and now Blythe—more examples of how a determined enemy can exploit our freedom to accomplish his deadly goals.

"I'm not going to wait any longer on this, Jeffrey," the President went on. "I've attended more funerals in the past several months than I ever thought possible, and I'm tired of standing up in front of crowds of angry and confused mourners, promising to do something more to stop terrorists from infiltrating our borders and conducting attacks against us." He took a deep breath before continuing: "I have been President during the three most deadliest terrorist acts ever on U.S. soil, events that make even Nine-Eleven

pale in comparison. I was hoping that the danger would have subsided, but I see now it has only intensified. I refuse to sit back and
worry about taking away rights while the evil in this world attacks
us with abandon."

President Conrad looked at the others around him, searching
their eyes or expressions for any sign of dissent or argument. He
found nothing but stone-somber faces and averted eyes. "Let Congress or the courts decide if what we do here this day violates the
Constitution we all swore to uphold," he said. "As the leader of the
Executive Branch of our government as well as this nation, which
has declared war on terrorism and has vowed to fight it wherever it
is found, with whatever weapon we have at our disposal, I will act.

"Gentlemen, the attack on our Border Patrol agents by these
highly trained and well-equipped assassins is a warning that our
borders are wide open and our country, our government, and our
people are vulnerable," he said. "I mean to do something about it,
and I want it done *now*. I want this program rolling quickly, efficiently, and positively.

"I'm staking my entire political future on this project, and I expect each one of my administrators and commanders to follow
through one hundred and ten percent," the President concluded.
"If you can't do it, I expect your resignations on my desk by the
time I get back to Washington. I want total commitment, or you
can find work elsewhere. Understood?" There was a muted cho-
rus of "Yes, Mr. President" around the room. "Let's get it on,
folks."

FIVE MILES SOUTH OF OCATILLO, CALIFORNIA
DAYS LATER

The five-mile gap between the steel border security fences between the Tecate and Mexicali border crossing points had been
filled in with a simple fifteen-foot-high chain-link fence, which

was laughably easy to climb. The fence was also cut into pieces in many areas, so much so that it was possible to walk through it without getting your clothes dirty or snagged. Messages and flags posted in various towns, villages, roads, and bus stations in Mexico also told the latest news about which parts of the fence were open, which cameras were active or broken, and where recent arrests had been made. Intel on crossing the fence was plentiful and mostly accurate.

Everyone also knew there were motion sensors buried in various places between the border, Route 98, and Interstate 8. The sensors would send a signal to the U.S. Border Patrol stations in San Diego or El Centro, alerting air and ground patrols. The Border Patrol planes had heat-seeking FLIR sensors, which could make out a warm body easily against the rapidly chilling ground at night. But at night the ground patrols took much longer to travel cross-country, if they came at all, so even with a plane up unless you were really unlucky and a patrol was already in the area, you were probably going to make it. Even if a Border Patrol vehicle did show, once the *pollos* scattered it was tough to round them all up again, so at night the majority of this group of twenty-five illegals crossing the border had a pretty good chance of making it to the interstate highway. A few would always get caught, but most would make it.

It was a numbers game most migrants were willing to play. The strongest and most dedicated of them would make it. The women, children, and the weaker ones had their own role to play too: they gave the Border Patrol someone to catch.

Once the migrants got to Ocatillo, there was a fairly sophisticated travel network set up to get the majority of them to their destinations. Many had relatives waiting for them; many used gypsy taxis and buses, many of them run by farm owners and driven by illegals themselves, to transport *pollos* to their jobs or to more migrant-friendly bus stations, ones not patrolled as frequently by Border Patrol or Immigration and Customs Enforcement agents. Once north of Interstate 8, the chances of evading the authorities and blending into the largely Hispanic population of southern California was much easier.

The trek for this group of twenty-five men and women went smoothly. They camped a couple miles from the border in a small gully until dark, out of sight of infrequent American patrols; then they crossed the chain-link fence, followed a circuitous path around known motion sensors, and hurried on, being careful to stay off established paths and roads where patrols and sensors would likely be.

By midnight the group was within sight of the town of Ocatillo. Another couple of hours to reach the outskirts of town, and then they would disperse. The group was excited, talking in soft but energetic voices. About a full day on foot, and they were safely in the U.S., ready to get to work. So far, no sign of any patrols or . . .

At that moment, they heard, *"La atención, ésta es la frontera de Estado Unidos patrulla. Permanezca donde usted está y tenga por favor su identificación lista demostrar a los oficiales. Gracias."*

"A la chingada! The Border Patrol is here!" one of the migrants cursed.

"Where? Where are they?" another asked. The Border Patrol rarely sneaked up on migrants in the field—they came in with lights on vehicles or helicopters blazing; their checkpoints were surrounded by lights that could be seen for miles, as if very demonstrably broadcasting a warning for the illegals to turn around and head back to the border.

"¿Quién cuida? Just run!" At that, eight men took off, five running east and the other three heading west. The rest of the group seemed confused and scared; a few "assumed the position"—squatting down, arms on their knees, and lighting up a cigarette, awaiting arrest—and several others headed off in random, mostly southerly directions, bumping into each other as they fled. A few dared not use flashlights, but most pulled out their "lucis," short for *luciérnaga,* or "fireflies"—small disposable flashlights to help them see in the pitch-black darkness, part of the discarded artifacts of the *pollos'* presence, along with water

bottles and plastic ponchos, which could be seen littering the desert by the thousands along the border region from California to Texas.

"No funcione por favor o usted puede ser dañado," the electronic voice said. Naturally, none of the ones running stopped. The only lights visible were the lights of Ocatillo far off on the horizon, and that direction had to be avoided. The runners simply put the lights of Ocatillo on their backs or left or right shoulders and ran as best they could, hoping that the Border Patrol would pick someone else to arrest.

The group of eight men running east shielded their "lucis" as much as possible to avoid giving away their position, but they still had trouble maintaining their balance as they half-ran, half-stumbled through the darkness. But the chase—the scratches from running into thorny bushes, the twisted ankles, the headlong tumbles down an unseen wash—was part of the game, and they played it well. The Border Patrol had their all-terrain vehicles, helicopters, dogs, and sensors—all the migrants had were their feet and their desire to make it safely to their destination. Most often they came out on top, proof enough to them that their exertion was worthwhile and justified. The farther they ran, the better chances they had of . . .

Suddenly they heard an electronic voice shout, *"¡Parada!* 'Stop!' "* directly in front of them, but they could see nothing in the darkness. Two men dodged left away from what they thought was the source of the voice . . . and ran headlong right into what felt like a steel wall. *"¡Madre del díos!"* one of them shouted. Dazedly he looked up, then flicked on his luci . . .

. . . just in time to see a large figure—not a man, but a man-shaped figure as big as a church doorway. The thing was about ten feet tall, with a ribbed frame throughout with a light gray covering underneath. Its arms were attached to broad shoulders, thinning down to a slender waist, but its legs and feet were wide and very steady-looking. Its head was bullet-shaped, with a variety of sensors attached all around it. But the most unusual thing about the robot is how it moved. It was remarkably agile and incredibly humanlike in all its movements, with every human nuance duplicated with amazing precision. As they watched, the thing darted away and was gone in the blink of an eye into the darkness.

One of the *pollos* tried to get up and run, but he stumbled into a thorny bush in the darkness, and the energy simply drained out of his body. The second man started scrambling across the desert on his hands and knees, but finally gave up as well and rejoined his dazed amigo.

Through his imaging infrared sensor, Captain Frank "Falcon" Falcone aboard CID One could see the desert landscape even clearer than in the shimmering, eye-burning daytime—and the migrants stood out even clearer, even at ranges in excess of two miles. "Two down here," he radioed. "I'm going after the group of five."

"We have a good eyeball on you, Falcon," Ariadna Vega said. She was back at the first Rampart forward operating location constructed as part of the presidential directive to fortify the U.S.-Mexico border, located about eight miles southeast. She was watching images broadcast from an unmanned reconnaissance vehicle called a Condor, orbiting overhead in a racetrack pattern in this often-used migrant border-crossing area. "The last guy in your group looks like he's giving up." She could clearly see the third runner with his hands on his head, walking in the direction from where he came. "The group of five have split up into two groups, Charlie and Delta. Delta looks like the group of three."

"Got 'em," Falcone said. Every time he moved his head, his electronic visor showed small lettered arrows where the Condor's targeting sensors had locked onto a person. "On the way." Falcone turned in the direction of the Delta arrow and started off in a fast trot, quickly reaching thirty miles an hour and catching up to the runners with ease. He ran past them, then stopped about fifty yards in front of their path and watched as they ran toward him. When they got closer he broadcast, "*Los hombres, éste son la fron-*

tera patrullan Operation Rampart. *Por favor parada. No le dañaré.*
'Please stop. I won't hurt you.' "

"*¡Déjenos solos, híbrido!*" one of them shouted. Falcone reached
out just as one was about to run past him and gave him a push,
sending him flying and crashing into the hard-baked earth. Another really big *pollo,* shining his flashlight on the CID unit before him, gasped aloud, swore, ran toward Falcone, jumped, and
kicked out with both feet as if he was trying to break down a
door. Falcone wasn't prepared for the jump-kick and didn't
brace himself; he staggered backward a few steps when the big
Mexican hit.

"*¿No tan resistente, eh, cerdo?*" the third man shouted gleefully.
"You messed with the wrong *toro* tonight, *culo!*" Out of nowhere
he produced an Intratec TEC-9 nine-millimeter semiautomatic
pistol, leveled it, and opened fire, pulling the trigger as fast as he
could. The second migrant screamed, trying to tell the third not to
shoot, then covering his ears and flattening himself on the ground
as the machine gun erupted.

"*Eso no era muy elegante, amigo,*" Falcone said through his electronic translator. The migrant's shots were running wild; Falcone
was sure he had not been hit; and the rusty sand-coated gun
jammed after the fifth or sixth round—but still, something happened to Frank Falcone in the next few milliseconds that he could
not explain. Maybe it was just piloting the CID unit; maybe it was
the excitement of the night patrol . . . he didn't think, he just reacted. Moving with breathtaking speed, Falcone rushed at the
gunman, and like a football linebacker running at full speed, tackled him with his right shoulder.

The Cybernetic Infantry Device robots were not heavy—the
CID unit with Falcone aboard weighed less than three hundred
and fifty pounds—but at the speed Falcone was moving, the impact was like getting hit by a car traveling over thirty miles an
hour. The entire force of the impact of the CID unit's shoulder
centered squarely on the migrant's left lung and heart, crushing
his sternum and rib cage and driving pieces of bone through both

organs. The man did not have enough breath to cough out the chestful of blood flooding his throat and right lung, and he died within moments.

"Oh, *Christ!*" Falcone cursed. "Control, CID One, I have a suspect down my position. I tackled the guy, and it looks like I really bashed him. I'm dismounting."

"We registered gunshots, One," Ariadna radioed. "Do not dismount until we can secure the area." There was no response. "CID One, do you read me? Falcon, answer up."

But Falcone had already climbed out of the CID unit and gone over to the gunman with a flashlight and first-aid kit from the CID unit's dismount container, a device resembling a fanny pack attached to the back of the robot. It did not take long for him to make an assessment—the guy was definitely dead. Falcone went back to the dismount container and retrieved a wireless headset. "Ari? Falcon. He's dead. Send a Border Patrol van with a medical examiner."

Ariadna was already talking excitedly when Falcone released the Transmit key: ". . . converging on your position, repeat, Frank, I see two unknowns moving in on your position! Do you copy?"

"I copy, Ari. Which direc . . . ?" He was interrupted by the sound of bullets ricocheting off the CID unit beside him. *"Shots fired, Ari!"* he radioed. "Where are they?"

"West of your position, Frank!" Ari responded. "Get down! Take cover!"

Falcone hit the ground and crawled behind the CID unit. He heard more gunshots, but no more bullets hit the robot or the earth around him. He tried to reach up to the dismount container to retrieve the wrist remote controller, but excited voices in Spanish and more gunshots made him duck again for cover. They were close, *very* close. Flashlight beams started to arc in his direction. "They're almost on me, Ari," Falcone said. "Take control of CID One and take 'em out!"

"Roger, Falcon," Vega responded. Moments later the hatch on the back of the CID unit snapped shut, and the big robot lumbered to life. "*¡Caiga sus armas! ¡Ésta es su advertencia pasada!*" Ariadna radioed through the robot via the satellite datalink. She raised the robot's hands and arms menacingly, steering the robot toward the oncoming migrants, hopefully enough to scare them off but not too far away to expose Falcone. The robot had no weapons, and the satellite downlink was very slow—the robot would be able to do little else but walk and talk under her control . . .

. . . and at that moment, it appeared as if the gunmen figured that detail out, for they immediately split up and started to flank the robot, circling it and moving closer to Falcone. Ari had no choice but to make the CID unit step back to protect Falcone.

"*¿Cuál es incorrecto, Señor Robot?*" one of the gunmen asked. "Not so tough now, are you?"

"*¡Mate al poli y salgamos de aquí!*" the other gunman shouted. "Send him to hell and let's . . . *aaiieee!*" Suddenly the second gunman's voice was cut off with a strangled scream. The first gunman swung his flashlight around toward his comrade and saw a large metal container of some kind lying on the ground next to the unconscious second gunman. The first gunman cried out, dropped his weapon, and ran off.

"You okay, Falcon?" Jason Richter radioed. A few moments later, CID Two ran up to where Falcone was still lying prone on the desert floor, and Jason dismounted.

"I'm okay," Falcone replied. They checked the unconscious gunman together. "What'd you hit him with, boss?"

"The only thing I had on me—the dismount container," Jason said. "Good thing the laser targeting system was still up and running. Where's the first attacker?"

Falcone showed him where the dead gunman was. "I recommend we bring weapons next time, boss," Falcone said.

Jason had seen his share of casualties in his short tenure as commander of Task Force TALON, but the condition of this corpse still made him a little queasy—it looked as if his chest had been flattened all the way to his spine, rupturing and smearing all of his internal organs throughout what was left of his body and all around him on the ground. There was no doubt, Jason thought ruefully, that no matter how violent these migrants had been, TALON was still going to take some heat for killing one like this.

"If there *is* a next time, Falcon," Jason said. "If there is a next time."

CHAPTER 3

RAMPART ONE FORWARD OPERATING LOCATION,
BOULEVARD, CALIFORNIA
THE NEXT MORNING

Army National Guard Captain Ben Gray of the 1st Battalion, 185th Infantry, finished his early-morning jog along Highway 98, poured some water from a plastic bottle over his head, then took a sip. It was barely an hour after dawn, and already it had to be in the low seventies here in the deserts of southern California. In another couple hours, he guessed, the pavement would be too hot to run on.

Gray, a California Highway Patrol Academy firearms instructor who lived near Fairfield, California, was an infantry company commander with the California Army National Guard, stationed in San Jose. Running was a way of life for him ever since he tried out for cross-country in middle school. After high school graduation he enrolled at the University of the Pacific in Stockton in prelaw, but his heart really wasn't into studying—he was meant for the outdoors. Operation Desert Shield, the buildup of troops in the Persian Gulf in response to the Iraqi invasion of Kuwait, gave him a good opportunity to get out of school, so he enlisted in the California Army National Guard.

Gray quickly discovered that he didn't want to be an enlisted man in the Army, so when he returned to the States after an eight-month deployment to the "Sandbox," he got his degree in criminal justice, applied for and received a reserve commission, and then, at the urging of many of his comrades in the Guard, joined the California Highway Patrol. It was a perfect fit for him. He quickly advanced in rank in both the Guard and the CHP. He didn't spend as much time as he wanted with his wife and two children back in Fairfield, but he was living the life he always wanted: two careers spent mostly outdoors, a good deal of responsibility but not unbearably so, and enough action to keep his life from getting mundane.

The place where he had stopped his jogging afforded him an excellent view of Rampart One, the small forward operating base he had been ordered to set up out here in the desert. Four days ago, Gray had led two mechanized infantry platoons, some elements of a transportation company, a security platoon, and an engineering platoon to the site about two miles south of the highway and just a few hundred meters north of the Mexican border, equidistant from the town of Boulevard, California, and the western edge of the steel border security fence around Calexico. His mission was to set up a patrol encampment to house personnel, security forces, construction crews, and aviation units for a long-term austere deployment.

Gray jogged back to his tent, showered, dressed, made his way to the mess, picked up a light breakfast of boxed cereal and a wheat roll, and went over to the commander's table, where he found his NCO in charge, Sergeant Major Jeremy Normandin, with two of the Task Force TALON cadre. "Good morning, sir," Normandin said, standing. "Hope you had a good jog. You get the report on the incident last night?"

"Yes. Sorry about your incident, sir, but it was bound to happen sooner or later."

"We were hoping it wouldn't, Captain," Major Jason Richter said somberly.

"Any word on who will conduct the investigation, sir?"

"FBI Director DeLaine herself will be coming out with investigators from the State and Justice Departments," Jason replied.

"I've received their equipment and facilities requisition list and we'll have it put together by later this afternoon, sir," Normandin said.

"Thanks, Sergeant Major," Gray said. To Richter: "Where's Captain Falcone, sir?"

"Still on patrol," Jason replied.

Gray looked as if he had swallowed a scorpion instead of a bite of his wheat roll. "Sir, SOP states that a soldier under investigation needs to be taken off duty until he's cleared by the investigation board, even an officer on detached assignment," he said, getting to his feet. "Besides, I think he should be receiving counseling after his incident. Being involved in a shooting incident that results in death is hard on anyone, even veterans."

"Frank said he was ready and able to resume patrol duties, and I believe him," Jason said. "We only have two CID pilots at this location. Besides, no investigation has formally begun. He'll cooperate fully with the investigation board, don't worry."

"Is he in the same robot . . . er, CID unit, sir? The investigators may want to examine it during their . . ."

"We downloaded all of the operating data and maintenance logs right after the incident," Ariadna Vega said.

"That might not be good enough," Gray said worriedly. "I'm a Highway Patrolman in the real world, and we impound vehicles involved in shooting incidents until well after the investigation is over—sometimes they're not even returned to service, depending on the . . ."

"This isn't the CHP, Captain," Jason interrupted. "This is part of the war on terror. We only have two CID units here at Rampart One and we couldn't afford to ground it. I don't take soldiers off the line because they engage and kill the enemy . . . do you?"

"No, sir, unless an investigation board has been convened," Gray said, matching Richter's glare with one of his own. "There's an investigation board on the way, so I would have pulled Falcone off the line in anticipation of the start of the investigation. It's just my advice and opinion, that's all. You're in charge of the task force."

"I appreciate your concern over the political and legal problems we might encounter because of this incident, Captain," Jason went on, "but until I receive orders to the contrary, we continue with our mission." He looked at Gray's concerned face, then added, "Captain Falcone will be off-duty when he returns—he will remain here at Rampart One until the investigation board releases him."

"Yes, sir."

Jason checked his watch. "Captain Falcone should be returning any minute now," he said. "I'm going out to the recovery pad to meet him."

"I'll tag along if you don't mind, sir," Gray said. "I'll grab us some water—it's going to be a hot one today." He and Normandin got up and followed Richter and Vega out of the mess tent and into the bright sunshine.

The Rampart One FOL, or forward operating location, was approximately forty acres in area, surrounded by electronic intrusion detection sensors and canine patrols instead of fences to save on setup time and cost. The mess tent was in the unit area, which included offices, barracks, and equipment and supply storage. The tents were standard desert TEMPER units—highly portable tents that used lightweight aluminum frames instead of center and side poles to make it easier to erect; they provided more interior space. The tops of the military personnel tents were covered with thin flexible silicone solar cells that change sunlight into electricity and were stored in batteries to power ventilation fans and lights.

"How often do you get supplies out here, Captain Gray?" Ari asked.

"Call me Ben, Dr. Vega."

"Only if you call me Ari, Ben," Ari responded with one of her patented man-killing smiles.

"Deal." Jason noticed with a smile that Gray was already hooked, landed, gutted, and filleted. "Once a day right now, Ari, but when we start getting some detainees here and the ops tempo picks up I'm sure it'll increase. I figure five hundred people here max, a minimum of eight liters of water each per day, plus water for the mess halls, showers, and maintenance areas—that's a minimum of two large tankers of potable water, or a tractor-trailer full of bottled water; plus a tanker of diesel for the generators and a tanker of Jet-A for the aircraft, per week. Add in rations for five hundred persons, spare parts, equipment—I figure two convoys a week, with four tankers and one to two tractor-trailers of supplies and equipment each. Half our manpower goes toward logistics and security for all this stuff."

They approached an area with a twelve-foot-high chain-link fence topped with razor wire. It was the detention facility, a complex of fences and tents to house migrants caught illegally crossing the border. He had seen the facility just last night, but it seemed as if the detainee population had doubled since then. "Man, I thought it would take a month or two to reach our maximum capacity—now it looks like it'll only take a few more days," he remarked. "We've only been open for business for three days!"

The detention facility had twelve TEMPER units set up, the same tent structures as the unit area. Each thirty-two-foot TEMPER unit housed sixteen individuals on cots; the plans called for sixteen TEMPER units at Rampart One. Access between units was strictly controlled with chain-link fence, so detainees entered and exited from the front of each unit only. In back of the tents was a fenced yard for basketball and soccer. Beside the exercise yard was a twelve-bed field medical clinic, a legal services tent, a small chapel, and a community latrine for men and women. Portable ballpark lights illuminated the compound at night.

Ariadna Vega definitely appeared uncomfortable looking around the place. "Pretty miserable, isn't it?" she remarked.

"I've seen worse, Ari," Gray said. "The TEMPER units are air-conditioned. The detainees will get three squares a day, water, and medical care while they're being processed; the kids will get free education; they'll have access to legal aid. We try to make them as comfortable as possible while they're here."

"I don't see very much privacy."

"No, I guess not," Gray said. "This is a detention facility, not a hotel. I've done the best I could here with the tools I'm given."

"I don't mean you're not doing enough, Ben," Ari said apologetically. "It's just . . . well, I've never been exposed to any of this before."

"This is light-years better than what we had in Kuwait during Desert Storm," Gray said. "I would've killed for a chance to wash my hair once a week then—here, the detainees can take a shower once a day if they like. The tents we had then were for shit—we couldn't keep the sand out no matter how hard we tried to seal things up. These TEMPERs are pretty tight."

They moved on to the next section of the detention facility. There were about two dozen chain-link cells with a cot, a "honey bucket" with a toilet seat, and a small open table next to the cot— no privacy whatsoever. The pens were covered with a large tent, which afforded a little protection against the sun and wind. There was also an open shower station with a few fiberglass shower stalls. Fifteen of the twenty-four stalls were occupied. "This area is for the violent or uncooperative detainees or any criminal suspects," Gray explained. "Security is a big concern, which is why these cells are completely open. We're hoping just the sight of these facilities will induce detainees to cooperate once they're in custody."

"Where are the gunmen from last night?" Jason asked.

"The two injured migrants were transported to the Border Patrol lockup in San Diego," Gray said. "Imperial County Sheriff's Department took the body of the dead migrant to El Centro; it'll be turned over to the FBI later this morning."

"Those cells are little more than damned dog-pens!" Ariadna suddenly blurted out disgustedly. "They remind me of the cages at Guantanamo Bay when the terrorist prison was first set up."

Now Ben Gray was starting to look perturbed at Ariadna's re-actions. "I guess they're pretty substandard to your way of think-ing, Dr. Vega," he said stonily, "but we put only the worst of the worst here. It's not meant to be comfortable—it's meant to keep the bad ones away from the other detainees and to keep our per-sonnel safe until they can be put into the justice system."

"Ben, I didn't mean . . ."

"We're in the middle of the desert out here, Dr. Vega," Gray in-terrupted. "I've been given a tough job and not a lot of time to do it in, and if I may say so myself my men and I have done a pretty damned fine job putting this FOL together. If it doesn't meet with your approval, then I suggest you take your suggestions or com-ments up the chain of command."

"As you were, Captain," Jason said. "Ariadna is just reacting out loud—she's not commenting on the good job you and your men have done out here."

"That's right, Ben," Ari said. "I'm sorry." Gray nodded coldly at her, unsure whether to accept her apology or not.

Jason looked at his watch, thanking the powers that be that it was almost time to meet the arriving team members—things were already getting pretty tense here. He wisely took the lead toward the clearing on the north side of the compound, which he knew would allow Gray and Vega to walk together. Ari took the oppor-tunity given her by her longtime friend and partner and touched Ben Gray's BDU sleeve: "Hey, Ben, I'm really sorry."

"Forget it, Dr. Vega."

"I can tell you're hurting too," she said. He turned halfway to her and gave her an irritated scowl. "The last thing I think you wanted to do in the Guard is build and run a detention camp, and here I come criticizing your mission."

"I do what I'm ordered to do," Gray said. "I don't have any ex-pectations or preferences—I do the job I'm assigned to the best of my abilities."

Ari trotted up to catch up, walking closely beside him. "That's it?" she asked gently.

"What do you mean, 'That's it?' What else is there?"

"I want to know how you feel about imprisoning foreigners in a place like this, out in the middle of nowhere in conditions hardly suited to farm animals, let alone human beings," Ari said. "Is this the America you swore to protect and defend?"

"It is now, Ari," Gray said perturbedly. "Listen, they know it's illegal to cross the borders at other than established crossing points . . ."

"Maybe they do, but they do it just for a chance to work, to make better lives for themselves . . ."

"The 'why' is just a mitigating factor, Ari—they're still doing something illegal," Gray said. "The 'why' doesn't excuse their actions, only lessens their punishment and allows them greater consideration. The reason why that entire detention facility isn't one big set of chain-link dog-pens is that few illegal aliens are like the ones that murdered those Border Patrol agents."

"But we're treating every illegal migrant the same when we throw them into facilities like this, aren't we?" Ari asked. "The vast majority of migrants are peaceful, God-fearing, law-abiding persons . . ."

"But they're *not* 'law-abiding'—the reason we're out here is because they're *breaking* the law!" Gray argued. "They're crossing our borders without permission, which in the United States is against the law. I'm a soldier, Ari. I swore to defend my country against all enemies, foreign or domestic . . ."

"*They* are not the enemy, Ben—the terrorists and murderers are."

"But the terrorists, murderers, and the migrants looking for work are all doing the same thing: crossing the borders of the United States without regard for the law or of national sovereignty," Gray interjected. "The migrants may not be a threat to the United States, but until we get a crystal ball that can tell us which ones are the workers and which ones are the terrorists, we need to stop all of them before the bad guys kill again."

Gray stopped and turned to Ariadna. "You say I might have

doubts about this mission, Ari, but you *sure* as hell do!" he said. "If you're so bugged about doing this job, why don't you just resign? It's as if you're trying to soothe your own conscience by indicting everyone else around you."

Vega didn't answer—which gave Jason Richter a chance to step over to the two and interject: "Is there an issue here, kids? If there is, let's lay it out right now." Neither of them said a word. "I promise, if either of you has a problem accomplishing this mission, I'll see to it you're reassigned, and there will be no repercussions whatsoever."

"No problem here, sir," Gray said flatly.

"I'm fine, J," Ari said in a low voice.

Jason looked at them both carefully, then clasped them both on their shoulders. "Be thankful Ray Jefferson isn't out here—he'd have you both for breakfast. Let's go."

The landing pad was simply a circular patch of desert about a half mile in diameter that had been cleared away, leveled, and covered with fiberglass mats to keep down blowing dust and debris. In the center of the circle was a retractable aluminum tower about fifty feet high, secured in place with guy wires. Off to the side of the dirt circle was a Humvee with a small satellite dish and various other antennae on top. Nearby was a transportable helicopter hangar constructed of tubular aluminum trusses and covered with thin, lightweight Kevlar; another slightly smaller hangar served as a maintenance and storage facility. The tanker with supplies of jet fuel and diesel were parked nearby, along with banks of wheeled generators.

A few minutes later both Gray and Ariadna received a message from the security patrols that their Condor aircraft was inbound, and they watched the task force's surveillance aircraft come in for its approach. From a distance it looked like a huge bird of prey coming in at them, and even up close it resembled an enormous seagull or eagle. It approached very quickly, a lot faster than Gray had ever seen a blimp travel. The thing was immense, with over a 120-foot wingspan. The wings curved upward from the body at least twenty feet, then curved downward again to the wingtips, then upward again at the very tip. It had a large propeller engine under each wing but was whisper-quiet, again unlike any blimp Gray had ever encountered. It had a long forward fuselage section, like a goose's outstretched neck, and a broad flat tail with long angled winglets at the tips. The fuselage was smooth, but as it got closer several camera ports and doors could clearly be seen.

But the most amazing thing was not the Condor's size or shape but its maneuverability. It came from the north-northwest at around sixty miles an hour, but as it approached the landing pad it made a tight, steeply banked turn to the west, directly into the wind, and all of its forward velocity seemed to disappear in the blink of an eye. When it was heading west right at the telescoping docking mast, it was going barely two miles an hour, and it nosed in precisely on a large electromagnetic docking attach point on the mast. Hovering overhead, the immense craft looked like a cross between a graceful seagull drifting on an ocean breeze . . . and a Klingon battle cruiser.

"That thing is just amazing," Gray exclaimed as he watched the immense airship dock itself. "Did you guys invent it?"

"It's been around for a few years as an experimental FEBA cruise missile radar platform," Ariadna said.

"Why not just use a regular blimp?" he asked.

"With carbon-fiber skin and structures, the Army was able to create an airship that did away with the typical blimp shape body," Ari replied. "Regular blimps are very susceptible to winds and have a huge frontal area, making them slow and not very stealthy. The shape of the Condor allows it to use air currents for propulsion, much like a sailboat sails against the wind—in fact, the stronger the winds aloft, the faster she flies. The Condor is almost twice as fast as any other blimp, its radar cross-section is a thousand times less than a blimp, it's far more maneuverable, and its payload is just as much as a large blimp while using less helium. This baby can carry almost two thousand pounds of sensors or personnel, fly as high as ten thousand feet aboveground, and stay aloft for almost two days."

"It was originally designed to carry infrared sensors and an airborne radar to detect low-flying aircraft like cruise missiles," Jason went on. "It's even fairly safe from small-arms ground fire—you might be able to take out an engine, but the Condor would probably survive the hit. It can fly just fine on one engine and return itself back to base with communications severed."

"Well, it's very cool," Gray said. He looked up, studying the immense underside of the huge airship. "It provides great shade too. It . . ."

At that moment, a hatch opened up on the belly of the center fuselage of the Condor airship . . . and a figure dropped through it. Before Gray could do anything but gasp in surprise, the figure hit the dusty ground . . . still standing, as if it had stepped off a porch step instead of jumping out of an airship hovering fifty feet overhead. The CID unit stepped over to Jason Richter and saluted. "CID One reporting in, sir," an electronic voice said.

"You like making an entrance in that thing, don't you, Falcon?" Richter commented, returning the robot's salute.

"Yes, sir, I do," Falcone replied. "It's the only time these days that I feel like I've got a working body." He stepped over to the Humvee at the edge of the landing area, dismounted from the CID unit, plugged it into the diagnostics and repair computers on the Humvee, and walked back to the others. "What's the latest on the incident last night, sir?" he asked Richter.

"Director DeLaine will be in later on today with whoever Justice, State, and the Pentagon chose to be on the board," Jason replied. "You'll be grounded from now on until the investigation board kicks you free. Don't talk to anyone except Ari and me about the incident until the board tells you differently. Understand?"

"Yes, sir."

They walked away from the landing zone as the retractable

docking mast lowered the Condor airship to ground level and maintenance crews began converging on it to do checks and refuel it. Falcone accepted a bottle of cold water from Jason and drained it in one chug. "How are you holding up, Falcon?"

"Okay, I guess," Falcone replied. "I appreciate the opportunity to go back out in the field after what happened—I'd hate to be cooped up in my rack just lying there thinking about it." He looked at Gray and added, "I know they're probably going to say it wasn't a good idea, me going back out on patrol."

"They didn't say, so I made the decision," Jason said. They reached the tent complex used by Task Force TALON and the Army National Guard as their headquarters. "You have nothing to worry about," Jason went on. "That migrant was shooting at you. That's enough reason for you to go on the attack. Your use of force was totally and completely appropriate and justified . . ."

"We'll be the judge of that, Major Richter," a voice from inside the tent said. Jason was surprised to see the large TEMPER complex nearly filled with people, some in suits and ties. The voice came from an older woman who wore jeans, a white shirt unbuttoned at the collar, and a hiker's vest. Jason caught a glimpse of a gun in a holster at her waist.

"Who are you?"

"Annette J. Cass, U.S. Attorney, southern district of California," the woman replied. She unclipped an ID wallet from her belt and showed him her badge and ID card.

"I wasn't advised of your arrival, Miss Cass," Jason said. "I apologize for not meeting you." She snapped the ID away before Jason could look it over and replaced it on her belt beside her gun holster. He smiled, trying not to look annoyed at having the ID snatched away before he could look at it, then extended his hand; Cass glared at his hand, obviously not expecting it, before accepting his greeting. He motioned to the others in the tent behind Cass. "And these nice folks?"

"Deputy Director Marta Fields from the San Diego office of the U.S. Border Patrol; Deputy Director Thomas Lombard of the Bureau of Immigration and Customs Enforcement in San Diego; Mr. Armando Ochoa, deputy consul general for investigation for the Mexican consulate in San Diego; plus some officers from the U.S. Marshals Service." Cass noticed Jason's eyes narrow when she mentioned the name of the deputy consul general, and she smiled knowingly.

"I wish you'd made an appointment first, Miss Cass," Jason said. "As you can see, we're in the middle of a shift change . . ."

"I'm handling the investigation of the incident last night. I'll expect your full cooperation, Major Richter," Cass interrupted. She looked at Vega and Falcone suspiciously, as if already deciding who was guilty and who was innocent. "I want to talk with Captain Falcone right away so he can give us a complete statement on the events of last night; all other personnel on duty last night will need to give us statements; and I want all operating data and recordings from last night from all of your Cybernetic Infantry Devices. Naturally all of your task force activities here will be suspended until further notice."

"Naturally—as soon as I get proper orders," Jason said.

Cass turned her green eyes on him and impaled him with an impatient, angry expression. "I just *gave* you your orders, Major Richter . . ."

"You gave me lots of orders, Miss Cass, but I'm not authorized to follow any of them."

"What did you just say?" Cass asked in a clearly threatening tone. "Major Richter, let me get this straight: are you *refusing* to comply with my instructions?"

"That's exactly what I'm doing, Miss Cass," Jason said.

"Do you have any idea what the penalty is for obstruction of justice, Major? Try five years in prison and up to a two-hundred-and-fifty-thousand-dollar fine. Your career would be over."

"Miss Cass, you're not in my chain of command, and I'm not in yours," Jason said. "Your orders are worthless on this installation without authorization from my superior officers."

"You're acting like a man with something to hide, Major," Cass said. "Are you trying to hide something? You do realize I'm here on official business?"

"You're not conducting an investigation here, Miss Cass—this is a plain old shakedown," Jason said. "Besides, you didn't even say the magic word, 'please.' So you've just worn out your welcome. You should all just pack up and get off my installation, right now."

"You're making a big mistake, Major," Cass said. "I'm giving you one last warning: obey my instructions or find yourself under arrest." She turned to the group of persons behind her. "Deputy Director Lombard and the U.S. marshals will secure this facility and begin my investigation. If you or any of your personnel do not cooperate, they'll be forced to take more drastic action."

"Miss Cass, the fact that you showed up here without any prior notice tells me that not only do you not have authority over me, but you initiated this visit on your own without any authorization from anyone—not even the Department of Justice," Jason said. He half-turned to Falcone and said, "Captain Falcone, make a note of the time, please."

"Yes, sir," Falcone said, surreptitiously checking the device strapped to his wrist.

"Dr. Vega, I would like you to call the White House from the secure radio in the command vehicle," Jason went on. "Advise them of the situation here and ask for instructions."

"Sure, J," Ariadna said a little worriedly, turning and heading for the exit.

"You're not going anywhere, Dr. Vega. Director Lombard." The ICE director motioned, and two men wearing black BDUs, black bulletproof vests emblazoned with the letters "U.S. MAR-SHAL" on the front, Kevlar helmets, and carrying suppressed MP-5 submachine guns quickly stepped forward to block the tent exit. "You've forced me to take drastic action, Major Richter. No one leaves, and no one makes any calls until I say so."

"What do you think you're doing, Miss Cass—trying to start a fight in here?" Jason asked. He wore a slight smile as he casually put his hands behind his back. "Why the guns? Aren't we all on the same side?"

"I will get your cooperation, Major, any way I must," Cass said seriously. "I heard how you treat those in authority, especially federal law enforcement agents, and it won't happen here. You could have done this the easy way. You want to be treated like an adversary, like you have something to hide—fine, you will be." The U.S. marshals took Jason's and Ariadna's sidearms away from them. "Now let's all go into your office, Major, while Director Lombard begins his interview with Captain Falcone. You will call in all of the personnel involved in last night's incident and have them report to us here immediately. I want your records, logs, technical data, and downloads from your robots, and I want them in the next five minutes or I will take this entire camp apart piece by piece until I find them."

"Five minutes?" Jason remarked, smiling. "I think we can have something for you a lot sooner than that. Captain?"

"Ready when you are, sir," Falcone said.

"Show Miss Cass what we have."

"Roger that, sir." Hidden behind Richter, Falcone pressed a button on his wrist device . . .

. . . and seconds later the top of the TEMPER module they were standing in ripped open, and one of the Cybernetic Infantry Devices peered inside. *"Everyone freeze and drop your weapons!"* a machine's electronic voice shouted. The CID unit immediately grabbed the marshals who were carrying weapons—one agent was grabbed by the upper arm, the other by his left shoulder. Both officers screamed in pain and terror as they were hauled up off their feet.

"What in hell . . . !" Lombard cried out, immediately reaching for his sidearm.

"No!" Jason said, still smiling. "No guns! It will detect guns and . . ."

But it was far too late. No sooner had Director Lombard's

gun cleared his holster than the CID unit walked quickly
through the nylon side of the TEMPER module and swung the
captured marshals at Lombard, knocking him off his feet. The
CID unit kept moving forward until Lombard was pinned
against the other side of the module, unable to move his hands
or arms, with the two U.S. marshals dangling painfully in mid-
air above him.

Falcone found Lombard's sidearm on the deck, unloaded it,
and stuck it into a flight-suit pocket, while Jason and Ari retrieved
their sidearms and the FBI agent's submachine guns, unloaded
them, and tossed them aside. "CID One, drop your captives," he
ordered. The CID unit's armored fingers opened, and the marshals clambered to the floor of the ruined TEMPER module beside Lombard, holding dislocated and bruised arms and shoulders.
"Ari, go get a doctor and a couple security guys to help these
clowns. CID One, back up ten meters and assume weapon guard
position."

"*Major Richter, are you insane?*" Annette Cass shouted. "You just
attacked *three federal agents!*"

Jason moved forward quickly and snatched Cass's weapon from
her holster—she was plainly too shocked to even notice her
weapon was gone. He unloaded it and tossed it aside. "And you
walked on to a TALON firebase and had the balls to draw down
on us? You're the insane one, Miss Cass. We're in an area already
known for heavy terrorist activity, possibly including the Consortium—the CID units are programmed to respond to all armed
threats with maximum force. You're lucky CID One used their
whole bodies as bludgeons and not just their limbs."

"J, more company," Ari radioed. "Two choppers inbound,
about a mile out."

"Any identification?"

"Nope."

"Where's the Condor?"

"I ordered them to launch the Condor immediately," she
replied. "They'll maintain surveillance on the base and send im-

agery to Cannon." Cannon Air Force Base, near Clovis, New
Mexico, was the home base of Task Force TALON.

"Good." To Falcone, he said, "Falcon, mount up. Get behind
those choppers and take them down if they attack."

"I don't have any weapons, boss—how am I supposed to take
them down?"

"Think of something—jump on them, toss a cactus at them,
distract them—just do it, Falcon." Falcone immediately ordered
CID One to assume the pilot-up stance, and he was inside the
robot and moving in less than thirty seconds, racing across the
desert out of sight. "Captain Gray, you expecting anyone?" Jason
asked the Rampart One commander.

"Negative," Gray replied. He was still breathless and bug-eyed
from the sudden and incredibly lightning-quick flurry of activity
that had just occurred right in front of his eyes. "Any inbounds are
supposed to get clearance from me or Top first through your headquarters or the White House."

"That's the FBI, Richter!" Cass exploded. "They're here to start
the investigation on the death of that migrant last night! Are you
hallucinating or are you on some kind of power trip?"

Jason ignored her. "Gray, take the injured to the infirmary and
the rest to the dog-pens and lock them up . . ."

"That consulate officer too?"

"The consulate officer too—until he can be positively ID'd, as
far as I'm concerned, he's Consortium," Jason said. "Have the rest
of your men on full alert until we figure out what's going on."
Gray issued orders to the physician, medics, and security forces
that arrived moments later, and Cass and the others that were with
her were hustled out. Jason keyed the mike button on his radio:
"Ari . . ."

"They're coming in pretty slow, J," she radioed from her command Humvee near the Condor airship's landing pad. "Staying in
formation . . . about a half-mile out . . . slowing even more. Looks
like they're starting to circle the perimeter. Wait . . . I see crests on
the sides of both choppers. One looks like an FBI patch . . . con-

firmed, and I can see the letters FBI on the tail. The other says U.S. BORDER PATROL on the side. They look like the real deal, J."

"TALON One, Rampart One," Ben Gray radioed a moment later. "Top just got a call from one of those choppers. The caller on board says she's FBI Director DeLaine. She apologized for not calling in first and is requesting permission to land. They gave the proper authentication."

Jason finally let out a nervous sigh of relief and holstered his own sidearm. "Let them in, Captain," he said wearily. On his command radio, he said, "CID One, stay out of sight until we verify everyone's ID out here."

"Wilco," Falcone responded.

"Ari, better get on the horn and tell Jefferson what's been going on," Jason said.

"I'm already on the line with him, J," Ariadna said. "He doesn't sound *too* pissed. He's calling the Justice Department and Homeland Security now."

"Swell," Jason muttered.

"TALON One, Rampart One, do you want me to release Cass and the others?" Ben Gray radioed.

"Negative," Jason responded.

"But we've got them in the dog-pens . . ."

"Let them cool their heels in your holding cells for a few more minutes," Jason said as he headed out to the landing pad. "I'll meet you over there in a few."

"Whatever you say, sir."

The two helicopters' rotors were winding down and all of the passengers were standing on the landing pad mats when Jason stepped over to them. FBI Director Kelsey DeLaine went over to greet him. "Hiya, Jason," she said cheerfully, giving him a firm, friendly handshake and a hug. She was dressed for action with a black nylon FBI jacket over a black T-shirt and bulletproof vest, black boots, BDU pants, an FBI ball cap, and a Beretta pistol in a holster. Jason saw a lot of energy in her step and in her smile and was pleased that Washington hadn't erased her genuine love for her profession. "Nice to see you again." She looked around. "Where's everyone else?"

"Were you expecting someone else?"

"Some folks from the U.S. Attorney's office in San Diego, maybe someone from Immigration and Customs Enforcement," Kelsey said. She noticed him looking questioningly at her. "They haven't arrived yet?"

"They're here."

"They didn't tell you we were coming? The security guy on the radio said we needed clearance to land first."

"They didn't mention you were coming. They didn't mention *they* were coming." He turned to look at the people coming off the second helicopter. "Who are they?"

"Investigators from Customs and Border Protection and some Spanish interpreters," Kelsey said. "We're participating in the preliminary investigation on Frank's incident last night." Kelsey was the cocommander of Task Force TALON when it was first organized less than a year earlier, and she was very familiar with its personnel, weapons, and tactics. "This visit should have been cleared last night or early this morning through the Justice Department. You received no word of our arrival?"

"I heard you were on your way to the West Coast to look into the incident here, but we received no requests for clearances and had no idea who was coming, or when."

"Well, it was pretty short notice—there must've been some snafu in communications along the line," Kelsey said, now sounding a little perplexed. "An assistant from the U.S. Attorney's Office assured me that all of the notifications *had* been made, through the White House as well as directly with the CO here; we didn't want to run into one of your monster blimps or get shot down by a ray gun or something. I should've checked myself." She looked at Jason carefully. "It's been a while since I've seen you, Jason, but I still recognize that 'cat with the canary in its mouth' look of yours. What happened?"

"Follow me."

Kelsey muttered something that Jason couldn't quite catch in the subsiding whine of the helicopters' turbine engines. She scanned the little base as she followed him toward the detention area.

"Jason, I'm not going to like whatever you've got to show me, am I?" Kelsey asked.

"Probably not."

"Uh, Miss Director . . . ?" one of Kelsey's bodyguards stammered. "Those persons in the small prisoner cells over there . . . is that who I *think* it is . . . ?"

"Jee . . . *sus,*" Kelsey exclaimed when she saw Annette Cass kneeling on the plywood floor in the middle of one of the dog-pen detention cells, her hands secured behind her with plastic handcuffs. "Jason, what in hell is going on here? *Do you know who that is?*"

"Do *you?*"

"Of course I do! That's Annette Cass, the U.S. Attorney for the southern district of California! What is she doing in that . . . that *cage?* Get her out of there immediately!"

Jason motioned to Gray, who unlocked the door to the chain-link cell and bent to help Cass up, but she pushed his hand away. "She and the others entered my base without permission and took away our weapons at gunpoint," Jason said.

"Jason, are you *crazy?* Did they show ID?" Kelsey didn't wait for a response, but hurried over to the detention cells, retrieving her ID and badge, showing it to Gray and his security guards, and then looping it atop her bulletproof vest so anyone could see it. "Open these cells immediately!" Gray looked over at Richter. "Don't look at him, Captain! I gave you a direct order—*open those cells!*"

"I want him *arrested!*" Cass shouted as soon as she joined the others. "I want Richter and all of his personnel arrested *right now,* I want my people released, and I want this base shut down *immediately!* I am going to put you away for twenty years for unlawful detention, false imprisonment, and abuse of power, Richter! Director DeLaine, you saw what he did to us!" She pointed at one of the other cells. "He even locked up an official from the Mexican consulate! This is going to create an international incident! This is a complete violation of international law and treaties . . ."

"Annette, calm down . . ." Kelsey tried.

" 'Calm down'? This Army officer attacked and nearly killed three federal agents with one of his robots, then handcuffed us and locked us in those pens! He's out of control, and I'm ordering you to arrest him!"

Kelsey's mouth hardened into a line. "That's enough, Annette," she said testily. "You can't order me to arrest anyone, let alone an Army officer on an Army installation, and you know it. I didn't observe any laws being broken . . ."

"He put me and my agents in those cells for no reason . . . !"

"The commander of an Army installation is allowed to put anyone on his base in his brig for any reason he deems necessary"— she looked over at Jason suspiciously, then added—"as long as it *was* absolutely necessary. He'll have to answer for his actions to his superior officer, which right now happens to be the President of the United States." She looked over at the detention cells. "And you say that's someone from the Mexican consulate? What's *he* doing here? You never said anything about bringing someone from the consulate!"

"He heard that Mexican citizens were being detained out here, and he demanded to see them," Cass said. "I agreed to allow him to accompany me."

"You never told me this," Kelsey said. "And what happened to getting us all clearances to come here? My two helicopters didn't have clearance to land!"

"Is that what Richter said? I wouldn't believe a word *he* says!"

"Annette, I didn't ask the major for confirmation—I asked my office in San Diego to verify our clearances from Homeland Security and the Army, the people who should have received your request to visit the base," Kelsey said. "They said the request was just received this morning and hadn't been processed because it was incomplete. I only landed here because I contacted the Attorney General directly myself when I learned we didn't have proper clearance. What's going on here?"

"Homeland Security delayed my clearance and told me to resubmit my application to visit this base," Cass argued. "I found that unacceptable. Any delay in getting here would've compromised evidence in our investigation and given Major Richter here time to coach or coerce witnesses . . ."

" 'Coerce witnesses?' " Jason retorted. "I'm not coercing anyone . . ."

"Now order Richter to release the consulate official and my men before there's hell to pay, Director DeLaine," Cass insisted, "or the next call I make will be to the Attorney General himself."

Jason could see Kelsey's jaw tighten. "Miss Cass, that's the second time you've ordered me to do something," Kelsey said, pulling out her cell phone. "I don't know how you do things in your district, but in the FBI we have procedures, and I'm not going to violate them just because you *order* it." Into her phone, she said, "John, this is Kelsey. I'm here at Rampart One . . . yes, the Army migrant reconnaissance base, in California . . . you've already received a call from the AG and from Homeland Security? I see. What's the word?" She listened for a few moments, then said, "Understood. Later."

"Well?"

"Major Richter, release all of Miss Cass's personnel immediately . . ." Kelsey said stonily.

"About time!" Cass remarked.

". . . and then escort her and her entourage off the base," Kelsey added, impaling Cass with an angry glare. "Turns out Miss Cass did not receive proper clearance to enter the base unannounced, although the Army should have done more to verify her identity and official business and reasonably accommodate her requests. Turns out the holdup was *your* demand to bring someone from the Mexican consulate with you. That request was forwarded to the State Department, and . . ."

"Miss Director, a Mexican citizen was *killed* last night by one of Richter's robots—the same one, I believe, operated by the officer, that attacked my marshals," Cass said. "Someone from the consulate deserves to be present during this investigation . . ."

"The incident happened on U.S. soil, Annette," Kelsey said. "The Mexican government does have a right to get involved— *after* our investigation has concluded, or at least after our investigation has *begun*. Whoever does the investigation has the duty to keep the Mexican government informed to the fullest extent of the law."

"I wasn't notified that my office was going to head the investigation, so I . . ."

"I'm not positive, Annette, but I don't think this is your jurisdiction."

"*Not my jurisdiction?* That's crazy! I'm the U.S. Attorney for southern California! If it's not me, who's going to do it?"

"The Department of Homeland Security," Kelsey said. "If they need any forensic help from the FBI or warrant authority from the U.S. Attorneys' Office, they'll ask; otherwise they handle it themselves."

"But what if there are criminal charges . . . ?"

"Those will be referred to your office if the suspects are not subject to the Uniform Code of Military Justice," Kelsey said. "Otherwise the Army handles it." She looked at Cass carefully, then added, "The State Department says it received no request from the Mexican consulate or embassy for any consulate officials or staffers to accompany you to this base, Miss Cass."

"I have the authority to bring along anyone I choose, including members of any foreign consulate in my district," Cass argued, "and consular officers have the right to make requests to travel as observers and go anywhere they like in the United States, especially on official business involving their citizens."

"I think the State Department and Attorney General may disagree with you, Miss Cass—that's not my department," Kelsey said. "But your conduct during this entire escapade of yours is starting to look more and more suspicious. A no-notice arrival with armed U.S. marshals and a Mexican consular official in tow? What were you trying to do, Miss Cass—shut down an entire Army base before anyone could stop you?"

"This is not an Army base, DeLaine—this is an illegal Army *prison*," Cass retorted, going over to help Lombard as he crawled painfully out of his cage, "locking up innocent civilians without due process and terrorizing people on both sides of the border with birds-of-prey airships and armored robots!"

"This base belongs to the Army National Guard and the Department of Homeland Security . . ."

". . . and it's in *my* federal district, and it has civilians in federal custody, which brings it under *my* jurisdiction," Cass interjected just as angrily. "All federal law enforcement matters in the southern district of California come under *my* review, and capturing and detaining suspected illegal immigrants is a law enforcement issue. And if there are Mexican nationals being detained here, consular officials have every right to meet with and speak to their fellow citizens, ascertain their medical, physical, legal, and political status, and ensure that all of their rights as Mexican citizens and American detainees are being preserved."

Kelsey fell silent—it was difficult, if not impossible, to argue with her reasoning. It was obvious that Cass thought she had gained at least an ideological advantage here, even though she was the one leaving. "We're not done here, Major Richter," she said. The two marshals, their arms and shoulders heavily bandaged, were escorted to waiting military ambulances while Cass's dark blue government Suburbans were brought for her. "You can't trample on the Constitution in my district like you did in San Francisco and Washington and get away with it. I'm going to see to it that you and your jack-booted storm troopers are removed from here, pronto."

"Sheesh, who peed in her cornflakes this morning?" Jason remarked as Cass and the other federal officials departed down the dusty access road.

"Jason, this thing is just getting started, and already we've got Americans battling each other," Kelsey said. "A little more restraint might be in order here."

"I hear you, Kelsey," Jason said, "but I've got my orders too, and they come right from the White House. The argument over who has jurisdiction is way above my pay grade. I was ordered to build reconnaissance and operations firebases, keep the border region under surveillance, and detain anyone illegally crossing the border, in support of the U.S. Department of Homeland Security. I'm not saying people like Cass are right or wrong, or what *we're* doing is right or wrong—but I've got a job to do and superior officers to report to, and they do not include U.S. Attorney Annette Cass, the U.S. Marshals Service, or anyone from the Mexican consulate."

"Well, we're all on the same side here—you might consider thinking twice before siccing your robots on fellow Americans, especially federal agents."

"I know no one will believe me, Kel," Jason said earnestly, "but I thought you were all Consortium, I swear to God. She came here unannounced with guys in bulletproof vests and submachine guns, and minutes later two helicopters swoop in. I thought we were goners." Kelsey could tell that Richter was being absolutely serious—she never questioned his feelings. She wasn't quite sure, but she thought she saw a little unexpected paleness in his face, and he swallowed nervously. "I never realized how vulnerable we are out here, Kel. They walked onto this base with guns and badges and no one even radioed us to tell us they were here. Maybe I panicked a little. Even when I saw their IDs, I felt . . . defensive, like I didn't do enough to watch my own back. I guess I got . . ."

"Scared? Hey, Jason, you have no idea how many times I was scared, working on the Task Force TALON, working in the FBI. You lose tactical control, even for a moment, and all you want to do is react, do *something,* until you *get* it back." She felt a sudden wave of concern wash over her consciousness, and without thinking she took his hand—and found it cold and clammy. "It's okay, Jason," she said gently. "It's over."

"TALON wasn't made to guard a base or stay in one place— we're hunters, not rent-a-cops," Jason said bitterly. "As long as TALON is here, we're sitting ducks for the Consortium. TALON was successful against the Consortium because we were aggressive and offensive—we took the fight to *them*. Here, they don't have to hunt us—they know exactly where we are, and they can take all the time they want planning an attack."

Richter's hands were subconsciously clenched into fists, and his voice was shaking with anger. "This will *not* happen again, Kelsey—I swear it," Jason went on adamantly. "I don't care who it is—federal agents, illegals, or terrorists—I *will not* allow this task force to work with its hands tied behind its back, *anywhere,* but *especially* on American soil."

"Ease up, Major," Kelsey said, her voice firm. "This is not a personal crusade, and Task Force TALON is not alone out here. You're part of a team—start *working* like it."

"That's what I'm doing here, Miss Director . . ."

"By having Falcone inside a CID unit grab two U.S. marshals and use them to club down *another* federal agent?" She didn't like Jason suddenly turning sarcastically formal on her, but he had it coming—he was still acting like Task Force TALON was his own private personal boys' club. She pointed to the ruined TEMPER units, surrounded now by National Guard soldiers starting to repair the damage. "What are you going to have your CIDs tear down next, Jason—the Border Patrol regional headquarters, after you get shut down? The federal courthouse, after they arrest Falcone for assaulting a federal officer? Are you going to take on the entire Justice Department because you want to run this assignment *your* way?"

She stopped and put her hands on her hips; Richter stopped but only half-turned toward her. "You haven't changed much since we began the task force, Richter—you haven't learned a thing. You're little more than a spoiled laboratory nerd out here playing army with your fancy high-tech toys. It's getting tiresome. Sure, you had some victories—but that's only when you worked with others like the FBI and the rest of the U.S. military. But now the stakes are higher—there are lives at stake here, not just terrorists but peaceful, unarmed, regular people. Maybe this job isn't for you."

"Bull, Kelsey. This *is* my job. TALON can do anything we're assigned . . ."

"Sure it can—but maybe *you* can't lead it," Kelsey said. "Maybe you ought to turn this assignment over to someone else and go back to your lab where you belong. In fact, I think I might recommend that to the AG. After this morning's incident, I think he'll do it to avoid a mutiny in his own department—at the very least, he'll have to do it to avoid an international incident and official government protest. Until the White House decides what to do with you, Major, I suggest you adopt an *extremely* low profile—for the sake of this operation as well as your own career."

"Kelsey, I may just be a nerd engineer with no field experience," Jason said, "but I was chosen to lead this task force, and my task force was deployed to this location, so I'm going to do the job I was assigned the best way I know how. The President or Ray Jefferson can shit-can me any time they feel like it, for whatever reason—or for *no* reason. Until then, I'm going to operate my men and equipment *my* way, following whatever guidance or directives I'm given. I'm going to . . ."

He was interrupted by a beep from his command radio: "TALON One, TALON Two," Ariadna radioed. "Condor has detected several large vehicles heading our way from the south across the border, about six kilometers out."

At the same time, Ben Gray radioed, "TALON One, we have a possible situation out here at the south perimeter."

"On my way," Jason responded. Both he and Kelsey hurried off. They found Gray standing on the roof of a Humvee, scanning the area to the south with binoculars. "Three armored personnel carriers, about five klicks south of us, spread out about two klicks along the border," he reported when Richter and DeLaine ran up.

"The one closest to us looks like an old World War Two half-track; the others are M-113s, with 12.7 mm machine guns mounted on the gunner's turrets. I see flags of Mexico on their radio antennae."

"Do they look like the real thing?" Jason asked.

Both Gray and DeLaine looked at Richter curiously—obviously neither of them had considered that they might *not* be official Mexican government vehicles. Gray scanned them again. "They look real enough to me," he said, his voice definitely a bit more strained. "They look . . . hold on . . . they're dismounting troops. I count . . . ten soldiers coming out of each vehicle carrying heavy packs and rifles."

"We're outgunned," Jason said. "All we have is small arms and the CID units against three APCs and a platoon of infantry. It's no better than even right now, and if we lost the CID unit, we'd be toast in minutes. Ben, better organize your security forces and stand by for action." Gray blanched slightly and hurried off.

" 'Lost the CID units'? What are you talking about, Jason?" Kelsey asked as Gray sprinted past her. "You think the Mexican army means to *attack* us?"

"I'm not assuming they're Mexicans," Jason said, "or if they are, they're not part of the Mexican army."

"Who do you think they . . . ?" Kelsey stopped—she finally figured out who Jason was worried about. "You think they might be *Consortium?*"

"Yegor Viktorvich Zakharov was a pro in recruiting local military personnel and getting his hands on all sorts of military hardware, all over the world," Jason said worriedly. "That slimebag recruited dozens of American military men and stole hundreds of millions of dollars of weaponry, including helicopters, armored vehicles, and even a multiple rocket launcher, to assault Washington, D.C., and the White House. The bastard even stole Secret Service uniforms and equipment and got his hands on the President of the United States himself during his attack on Washington. If he could do that, he can certainly get control of Mexican military hardware and personnel." He clicked the mike button on his command transceiver. "Ari . . ."

"I've got a call in to Jefferson at the White House, J," Ariadna said. "They told me to stand by. I'm sending Condor imagery to TALON headquarters at Cannon to see if we can identify any of those soldiers."

"What do they think they're going to do?" Kelsey asked. "Are they going to assault the base?"

"It's a possibility," Jason said. "If it's the Consortium, and their attack is successful, they could throw the entire continent of North America into a terrorism panic." He changed channels on his command transceiver. "CID One."

"I'm receiving the downlink from the Condor," Falcone responded. "I'm in the aircraft maintenance hangar. What's the plan?"

"Stay out of sight until we see what they're going to do," Jason said.

"Wilco."

"Break. CID Two."

"I've got them on my datalink too, sir," Sergeant First Class Harry Dodd, U.S. Army, piloting the second Cybernetic Infantry Device, responded. "I'm eight point seven miles east of Rampart One. I can be there in thirteen minutes."

"Negative. Hold your position for now. You're guarding our east flank. Sound off if you see anything going on."

"Roger."

"This might just be a show of force, or some kind of probe," Kelsey said. "They *must* know about our CID units . . ." But she fell silent—she knew she could not afford to assume anything right now.

"Jason, we're picking up air targets—slow-moving, probably helicopters," Ariadna said. "Closest one is about six miles out."

"Where from?"

"All sides—six from north of the border, two from the south," the civilian Army engineer said.

This was quickly getting way out of hand, Jason thought, try-ing to choke down a growing bolus of panic rising in his chest. "Any air traffic control codes?"

"Stand by . . ." It was the longest wait Jason could recall in a long time. "Negative, Jason, negative on the air traffic codes," Ari finally reported breathlessly. "I'll try to coordinate their tracks with the Domestic Air Interdiction Coordination Center at March Air Force Base to find out where they're from." There was an-other interminable wait; then: "Jason, the DAICC duty officer just blew me off. He said, and I quote, 'Tell Richter that his friends at the Border Patrol said unable at this time: don't call us, we'll call you.' "

"Jerks," Jason said. "Put in a call to Los Angeles Center and Riverside Approach, request some kind of track correlation and point of origin, and tell them it's urgent. And keep on broadcast-ing warning messages to stay at least five miles away from the base or they could be attacked without warning. If we can't fight 'em, our only chance is to bullshit them. And radio Cannon and tell them to bring some weapon packs out here."

"You got it, J."

This was definitely starting to get tense. "Rampart One, TALON One, did you copy about our visitors?"

"Affirm," Gray responded. "I'm briefing my security platoon now. Stand by." A few moments later: "TALON One, my guys are recommending we take any infantry units that move in on us; have your CIDs take the armored personnel carriers, if they move in."

"And the helicopters?"

"All we've got are small arms, sir," Gray reminded him. "If they try a gunship air-to-ground attack, we'll just have to hunker down, stay out of sight, and wait for the infantry to try to engage us. We're relying on your robots to put the fear of God into them."

"That's exactly what we intend to do," Jason said. "Break. CID Two, start heading back to Rampart One. Defend yourself using any means necessary."

"CID Two copies," Dodd responded.

"Break. Ari?"

"Still on hold with Los Angeles ARTCC," Ariadna said. "The nearest helicopter is three miles out."

"They're ignoring the TFR," Jason said. The TFR, or temporary flight restriction, was a cylinder of restricted airspace established around the base and the Condor airships to prevent aircraft from overflying them. The Condor airship had a civil aircraft transponder that broadcast identification signals to other aircraft to try to prevent a mid-air collision, since it was almost impossible for the unmanned Condors to maneuver out of another plane's way. "Rampart One, they're inside the TFR. Weapons tight until you see a gun, then repel all invaders."

"Rampart One copies. All Rampart units, this is Rampart One, weapons tight, repeat, weapons tight. Sound off immediately if you see weapons or encounter hostile action. All squads acknowledge."

"Inside two miles, J, bearing two-five-five," Ari radioed.

Jason scanned the sky and saw a helicopter in the distance. "Got a visual," he radioed on the command network. "Doesn't look military—looks like a civilian aircraft, a Bell JetRanger or similar. Paint looks civilian."

"Second aircraft bearing one-nine-five, two miles."

"No contact," he said. He swung around and focused on the first helicopter again. This was going to be a tough decision. If he guessed wrong, and the helicopter was hostile, it would open fire any second—but if it was not hostile, he'd have his men open fire on an unarmed aircraft. There really wasn't any other choice—he just hoped to God he'd make the right one. "All Rampart units . . . dammit, weapons tight, repeat, weapons tight. It's a civilian helicopter. Looks like it's turning away."

"Third aircraft bearing three-one-zero, two miles."

"I got a visual on number three," Gray radioed seconds later. "The sucker's coming right for us." Jason could now hear the third helicopter, and sweat broke out on his upper lip. "It's moving in . . .

it's . . . shit, it's a *media helicopter*. It says TV-12 on the underside. It looks like it has a zoom camera on the belly . . . I can see a TV logo on the side . . . I recognize that chopper. It's a TV station chopper from San Bernardino."

At that moment, Ariadna radioed: "J, just got the word from L.A. Center. They're *media* helicopters—three from Los Angeles, two from San Diego, one from San Bernardino. The two on the Mexico side are also media, both from Tijuana." It felt as if it was the first time in several minutes that Jason was able to take a normal breath. "L.A. Center asked one of them if they were aware of the TFRs in the area that they were headed directly for, and the pilots said no. L.A. Center told them to turn back, but . . ."

"But no TFR is going to get in the way of a good story," Jason said. "Swell."

"This is turning into a heck of a cluster-f— Well, you get the idea, J." But Jason wasn't in a joking mood. If he was a leader in the Consortium, this is precisely how he would organize a sneak attack: get a swarm of media aircraft overhead to confuse the scene, then strike. The three armored personnel carriers less than two miles away were still major threats—if they attacked, there was very little Richter's forces could do about it. CID Two might be able to get back to base in time to help, but if he didn't, or if he was ambushed by another strike team, the losses could be horrendous . . .

. . . and if the attackers had nuclear, biological, or chemical weapons, all of which the Consortium had used in the past, the fight would be over in moments.

No! Jason screamed at himself. It wasn't the Consortium! It was just a bunch of reporters, out to cover a story that obviously the San Diego U.S. Attorney's office had just planted. Overreacting now could kill Operation Rampart before it got started.

"All units, this is TALON One, stand down, repeat, *stand down,*" Jason radioed on the command network. "I believe the aircraft and vehicles are here to document this task force looking belligerent and dangerous—let's not give them a headline. All Rampart units, acknowledge."

"Rampart One acknowledges," Gray radioed, then relayed the orders through his squads and got acknowledgments from all of them, keeping them on high alert but having them shoulder and holster their weapons.

"CID Two, I copy all," Dodd responded. "Resuming my patrol. Negative contacts."

"Rampart One, I want N-numbers and descriptions of every aircraft that comes within the TFR," Jason said. "Those aircraft and their pilots' asses are *mine*."

"With pleasure, sir," Gray responded.

It was almost comical to watch. The first helicopter seemingly "tiptoed" toward the base, turning suddenly as if suddenly realizing it was in restricted airspace; then a second helicopter would move in a few hundred yards closer, then turn away; then a third would come in closer still. Soon the helicopters were hovering almost right overhead, less than five hundred feet above them—one helicopter dipped to less than a hundred feet to get pictures of excited migrant children waving in the exercise yard, women with babies running for cover from the swirling dust the helicopters kicked up, and men coming out of the latrines, tying ropes around their waists to keep their pants up.

"TALON One, you're on the tube," Ari radioed a few moments later. "Better go take a look."

Jason walked over to the mess tent, which had a large flat-panel TV set up with satellite TV access. The TV was already set up to one of the all-news channels—and there, in high-definition color, was an image of Jason walking across the base, taken just moments ago. The camera quickly panned back to the detention area, showing in closeup detail the razor-wire-topped chain-link fences, housing units, latrines, and finally the chain-link dog-pen detention cells.

"Well, so much for keeping a low profile out here," Jason muttered. He picked up his command net radio: "Ari?"

"He was just called to a meeting in the White House," Ari said immediately, referring to National Security Adviser Jefferson. "He said to stand by at a secure line in case they want to conference you in."

"Great. Just great," Jason said. The command tent was still being repaired, so he'd have to wait in the Humvee. This morning was truly shaping up to be a real headache.

THE OVAL OFFICE, THE WHITE HOUSE,
WASHINGTON, D.C.
A SHORT TIME LATER

"Is the whole damned world going stark raving *crazy?*" the President of the United States thundered. Like a high school principal who had just heard explanations from three of his pupils who had just been caught drag-racing in the school parking lot, President Samuel Conrad had Ray Jefferson, Attorney General George Wentworth, Secretary of Homeland Security Jeffrey Lemke, and Brigadier General Ricardo Lopez, commander of Operation Rampart, standing before his desk. He had just received reports from his four advisers on what had just happened in southern California. "Are your people all totally out of control, or just plain *stupid?*"

"Mr. President, will all due respect to this office, I *will not* allow what has happened out there today to stand," Wentworth said angrily. George Wentworth was one of the most experienced and respected elder statesmen in Washington—he was so respected by both major political parties that no one was surprised that he stayed on after the administration's shakeup following the Consortium terror attacks in the United States, even though the FBI and Justice Departments were roundly criticized for not protecting the nation better. "Three federal agents were physically assaulted by one of Jefferson's task force members, and several of my people, including a district U.S. Attorney, were put into cages like *stray dogs!* Richter's men are totally out of control out there, and they need to be recalled and prosecuted *immediately!*"

"I agree, Mr. President," Secretary of Homeland Security Lemke said. "We don't know all the details of that encounter, but once the international press gets hold of this story, they'll murder us." He motioned to the flat-panel TV in the cabinet to the right of the President's desk. "It's only a matter of time."

"Those choppers are not supposed to be overflying that base," Ray Jefferson said, glancing at the TV screen. "That's restricted airspace."

"What do you want to do about it, Jefferson—shoot them down?" Wentworth asked.

"What would you do to any media helicopters that flew within a mile of *Air Force One*—have the FAA slap their wrists?" Jefferson asked. "The temporary flight restriction zone was set up around that base for a reason . . ."

"And it appears the reason is to keep the world from witnessing the human rights *atrocities* that are being performed out there!" Wentworth argued. "That's what the press is going to say, you can bet on it!"

"All right, that's enough," the President said, holding up his hands. "Listen, we all knew we were going to take a lot of bad press about this plan." He gave Wentworth a glare, then added, "But I don't want the source of a lot of bad press to be my own cabinet. George, you told the cabinet when we implemented this plan that we were legally authorized to set up those detention facilities; you also said that we could establish that restricted airspace over those bases and around those bird-looking blimp things. Are you just talking about objections to the sight of those facilities, or are you warning us about serious legal challenges to the plan?"

"There are bound to be numerous legal challenges to the plan, Mr. President," Wentworth replied. "I assume Justice and your counsel's office will be quite busy in the months ahead. But sir, I was *horrified* at the sight of those chain-link fences and cages—

and I was part of getting this plan put into action! I can't begin to imagine the international outrage when the world sees those things on American soil!

"I'm also angry because of Major Richter's treatment of my U.S. attorney and marshals," he went on. "My God, sir, one of those robots—manned by the same officer who killed that migrant last night—nearly ripped one of the marshal's arms off, and he used the marshals' bodies to club down the other! It's unacceptable behavior . . . !"

"About the reason why the U.S. Attorney and the marshals were there in the first place . . ." Jefferson began.

But Wentworth held up a hand. "I know, I know, Cass didn't say 'pretty please,' " he said irritably.

"George . . ."

"There is some confusion about whether Miss Cass properly requested permission to enter the facility, or tried to do so under her own authority," Wentworth said to the President. "And yes, perhaps she started throwing her weight around when she didn't have any to throw around. She may be guilty of bad judgment and sloppy paperwork. But that Task Force TALON officer, Falcone, is guilty of three counts of assaulting a federal officer, and Richter is guilty of false imprisonment . . ."

"George, I respect your wisdom and experience," the President interjected, "but I'm telling you again: stop making definitive statements that undermine our own programs before we know all the facts. Falcone and Richter are not 'guilty' of anything. At a later date, when I give the okay, you can charge them if you want, and we'll let a circuit court judge or the Supreme Court decide who has jurisdiction. Until that time, the words you need to remember are 'We're investigating, so I have no comment.' Understood?"

"Of course, Mr. President," Wentworth said. "But we can't keep those task force members out there any longer. The operation can continue—there's no legal reason I can surmise that prohibits us from patrolling our own borders—but the presence of those robot contraptions will only terrorize the citizens on both sides even more."

"That's part of the plan, isn't it, General Wentworth?" Ray Jefferson asked.

"You know very well it isn't, Jefferson . . . !"

"I know nothing of the sort, Mr. Wentworth," Jefferson retorted. "First of all, we can put anything we care to on the border to perform whatever tasks we wish, especially homeland security and border protection. I'm not saying Richter's or Falcone's action with your agents was proper, but if the sight of those manned robots and detention facilities forces illegal migrants to sign up for a guest worker program, it's done its job."

"So that was our plan, Jefferson—*terrorize* the Mexicans into not crossing the border? I don't remember that as part of the game plan, Sergeant Major!"

"Look at the televisions, Mr. Wentworth," Jefferson said. "We have thirty U.S. soldiers at Rampart One, plus two CID units and two Condor unmanned reconnaissance airships. The Mexican Army has just deployed a similar number of troops in that same area, with armored personnel carriers and patrol helicopters instead of CID units and airships. I don't think any illegal migrants will be crossing the border at this location for a while, do you?"

"You've got to be *kidding* me, Jefferson!" Wentworth exclaimed. "It's a madhouse out there! Someone is going to make an awful mistake, and there could be a shooting war breaking out at any moment! Don't tell me this is *acceptable* to you, because it certainly is not acceptable to the Justice Department!"

"All right, all right," the President said, raising a hand. He turned to Brigadier General Lopez. "Okay, General, let's hear it. What's going on with you and TALON?"

"Sir, it was my decision to leave TALON completely in the hands of Major Richter," the one-star Army National Guard flag officer responded. Ricardo Lopez was a bear of a man, six feet two inches in height, broad-chested and imposing, with close-cropped salt-and-pepper hair, square jaw, a perpetual five o'clock shadow, and dark features. "My staff is directing the construction of forward operating bases in California and deploying support personnel, but I'm not up to speed on those Cybernetic Infantry Devices or their capabilities."

"Didn't Major Richter brief you on their capabilities, General?" the President asked.

"Yes, sir, he did. But getting briefed on them and knowing enough about them to deploy them effectively are two very different things. Given the short time frame given to have the first base set up, I decided the best way to handle it was to assign Major Richter the task of directing his men and equipment as he saw fit. I approved his rules of engagement orders; he coordinates all his movements with my staff on a regular basis; and he personally delivers a status report four times a day."

"Do you think turning over control to Richter was a smart idea, General?" Attorney General Wentworth asked.

"Major Richter is a fine officer, and he has an enthusiastic and dedicated staff behind him," Lopez said. "Richter may be . . . unconventional, to put it mildly, but he gets the job done. He's not the problem."

"Oh?"

"No, sir. The crazy idea here was using those CID robot things in the first place. But I believe I was not given a choice in making that decision."

"So you're not taking responsibility for what's happened out there . . . ?"

"No, Mr. Wentworth, I take full responsibility for whatever happens with Operation Rampart," Lopez said immediately. "I'm just explaining my decision-making matrix, as I've already explained to Sergeant Major Jefferson."

Wentworth turned to Jefferson. "You never told us that the commander of Rampart objected to using the robots, Jefferson."

"I noted his objections, Mr. Wentworth," Jefferson said, "but given the time constraints, TALON's capabilities, and the problems associated with mobilizing the required number of National

Guard forces, I directed General Lopez to utilize TALON to the utmost extent possible anyway. General Lopez assured me he would educate himself and his senior staff on TALON's capabilities as quickly as possible. That was good enough for me." ◦

"What's your plan, General?" the President asked.

"Very simple, sir: augment National Guard troops into regular U.S. Border Patrol operations, just like we do with Customs Service port inspection assistance teams," Lopez said. "Each Border Patrol sector gets a National Guard infantry or cavalry platoon and a helicopter element for support, along with their equipment, for deployments that last no more than a week. We can augment other forces such as reconnaissance, communications, or intelligence as necessary, but I feel that wouldn't be necessary—the Border Patrol has all of that already. All our units deploy from Border Patrol offices and travel under the direction of Border Patrol field units—we wouldn't have to build any bases, jails, detention facilities, or anything else. The Guard gets on-the-job training by the Border Patrol, so we don't have to reinvent the wheel. Plus, since the National Guard works in a support role, there are no Posse Comitatus conflicts."

"And this was rejected . . . *why*, Jefferson?" Wentworth asked incredulously. "Sounds like the perfect plan to me."

"It wasn't rejected—in fact, the plan is being put into motion," National Security Adviser Jefferson replied. "An urgent request has gone out to every state governor and adjutant general requesting support for the plan. We've received requests for more information—mostly on who's going to pay for it—but so far no takers."

"What do you mean, 'no takers'?" Kinsly asked. "Why can't we just order them to give us the forces we need?"

"We need a presidential directive ordering the federalization of the National Guard if we wish to put those forces under our direct control," Jefferson said. "Otherwise, we can only *request* support. We have a budget for the construction of four forward bases for Rampart operations; most of that money went to the state of California for their National Guard engineering units to build the bases."

"How long would it take to implement the program General Lopez has described, Sergeant Major?" Secretary of Homeland Security Lemke asked.

"The governor of California tells us that he is in favor of the proposal but he wants to feel the pulse of the legislature and the people before he commits the California Guard," Jefferson replied. "Initial polling results suggest that most Californians wouldn't want their National Guard involved, that it's a job for the FBI and Homeland Security, not the military."

"That's not surprising," Kinsly interjected. "California is almost thirty percent Hispanic, and they aren't minorities in all of the counties in southern California."

"Arizona, New Mexico, and Texas haven't responded officially, but the governors are generally in favor of the program as well, with reservations," Lopez said. "They are all in favor of Rampart if it means bringing their Guardsmen home from overseas duty."

"The Pentagon won't like that notion," Lemke pointed out. "We're stretched to the breaking point already—removing the Guard from overseas deployments will hurt."

"So if the request is denied, our only option is to federalize those forces," Jefferson went on. "General Lopez has current data on each unit's readiness and deployability—some units could be ready in days, while others might take weeks. Integrating the forces with Border Patrol sectors would take a few weeks at best, mostly to cut orders, reroute units scheduled for overseas deployment, arrange transportation and lodging, and set up a training program."

"The bottom line, sir: we can do it, without the help of Richter and his robots," General Lopez said, giving Jefferson an exasperated glare. "They should be pulled out of there right away and Rampart turned over to the Border Patrol for operational control. The reconnaissance stuff is great: we are getting good support from those big sensor airships, but the robots are overkill . . . uh, excuse the pun, sir."

"Looks like we may have pushed Rampart into existence too quickly, eh, Sergeant Major?" the President asked. "Maybe Richter wasn't up to it."

"Rampart has detained hundreds of illegal migrants in just a few days' time, Mr. President," Jefferson pointed out. "Last night's incident was unfortunate, but an aberration—and it happened on the U.S. side of the border, with persons who refused to comply with the CID unit's orders. Persons who are confronted by the CID units and don't resist are treated the same as any other detainee apprehended by the Border Patrol. They are . . ."

"Oh, God," Chief of Staff Thomas Kinsly interjected. The President followed his surprised look at one of the TV monitors—which showed the Minister of Internal Affairs, Felix Díaz, speaking in front of TV cameras. Kinsly turned up the volume, and they heard Díaz say, in excellent English, ". . . an absolute outrage. Mexico and the United States have enjoyed an unarmed and peaceful border for over eighty years, and both nations have shown the utmost respect for each other's sovereignty, for the rule of law, and for the rights of all free men. Now look at this: a military base, less than three kilometers from the border, where Mexican citizens, among others, including women and children, are being held without being charged with a crime, in completely inhuman and degrading conditions.

"Last night, the inevitable happened: one Mexican national was killed, and two others seriously injured, by a U.S. military manned robot called a Cybernetic Infantry Device along the border region," Díaz went on, referring to a notecard to pronounce the name of the offending weapon correctly. The cable TV news network promptly showed a picture of a CID unit, complete with twenty-millimeter cannons blazing, taken during the Consortium's attacks in Washington, D.C. "The whereabouts of the dead and wounded are unknown. This is no less than a horrific and brutal crime, and I hold President Samuel Conrad as commander in chief of the American armed forces completely responsible."

While Díaz was talking, a light had been flashing on the phone on the President's desk; after some minutes, Kinsly finally answered it. "What is it, Gladys, the President is ..." He paused, and the others saw his face sink. "Stand by." He put the call on hold. "Mr. President, it's President Maravilloso," Kinsly said. "She's on the phone."

The President paused for a few moments, then sighed resignedly and motioned for the phone. "Put her on, Gladys," he said into the receiver. A few moments later: "Madam President, this is Samuel Conrad."

"Mr. President, thank you for speaking with me," Maravilloso said, her voice edgy, not friendly at all. "As I'm sure you and your advisers there in the Oval Office are aware, I would like to speak to you about the situation on the border. I assume you are watching the news coverage of the disorganized and highly illegal activities here."

"I am being kept fully informed of the *facts* of recent activities in that area, Madam President, yes. What can I do for you?"

"I will make my wishes plain for you, Mr. President—I request that you release *all* of those Mexican detainees from your prison camp *immediately* into my custody," Maravilloso said sharply. "They will all be confined and supervised by the Mexican federal police—if they are guilty of a crime, I assure you they will not go unpunished."

"Madame President, I cannot do that. I ..."

"You mean you *will not* do it."

"Those detainees have been observed crossing the U.S. border at other than a legal border crossing point," the President said evenly. "That is a crime in the United States, and so they have been arrested and are being detained until ..."

"Mr. President, you must understand, this cannot be allowed to stand," Maravilloso retorted. "That facility you built as part of Operation Rampart, the one called Rampart One, is nothing more than a chain-link concentration camp for innocent Mexican citizens. What's even more egregious, even more *horrifying*, is how those citizens are being treated by American military forces! We have received reports of torture, cruelty, and total disregard for basic human rights, let alone rights guaranteed to all under the American constitution. This must stop immediately, Mr. President!"

"The American government will thoroughly investigate any and all charges of torture or cruelty to . . ."

"Then you admit that these cases exist?"

"I admit nothing, Madam President—in fact, I have received no reports of . . ."

"We have eyewitnesses to such acts, Mr. Conrad—in fact, one of the eyewitnesses was also a victim of such cruelty and illegal treatment, the consul general of the Mexican consulate in San Diego," Maravilloso interrupted. "He was just recently captured, arrested, and falsely imprisoned in a cage so small that he was forced to stoop on his hands and knees until he was released at the orders of your director of the Federal Bureau of Investigation, who was also a witness to this unspeakable action! The consul-general, a well-known, fully credentialed, and well-respected member of the Mexican diplomatic corps—forced to be imprisoned in a cell barely large enough for a *dog*?"

"The results of our investigation will be released as soon as possible, Madam . . ."

"That is not acceptable, sir!" Maravilloso cried. "We have reports not just from our people, but from very high-ranking American Justice Department officials, attesting to the accuracy of these charges!"

"Madam President," Samuel Conrad tried, "I don't have time to listen to speeches . . ."

"Mr. President, I respectfully request that you release all Mexican citizens into my custody *immediately,* or you risk creating an international incident and ruining the peace and trust between our countries," the Mexican president said angrily. "If you refuse, I will immediately file protests with the Organization of American States, the United Nations, and the World Court, and I will ask American advisers to request that Amnesty International and the American Civil Liberties Union file lawsuits against the United States requesting injunctions to stop this gross violation of human rights."

Samuel Conrad hesitated—and the reaction to that silence was as if a large cannon had been set off in the Oval Office. "Sir, tell her to mind her own business!" Jefferson said quietly but emphatically. "She knows she has no legal recourse here, or else she would've taken action already, not just threatened us like this . . ."

"It may not get her anywhere legally, but she'll succeed in getting the entire world's attention," Secretary of Homeland Security Lemke said.

"Madam President, the United States asserts its right to secure its borders and enforce its laws," Conrad said into the phone. "No legal or human rights are being violated: they have full access to legal representation, religious facilities, privacy, food and water, and medical care. They are . . ."

"Oh no," Kinsly moaned again. "What in hell is he doing *now?*"

The President looked—and saw Minister Felix Díaz with a bullhorn to his lips, shaking his fists as he led a chant directed at the detainees at Rampart One! "What is he saying, Thomas?" he asked.

"I'll get a translator in here . . ."

" *'¡Usted es héroes mejicanos! ¡Lucha para su libertad!'* 'You are heroes of Mexico! Fight for your freedom,' " Ray Jefferson said.

"My God, he's inciting them to *riot!*" Attorney General Wentworth exclaimed. "Can they hear him?"

"I don't think so," Jefferson said, "but they have radios and televisions in that facility—I'm sure he's being broadcast to them."

"Well, pull the plug!" Kinsly said. "Shut off those transmissions, or confiscate those radios!"

"It's too late, Mr. Kinsly," Jefferson said evenly. To the President, he said, "Sir, it might be too late to stop whatever happens next. We shouldn't overreact. We can make full repairs to the base, but we'll need to increase manpower at this and all other bases, especially for security at the detention facility. Our forces there need to be armed and authorized to oppose any action by the Mexican authorities."

"What are you talking about, Sergeant Major?" the President asked absently. "What do you think is going to hap . . . ?"

"*Look!*" Kinsly blurted. In response to the Mexican minister's loudspeaker calls, several dozen men and boys had jumped on the chain-link fencing surrounding the detention facility and had begun swinging on it. At first the fence looked plenty sturdy enough, but it did not take long for the swaying to become wider and wider, until it was apparent that the fence was weakening— and the more the fence weakened, the more detainees jumped on it and joined in, causing it to weaken faster.

The camera swung back to Díaz, who was now getting into one of the news helicopters that had landed a short distance away. The helicopter lifted off, and soon his sound-amplified voice could be clearly heard on the broadcast. "He keeps shouting 'freedom, freedom,' " Jefferson said. His cellular phone vibrated; in a major breach of Oval Office etiquette, Jefferson stepped away from the President and the others after checking the caller ID. "Go ahead . . . yes, we're watching it, Major," he said.

"Order Richter to get those people off that fence!" Lemke shouted.

"But don't use that damned robot, for God's sake!" Wentworth added.

Jefferson said nothing but continued to listen. Finally: "I concur, Major," he said. "Proceed. Keep me advised."

"Was that Richter?" Lemke asked. Without waiting to hear the answer, he said, "You didn't order him to get those people off the fence?"

"No, Secretary Lemke," Jefferson said. "He recommended that we establish a full defensive posture, and I concurred."

"*Defensive?* You mean you're not going to do *anything* but watch those detainees break out? They're *rioting* out there! What do you intend to do about it?"

"Nothing, except guard what we can and minimize the damage," Jefferson said simply. He answered his cell phone again, listened, then closed it. "Rampart One reports that Díaz's helicopter is now *in* U.S. airspace, and is heading straight for the base. He is broadcasting on a PA system on the helicopter and can easily be heard by everyone at Rampart One."

"For God's sake . . ." the President muttered. He picked up the telephone on his desk. "Get the Secretary of State over here right away."

"Mr. President, we have to call out the National Guard . . . we have to bring in troops to secure that area," Jeffrey Lemke said. "We cannot allow the Mexicans to freely fly across the border like this and spring those prisoners!"

"Mr. President, again, I'm urging restraint," Ray Jefferson said. "It's too late to do anything at Rampart One now."

"Too late . . . ?"

"By the time we move one Marine from Camp Pendleton or one soldier from Yuma or El Centro, it'll long be over, Mr. Lemke," Jefferson said, more firmly this time. "We're outgunned. We can launch some Cobra and Apache gunships from Twenty-nine Palms . . ."

"Are you *crazy,* Jefferson?" Kinsly asked incredulously.

"We're fully within our rights to chase away any aircraft inside that TFR, Mr. Kinsly," Jefferson said. "I'm not saying we engage those helicopters, but maybe just the sight of an armed helicopter will defuse this incident . . ."

"And if someone gets a twitchy trigger finger, it'll escalate it," Lemke interjected. "Just because we have the *right* to do something doesn't mean we *should.*"

Jefferson could do nothing else but nod in agreement. The President angrily slapped a hand on his desk, then shook his head and chuckled gloomily. "President Maravilloso and Felix Díaz took a chance, and it paid off," President Conrad said resignedly. "Like you said, Sergeant Major, I'm damned either way, right?"

"We'll make sure we don't get caught defenseless when we set up the next base, sir," Jefferson said. "We were ready to deal with violence from migrants, smugglers, and detainees, not from the Mexican government. That will not happen the next time."

"If there'll *be* a next time," Lemke said.

"Sergeant Major Jefferson, make sure that the personnel at Rampart One defend themselves to the utmost—they can use Richter's robots if absolutely necessary," the President ordered. "But no one interferes with the Mexican Army or the detainees. I don't want a gun battle breaking out."

"I'll pass the word, sir," Jefferson said, and he immediately picked up a telephone in the Oval Office to issue the orders.

It did not take long for chaos to erupt at Rampart One. The detention facility fence finally came down, injuring two men; several persons were badly cut when the tidal surge of detainees tried to run over the chain-link fencing and razor wire on their way out—it almost seemed as if some human bodies were being used by the crowd to bridge the wire. Women carrying children and old men were roughly pushed aside by the younger men on their scramble to freedom; dozens of detainees were screaming in pain. Detainees who hadn't yet left the yard started running into other housing tents, emerging moments later carrying blankets, jugs of water, and personal items.

Outside the toppled fencing, Gray had stationed his men around the headquarters unit, maintenance facility with its power generators and fuel storage, medical unit, and the cages in which the more violent or criminally suspect individuals were kept—all other areas were unguarded, as the escaped detainees quickly discovered. The mess tents, barracks, legal aid unit, and personnel break units were completely overrun. The escapees filled their arms and pockets with food, bottles of water, and any personal effects they could find, like clothing, radios, game machines, and computers; the ones who emerged from the tents with nothing ransacked the place on their way out.

"*¡Allá!* Over there!" shouted Díaz's voice from a loudspeaker on the helicopter. He began gesturing toward the dog-pens as his bodyguards struggled to keep him from falling out of the helicopter's open door. "More of our people are being held prisoner! *¡Láncelos!*"

At Díaz's urging, a dozen men approached the prisoner cages, grabbing anything they could use as a weapon—chairs, shovels, kitchen tools, and pieces of pipe from the collapsed fencing. The National Guardsmen guarding the pens quickly found themselves outnumbered. "Rampart One, this is Seven, we have a situation here, am I cleared to engage?" one of the fearful guards radioed. *"Am I clear to fire?"*

"Sir?" Ben Gray asked.

"Negative—not yet," Richter replied. On his command radio, he spoke: "CID One, respond to the prisoner cages, protect the Rampart personnel, and do not allow any prisoners to be freed. Use minimal force if possible."

"Roger," Falcone responded immediately. Within moments he was at the cages, standing between two guards. One of the guards had his rifle shouldered and had a tear gas canister launcher ready; the other guard still had his M-16 rifle at port arms.

"Rampart Seven, this is Rampart One, *weapons tight,* don your gas masks," Gray ordered. The two Guardsmen complied immediately, shouldering their rifles and hurriedly donning their M40A1 gas masks. The angry escapees immediately began to throw their weapons at them, and the Guardsmen stepped behind the CID unit to avoid being hit by the projectiles.

"Seven, this is Condor!" Ariadna shouted on the command net. She had been scanning the area as the detainees fled, then the area in front of the cages as the angry escapees approached, and had just zoomed out for a wider look. "Several detainees approaching your position from behind! *Look out!*"

But her warning came too late. A group of five men had

sneaked around behind CID One and the distracted Guardsmen. Before they could react, the men grabbed for their rifles, and after a brief struggle managed to wrestle them away from the soldiers. A tear gas canister ignited, covering the area with yellowish smoke.

"They got the rifles!" Ariadna radioed. "Watch out! Falcon, two beside you . . ."

"I've got 'em, Ari," Falcone said. But it was not as easy as he thought. He was instantly pounced upon by the escapees, with as many as three men holding onto one arm. It was impossible to move slowly and carefully anymore with so many escapees on him—Falcone had no choice but to use the CID's strength to flick the men off. Bodies started flying everywhere, and he couldn't tell if the persons he was throwing around were attackers or onlookers, men, women, or children. Gunshots erupted, first just a few, then several on full automatic. Agonizing screams soon mixed in with the gunshots.

The helicopters overhead no longer avoided overflying the base—they circled right overhead now, their rotor wash helping to clear the tear gas. When the smoke cleared moments later, the television cameras saw the Cybernetic Infantry Device . . .

. . . surrounded by two dozen prisoners and escapees strewn about like debris after a tornado, none moving. It was a scene of absolute horrific carnage. Blood covered everything. Some of the bodies looked mangled, their limbs twisted in grotesque angles; one detainee was stuck on CID One's left knee, his dislocated arm caught in one of the robot's joints, being dragged around like an errant leaf or scrap of paper. When Falcone finally noticed the person stuck to him, he reached down and pulled the man off, leaving part of his hand and wrist still jammed on the robot, blood spurting everywhere like a leaky garden hose. Unthinking, Falcone tossed the man aside as if the body was nothing more than a piece of paper stuck to the bottom of his boots.

It was all captured on international television, live.

"Oh . . . my . . . God . . ." the President breathed as he watched the ghastly sight on his TV monitors. All of the major broadcast, cable, and satellite stations were playing the live video now.

"Mr. President, we're going to need to clear that airspace so we can get emergency medical units out there," Ray Jefferson said. "I suggest we request the California Highway Patrol respond first until we can get the National Guard out there."

"Do it," the President said in a whisper. He moved to the window behind his desk and stared out the window. Jefferson picked up a phone to issue instructions.

"Falcone . . . he's getting out of the robot," White House Chief of Staff Kinsly remarked. "This is the most horrible thing I've ever seen on television. I still can't believe what I just saw."

"Falcone has got to be prosecuted," Attorney General Wentworth said. "The Mexican government . . . no, the *world* will demand nothing less." A moment later, he asked, "So what's he doing now, Jefferson?"

"Sergeant Major, have that man placed under arrest," the President said, still staring out the window into the Rose Garden.

"No need, Mr. President," Jefferson responded.

The President whirled around and stared in utter disbelief at his National Security Adviser. *"What did you say to me, Jefferson?"* he roared. "I ordered you to place Falcone under arrest! He's got to be a lunatic! Even if he didn't kill any of those people, he precipitated this entire episode by his actions! He's going to go to prison for a very, very long time. He . . ." The President stopped, finally noticing that everyone else in the Oval Office was staring at the TV monitors. "What in hell is going on?"

"We're about to see the last casualty in this debacle, sir," Jefferson said stonily, sadly.

They all watched as Frank Falcone wandered, seemingly dazed and disoriented, through the piles of battered and bloody bodies around him and his Cybernetic Infantry Device. He stopped, zipped his flight suit all the way up to his chin, then stood limply, his arms hanging straight down, his head bowed. After a few moments, he looked up, reached down, retrieved a blood-covered M-16 rifle from the ground, pulled the charging handle to make sure a round was in the chamber, checked that the safety was off, turned it around, inserted the muzzle in his mouth . . . and pulled the trigger.

CHAPTER 4

WHEELER RIDGE,
SOUTH OF BAKERSFIELD, CALIFORNIA
DAYS LATER

The man jumped when he saw the American military officer blow his head off on the taped replay being broadcast again on TV, but the next thing he felt was . . . intense amusement, almost glee. *"Yop tvayu mat! Usrattsa mozhna!"* he swore in Russian, being careful not to be too loud—these motel cabin room walls were paperthin. The men and women behind him were stunned into silence, not daring to believe what they'd just seen on TV. "That guy must have really been fucked in the head—of course, now he does not even have a head anymore!"

"Chto sluchilos', Polkovnik?" Ernesto Fuerza, known as Comandante Veracruz, the man standing watch by the back door and windows, whispered in good Russian. "What is it, Colonel?"

"I am watching the self-destruction of the American idiots trying to put military forces on the Mexican border, *Comandante,*" Colonel Yegor Viktorvich Zakharov said. "They cannot seem to get out of their own way. That poor bastard, Falcone, was probably the only one committed enough to do the job, and he has just blown his silly head off with an M-16 assault rifle—and not because of anything he did, but because he felt sorry for the prisoners he killed who were *also* stupid enough to shoot themselves trying to escape!"

Fuerza got another one of the men in the room to take his post, then stepped into the room—not to watch TV, but to watch Zakharov. The ex–Russian military officer always wore sunglasses, with the right lens slightly lighter than the left; he would occasionally dab under his left eye also, so he obviously has suffered some sort of injury. He drank like a damned fish, mostly chilled vodka or anything he could get his hands on, but he never seemed drunk or even impaired. He definitely liked his women too—he enjoyed the company of any number of prostitutes who always seemed to be nearby at every camp, hostel, or safe house they visited.

"Some of those 'stupid' prisoners were my people, Colonel," Fuerza said irritably.

"Which ones are you referring to, Fuerza—the ones that were stepping over old men and women as they tried to escape, the ones that listened to your president's brave orders to try to release those prisoners with two armed soldiers guarding them, or the ones who decided it was a peachy idea to attack that robot?" Zakharov's demeanor was still ebullient, but his mood had changed—everyone could feel it. He definitely didn't like being challenged.

"Fuerza, 'your' people are dead because they were stupid. They were *free,* for God's sake—in twenty minutes or less they could have strolled back across the border to safety, and all the Americans would have done was wave bye-bye to them. Instead they decide to turn *back* toward the prison they just escaped to release some criminals that they would never associate with anyway. Are those the ones you feel sorry for?"

"Colonel, all those people want is freedom and prosperity in exchange for hard work," Fuerza said. "Coahuila—what they now call Texas—Nuevo Mexico, and Alta California are home to them, even though a U.S. flag flies over the land. It belongs to us—it will *always* belong to us. It will one day . . ."

"Fuerza, please, you are boring me," Zakharov said, downing another shot of vodka. "I really do not give a shit about your struggle or about your claims. Your followers may believe that nonsense, but I do not. You call yourself Comandante Veracruz as a reminder of the bloodbath that accompanied the American invasion of Veracruz in 1847; you strut around like some wild-eyed Muslim fanatic inciting the people to rise up and take what is theirs. But it is all for show. You get your picture on the cover of *Time* Magazine and you think you are a hero. In reality, you are nothing but a drug and human smuggler with a simple, effective message that has captivated the imagination of some otherwise mindless Americans. I cannot abide patriots or zealots—criminals, I can deal with."

"Then I have a deal I wish to discuss with you, Colonel," Fuerza said.

Zakharov looked to refill his glass, found the vodka bottle empty, then tossed the shot glass away with disgust. "What do you have in mind—gunning down more Border Patrol agents and corrupt sheriff's deputies? Becoming a drug dealer, like you?"

"You want money—I have plenty of it," Fuerza said. "What my men and I need is training and protection. You have experienced professional soldiers, and you want to bring more of them into the United States. Until your army is ready for whatever havoc you intend to create here, I have need of your services." He searched a box of supplies on the floor, found another bottle of vodka, retrieved the shot glass, and gave them to Zakharov. "*Napitok, tovarisch polkovnik.*"

"I do not drink warm vodka, and I do not make plans with drug dealers," Zakharov said, putting the unopened bottle in the tiny freezer section of the cabin's noisy old refrigerator. He looked over at a corner of the cabin, where a man was setting up a plain white bedsheet and adjusting some lights, and shook his head with amusement. "Time for another videotape, I see?"

"It is the best way to keep the people of the world aware of our struggle on their behalf," Fuerza said. "One Internet message can travel around the world in an hour these days."

"It will also be the best chance for the American FBI to catch you," Zakharov said. "They can analyze the tiniest background noises in a recording and identify the characteristics of any digital or audio recording; they can pinpoint any IP address in the world within moments; they can trace the origin and path of any package put in the mail anywhere in the world. Why give them any more clues to investigate?"

"The reward is worth the risk, Colonel," Fuerza said confidently. "We get dozens of new recruits, tens of thousands of dollars in cash donations, and hundreds of thousands of dollars' worth of free publicity every time we post a tape on our Web site, and even more when it is rebroadcast by the Mexican and American media. My messages are even rebroadcast overseas on Al-Jazeera and the BBC. We have received donations from as far away as Vietnam."

"I will be sure to stay as far away from you as possible while your messages are uploaded to the Internet and mailed out to the media—sooner or later the FBI is going to swoop down on you, just like they did to Bin Laden and al-Zarqawi. You cannot avoid scrutiny if you decide to play out in the open."

"As far as assisting your operation, Colonel, we will remain secret and concealed," Fuerza said, "but as for my battle, I prefer to do my fighting out in the open."

Zakharov took the bottle of vodka from the freezer and downed another shot. "Oh, really? Is that why you wear that fake hair, wear sunglasses even indoors at night, and disguise yourself to look like three or four different nationalities?" He saw Fuerza frozen in surprise and smiled. "You actually think no one sees you are wearing a disguise? It is good, but not *that* good. You look like some ridiculous Hollywood cross between Pancho Villa and Muhammar Qaddafi."

"This disguise is *my* affair, Colonel," Fuerza said. "The Mexican people need a symbol of our struggle for freedom, and I find it easier and more effective to do it in disguise." Zakharov shrugged. "I have found using the media to enflame public opinion works much better in this country than the gun. The revolution *is* coming, Colonel. The power of the people is absolute and real."

"Courageous and defiant . . . to the last."

" *'My ne mozhem ubedit'sja iz nalichija koe-chego, chtoby zhit' dlja togo, esli my ne zhelaem umirat' dlja etogo.'* 'We cannot be sure of having something to live for unless we are willing to die for it.' Ernesto Che Guevara," Fuerza quoted in Russian.

"Your namesake, I gather? How touching."

"He recognized early on that the source of most of the oppression and poverty in the world is imperialism and capitalism, and the number-one proponent of both is the United States of America," Fuerza said. "Ernesto Guevara was one man, a man of education and privilege, a trained physician who could have had anything in life he wanted—yet El Che chose instead to go toe to toe against the American Central Intelligence Agency to fight capitalistic aggression in South and Central America and the Caribbean . . ."

"Until he was sold out by Castro and captured by the CIA in Bolivia."

"El Che dared to criticize Castro for selling out to the Soviets for money—in doing so, he became a martyr to the socialist movement," Fuerza said. "His truth has been borne out by history: Cuba is nothing but a stinking Communist shithole exploited by Castro; Mexico is little more than America's whore because the government sold the workers out just to line their own pockets. El Che is a hero to us all. I hope to be half the man he was."

"Well, who knows what Guevara could have done with videotapes and the Internet," Zakharov said. "But Guevara's problem was he expected too much from the people of the Congo and Bolivia . . ."

"Not the people—the *people* were solidly behind him. The corrupt government in Brazil fought him; then, when El Che's revolution looked like it might successfully overthrow the government, the Bolivians paid Castro to betray Guevara. But Castro didn't have the guts to assassinate Guevara himself, because El Che was as much a hero of the Cuban workers' revolution against the corrupt Batista regime as Castro himself. So Castro ratted him out to the CIA, who was more than happy to do Castro's wet work for him."

"Thank you for the history lesson," Zakharov said drily. "Where are the damned weapons you promised me?"

"Five thousand dollars a day for you, a thousand per day for your men, free travel across the border, and all the weapons you want," Fuerza said. "A few security and enforcement chores, keeping the rival cookers and the corrupt cops like Nuñez back there in line. That is all."

Zakharov looked as if he wasn't listening, but a few moments later he shook his head. "Ten thousand a day for me, two for my men . . . and one hundred thousand dollars as a signing bonus." Fuerza's eyes widened in anger. "Take it or leave it, Comandante. Or else go back to using your own *banditos* and paying off corrupt cops to secure your drug empire. They do such a good job for you, no?"

Fuerza thought for a moment—actually, he thought about whether he could get away with executing Zakharov, but the Russian's men were too loyal to try to pay off and turn on their leader, at least right at this moment—then nodded. *"Prevoshodnyj, tovarisch polkovnik,"* Fuerza said. He extended a hand, and Zakharov clasped it. *"Spasibo."*

"You do not have to thank me—you have to *pay* me," Zakharov said.

Fuerza watched as Zakharov turned to look at the television again, and he could almost feel Zakharov's body temperature rise when the helicopter cameras tracked a man and two women running from an enclosure out to where the dead officer that had piloted the robot lay. "Who is he, Colonel? He is the one you want, is he not?"

Zakharov half-turned toward Fuerza and chuckled. "You are very observant, Comandante," he said. "Yes, that is Major Jason Richter, commander of Task Force TALON, the one that defeated my forces in Egypt and Washington. With him is his assistant, Dr. Ariadna Vega, Ph.D."

"*Ariadna Vega?* That is the name of a famous guerrilla fighter during the Mexican War of Independence," Fuerza said, his face transfixed in surprise. "She is one of the most celebrated women in Mexican history."

"Well, she's one tough *minino,* that's for sure," Zakharov said. "I all but killed her in Brazil, and she was back in the fight just a few days later. The other one is Richter's former partner and now the director of the Federal Bureau of Investigation, *Kelsey DeLaine.* Learn their names and faces well—they will undoubtedly be after both of us. They must be defeated at all costs."

Fuerza was staring at the television until the camera zoomed in on the decapitated body, cutting Vega from view. "So. Was Richter the one who shot out your left eye, Colonel?"

"He did *not* shoot out my eye, Fuerza," Zakharov snapped. "He missed by a mile—the bullet ricocheted off my helicopter's rotor, and a fragment lodged in my eye. A hack doctor in Havana told me the eye had to be enucleated or the uninjured eye would sympathetically shut down." He removed his sunglasses, revealing an empty eye socket. Fuerza did not—rather, *dared* not—look away, afraid of appearing squeamish at the sight of the horrible injury. "I took one of *his* eyes in exchange for the one he unnecessarily took from me—unfortunately, his did not fit me, and it was too late to give it back to him."

"Why do you keep it open like that?"

Zakharov chuckled. "It puts great fear into my adversaries, Comandante, forcing them to look into another man's skull."

"But the pain . . . ?"

"The pain helps keep me focused on my objective."

"Which is?"

"*Acercamiento de camión, capitán,*" the lookout at the window said. Everyone drew weapons, including Zakharov. Fuerza went to another window and watched as the pickup truck with a camper—a familiar sight in this part of rural southern Bakersfield, at the foothills of the Tehachapi Mountains. They trained their weapons on it carefully, looking for any signs of danger, even after the driver flashed the headlights in a coded "all clear" signal. Fuerza requested and received a coded "all clear" from his lookouts around the perimeter before signaling that it was safe to approach the cabin.

While two men kept watch on either side of the camper, three more men began unloading. They brought in two coffin-looking fiberglass canisters and several wood and metal boxes of assault rifles, pistols, and ammunition. The men quickly opened the crates and distributed guns and ammo to each other to check over, while Zakharov and Fuerza concentrated on the "coffins."

It was their best and most potent weapon since beginning this operation months ago: a Russian-built advanced man-portable air defense system, known in the West as an SA-14 Gremlin and in the East as a 9K34 Strela-3. An advanced version of the venerable SA-7 Grail MANPADS, the SA-14 had a larger warhead, a broader detection and tracking window, better countermeasures discrimination, and improved reliability. Each coffin contained the weapon stock, which included the pistol grip, shoulder stock, electronics, fixed and optical sights, and battery holder; two missile launch tubes; and two spherical battery-gas generator canisters.

"*Prevoshodnyj,*" Fuerza said. "They look to be in excellent shape."

Zakharov examined each one carefully. "They were painted to look new, but the data plates are missing—I would estimate the gas generator is at least twenty years old, maybe twenty-five," he said. "And if they used regular lead-based paint on those gas generators, the heat could cause them to catch on fire as soon as the operator pulls the trigger."

"Are you sure, Colonel?" Fuerza asked angrily.

"I *do* know my Russian-made weapons," Zakharov said drily. "Trust me, I know what I am talking about." He continued his examination. "Overall the electronics and components look to be in good order, but the data plates are missing from the missiles as well, so I would guess they are as old as the gas generators. That means they are at least five and probably ten years over their service life. If you paid more than a thousand dollars apiece for these, Comandante, you got ripped off."

Judging by the color in his cheeks and the bulge in his eyes, it was obvious Fuerza had paid much more than a thousand dollars for the missiles. "I do not get 'ripped off,' as you say, Colonel—I get *even,*" he said darkly. "The dealer who sold me these weapons will gladly give me a full refund and suitable replacements—especially if he wants to keep his fingers and balls intact."

"I think you should take one or two fingers anyway just to ensure he does not try to steal from anyone else," Zakharov suggested. "We have been here too long already, Fuerza. I suggest we split up until it is time to rendezvous again to carry out our next operation."

"*Soglasovannyj,*" Fuerza said. "Agreed. You are the chief of security now."

Zakharov examined the other boxes of weapons, found the ones he was looking for, opened six of them, looped two small cylindrical canisters over his shoulders and gave the other boxes and canisters to an aide. "I will have need of these, I am sure of it," he said. "My next two squads are scheduled to arrive at the rendezvous point at Esparanza in two days. You will arrange the border crossing for them and transportation to Amarillo, Texas."

"Two days? Impossible, Colonel," Fuerza said. "The entire El Paso and Fabens border crossing area will be swarming with American Border Patrol and Mexican Internal Affairs border patrols for at least a week, maybe more." He thought for a moment; then: "The best chance for a crossing in that time frame will be Arizona," he said, smiling. "Have your men go to the rendezvous point in Nogales and await my signal. They will . . ."

"*Nogales!* That's at least six hours west of the original rendezvous point!"

"Your first assignment, Colonel," Fuerza said. "Perhaps your men will get a little field training and target practice in at the same time."

"What are you babbling about?"

"Your men will come across others on the trail," Fuerza said. "If and when you do, you must deal with them . . . appropriately."

"More Border Patrol agents, Fuerza?" Zakharov asked irritably. "They will be ready for us this time. Pick a different crossing point, Fuerza. What about Agua Prieta or Palomas?"

"Western and central New Mexico are already overrun with migrants," Fuerza said, smiling. "My intelligence reports indicate that the Border Patrol and perhaps some civilian border patrol groups will concentrate their efforts there."

"Civilians? You mean the vigilantes? You are going to put my men on the same trail as some of those American commando wannabes?" As Fuerza expected, the Russian terrorist broke out into a grin. "Well, that's different, Ernesto. My men would enjoy an easy night of target practice."

"I thought you might enjoy it," Fuerza said. "But you must deal with them carefully."

"My men and I are *always* careful . . ."

"Do as I suggest, Colonel, and I will create an atmosphere of paranoia and fear that will cause the entire border security debate in America to shatter," Fuerza said.

"Explain."

"The Americans are going to put more robots on the border and, if that fails as it appears it has, they will bring armed troops in," Fuerza replied. "They will do this because they think *they* have the upper hand."

"Militarily, that is unquestioned."

"But in every other respect, they do not," Fuerza said. "Perhaps on the question of their right to secure their borders from terrorist monsters like *you,* they win. But in moral, social, political, economic, humanitarian, and cultural terms, they fail. When the Americans realize they do not control what happens on their own immense borders, they will rush to return to the status quo, just as the American people's response to your attacks just a year ago has been to simply return to the status quo."

"This is gibberish, Fuerza," Zakharov said, pouring himself more vodka. "I am not playing along with this cultural psychobabble. You want to kill some American vigilantes, do it yourself."

"At the very least, you get to practice your night-hunting skills, and save some money on border-crossing fees," Fuerza said. "At most, you will start an insurrection in this country that I guarantee will result in the borders being thrown wide open for you."

Zakharov thought for a moment, then nodded. "Very well, Fuerza. But if we expend any ammunition or lose any men or equipment, it comes out of *your* pocket, not mine."

Fuerza fell silent himself, but only for a moment: "Very well, Colonel, it is a deal." They shook hands, both eyeing each other warily as they did so. "Nice to do business with you, Colonel," Fuerza said; then he added, "You still did not tell me what you and your men intend to do in this country, Colonel," he said. He motioned to the television. "You want those robots, do you not?"

"First I want Richter and Vega as my prisoners, and *then* I want those robots," Zakharov said. "They will teach me how those robots are maneuvered and controlled. I will use the robots to capture other robots and other weapons, and soon I will be the most powerful mercenary warlord in the world."

"Such a force would be extremely valuable to me, Colonel," Fuerza said.

"Use my robots to protect your dope deals, Fuerza? Not a chance. There are dictators that will pay me a hundred times what you are paying me now to have those robots fighting for them."

"So you want to capture some of those robots to form a mercenary fighting force?"

"A fighting force, yes," Zakharov said. "A 'mercenary' force—no. I have one specific objective in mind."

"In Amarillo, Texas? More oil refineries, I assume?"

"You should assume nothing, Comandante," Zakharov warned, "or if I am discovered, I will 'assume' that *you* told them, and if I survive I will be coming after *you*." He paused, then murmured, "They have some things in Amarillo that belong to me, and I want them back."

"Perhaps I can be of assistance," Fuerza said. "I have excellent contacts throughout Texas, and of course I do a great deal of business there."

"We will see how good your information is in Arizona first," Zakharov said. "But perhaps you can be of help to me later on."

"We will talk, Colonel," Fuerza said. "If it is money you want, I can get it for you."

"Keep your end of the bargain and don't try to screw me, Fuerza, and then you can talk to me all you want." He got on a small walkie-talkie, checked in with his security detail to be sure the way was clear, and departed.

As soon as the Russian departed, Fuerza ordered, "Keep an eye on them. I do not want those bastards coming back for this money. They have enough weapons now to lay waste to this entire county."

"No confío en aquel ruso, Comandante," one of Fuerza's men said. "I think he would turn us in to the *federales* in an instant."

"Concordado," Fuerza said. He nodded toward the duffel bag filled with money. "Zakharov thinks he has bought our cooperation as well as those weapons. But we do not need his help. We will use him as much as possible, then dispose of him."

He went into the living room, moved a couch, a rug, and several pieces of plywood, revealing a hidden door. He carefully removed a trip wire on the handle to deactivate a booby trap explosive device, then opened the door. One by one, he started handing out kilo bags of white powder, securely wrapped in duct tape, and more bundles of cash. "Guns and missiles are good," Fuerza said as he handed the bags out to his men, "but they are a dime a dozen in this country. Get control of the money, and you get the real power." He held up two bags of cocaine, worth several thousand dollars each. "This is the real currency in the United States of America, not guns—and certainly not nationalism or revolution. Get the money, and you get the power."

FBI FIELD OFFICE, SAN DIEGO, CALIFORNIA
THE NEXT MORNING

"Getting fired seems to be part of your regular routine now, eh, Jason?" FBI Director Kelsey DeLaine said with only just a hint of humor in her voice. With her was her assistant, Special Agent Janice Perkins, a friendly and rather demure blonde who was very quick with a smile and a handshake and who, armed with a seemingly endless array of PDAs and smart cell phones, always seemed to have any person or every bit of information requested of her instantly at her fingertips. They were approaching the FBI's San Diego field office headquarters north of San Diego near Montgomery Field Airport on a bright, clear California morning.

"I don't see the humor in it, Kel," Jason said somberly. With him was Ariadna Vega, looking beautiful as always although she dressed down in a plain pantsuit and casual jacket against the chill of the gradually lifting morning marine layer, still visible to the west toward San Diego's Pacific coastline. "What are we doing here, anyway? We've been debriefing you guys for the past eighteen hours already."

"I have some folks I want you to meet," Kelsey said.

"What for? We're not part of Operation Rampart anymore."

"And you shouldn't be . . . you said so yourself," Kelsey said. "For once, I agree with you: as you said, you need to be out in the field chasing down the bad guys, not waiting for them to come to *you*." She looked at Jason earnestly and added, "And frankly, I think Task Force TALON was a great success. The FBI can sure put your capabilities to good use." Jason made a show of clearing out his ears as if he hadn't heard her correctly. "Kiss my ass, Major. I still think *you're* a loose cannon, but Task Force TALON is for sure the future of special operations and high-risk law enforcement."

"I'm touched by your concern for me, Kel."

"It's nothing personal, Jason—some men can lead, others can't," Kelsey said matter-of-factly.

"Don't hold back, *friend:* tell me how you *really* feel."

"Your training, education, and background have been in research and development, not leadership. You've always come through in the end, but usually at the expense of one or two of your best people. To me, that's not true leadership."

Kelsey's last comment hurt—Frank Falcone's horrifying suicide was just a couple days earlier, and he and Ariadna had been grilled about it and all the events leading up to the riot at Rampart One for most of yesterday. "So *you* want to take over?" Jason asked bitterly. "You want to make TALON a big bad FBI terrorist-hunting force?"

"As FBI director, I'm in a great position to see to it that TALON gets the funding, equipment, support, and taskings that can quickly turn it into the world's most high-tech and fearsome security, interdiction, and law enforcement team," Kelsey said. "I'm not trying to cut you out—there'll always be a place for you on TALON . . ."

"Just not as commander, right?"

"As technical team leaders, designing, building, and deploying the latest weapons and technology, there's no one that could replace you and Ariadna. As tacticians and field commanders . . ."

"You think we suck."

"I think you need to learn how to *build* a fighting team, rather than slap on the armor yourself and rush out into the middle of a firestorm—or, worse, *creating* a firestorm," Kelsey said. "I think I can do that. Now that I better understand how your technology works and what it's capable of, I think I have the organizational skills to take TALON to a much higher level."

"And that would sure make you look good, in or out of the FBI, wouldn't it?"

"I'm not doing this to make myself look good," Kelsey snapped. "Sure, it would be a great legacy for me to bring that force up to full operational status as quickly as possible before I leave the Bureau. But I really believe in Task Force TALON too. I think it can be as big and as important as the U.S. marshals—heck, I think it could eventually *replace* the U.S. marshals."

Jason had to admit to himself that he had never thought of TALON in that way before: TALON becoming its own federal law enforcement agency. He had only thought of it as a tool of the FBI or the armed forces, like choosing a different gun or vehicle to do a specific task. "Are you willing to take the added scrutiny?" he asked.

" 'Scrutiny'? I call it 'universal condemnation,' " Kelsey said, only half-joking. "But to answer your question: yes, I'm willing to take it. To tell the obvious truth, I'm already tainted by my actions with TALON—I'm not long for the directorship. I was nominated because of what I did to help hunt down the Consortium. But I don't play well with Congress, the Attorney General, or the Washington bureaucracy, the three players that you need to win in that town. So I might as well help TALON hunt down whoever is invading America now, then take my retirement and head off to a nice comfy private sector consulting job."

She took off her sunglasses and looked around. "And this would be a nice place to base my consulting firm," she added. "Nice weather year-round, far enough away from the ocean to avoid the fog, but close enough to still enjoy the coast; great airport, great facilities. Nothing against Clovis, New Mexico, but this area puts it to shame."

"I'm surprised to hear you talking like this, about getting out of government service and hanging out a shingle," Jason remarked. "Doesn't sound like you."

"I can read the handwriting on the wall, Jason—my honeymoon with Washington is just about over. They'll want a more experienced, hard-nosed *man* in the directorship soon. I think it's smart to make plans. If you're smart, you'll do the same." She looked at him carefully and added, "Maybe even join my team."

"You and I . . . working *together?*"

"I didn't say that. It's my firm—you'd be working for me."

That, Jason thought, was the no-nonsense, plain-talking Kelsey DeLaine he knew. He saw the surreptitious glance that Ariadna gave him and knew that she was thinking the same thing. "But I'd put your *real* talents to good use, and I'd guarantee the pay, benefits, and perks would be well worth it."

"Sounds like you have it all worked out, Kel."

"Times change—you gotta change with them," Kelsey said. "Think about it."

As she stepped ahead to greet the woman standing just outside the FBI field office, Ariadna walked up to him and said under her breath, "You, in a *suit* and *tie,* working for *her?*"

" 'Times change—you gotta change with them,' " Jason parroted.

"I'd rather go back to Fort Polk and eat crawdads."

"Now you're making me hungry."

Kelsey was met by the Special Agent in Charge of the San Diego field office, Angelica Pierce, a tall and striking brunette with bright blue eyes and an unmistakable upstate New York accent. "Welcome to San Diego, Miss Director," Pierce said, shaking first Kelsey's hand, then greeting the others. "I understand you'll be heading out right away, and I know you've had a long night. Everything's ready; coffee's waiting."

"Thanks, Angelica," Kelsey said. "I appreciate your office's hustle on this. Your support has been outstanding."

"Thank you, ma'am," Pierce responded. Her tone became much more serious—pleasantries were over, time to get down to business. "We're at full security posture, as you know, which is why you had to park so far away from the building. We won't be bypassing entry security either; sorry in advance for the delay." They surrendered their ID cards before entering the building, then entered an entrapment area together while low-power X-ray scanners scanned for weapons and explosives, then entered the inspection area one at a time, where they were hand-wanded with metal detectors to locate their weapons. Everyone but Jason and Kelsey were surprised that Ariadna was carrying a weapon, her standard SIG Sauer P220 .45 caliber semiautomatic pistol—but everyone but Kelsey was surprised as they watched cheerful, friendly, smiling Janice Perkins go through security: she was carrying no less than three guns, including a remarkably small Heckler & Koch .40 caliber UMP submachine gun on a shoulder rig under her coat.

"Sheesh, I never would've guessed," Jason remarked. "Wonder how well armed your *bodyguards* would be?"

"Janice *is* my bodyguard," Kelsey said. "She can take dictation, type eighty words a minute, can make any computer turn cartwheels, and can put thirty rounds inside a twelve-inch diameter target at sixty feet on full auto. She's also an attorney. She was a JAG in the U.S. Marines before joining the Bureau."

They took an elevator down one level to a detention facility, checked their weapons in with the jailers, then entered an interrogation room, with a long metal table bolted to the floor, several chairs, and two walls with one-way mirrors on them. Coffee and sandwiches were brought in, which Richter, Vega, and DeLaine hungrily devoured. A few moments later there was a knock on the door, and an agent brought in an older white male, with several days' growth of gray facial hair and unkempt gray hair, wearing an orange prisoner's jumpsuit. The agent made sure the inspection shutter on the door was closed, removed the prisoner's handcuffs, and closed the door behind him on his way out.

Special Agent in Charge Pierce went over and shook the man's hand. "Welcome, Paul," she greeted him. "Hope you don't mind the masquerade. We have too many folks in this facility that might recognize you."

"No problem at all, ma'am," the man replied.

Pierce turned to the others in the room. "Paul Purdy, this is FBI

Director DeLaine, her assistant Special Agent Perkins, Major Jason Richter of the U.S. Army, and his deputy Dr. Ariadna Vega. Folks, this is . . ."

"Paul *Purdy?* The U.S. Border Patrol agent who was reported killed by those terrorists near Blythe?" Kelsey asked. She stepped forward and shook his hand. "Glad to see you're really alive, Agent Purdy."

"No one more'n me, Miss Director," Purdy said in a rather "aw-shucks" down-home southwestern country twang—not Texas, not southern California, but somewhere in between. Kelsey was immediately certain Purdy had adopted the accent to make anyone he encountered underestimate him—she had to be careful, she reminded herself, not to do that.

"What happened?"

"They shot me in the back as I was helpin' the migrants we caught out of my patrol truck," Purdy said. "Like an idiot, I didn't have a shock plate on the back of my vest, like I do in front, and the bullet knocked the wind outta me. I landed face-down in a ditch, and I guess they left me for dead. I came to in the hospital."

"And you announced to the world that he was killed?" Jason asked. "Why? To keep his family safe?"

"Paul was a BORTAC agent and used to do some undercover work in his early years in the Border Patrol, and his Spanish is very good—we thought about having him go undercover again," Pierce said.

"BORTAC?"

"Border Patrol Tactical units," Pierce explained. "The top one percent of the Border Patrol, chosen to undergo special training in covert surveillance, high-risk captures, hazardous warrant service, assault, and special weapons. They put members of the FBI's Hostage Rescue Teams, U.S. Marshals Special Ops Group, and most big-city SWAT units to shame sometimes. Purdy was one of the Border Patrol's top BORTAC agents in the early years of the program."

"My family's pretty small and spread out, and I'm definitely not made of money—the terrorists should have bigger fish to fry, Major," Purdy said. "I'm not one for hidin' out, either—if they want to get to me, let 'em come. I'll be ready for 'em next time." Jason smiled at the guy's tenacity—he was ready to take on the Consortium all by himself. Purdy looked at Richter and Vega. "You the people trying to use those big robot things on the border, aren't you?"

"That's right, Agent Purdy," Ariadna replied.

Purdy reached out and shook both their hands. "Thank God we're finally getting some firepower to back up our patrol forces," he said. "Every swingin' dick on the wire is dead meat otherwise."

"I hate to tell you this, but we've just been reassigned," Jason said. "My team's been taken off the project—just regular Border Patrol units and a few National Guard out there now, although they are better armed and have better surveillance equipment now."

"That's just because your gadgets scare the livin' shit out of everyone, especially those pasty-faced pencil-pushers in Washington." He paused, looked at Kelsey in embarrassment, then decided he really meant it and shrugged. "No offense, ma'am."

"I think you well deserve to speak your mind, Agent Purdy," Kelsey said.

"Tell the major and Director DeLaine who you think attacked you, Paul," Pierce prompted the rough-looking Border Patrol veteran.

"Russians," the old guy said simply. Kelsey's mouth dropped open in surprise; Jason nodded knowingly. "Expert, well-trained, and stone-cold killers. They popped my partners and the other migrants as casually as if they were squashin' *cucarachas*."

"Are you sure, Agent Purdy?" Kelsey asked.

"Sure I'm sure, ma'am. I spent four years in Air Force intelligence before I joined the Border Patrol, two of 'em in West Germany. I spoke with plenty of Russians—I learned to speak it pretty well, if I do say so myself. Another one of the terrorists yelled at the one speakin' Russian, telling him in Spanish to quit talkin' Russian."

"You were right, Jason," Kelsey said. "It's got to be the Consortium, trying to infiltrate back into the country—except this time they're sneaking across the border instead of using fake passports."

"There's no 'trying' about it, ma'am—I'd say they had at least a dozen, maybe two dozen, inside Ernesto Fuerza's truck, fully armed and equipped like front-line infantry," Purdy said. "They mowed down their targets as easy as waterin' the lawn. Who knows how many more of those trucks made it across? We only nab one out of ten *pollos* on a good day. If ten more trucks like that one made it across that night, they'd have an entire company of shock troops or *Spetznaz*—Russian special ops forces—in the country right now. I didn't see anyone come out of Flores's truck except Hispanics and one other . . ."

"*Fuerza* was there?" Ariadna Vega interrupted incredulously. "Ernesto Fuerza? Are you sure, Agent Purdy?"

"Sure am, Dr. Vega," Purdy said. "The one smuggler I've never been able to nab—I'm not sure if I could hold him either, since every civil rights and immigrant rights attorney in the southwestern United States and northern Mexico would sign on to represent him. The Hispanic community thinks he's Mexico's Fidel Castro or Yasser Arafat and will eventually lead them to a pan-American homeland, free of persecution. To me he's just another coyote. I personally recovered dozens of kilos of drugs during one bust, but he got away . . ."

"He says he's not a drug smuggler anymore," Ariadna said.

"Once a drug smuggler, always a drug smuggler," Purdy said. "The money is just too good to ignore. I wouldn't make the mistake of giving him the benefit of the doubt if I were you. And now that he's been seen traveling with a bunch of Russian commandos, I'd say he might be into infiltrating terrorists and guns into the U.S. too. I'd love to put that bastard away for good." Purdy smiled at Ariadna's grim expression. "Sorry to burst your bubble, Doc, but Fuerza is a serious bad guy. I don't think he's the freedom fighter everyone makes him out to be."

"He has done some remarkable, important things for the migrant community, Agent Purdy," Ariadna said. "I'm not questioning your knowledge and experience, but I'm pointing out that the good he's done can't all be discounted."

"Oh yes it can, missy," Purdy said. "First of all, the 'good' you're talking about—helping foreigners sneak into the country illegally—is a*gainst the law*. Maybe we should be changing the law to make it easier for workers to come to this country legally, but until it *is* changed, Fuerza is breaking the laws that I swore to uphold, and I'm going to stop him.

"Second: maybe back whenever he supposedly renounced his evil days of drug smuggling and switched to migrant smuggling he did it because he really did want to help his fellow Mexicans find a better life in America. But that was *then*. These days, he takes on any client and any cargo as long as they got the cash. It looks to me like he brought in terrorists with serious heavy weaponry—and those terrorists used a bunch of migrants as human shields to gun down my buddies."

"But you didn't see *Fuerza* shoot anybody, did you?"

"No, but he certainly didn't warn my buddies that they were about to get blown away now, did he?"

"Maybe he didn't know they were going to . . ."

"Sure, Doc—a guy loads a truck up with a squad of guys in body armor and automatic weapons, and he's just going to take them to the local farm so they can go pick some vegetables," Purdy shot back acidly. His features softened a bit when he saw Vega's expression turn from defiance to hurt and shame. "Hey, Doc, I'm not tryin' to pick a fight with you, okay? A lot of folks all over the world, including some very smart politicians, lawyers, and talkin' heads on TV, think Fuerza is a hero. I just can't help but notice that I don't see *those* people out on the wire with me and my guys very often." He smiled reassuringly. "But *you're* out here, Doc, and I respect that. We'll make a good team, and we'll see what we see."

Ariadna nodded and tried to smile, but her face looked grim and she averted her eyes and said nothing.

"What else do you remember about that night, Agent Purdy?" Kelsey asked. "You mentioned Russians—can you give us a description?"

"Just of one of them, the one that I think came in with Flores—I couldn't ID the military ones that jumped out of Fuerza's truck, 'cause they were wearing balaclavas and helmets," Purdy said. "Big guy, about six-two, square and solid but not fat, shaved head, wearing sunglasses."

"Zakharov," Jason breathed. "It has to be."

"*Zakharov? Yegor Zakharov?*" Purdy asked incredulously. "The guy who planned those terrorist attacks on Kingman City, San Francisco, and Washington? *He was right in front of me?* My God, I actually *saw* Yegor Zakharov . . . I even got a bead on the motherfucker until his troopers started shooting up the place!"

"Are you sure about your description, Agent Purdy?" Kelsey asked.

"Positive, ma'am—I hit him square on with my lights, and he turned and faced me as soon as I did. Zakharov came with Flores in his Suburban with a small group of migrants, and Fuerza brought the big truckload of terrorists."

"Wait a minute, wait a minute—you keep on mentioning this Flores," Jason interrupted. "Who's Flores?"

"Flores. Victor Flores. He was the second smuggler in the group." He looked questioningly at Special Agent in Charge Pierce. "You didn't recover the body of a young kid, seventeen or eighteen years old, near the shot-up Suburban?"

"No," Pierce said. "You never mentioned him."

"I assumed he was among the dead," Purdy said.

"There was a young boy killed, maybe eleven or twelve, but not a teenager . . ."

"When I arrived on the scene I arrested a coyote named Victor Flores," Purdy backtracked excitedly. "He was separate from Fuerza. Fuerza brought the big truck with the commandos in it, the one that the second Border Patrol unit rolled up on. I rolled up on Flores and his Suburban. I know the kid—I've caught up with him many times, but never arrested him. But he was *there*. I had handcuffed him to the door of his Suburban but cut him loose just after the shooting started." He looked at the others in surprise. "He must'a gotten away!"

"There's another witness out there," Jason said. "Another guy who could positively ID Zakharov."

"ID him? Hell, I think Flores *brought him into the country!*" Purdy exclaimed. "When I rolled up behind Flores, before I hit my lights, Zakharov had just finished talkin' with Flores and was walkin' with Fuerza toward Fuerza's truck. It looked like a meet."

"They must've come in separately—Zakharov with Flores, and the commandos with Fuerza," DeLaine said. "Good operational security technique."

"But if you didn't recover Flores's body, he might still be around," Purdy said. "We gotta find him before Zakharov or Fuerza do." He looked at Pierce and DeLaine. "Give me another chance at them, ma'am, Director. Let me out of here."

"If it's the Consortium, and they find out you're alive, they'll kill anyone in their way to get to you," Kelsey said. "It's too dangerous."

"I didn't sign up for the Border Patrol to be safe, ma'am," Purdy said. He looked over at Richter and Vega. "Put me in with these guys. I'll help them track down Zakharov and whoever is in on this."

"We've been shut down, Agent Purdy," Ariadna said.

"Well, open back up again," Purdy said testily, suspicious about all the resistance he was getting from the supposedly gung-ho Army guys. "Your robots are the only thing that can stop these nutcases from killin' more agents. Those Russians are just as well equipped and effective as any U.S. Army light infantry unit I've ever seen, and they're gettin' stronger every day. They'll blow any Border Patrol agents away easy." He turned to Pierce and said, "I can help track those terrorists down. I know the migrant worker community, ma'am . . ."

"They know who you are. They won't cooperate with you."

"They know I'm fair and don't try to bust their balls, ma'am," Purdy said. "They probably don't know how dangerous those Russians are—if the migrants knew who they were hiding, they might welcome our help in shutting them down."

"You're still *La Migra,*" Pierce said. "If the Consortium is living and moving among them, the migrants might just turn you in to ensure safety for themselves and their families. Do you have anyone in the community who could help you?"

"I might be able to contact some of my informants . . ." Purdy replied, but from his expression it was obvious he couldn't trust them either. He turned to Ariadna. "But Dr. Vega here could help me. She knows the language better than me, and she's a helluva lot better-lookin'."

"I'm second-generation American," Ariadna said uneasily, her eyes lowered apologetically to the floor. "I've never been part of the Hispanic community. I'm not sure if I could help you. Besides, I've got my hands full with the task force."

"Hey, Dr. Vega, you look pretty tough to me," he said, "and from what I heard you did in Brazil and Egypt, I think you can handle yourself. Besides, the Hispanics usually don't rough up or squeal on the women, even if they're not from their community— it's not very macho to put a lady in danger, even a lady cop." In pretty good Spanish, he added, *"Ellos no pueden parar mi Veracruz y su belleza, señorita."*

"Gracias, señor," Ari said, adding tentatively, "But I don't think I can do it."

Purdy looked at Ariadna carefully, quietly trying to gauge the real meaning of her response, then shrugged. "I'm stuck, then," he said. "I'll just have to do it the old-fashioned way—pound the pavement, kick a little ass, and pass around a lot of cash. Give me a couple BORTAC squads and I'll have enough firepower to handle anyone." He looked wistfully at Jason and added, "Except the

Consortium. For them, I'm sure I'll need the Marines or Special Forces, if I can't get the robots."

"It might be too late anyway, Paul," Pierce said. "I'm sure Flores has hightailed it back to Mexico by now."

"He might have, but I don't think so," Purdy said. "Flores is not Mexican. He's an 'angel baby'—his parents were Mexican migrant workers, but he was born in the US of A, an instant citizen." From Pierce's expression, she obviously didn't know this bit of information. "I'm sorry, ma'am, but you don't show us yours, so we don't show you ours. That's gotta change if we hope to get any real work done.

"Anyway, Flores's parents were migrant farmworkers, but *he* was born in southern California, Coachella Valley, JFK Hospital, I think—I've seen his jacket. Hell, nowadays more than half of all kids born in southern California have parents who are illegals, but seventeen years ago, that made you special—an 'angel baby.' I'll bet you dollars to doughnuts he's still in the area. He helps the migrants but he's one hundred percent American—I don't think he would run to Mexico." He turned again to Jason and Ariadna. "Give me these two and their gadgets, and I'll find Victor Flores, I guarantee it."

Kelsey looked at Jason, then said, "There's no way the White House is going to approve using TALON to hunt down one young man," she said.

"You're the freakin' director of the FBI, ma'am—*tell 'em* what you want and what you're plannin' on, and they'll do it—if they're smart," Purdy said. "You meet with the President all the time, right? You used to work for the new Secretary of Homeland Security, and if I'm not mistaken you reported directly to the new National Security Adviser and that rat bastard traitor Chamberlain when TALON was first stood up, right? Excuse me, ma'am, but what's the question here? You got more insider avenues than Martha Stewart."

"TALON wasn't designed as an investigative system, Agent Purdy," Jason said. "TALON is a high-tech individual motorized infantry unit, equivalent to a heavy rifle, missile, or mortar squad. It's better if it . . ."

"You guys are killin' me," Purdy said, shaking his head in pure exasperation. "You're tellin' me you have a gazillion-dollar robot and all these fancy unmanned reconnaissance aircraft out there and you can't help me find one damned kid in an artichoke field in the Coachella Valley? You"—he went on, turning to Kelsey— "can't requisition these guys to help you track down the one other survivor of a terrorist assassination, the guy that may lead us to the whole gang?" He glared at them both. "With all due respect: what kind of pansies are you guys? That's all you do all day is whine and tell your subordinates no, no, no?"

"You've never seen a CID unit in action, Agent Purdy . . ."

"I've seen 'em on TV enough to know they're a hell of a lot faster, stronger, and tougher than those Russians that shot me in the back," Purdy interjected. "Yeah, sure, robots aren't your *typical* undercover agent. But that doesn't mean we can't put them and the rest of your stuff to work. It just takes a little imagination and brainpower, Major. What's the matter—the Army not issuing creative thought to its field grade officers anymore?" Jason smiled and nodded in surrender; Purdy nodded in satisfaction and turned to Kelsey. "And you, Miss Director—I don't want to hear the words no or I can't do that in my presence, with all due respect. If you don't want to use your power or authority as director of the freakin' FBI, hand it over to me—*I'll* show you how to get the job done."

"Keep it in check, Agent Purdy . . ." Angelica Pierce warned.

"No, he's right, Angelica," Kelsey said. She looked at her watch, then at Janice Perkins. "Janice . . . ?"

She had her personal digital organizer out before Kelsey asked the question. "We'll be taking status reports from the SACs and the foreign bureaus on the flight back to Washington," she said immediately. "Meetings in Washington start at thirteen hundred hours. The first one is with the intelligence staff, followed by the meeting with the directors of national intelligence and central intelligence at Langley. We'll have one hour after that to prepare briefings and recommendations. We brief the AG at sixteen hundred hours, the National Security Adviser and Chief of Staff at sixteen-thirty, which I think will go at least two hours, and then we brief the President. He may ask for it earlier because he has the speech to deliver at Annapolis."

"That's *way* too much information, Agent Perkins," Purdy said. "No one wants to know how the damned sausage is made, for Christ's sake."

Kelsey thought for a moment, then nodded resolutely. "Janice, I need you to . . ."

"Have the deputy director take the status reports and report any unusual or significant activity to you," Janice interjected, making notes on her PDA with amazing speed, "because you'll be in a strategy meeting with Major Richter, Dr. Vega, and the charming Agent Purdy, preparing a plan to utilize Task Force TALON to apprehend suspected Consortium terrorists that you think have infiltrated into the southwestern United States with the use of Mexican human smugglers."

"Tell me you can cook and I'll marry you tonight, sweetheart," Purdy said to Perkins.

Janice only winked at the veteran Border Patrol agent in reply, then asked, "Are you going back to Washington, ma'am?"

"Back to all those damned fool boring-ass meetings?" Purdy mumbled under his breath. "How can she bear to miss any of them?"

"I'll be back for the meeting with DNI and DCI," Kelsey said. "The deputy will have to take over all other chores until I return."

"That's what assistants are for, ma'am," Purdy said.

"Thank you for your insights, Agent Purdy," Kelsey said, letting a little exasperation show in her voice. "I just gave you one hour of my time to put together a plan of action to use Task Force TALON and the FBI to assist you in tracking down the terrorists that killed those Border Patrol agents. Now, if you're not all jokes and hot air, you had better start talking to me, and it better be good. Jason, Ari, have a seat. When I get on my plane for Washington, I want a plan in place and all the players tagged and ready to go as soon as I get the word from the White House."

Paul Purdy slapped his hands together and rubbed them excitedly. "Now *that's* what I was waitin' to hear, ma'am!" he exclaimed. "It won't take ten minutes to tell you what I want to do to track down those bastards that killed my friends and slaughtered those innocent people. Then, *you* tell *me* how you can help me do my job.

"This isn't the Army, my friends; it ain't the FBI; it ain't even the Bureau of Customs and Border Protection," he went on seriously, looking at each one of them in turn, then settling his gaze on Ariadna's worried expression. "I'm talkin' about the Border Patrol, the *real* Border Patrol. We been around a long time, doin' our jobs the best we could. We do things a little differently out in the field. You follow my lead and help me do my job, and we'll nail those murderous sons of bitches *soonest*."

He looked Jason up and down with a smile on his face, then slapped him on the shoulder. "You'd better get busy growin' some facial hair, young fella—if you can," he said. "You look *way* too clean-cut for where we're goin'."

CHAPTER 5

CORONADO NATIONAL FOREST,
SOUTHEASTERN ARIZONA
TWO NIGHTS LATER

"Welcome to a very special edition of *The Bottom Line,* my friends and fellow Americans. I'm Bob O'Rourke, speaking to you from the Coronado National Forest about thirty miles southwest of Tombstone, Arizona, the site of the infamous Gunfight at the OK Corral and the home of tough-as-nails lawmen like Wyatt Earp and Bat Masterson. This is being taped for broadcast tomorrow morning. My voice may sound weird to you because I'm speaking into a special microphone mask that muffles my voice so it can't be heard by others, which might reveal our presence. I'll explain why I need this in a moment.

"I'm here with my sound engineer, Georgie Wayne, who has done stevedore's work helping me haul our gear up these mountain passes tonight. It was quite an exhausting hike for me, and I only carried a light backpack—Georgie carried the rest of our stuff, and I give him all the credit in the world for humping all this gear for me. My tree-hugging producer, Fand Kent, is back in the studios in Las Vegas—she doesn't have the legs or the stomach for this kind of work.

"We're way up in the Huachuca Mountains, at about six- to seven-thousand feet elevation. It's rocky, with lots of trees and scrub brush—easy to hide in, as countless generations of fugitives, gangsters, Native Americans, and outlaws well know. Nearby Millers Pass rises to an elevation of over 9,400 feet. The air is cool, even though the daytime temperatures exceeded ninety degrees, and the air is very still. There is a very thin moon out tonight. It's a perfect night for an ambush.

"But it's us who will be doing the ambush. I'm here with Alpha Patrol of the American Watchdog Project, the world-famous group of volunteers from all over the United States who have taken it upon themselves to do what the federal government and the military are apparently unwilling or—in the case of the abortive attempt by Task Force TALON in southern California recently—*unable* to do: patrol and protect America's borders. We're here tonight because we have credible, actionable information gleaned from informants and from the Watchdog's own network of watchers, both on the ground and in the air, that a large number of illegal migrants will be heading this way to cross into the United States. With me on a wireless microphone is the American Watchdog Project's commander, Herman Geitz. Can you hear me okay, Commander?"

"Loud and clear, Mr. O'Rourke," Geitz replied. He was almost a foot taller than O'Rourke, with a bushy beard and large craggy features, wearing camouflaged forest hunting clothes, a Camel-Bak water bottle in his pack, and a web utility belt with a sidearm holster, flashlight, and other gear.

"Thank you for allowing *The Bottom Line* to accompany you on this mission, Herman. My first question is obvious: if your information is so accurate, where is the Border Patrol? Why aren't they in on this?"

"Thank you for being here tonight with us, Mr. O'Rourke," Geitz said. "To answer your question, the Border Patrol *is* here. The closest unit is down the trail about ten miles away at the base of the mountain, probably patrolling Route 83 and the Coronado

Trail Road. The Border Patrol has about thirty agents that work
in three shifts to patrol southwest Cochise County and half of
Santa Cruz County, roughly between Nogales and Bisbee up to
Interstate 10."

"And how much territory is that?"

"That's about a hundred and sixty square miles, Bob."

"One hundred and sixty square miles of some of the most
rugged, inhospitable, and dangerous land in the United States,"
O'Rourke said. "Ten agents—basically one agent for every sixteen
square miles."

"It's actually two agents per patrol," Geitz corrected him, "so it's
five units plus a roving supervisor per shift for the entire patrol
area."

"How do they do it, Herman?" O'Rourke asked. "How is it
possible to cover that much territory with only ten men per shift?"

"Like most small tactical units, Mr. O'Rourke, the Border Patrol relies on intelligence information and sensors, whether they be
ground vibration alarms or helicopter patrols using infrared sensors," Geitz replied. "In essence, the patrols position themselves
according to the latest information they receive; and they respond
to alarms, like a private security company patrolling a large gated
community. Unfortunately, in this case, the 'gated community' is
very large and very rugged, and there are no gates—the illegals
can cross the border anywhere within twenty to thirty miles from
where we're standing, and if the Border Patrol's not close by when
they trip an alarm, they can make it without getting caught."

"Sounds like an impossible task."

"They're backed up with two helicopters assigned to the Tucson Border Patrol sector, and they can call on local law enforcement and even Army soldiers from Fort Huachuca if necessary."

"Ever see soldiers out here helping the Border Patrol, Herman?"

"I've seen one Army helicopter used to medevac an agent when
he rolled his Ramcharger," Geitz replied.

"How about the sheriffs' department?"

"They help transport any detainees and provide the lockup until the Border Patrol transports prisoners to Tucson for processing."

"So in essence it's just five patrols and a supervisor to patrol this entire mountainous area . . ."

"And the Watchdogs," Geitz said proudly. "We have almost a hundred volunteers out here patrolling the Coronado National Forest tonight. Stand by." Geitz swung one microphone away from his lips, spoke quietly into another headset microphone, then brought O'Rourke's mike back. "One of our patrols has made distant contact with a very large group of individuals moving through the Khyber Pass. Looks like our information is right on."

O'Rourke's voice quivered in excitement. "What's the Khyber Pass, Herman?"

"As you know, Bob, the real Khyber Pass between Pakistan and Afghanistan is an important and well-used route of travel, used for centuries as a link between central Asia and the Indian subcontinent," Geitz said. O'Rourke nodded impatiently as if he knew all about what Geitz was saying. "Alexander the Great used the Khyber Pass three hundred years before the birth of Christ to invade India. Centuries of traders, soldiers, smugglers, and travelers used that route freely because there was virtually no way to patrol or regulate it. We call this particular trail over the mountains the Khyber Pass because it is by far the busiest route for illegals to travel between the state of Sonora in Mexico and southern Arizona. The Watchdogs have made dozens of intercepts on this trail since our formation two years ago."

"What do the Watchdogs do up here, Herman?"

"We sit, wait, observe, and report, sir," Geitz replied. "Nothing more, nothing less."

"So you spot someone walking on this trail. There's nothing illegal about that, is there?"

"No, sir, there isn't, and we don't treat everyone we encounter up here as illegals," Geitz said. "Only the ones we definitely know traveled across the border are classified as illegals."

"And how do you do that?"

"Most times, it's just watching," Geitz said. "We station our-selves along the border, which is carefully surveyed and verified, and watch them come across with our own eyes. Sometimes we have Fido observe them coming across."

" 'Fido?' What's that? A dog?"

"Our unmanned reconnaissance drone," Geitz said. "It's actu-ally a war surplus Pioneer drone used by the U.S. Navy and Marines during Operation Desert Storm to pick out artillery and shore bombardment targets. The Iraqi soldiers knew the Pioneer drones were used to spot artillery targets and actually surrendered to the drones in very large numbers. It's been invaluable help in telling us where and when a group will come across. When we see activity, we'll go out to make contact."

"But when you make contact, you don't actually *know* for sure they're illegal immigrants, do you? How do you *know* they're illegals?"

"Most times we actually see them cross the border—we have it carefully surveyed and mapped relative to our observation posi-tions, so there's never any doubt," Geitz explained. "Anyone who crosses the border at other than a border crossing point is in viola-tion of the law, no matter what their nationality is—even natural-born Americans can't legally do it. But it's not our job to know or to find out if they're illegal or not. Only law enforcement has the right to stop them, ask for identification, and ascertain their citi-zenship or immigration status. Again—and it's the main point that so many of our critics miss—all the American Watchdog Project does is observe and report. We help the Border Patrol do their job."

"So when you come across a group of illegals . . . ?"

"We photograph them with our infrared and low-light cam-eras, send the images to a relay van down on Route 92 to upload our contact images to the Internet, and have the guys in the van contact the Border Patrol. The control unit will then relay any in-structions received from them to us."

"Instructions? What do they tell you to do?"

"They usually tell us to leave the illegal migrants alone, Mr. O'Rourke," Geitz replied.

"*Leave them alone?* Let them just *stroll* into the United States?"

"That's right, sir," Geitz said. "We report their location, numbers, general physical description, and any other information we can gather. Sometimes we'll follow them; many times, if we feel they're dangerous or if we recognize them as repeat offenders, we'll escort them all the way down the mountain and try to have the Border Patrol rendezvous with us."

"You said 'try' to have the Border Patrol meet up with you?"

"They just don't have the manpower to respond to us every time—and frankly, I don't think they always have the desire," Geitz said. "Simply put, we make them look bad sometimes. We're a bunch of volunteers that intercept just as many illegals as they do—that doesn't look very good in the press."

"So you're out here doing intercepts and surveillance and reconnaissance—sounds like a military operation to me," O'Rourke said. "You call yourself 'Watchdogs' but you do a lot more than just observe. Bottom line: aren't you all just a bunch of vigilantes?"

"No more than a neighborhood watch group would be—our 'neighborhood' just happens to be popular immigrant smuggling routes in the mountains and deserts of America," Geitz replied. "Vigilantes take the law into their own hands, the *entire* law—they become the police, prosecutors, judge, jury, and sometimes the executioner. We don't do any of that. Think of us as a neighborhood watch program: we observe and report, nothing more.

"But this is our home, so we act like neighbors as well. We live here, but this is also public land, and anyone can travel through these parts. Outsiders are not treated like intruders or criminals unless we observe and *know* they are breaking the law—merely walking through this area is not illegal, and we don't treat those we find as illegals. We've offered rides on our four-wheel ATVs in case anyone is injured or having trouble keeping up with the others. We offer water, some food, and first aid, just as we would if we encountered any other hikers on the trail."

"What does the Border Patrol do after you give them a report on what you've found?"

"If they have a unit available, they'll meet them down at the end of the trail and detain them," Geitz said. "If they don't, they get away."

"Get away? Even if you tell the Border Patrol exactly where they are, they still get away?"

"It's a matter of manpower, sir. If they don't have a unit available, they get away."

"What do the Watchdogs do in that case?"

"Nothing," Geitz said. "We let them go too. We'll report their direction of travel, whether or not they were picked up by anyone and a description of the vehicle, but we let them go. We don't have the power to arrest or detain them unless we actually see them breaking the law. Even then, we tread very lightly."

"What do you mean by that?"

"Well, for example, if we actually observe and record a person crossing the border in this area, we *know* that's an illegal act, because you are only legally allowed to cross the border at a border crossing point. But even if we positively identify the offender and have incontrovertible proof he broke the law, we don't know all the ramifications of why he did what he did."

"I don't understand what you mean. What 'ramifications'?"

"For example, Mr. O'Rourke, you can legally cross the border at other than a border crossing point if you feel your life is in danger, or if you are fleeing political persecution," Geitz said. "A lot of times I know the migrants *claim* all that just to hope to avoid deportation; it may or may not be true. The point is, however, that the Watchdogs don't make that call. Everyone is innocent until proven guilty in our eyes, and we strictly enforce that. We simply observe and report—the rest is up to the authorities."

"Reports say you try to make citizen arrests on them."

"Absolutely not true," Geitz insisted. "Although I *know* they're breaking the law, and I have incontrovertible proof of it, the Watchdogs do not make arrests."

"But you and your men are armed. I see plenty of shotguns and rifles, and almost everyone I've seen carries a sidearm. If you intercept someone out here in the dark carrying weapons, couldn't that be considered an arrest?"

"First of all, sir, I must emphasize that everyone who carries a weapon must have the legal right to do so," Geitz said. "We do not carry concealed weapons, and we do not brandish weapons—show, operate, or handle them as a means of intimidation or coercion—under any circumstances. We conduct firearms safety courses for everyone in our organization; everyone who carries a weapon is fully trained in gun safety and field procedures as well as marksmanship. Discharging a weapon except in self-defense is strictly prohibited and will result in immediate dismissal and being reported to the sheriff's department."

" 'Self-defense'? From animals . . . or human beings?"

"Anyone or anything that threatens us, Mr. O'Rourke, but mostly animals. Many of our patrols have encountered snakes and other predators out here. Most times using a firearm is not necessary—a bright light, a noisemaker, or simply leaving the area does the trick better than shooting a gun off in the dark that might endanger other patrols. Most folks that carry weapons carry only 'snake loads'—ammunition containing small pellets instead of bullets that are good only at short range and probably wouldn't kill a person, best suited for killing aggressive varmints."

"Varmints are one thing, but what about some of the illegals you intercept?" O'Rourke pressed. "You have arrested illegals before, Herman—I've seen the reports. Have they gotten violent? Have they threatened you? Is that the real reason you and your members carry guns?"

"As I said, sir, no member of the American Watchdogs may discharge or even brandish a weapon except in self-defense," Geitz said. "Whenever we make an intercept and a person unknown to us is carrying a weapon, we order him or her from the cover of darkness to drop the weapon. This is for our safety and the safety of our fellow citizens. That's what some in the media have been calling 'arrests.' "

"And then what?"

"If they drop their weapons, we inspect the weapons and search the individuals to make sure they don't have any more weapons, and then we report the contact to the Border Patrol and sheriff's department," Geitz said. "We comply with whatever instructions we receive from the authorities, which is usually to stop what we're doing and wait for help. If the migrants don't comply with our orders, we don't approach them, but we try to keep them in place until the authorities arrive."

"In other words, you arrest them."

"We make it clear to them that for our own safety, they will not be able to leave until it is safe for us to allow it," Geitz said. "They don't have to attack us first for us to be fearful for our lives. We won't let a stranger with a machete just walk away from us with the thing still in his hand—that wouldn't be too smart. If that's what the media calls an 'arrest,' so be it."

"What if they're carrying guns?"

"We don't allow them to take any firearms," Geitz said firmly. "Absolutely not. That's too dangerous for everyone involved. We confiscate all dangerous weapons and turn them over to the Border Patrol or the sheriff's office. We've turned in hundreds of weapons, everything from swords to bombs to machine guns."

"But what about *their* protection from animals and predators?"

"Mr. O'Rourke, I'm more concerned about the safety of *my* members. This is *our home*. An unidentified alleged illegal immigrant carrying a firearm or any other dangerous weapon near my men and women will not be tolerated. I may not have the legal right to take away another man's freedom or weapon on public property, but I am legally permitted to defend myself if I feel my life or property is threatened, and I will do so. Without hesitation."

"I commend your bravery and honesty, Commander Geitz."

"Fortunately, we haven't run into too many illegals with firearms," Geitz said, "and the ones that do have them surrender them to us without incident. The sheriff tells me that if I take any kind of possession whatsoever—a backpack, knife, handgun, bazooka, or even a nuclear bomb—from anyone, that person has the right to swear out an arrest warrant for armed robbery and assault and have me thrown in jail. But so far no one has done that," he added with a satisfied chuckle.

"But what if some human rights, civil liberty, or migrant advocacy group goes after you with an army of their attorneys?"

"I'm not too concerned with what an illegal or their lawyers might do to me," Geitz said confidently. "Frankly, I'd welcome a day in court. We have nothing to hide here, and we're doing a public service. We document every second of every intercept with both video and audio, beamed to our relay unit and digitally recorded before it's uploaded to our Web site. We use GPS technology to pinpoint our location, so there's no . . ." Geitz froze, listened in his headset, then said, "Time to get ready, Mr. O'Rourke. They're almost here."

Bob O'Rourke was quivering with excitement as he dropped the microphone mask and stowed his gear. "Now remember, our men have tiny blinking red identification lights on the back of our belts, so you should be able to follow us in the dark if you stay close," Geitz said into his whisper mike. "In case you do get separated, all you have to do is stay put, wherever you are, and wait for us to come back for you." He pulled several plastic tubes from a utility belt pouch, bent them almost in half, shook them vigorously, then handed them to both O'Rourke and Wayne. "Put these around your neck. They're identification ChemLites."

"Mine's not working."

"You can't see the light unless you're wearing night vision goggles, as all of the Watchdogs are," Geitz said. "But we can see *you* as clearly as if you were carrying a flashlight."

O'Rourke held his ChemLite up to his face as if looking closer would allow him to see the light, but he couldn't see a thing in the darkness. He could hear the sounds of men getting ready to move all around him, and he could barely contain himself. "Damn," he muttered, "*now* I have to take a piss."

"It happens all the time—the excitement of the hunt," Geitz said gleefully, like a kid getting ready to get on the rope swing for the first time. "You have to hold it until we make the intercept and take control of the targets. Don't be embarrassed to piss in your pants if it gets too uncomfortable—you wouldn't be the first one to do it, I guarantee it. It won't be long now—they're coming right at us." The thought of any of these rough, tough Watchdogs seeing him, big-time radio celebrity Bob O'Rourke, with urine-stained pants was unthinkable, and he strained harder to hold it in.

In a sudden flurry of activity, the Watchdogs ran into the darkness for several dozen yards, then stopped suddenly. "I . . . I'm following Commander Herman Geitz of the American Watchdogs as best I can—they're moving quickly down a path that is completely invisible to me." O'Rourke spoke into his microphone mask, trying but failing not to breathe too heavily and reveal how completely out of shape he really was. "My legs feel as if they've been bull-whipped by running through the scrub brush. Good . . . good, we've stopped." He whispered for Geitz, who turned back to O'Rourke. "Why did we have to run all of a sudden like that, Commander?"

"A little confusion, sir," Geitz whispered, raising his night vision goggles away from his eyes. He pulled a small GPS map device from a pouch and checked it. "Our lookouts initially reported the migrants' position on one trail. But Fido positively identified the migrants on a different trail, so we had to move quickly to intercept."

O'Rourke looked skyward as if expecting to see the drone watching him. He felt somewhat reassured that the electronic eyes were watching them, although it still didn't prevent things from getting a bit chaotic. "So we have *two* groups of migrants out here tonight?" he asked nervously.

"It appears so," Geitz said, a bit of concern evident in his voice. "More than likely the first group split up. But the group we're headed for is very large—the tactical reconnaissance operators in the mobile control van count at least twenty individuals on foot. As soon as we intercept the first group, we'll turn our attention to the others."

"Shouldn't you order your second unit to intercept the other group?" O'Rourke asked. He noticed the worry in Geitz's voice, which made him doubly concerned. "What if they get away? They could be the smugglers."

"We'll use Fido to keep an eye on the smaller group." Geitz turned back to his radios, leaving O'Rourke alone with his fears. This just wasn't smelling right.

Thankfully they were apparently in the right position, because they didn't have to run off again. In just a few minutes the night got very still again. All O'Rourke could see in the total blackness was the tiny blinking red light on Geitz's belt—staring at it seemed to make it revolve in slow clockwise circles, which was starting to make him a little nauseous. He felt his canteen on his hip—the one filled with bourbon, not water—and thought about reaching for it when he heard . . . voices. He froze.

They were *right in front of him,* O'Rourke realized with shock. He could hear their feet scraping the rough earth, hear their anxious voices, hear someone spit, hear another stumble and curse. They sounded rather . . . workmanlike, like you would hear a group of factory workers or farmers walking together on their way to the entry gates or the barns, getting ready for a hard day ahead. O'Rourke had expected them to sound like guerrilla fighters carrying machine guns and ammo discovered by Special Forces along the Ho Chi Minh trail, not worker bees carrying their lunch pails and thermos bottles.

"I . . . I can hear them." O'Rourke spoke into his microphone mask. "I can't see them, but I can hear them. Commander? You're using night vision goggles: what do you see?"

"It's a group of . . . I count twenty-three individuals," Geitz whispered, his strained voice barely audible. "I can make out two women. Those on the Internet will be able to view our night vision images on our Web site in just a few minutes. I see the usual assortment of backpacks, garbage bags, numerous one-gallon jugs of water, and rucksacks the migrants carry while traveling. It's hard to tell their ages, but they look pretty young. I don't see any children this time."

"What about calling the Border Patrol?" O'Rourke asked nervously.

"Our tactical control van is relaying the information now," Geitz said. "We haven't heard a response about whether or not they'll head up here yet."

"Are they carrying any weapons? This sounds very dangerous, Commander . . ."

"I don't see any weapons, but I see several persons carrying suspicious bags that could contain weapons, so we'll have to confront these individuals and do a citizen's search of their belongings for weapons." Geitz swung O'Rourke's microphone away and spoke into his tactical radio.

"Commander Geitz is relaying instructions to his teams," O'Rourke said. Geitz reached behind him and touched O'Rourke's arm, telling him to be quiet. "I've been told to be quiet," O'Rourke whispered into the mask. "I don't know if they can see us, but I'm sure as soon as Commander Geitz judges it's safe, I'm sure he'll . . ."

"*Attention! This is the American Watchdog Project!* You are surrounded!" Geitz suddenly shouted, using a bullhorn. Then, in stilted but understandable Spanish, he ordered, "*¡Levante sus manos y no harán daño a usted de ningún modo!*" Powerful flashlights popped on, illuminating thirty or forty feet of the trail. The men and women blinked at the lights in confusion and slowly raised their hands. The coyote in the lead of the column of migrants had two cloth pouches over his shoulders. "Drop those pouches, señor," Geitz ordered. "*Deje caer todas sus posesiones!*"

The *pollos* started to comply, looping their backpacks and trash bags off their shoulders. "This is incredible!" O'Rourke said, switching from his microphone mask to a regular handheld mike. "We've just burst out of the darkness and surrounded this group of migrants. We have eight men plus Georgie and myself, Geitz's Alpha Team plus the Bravo Team on the other side of the trail, just carrying flashlights. We're not showing any weapons, none at all. But the migrants are giving up. They're stopping and raising their hands in surrender."

The coyote was a little more defiant. "Hey, whoever you are, *vete a la mierda!*" he shouted. "We don't answer to you or nobody!"

"I am Commander Herman Geitz of the American Watchdog Project," Geitz said over the bullhorn. "Your presence is being reported to the U.S. Border Patrol right now. There is no use running. *La permanencia y nosotros le daremos el alimento, el agua, y la medicina.*" More migrants began to find a place to sit on the rocky trail—it was obvious they had had enough. "If you try to travel north into the United States, we will track you and continue to report your whereabouts to the U.S. Border Patrol."

"And if you do not leave us alone, *hideputa,* you will feel the wrath of Comandante Veracruz and all who honor freedom!" the smuggler shouted back. "Now get out of here! Leave us alone!"

"Alpha Team, this is Fido Control," came a message from the Pioneer unmanned observation plane's control team. "How copy, Alpha?"

"Stand by, Fido," Geitz radioed back.

"Just be advised, Alpha, video is intermittent from Fido, repeat, we're losing video. Very strong interference. Will advise when it's back online."

"Commander Geitz has just offered the migrants food, water, and medicine if they give up and wait for the Border Patrol," Bob O'Rourke said, after getting a translation from Georgie Wayne. "The leader of this group is a young man with long dark hair, what looks like a green military-style fatigue cap, a red bandanna around his neck, and military-looking boots, probably in his early to mid-twenties. He is carrying two canvas satchels and he hasn't dropped them yet like most of the migrants have done. He is obviously the coyote, the smuggler. But he is quickly losing control of his clients. Commander Geitz seems very nervous about this young man, mostly because he's still got those satchels and they look like they could hold a lot of guns and ammo. The situation appears to be getting very tense now."

"*¡Déjenos en paz!*" the smuggler shouted. "*¡Veracruz de comandante dice que estamos en el suelo mejicano!*"

"What did he say?" O'Rourke asked.

"Something about someone called Commander Veracruz saying he is on Mexican soil," Georgie replied.

"Is he high? Is he crazy? This is America, not Mexico!" O'Rourke said acidly. "This Veracruz guy is nothing but a rabble-rouser and drug dealer who thinks he's some hot-shot Mexican version of George Washington."

"I say again, drop those bags immediately!" Geitz said over the loudspeaker, ignoring the radio call from his observation team. "*Usted no será dañado, prometo.* You will be allowed to pass after we have searched your possessions for weapons."

"Screw you, gringo!" the smuggler shouted. "You don't have no right to do this!"

"Alpha Team, this is Fido. Be advised, we've lost our video downlink, but we saw two separate contacts approaching east and west of your position, range less than thirty meters. Recommend you use caution; repeat, we lost the downlink. Do you copy, Alpha?"

"I said, drop those bags, *cagado!*" Geitz shouted, shining his flashlight directly into the young man's eyes to try to disorient him.

"I . . . I think Commander Geitz just called that guy a coward, boss," Georgie Wayne said. "He ain't gonna like that."

"*¡Me cago en la leche de que mamaste!*" the coyote shouted angrily, and he reached into the right satchel.

"*He's reaching for a gun!*" O'Rourke screamed, his voice rising several octaves in pure terror. "*Watch out! He's got a gun!*"

Everything was a blur of motion at that moment. Georgie

Wayne was right beside O'Rourke with his left hand on his shoulder, trying to get his attention, and when the first shots rang out he immediately pulled the radio personality to the ground and lay on top of him. Men were screaming all around them. The gunshots sounded like firecrackers, punctuated occasionally by a loud "BOOOM!" from a heavy-caliber gun.

It seemed like the shooting lasted an hour, but in reality it was only seconds. O'Rourke waited until all the shooting had subsided; then, with all the courage he could muster, said to Wayne in a low voice, "Get off me, dammit!"

"Stay down, boss . . ."

"We're not here to hide like chickens, Georgie! Get off me!" Georgie reluctantly slid off him—O'Rourke found himself committed now to get up, even though his legs were shaking so badly that he might not have been able to make it. "What happened? Did the smugglers open fire?" He looked up and saw Herman Geitz walking beside him, with his sidearm still smoking in his right hand. "Geitz! What happened? Were we attacked by the smugglers?"

Geitz looked down at O'Rourke and opened his mouth as if he was going to reply . . . but instead, a torrent of blood rushed from his open mouth, his eyes rolled up into his head, and the man pitched over and landed face-first on the rocky ground.

"Oh . . . my . . . God!" O'Rourke gasped. Years of experience taught him to never say a word unless he had a switched-on microphone in his hand, and the flood of emotions that came forth were all caught on tape. "Jesus, Commander Geitz has been killed, shot in the head . . . God, the whole back of his head is *gone,* it's just one big massive bloody hole . . . the smell of gunpowder is unbelievable, almost overpowering . . . Georgie, are you okay? Are you all right?"

"Yes, boss, yes," Wayne responded. "I'm going to see if anyone else needs help."

"*No!*" O'Rourke blurted out, a lot more fearfully than he'd intended. "Don't leave me . . . I mean, the smugglers could still be out there! Stay down!"

But Georgie had already taken his recording gear off and was low-crawling along the trail. The members of the American Watchdogs were standing around in dumbfounded shock and disbelief, weapons smoking in their hands, flashlight beams jerking and darting aimlessly in all directions. Wayne moved carefully, not wanting to startle them in case they might start shooting again. He didn't move very far before he discovered a body. "Oh, Christ, one of the migrants . . . a woman. Shot in the belly. Another migrant . . . Jesus, looks like they're *all* dead, every one of the migrants."

"This . . . this is unbelievable," O'Rourke repeated hoarsely into his microphone. "There has been a massacre on this trail tonight, my friends and listeners, a massacre on an enormous scale. Eight members of the American Watchdog Project, volunteers, men who risked their lives to help patrol this remote and dangerous border region, have . . . have apparently shot and killed a group of about twenty migrants on this trail. When Commander Herman Geitz ordered the migrants to put down their bags so they could be searched, one of the migrants apparently opened fire, and the Watchdogs returned fire. More shots rang out—shotguns, handguns . . . the noise and confusion was horrifying. It . . . it is just plain impossible to put into words.

"Now, just moments later, it appears that everyone . . . *all* the migrants on this trail are *dead*. Twenty or so illegal immigrants who sneaked across the border and were attempting to infiltrate into the United States of America have been killed, along with the commander of the American Watchdog Project. The smuggler leading this group was afraid of being caught with weapons, afraid of what the Border Patrol might do to them after the horrible assassinations near Blythe, California just a few days ago, afraid of being sent to prison instead of just being released again into Mexico a few days from now, and they were determined not to be taken into custody. So he pulled out a weapon and began firing, and in the confusion, the Watchdogs returned fire, and

now . . . now . . . my God, the migrants all appear to be dead, every
one of them."

RAMPART ONE FORWARD OPERATING BASE,
OCATILLO, CALIFORNIA
THE NEXT MORNING

The Mexican Army forces stationed on the border south of Rampart One had just raised their flag, played the "Himno Nacional
Mexicano," and were now policing up their encampment when
the new unit arrived. An additional six M-11 ULTRAV armored
reconnaissance vehicles and HWK-11 armored personnel carriers,
and thirty-three infantrymen, pulled up to the encampment in a
cloud of gray dust and noise.

The commander of the new unit, Major Gerardo Azueta, dismounted from his American-made Humvee and stretched his
aching legs. Azueta was way too tall and thin to comfortably ride
in the bumpy, creaky Humvee, but any opportunity to get out of
the garrison and into the field was welcome, especially on a low-
risk, cushy, and high-visibility assignment such as this. The current unit commander greeted him with a salute. "Welcome,
Major," Lieutenant Salinas said, introducing himself. "Lieutenant
Ignacio Salinas, commander of this detail. Good to see you again,
sir." All officers in the Mexican armed forces were graduates of
Chapultepec, the Mexican military academy in Mexico City; the
officer cadre was very small and officers in the same state knew
and saw each other often. "How was your trip from Mexicali?"

"A nightmare, as usual," Azueta replied, brushing dust off his
olive green uniform. "General Cardenas did not want to send
any more companies from state headquarters, so we had to move
almost the entire force from Ensenada. It took all day. The regimental commander there said he could not spare any infantry to

go along with the vehicles, so he rounded up a bunch of Rural Defense Force militia to accompany us. They are worse than conscripts."

"We have several in my detail, sir. They shape up quickly when they are away from the garrison."

"I know you and your men are anxious to get home, Lieutenant, but I am afraid these militiamen are going to go berserk if there is any trouble," Azueta said. "It will only be for a few days, a week at the most."

Salinas had already received the notification from his company commander. Most men liked duty in the garrisons, but Salinas was young and liked assignments that took him away from town, no matter how trivial or menial the task. He motioned to a nearby tent and offered the senior officer a canvas camp chair and a plastic bottle of water, which Azueta accepted eagerly. "No problem at all, sir. We are happy to assist."

"Thank you, Lieutenant. Status report, please."

"Things have calmed down considerably these past couple days, sir," Salinas began. "I am sure you are aware of the recent incident in Arizona."

"Yes. A bloody act of murder, plain and simple. The American government is entirely to blame, allowing those vigilantes to operate in the border region."

"I agree completely, sir," Salinas said. "I hope the president does not let up on her pressure on the Americans to stop this campaign of violence. Fortunately, despite that brutal incident, the situation is quiet here. The American military presence is all but nonexistent as far as we can tell from our position and from American news reports. They are making some attempts to repair and rebuild the facility, but it does not look like the base has been fortified, and there has been no sign of those manned robots. We see the reconnaissance airships and unmanned drones on occasion, and we must assume they and the regular Border Patrol units are operational."

"And the media?"

"They haven't been back since yesterday," Salinas responded, "although I would expect them to return for comments on the murders in Arizona."

"Let me handle the media now, Lieutenant."

"With pleasure, sir."

"What about smuggler activity?"

"None in our entire patrol sector, sir," Salinas said, "which was expected. Having smugglers push all the way to remote sections of Arizona was fully expected; and after the incident here, I would have expected much American vigilante activity. Of course, Mexico will be blamed for what has happened here and in Arizona."

"It was only a matter of time before someone else got killed by vigilantes or right-wing extremists," Azueta agreed. "The Americans are not stopping the level of violence whatsoever. That will be our biggest challenge: keeping the violence down until the politicians get off their fat asses and come to some sort of agreement." Salinas nodded. "Let us go inspect the camp, and then we will inspect the border area. Maybe I will even get to meet one of those infamous robots."

Salinas recalled the armored personnel carrier patrols so Azueta could meet every one of the men in the detail. He was tough but not as tough as in the garrison—he understood the need for discipline, and demanded it, but he also knew they were in the field and certain things, like keeping boots perfectly polished or uniforms perfectly spotless, was going to be difficult at best. He loudly and harshly admonished the noncommissioned officers and men for missing equipment, dirty weapons, or men sleeping at their posts, but he was careful not to openly criticize anyone for not shaving or for rolling up their sleeves in the desert heat. There would be time enough for that back at base.

After the equipment inspection, they got back into the Humvee again and began to drive toward the border area. They hadn't gone very far when Azueta ordered the driver to stop. He immediately got out of the vehicle, stood on the hood, and peered north. "Lieutenant, when was the last time you did a tactical map of the border and scouted out all of the American patrol units and emplacements?" he asked.

"We redo the map every three hours, sir," Salinas responded. "The last one should have been done an hour ago."

"Either your men are liars or they thought they were going to be relieved and did not do it," Azueta said. "Get up here and take a look." Salinas did as he was told . . . and although Azueta handed him his binoculars, he didn't need them to see the change.

"Two . . . three . . . I count three Humvees to the west," Salinas breathed. "My God, they were not here at daybreak, sir!"

"I count two more to the east, spread out about a kilometer apart," Azueta said. "They appear to be up-armored scout vehicles with .50 caliber machine guns mounted on the . . ."

"And TOW missiles, sir," Salinas interjected excitedly. "It appears every other unit to the west has TOW missile launchers on the gun turrets!"

"That explains their deployment—they are spread out just far enough to have overlapping fields of fire for their TOWs," Azueta said. "It is the same to the east." He lowered his binoculars. "Well, well. The Americans have raised the stakes out here. We have a report to make to Mexico City, Lieutenant."

CHAPTER 6

"Mr. President, I must protest this latest move of your military," President Carmen Maravilloso of Mexico's voice cried over the speakerphone, echoing throughout the historic room. Even the usually unflappable National Security Adviser, Raymond Jefferson, was startled when he heard the voice as he entered. "Again, you have put armed military forces on our border without consulting or even notifying us beforehand! This is not right, sir! This is not the action of a good and peaceful neighbor, sir."

"Madame President, as you well know, the United States is not obligated to report the movement of its military forces to Mexico or anyone else, no matter how close to the border." U.S. President Samuel Conrad responded as calmly as he could. He had been expecting this phone call since issuing the order to Secretary of Defense Russell Collier minutes after receiving the report of the massacre in the Coronado National Forest in Arizona, and he had his cabinet and their staffs working since then to bring him up to speed on the myriad of treaties and agreements regarding military and police action on the U.S.-Mexico border. "This troop move-

ment is in direct response to the murders of twenty-three Mexican
nationals in the . . ."

"I am very well aware of what has occurred, sir," Maravilloso
interrupted, still refusing to use President Conrad's official title.
"But I would have expected an investigation by the local sheriff's
office, perhaps assisted by the FBI or the Arizona State Police, not
the American Army National Guard—and certainly not in California. What do you intend to do, sir—invade Mexico with the
California National Guard? Those troops on our border have missile launchers! *Missile launchers!* What will be next—ballistic missiles and stealth bombers?"

"Madame President, the United States intends on pursuing all
legal options available to us to ensure the safety and security of our
citizens, our nation, and any who are here legally . . ."

"Do you intend on using the National Guard to hunt down
Mexican citizens whose only goal is to do the work that Americans
do not want to do themselves?" the fiery Mexican president asked.
"That is a hateful and brutal policy, sir, akin to totalitarian regimes
in North Korea or Myanmar. The people of Mexico are honest,
hardworking, nonviolent, and law-abiding people. True, a few—
a *very* few—have been corrupted by drug dealers to carry drugs;
others respond to abuses by gangsters, white supremacists, and
corrupt law enforcement officials by arming themselves. Will you
condemn them all just for the actions of a few?"

"Madame President, a horrible crime has been committed in
Arizona last night," the President said. With him in the Oval Office was his Chief of Staff, Thomas Kinsly, the Secretaries of Defense, State, and Homeland Security, the President's National
Security Adviser; and the one-star general in charge of deploying
those National Guard forces to the southern border, all listening
on a listen-only speakerphone. "It was broadcast around the world
on the Internet. Nearly two dozen persons were horribly murdered by unknown assailants. The only evidence we have so far is
the American Watchdog Project's own Web broadcast . . ."

"Do you refer to the right-wing radio instigator Bob O'Rourke and his lackey?" Maravilloso asked incredulously. "Surely you would not for a moment consider them credible witnesses, sir? Bob O'Rourke is one of the world's most well-known and well-documented racists, a man who has been calling for the elimination of all nonwhites from the border region on his radio show for years. I am *positive* that he orchestrated this entire murder campaign in order to stir up a campaign of hate against all persons of color . . ."

"I don't think that's an accurate characterization of his opinions, Madam . . ."

"You *agree* with this racist? You support his contention that all Mexicans should be hunted down and forcibly removed from the United States?"

"That's not what he . . ."

"Obviously you do, because you are doing precisely what Bob O'Rourke has been calling for: putting the military on the border, repealing Posse Comitatus, and removing all Mexicans from the United States. You, sir, are following his hysterical xenophobic fascist ranting to the letter! Please, Mr. President, I urge you: get control of this situation quickly before it gets out of hand."

"Madam President, I assure you, I'm doing all I can to defuse the growing crisis and deal with the illegal immigration problem," Conrad said. "Placing National Guard forces on the border is a temporary measure until Congress approves a more comprehensive immigration reform package."

"Sir, Mexico is here to assist you any way we can," Maravilloso said, "but it is hard to support you and your government when you make bold, radical moves such as this without consulting us first. You can help me help you by conferring with us beforehand. Good day to you, Mr. Conrad." The connection terminated abruptly.

"Who does she think she is, speaking to another foreign leader like that?" Thomas Kinsly said as he deactivated the listen-only receiver he had been using to monitor the call.

"She's using these circumstances to full political advantage, that's what," the President said, rubbing his eyes wearily. "I'm getting hammered, and she's looking like a tiger. She's taken the complete moral high ground here, and there's not a damned thing I can do about it."

"Why not let State handle her calls from now on, Mr. President?"

"Because heads of state talk to each other, not to the bureaucracy," the President replied. "I'll handle her calls just fine. She's looking for anything I say to use against me—if I didn't talk to her, no matter how rude she becomes, I'll be the coward who didn't take her call." Kinsly had no response. The President turned to Attorney General Wentworth. "What do you have on the investigation, George?"

"The FBI is still collecting evidence," Wentworth said, "but it appears that the migrants *were* shot by the Watchdogs. The caliber of the weapons used matches the ones the Watchdogs were carrying."

"Oh, Christ . . . !"

"Has there been an actual match with the weapons, Mr. Wentworth?" National Security Adviser Ray Jefferson asked.

"Not yet. Those results will be in later today." He looked at Jefferson closely. "The caliber matched the weapons the Watchdogs were carrying. Why do you want an *exact* match?"

"Those weapons could have been planted."

"C'mon, Sergeant Major, that's overly far-fetched, especially for you," Kinsly said. "Let's stick to the facts, shall we?" He turned to the President. "We have *got* to keep this quiet. If word gets out that the Watchdogs slaughtered those migrants, all hell will break loose."

"But the video was tracking another group of unknowns," Jefferson said. "Geitz said they were more migrants, part of the original large group that just split up. What if they *weren't* migrants?"

"Who, then?" Kinsly paused, then rolled his eyes. "Oh, you think it was the Consortium, right?"

"I think it's not just possible—I think it's *probable*," Jefferson said. He raised a message form he held in his hands. "I have an important report from Task Force TALON commander Richter . . ."

"He's not still out in the field, is he, Sergeant Major?" Chief of Staff Thomas Kinsly groaned.

"Major Richter met with FBI Director DeLaine yesterday in San Diego, after being debriefed by the FBI and Justice Department after the incident at Rampart One. They spoke with a survivor of that attack on the Border Patrol agents."

"Say again, Sergeant Major?" the President remarked. "There was a *survivor?*"

"A veteran Border Patrol agent, shot in the back by the terrorists," Jefferson said. "Name's Paul Purdy. He had the wind knocked out of him and fell into a ditch, where he was left for dead. But he's positive that he heard some of his assailants speaking Russian, and he identified two of the individuals at the scene of the shooting: the Mexican insurgent known as Ernesto Fuerza, and . . . Yegor Zakharov."

There were a few moments of stunned silence; then: "Is he positive, Sergeant Major?" the President asked.

"Not one hundred percent, sir, but close. It was dark, and he saw them only at a distance, but Purdy is a reliable, trained eyewitness . . ."

"It's not enough to link Mexican insurgents with the Consortium," Chief of Staff Kinsly said, shaking his head. "It doesn't prove anything."

"There was another survivor: the smuggler that brought one of the terrorists across the border, the one identified as Victor Flores," Jefferson said. "Director DeLaine wants to go after that smuggler. Purdy thinks he still might be in the United States, where he was born, possibly somewhere in the agricultural region of southern California. If they find the smuggler, he may be able to gather information on where the others were heading."

"What does Richter have to do with any of this?" Attorney General Wentworth exclaimed. "He shouldn't be involved in this operation any further."

"Director DeLaine has requested Task Force TALON's assistance in hunting down Flores and the ones that were smuggled into southern California," Jefferson said. "She wants full authority over TALON to provide the high-tech surveillance support and firepower she needs to take on the terrorists."

"Those robots—in the hands of the FBI?" Kinsly retorted. "No way, Jefferson."

"The FBI has plenty of firepower of its own already," Wentworth said. "They don't need TALON. TALON was designed for military operations . . ."

"TALON was designed to replace a light armored cavalry unit or special ops platoon with a single, highly mobile, highly effective weapon system, General Wentworth," Jefferson said. "The FBI's Hostage Rescue Teams are the best of the best, but they don't have nearly the capabilities of a Cybernetic Infantry Device. Judging by what we've seen in southern California and now in southern Arizona, I think CID is exactly what we need. And if the Russians Purdy identified turn out to be Zakharov and Consortium terrorists, we're going to need all the firepower we can get out there." He turned to the President. "This episode in Arizona could have been one massive setup. The Consortium had plenty of time to plan this ambush in order to make it look like the Watchdogs killed those migrants. They could have even jammed the transmissions from the unmanned aerial vehicle the Watchdogs used to monitor their operation . . ."

"That's really stretching credibility, Sergeant Major," Kinsly said. "No use in speculating until we get more information from the FBI."

"Until then, we need to prepare in case the word *does* get out and it does precipitate unrest," the President said. He turned to the one-star Army general standing in the center of the Oval Office. "General Lopez, I'm impressed you were able to deploy those troops so quickly."

"Thank you, sir," the commander of Operation Rampart replied. "I had seven Army National Guard units standing by with orders to deploy on short notice. They were all units previously tasked for border protection duties with Customs and Border Protection—I just put them on a higher readiness level. The California unit was on the highest readiness level and was able to roll within two hours of the incident in Arizona. The Arizona Guard units are rolling now. We'll have two additional Guard companies on the border in California and Arizona within eight hours, and another seven units in place in all of the border states within seventy-two hours."

"Outline the plan for me, General."

"Yes, sir. The plan is simple: reinforce Border Patrol sectors with Army National Guard infantry, reconnaissance, intelligence, and light armored cavalry forces as quickly as possible in order to better patrol the U.S.-Mexico border," Lopez said. "Our goal is to assign one National Guard company to each sector within the next seventy-two hours. Each company is generally comprised of between seventy and one hundred soldiers, which on average is an increase in manpower of ten to twenty percent in each sector, dedicated solely to field operations.

"Each company fields between six and twelve vehicles. To save on cost and increase maintainability, we rely mostly on reconnaissance and light mechanized infantry units that use the M-998-series Humvees. Each Humvee has two soldiers on board, although for special missions or situations it can have as many as six. They are lightly armed, mostly with infantry weapons such as rifles and sidearms. Their job is to observe, report, and act as directed by the Border Patrol sector commanders."

"What missiles was Maravilloso talking about, General?"

Lopez looked down at his spit-shined tanker boots for a moment, then stood straight as he replied, "My decision was to beef up the El Centro Border Patrol sector that has those Mexican armored vehicles stationed on the border near Rampart One, sir. I sent in a platoon of Humvees with TOW antitank missiles on board. I thought it was important to counterbalance the Mexican force quickly and effectively, but not raise the ante too much."

"Christ, no wonder she's pissed," Kinsly breathed. "That's a major provocation!"

"I don't hear anyone accusing the Mexican Army of a major provocation by sending in armored vehicles across from Rampart One, Mr. Kinsly," Secretary of Defense Collier said, scowling at the President's Chief of Staff. "General Lopez did recommend sending Humvees with TOW missiles on them, and I approved the idea, Mr. President. I was more concerned about evening the odds than what Maravilloso or the media might think."

"Rotate the TOW missile vehicles out of there as soon as possible, General," the President said. "We're not trying to start a war here. The Mexican Army isn't going to attack us. Machine guns and rifles are okay."

Lopez shuffled uncomfortably and glanced at Collier. The Secretary of Defense stepped closer to the President. "Sam, do you think it's a good idea to second-guess your field generals at this early stage of the game?" he asked in a low voice.

"You think I'm micromanaging this thing now, Russ?"

"That's what it sounds like to me, yes, sir. Telling a one-star general which guns his infantrymen can carry . . . ?"

"I'm responsible for what happens out there, Russ . . ."

"Trust your generals, sir. If Lopez thinks we need TOWs on the border to put the fear of God into the Mexican Army, let him. You put Lopez in charge—let him *be* in charge."

Conrad thought for a moment, then shook his head. "This whole operation is controversial enough, Russ—I don't want to complicate it further by putting major offensive weapons on the damned border. I'm taking enough heat by approving those robots out there—I'm not going to repeat the mistake by putting guided antitank missiles out there. Pull them out—quietly, but get it done." Collier nodded and stepped back. "General, what's your next move?"

"Sir, my staff and I feel that the activity at Rampart One has forced smugglers east into the Arizona deserts," Lopez replied, "so we're going to concentrate our next deployments in western and central Arizona. The Border Patrol will intensify patrols at the most well-known trails and watering holes, and the National Guard will start patrolling the border region itself."

" 'Watering holes?' Are you talking about bars and taverns?"

"Sources of drinking water, sir," Lopez explained. "There are hundreds of watering holes throughout the deserts in the American South and Southwest. Some are over a hundred years old, set up by miners, ranchers, and conservationists. Some are deep year-round wells; others are little more than mud holes. Over the years various human rights or immigrant rights groups have set up solar-powered wells and portable water tanks to assist immigrants traveling through the deserts. Since they are obvious destinations for immigrants and smugglers, the Border Patrol watches those locations carefully; as a result, human rights groups move the tanks from time to time to throw off *La Migra*—what the illegals call the Border Patrol. The groups pass the word on the new locations through the migrant information grapevine."

The President shook his head in frustration. "It's damned hard to try to put a cap on illegal immigration when citizens in your own country are helping the ones we're trying to control."

"We'll deploy three companies, nine platoons, of Arizona National Guard mobile troops to this next operating area, along with unmanned aerial reconnaissance aircraft and support forces," Lopez went on. "Each platoon is responsible for patrolling roughly one hundred square miles of the border region. It's not much: that equates to just one Humvee, two men, patrolling that acreage on each eight-hour shift, with the other units in ready position."

"Seems like an impossible task, General."

"We'll concentrate on known trails and rely on UAVs to spot migrants over the horizon," Lopez said. The tone of his voice definitely indicated that he agreed, but he would never admit that to the commander in chief. "The more troops we have, of course, the better, but we think we can do the job at this current manpower level."

"We have very little choice, sir—we're stretched pretty thin as it is," Ray Jefferson interjected. "General Lopez is already talking about ten National Guard companies, about a thousand soldiers, deployed to the border region—but that's for a maximum of thirty days, and a recommended tour of two weeks. So we need at least two thousand soldiers a month at our current manning level, which as the general said is only a ten percent increase."

The President thought for a moment, then looked directly at each of his advisers in the Oval Office. "What are the alternatives, gentlemen?" he asked. "Sergeant Major?"

"In my opinion, sir, General Lopez doesn't have enough of the tools he needs to get the job done," Jefferson said immediately. "His plan calls for the use of only seven National Guard battalions—two from California, three from Texas, and one each from Arizona and New Mexico. Although we'd only be using each company for two weeks, and by law we can use these forces for up to sixty days on an 'emergency' basis, they'll be exhausted after just one or two rotations. We need more troops to maintain even this low level of commitment."

"So what's your recommendation?"

"My previous recommendations stand, sir: transfer the Army and Air National Guard bureaus into the Department of Homeland Security instead of the Pentagon; federalize as many units as the states think they can support; and completely reinforce the northern and southern borders and the coastlines."

"And I'll renew my disagreement with that recommendation, Mr. President: we can't just yank *over four hundred thousand* Army and Air National Guard troops away from the Pentagon, even for something as important as homeland security," Secretary of Defense Russell Collier said. "It would throw our entire ground military force structure into complete chaos."

"We're in a declared state of war since the Consortium attacks, sir—this is the perfect time to make that commitment," Jefferson said. "I'm positive we're in a fight against the Consortium, but the Consortium's activities have switched from attacks against Trans-

Global Energy facilities to massive and violent border incursions in order to infiltrate large numbers of men, weapons, and supplies covertly into the United States . . ."

"There's no evidence yet of any massive incursions, Jefferson, and scant evidence that the Consortium is involved," Attorney General George Wentworth interjected. "Yes, the incursions have become more violent recently, but I believe that's in response to us arming the border. They're still going to try to come across—but now they're arming themselves and shooting back."

"And that is unacceptable to me, General Wentworth . . . !"

"As it is to me—but adding more fuel to the fire by sending in more troops is not the answer."

"Then what do you suggest, George?" the President asked. "Let's hear it."

"Cancel the National Guard deployments immediately; stand down the units already in the field; ask Congress for an immediate appropriation for ten thousand new Border Patrol agents over the next three years, plus increased funding for unmanned aerial reconnaissance, electronic monitoring, and support from the Justice Department for more judges and detention facilities," Wentworth responded immediately. "We don't need the military to secure our borders. We've relied on the Border Patrol to do it for over eighty years—let's beef them up and support them better, but have them continue their work. We can get congressional approval for such a plan—they'll never buy off on an increased military presence on the borders."

The President paused again, then looked at his Chief of Staff. "Tom?"

"Putting the military on the border is going to become an increasingly tense and difficult political and foreign relations problem, Mr. President," Kinsly said. "With all due respect to the Border Patrol agents that were killed and the Mexican citizens and the American killed last night, I believe we're overreacting by placing troops on the border. As General Lopez and the sergeant major have said, even if we fully implement a military response to this crisis, we won't be able to completely cut off the flow of illegal migrants—they'll just find another way to get in. There's a societal and cultural dynamic here that we won't be able to solve with government or military intervention."

"And your recommendation?"

Kinsly glanced at the Secretary of Defense, then said, "Politically we can't afford to stand down those troops already deployed to the border—it'll make us look weak, like we caved in to President Maravilloso's demands. They have to stay, at least for a month or two, assuming there are no more serious acts of violence. But after the furor dies down, they should be quickly and quietly withdrawn. No more military forces on the border"—he looked directly at the National Security Adviser and added—"and especially *not* the robots.

"I believe our policies should concentrate on fully implementing the guest worker visa program, and tougher penalties for employers who hire outside it," Kinsly went on quickly. "We can continue to build detention facilities in the desert, but make it clear that we will follow the usual immigration and deportation guidelines. We can announce an expanded detention program for the OTMs—the 'Other Than Mexicans,' the ones from countries all over the world who we usually release with orders to appear, but who usually *don't*. General Wentworth's suggestion of about ten thousand more Border Patrol agents over three years is based on a legislative analysis taken not too long ago, indicating a lot of congressional support."

"Mr. Kinsly, none of those programs solve the problem of terrorists and killers coming across the border," Ray Jefferson said. "We can take on illegal immigration, sovereignty, border security, and antiterrorism problems all with one move: maintaining a large paramilitary presence on the borders . . ."

"We're still not sure if we have a terrorist problem here, Sergeant Major, despite your enlightened guesswork," Kinsly said. "With all due respect to the Border Patrol agent that survived and your instincts and hunches, I don't think the United States can afford to mobilize tens of thousands of troops and place them on our borders without concrete evidence."

It was obvious the President was quickly being swayed. He turned to the Secretary of Homeland Security. "Jeffrey?"

Jeffrey Lemke shook his head. "I hate to be so wishy-washy, Mr. President, but I think the sergeant major goes too far, and the Chief of Staff and Attorney General don't go far enough," he said. "I'd sure like to see all of my border security and immigration bureaus get more manpower and funding, of course, but I don't think putting the National Guard on the borders except to assist the Border Patrol is appropriate. And I sure as heck wouldn't want the headaches I foresee with gaining four hundred thousand National Guard troops. Homeland Security took two years to finally integrate just forty thousand members of the Coast Guard, and that's still not fully completed.

"My recommendation is to use the National Guard on a limited basis to assist the Border Patrol, like we do with Customs and the Coast Guard," Lemke went on. "My own studies, which I haven't sent out for congressional opinion, point to the need for funding for twenty thousand more Border Patrol agents within five years. That's a more appropriate level. That's the same recommendation put forth by General Lopez when he was assigned command of Operation Rampart, and it's a good one.

"Strategically, without definite actionable information on a specific threat to the United States, we should try to find a political and legislative solution rather than adopt a defensive and clearly threatening posture. Many of Mr. Kinsly's suggestions sound good to me: a limited guest worker program, more punishment for violators, no 'catch and release' for OTMs, longer detention stays, more detention facilities. I feel we're overreacting to recent events, and we're in danger of having this situation spin out of control." He glanced at Jefferson, then added, "I continued to be impressed by the sergeant major's CID robots and his ambitious plans to deploy them, and I do believe Operation Rampart was a victim of a series of unfortunate mishaps and doesn't reflect Task Force

TALON's capabilities. But we're hurting, plain and simple, and I see no downside in drawing down the military aspect and steeply ramping up the legislative and political responses."

"Sir, it sounds to me like we have a meeting of the minds, if not a full consensus," Chief of Staff Kinsly said to the back of the President's head. "Defense says he can't support a major mobilization or move of the National Guard for border security; Homeland Security doesn't seem to want them anyway, at least not as part of their roster, but suggests some limited assistance; Justice is in favor of increased Border Patrol manpower. I suggest we draft resolutions and start putting together a plan of action to push these resolutions through Congress. In the meantime, we gradually draw down the National Guard forces on the border in order to quiet the tension ratcheting up around here."

"I'm in favor of drafting resolutions to support more detention facilities, additional funding for the Border Patrol, a guest worker program, more sanctions against employers who hire undocumented aliens, and all the rest, Mr. President," National Security Adviser Jefferson said, "but I feel we need to make those moves in an atmosphere of strength and resolve, not weakness. General Lopez's move to put those Guard forces on the border so quickly after the Arizona incident was a bold, audacious, resolute one— we shouldn't lose the advantage of surprise and shock it gave us." He paused for a moment, then added, "And if FBI Director De-Laine thinks she can use Task Force TALON to help her track down any terrorists that may have sneaked across the border, I think we should give it to her."

"Your loyalty to that group astounds me, Sergeant Major," the President said. "They've done nothing but be a royal pain in the ass to everyone involved ever since that bastard Chamberlain put them together—a move, need I remind you, *designed from the beginning* to make the government look bad. They've done nothing but look bad since day one."

"Sir, they may *look* bad, but they've been highly successful in their given mission," Jefferson said. "They may not do the job neat and pretty—no truly effective combat unit or special ops team is known for their tidiness—but they get the job done. They took on the Consortium and other terrorist groups all around the world, and they caught three hundred percent more illegals crossing the border than the Border Patrol."

"Mr. President, I'm not going to try to support or condemn TALON," Kinsly said. "I have to admit they've had some spectacular successes—unfortunately, their heavy-handed blunders have only served to obscure those successes, at least in a political and public relations sense." He swallowed when he noticed Jefferson's glare, but went on: "Speaking as your chief political adviser, sir, I believe TALON is a much bigger liability than they are an asset, because it makes you appear as if you're not in total control."

"Well, sir, I'm not a political adviser," Jefferson said, "but let me try to approach this problem from a political direction: should TALON be placed in the control of the FBI? Right now TALON reports directly to me, which means they report to *you*. If that's too *politically* distasteful, then putting them under Director DeLaine's authority might be a good thing. It's an added layer of political insulation from this office."

"You sure are *sounding* like a political adviser, Sergeant Major," the President remarked.

"I'm not sure if that's a compliment or an insult, sir," Jefferson said.

"It's a warning: don't get in over your head."

"Message received, loud and clear, sir." Jefferson looked at Kinsly and asked, "Does Director DeLaine suffer from the same adverse political appearance as TALON? My guess is, she does not."

Kinsly shook his head. "In fact, Director DeLaine polls out extremely well with the public, Congress, and the media," Kinsly said. "She's talented, knowledgeable, well spoken, professional, experienced, articulate, and considered a team player by a majority of respondents."

Jefferson rolled his eyes at the mass of polling data being so easily regurgitated by the White House Chief of Staff—he couldn't. help worrying if that's what he spoon-fed the President on a daily basis, and how many decisions were made from this office on that basis. "I suppose it doesn't hurt that she's young, good-looking, curvy, and unmarried," Jefferson added sarcastically.

The Chief of Staff looked uncomfortable. "In fact, she tested out well in all those areas too," he admitted.

Jefferson shook his head sadly. "Goes to show you what the American public *really* cares about."

"Point taken, Sergeant Major—now drop it," the President said irritably.

"Sorry, sir."

The President fell silent again, but only for a few moments this time: "Tom, issue instructions to General Lopez that he should plan for a complete withdrawal of National Guard forces from the border within sixty days," the President ordered. "I'll leave the decision as to which weapons he wants to use to him, but it is my clear desire to use the absolute minimum firepower necessary for self-defense. We're trying to secure the borders from illegal entry, not defend against a massed armored invasion.

"I want to see a draft resolution for a temporary worker program on my desk by the end of the day today, ready to present to Congress for sponsorship," the President went on. "I want the bill to include tough penalties for employers who hire undocumented workers after the law goes into effect. I also want draft resolutions for emergency funding for twenty thousand additional Border Patrol agents, a greater number of detention facilities and judges to hear immigration and deportation cases, and more provisions for detaining more OTMs and making sure they appear for immigration hearings. I'm going to table discussions—for now—on having the Guard transferred to Homeland Security and changing the Constitution to prohibit granting citizenship to children born in the U.S. of illegal immigrants, but you can leak it to the press that the White House is looking into those two topics for near-future legislation."

Kinsly had his PDA out and was wirelessly transmitting notes furiously to his staff. "Got it, Mr. President," he said.

The President then turned to Ray Jefferson. "Okay, Sergeant Major: convince me that the FBI needs TALON."

"One name: Yegor Zakharov," Jefferson responded immediately. "Agent Paul Purdy may not have made an absolutely positive ID, but I believe that's who we're dealing with. I think forensic evidence from the shootings in Arizona will reveal Zakharov's handiwork—as we know, he's an expert marksman, with a rare and easily identifiable Russian sniper rifle as his weapon of choice. If Zakharov and the Consortium are still in the U.S., it'll take more than an FBI Hostage Rescue Team or a police SWAT unit to take him down. We'll need either a Delta Force company, an entire SEAL team, a Marine Special Purpose Force platoon— or *one* Cybernetic Infantry Device."

The President paused, looking carefully at Jefferson, studying him, trying to think of another question that the senior Army noncommissioned officer wasn't prepared for, but finally gave up. "Tom, I want a video conference with the Attorney General, FBI Director DeLaine, and Major Richter as soon as possible."

"Sir, I would advise against that," Kinsly said evenly. "The assaults on the federal officers, the killing of that migrant, and the multiple killings at Rampart One are still fresh in people's minds. Now you want to put those robots on the streets and give them an FBI badge . . ."

"And a judge's warrant," the President added. "That's exactly what I want to do." To Jefferson, he said, "Sergeant Major, I'm not relieving you of responsibility for Task Force TALON. You keep them under tight control, or you bring them in and shut them down. Do I make myself clear?"

"Yes, sir," Jefferson replied.

At that moment the President's assistant entered the Oval Office and gave Kinsly a folder. The Chief of Staff reviewed the cover letter quickly, his eyes widening in concern as he read. "Tom . . . ?"

"Transcript of another videotape message by that Comandante Veracruz guy," Kinsly announced, "distributed to several U.S. and international media outlets, reporting details of the killings in Arizona and calling for a general uprising and retaliation against the U.S. government. The cat's out of the bag, Mr. President, and Veracruz announced it before we did—that'll make it look even worse for us."

The Oval Office erupted into sheer bedlam. Kinsly gave the folder to Jefferson, who speed-read through the transcript. "Detailed, accurate account . . . no doubt in my mind the Consortium, or Veracruz himself, staged the ambush."

"That's absurd!" Kinsly said. "We're not going to respond to this horrible incident by stating that Veracruz allowed *his own people* to be killed, when the evidence so far shows that *Americans* did it! That's political suicide!"

"It's the only explanation, sir," Jefferson said.

"How could Veracruz do it? What did he do . . . analyze every weapon those vigilantes carried and used only those same weapons to shoot the migrants?" Kinsly asked. "That's stretching credibility, Jefferson."

"It's no secret what weapons they carry, Mr. Kinsly—it's all on their Web broadcasts and ops report they publish online, in exact detail," Jefferson said. "It's possible . . . ."

"The fact is, Jefferson, that when the tape gets broadcast on TV, *everyone* will believe what this Veracruz guy says," Kinsly argued. "And the media *will* broadcast the tape, even if they don't check its authenticity first. The American Watchdog Project will be called racist murderers, and we'll be blamed for allowing them to be out there doing the Border Patrol's job—or, worse, charging that they're working *with* the Border Patrol to execute illegal migrants."

The President thought for a moment; then turned to Ray Jefferson. "Sergeant Major, get TALON moving out there to find this other eyewitness so we can prove that Zakharov is still in the country and working with Veracruz . . ."

"But, sir," Kinsly protested, "if the press sees those robots out there, and they're even *seen* anywhere near the illegal immigrant population, it'll look like we're organizing a government-sponsored vigilante terror campaign against them, first with the Watchdogs and then with Task Force TALON. We'll be roasted alive by the press and . . ."

"If it *is* Zakharov out there attacking the Border Patrol and working with Veracruz to incite violence, we're going to need all the firepower we can get," the President said. "I'm not going to run and hide while some Russian terrorist and some drug-smuggler punk create a nationwide race riot in the United States. Task Force TALON may be America's bull in the china shop, but they get the job done. I just hope they can find Zakharov and Veracruz before it's too late."

He turned to Jefferson and jabbed a finger. "But they do it by the book, Ray—that means search warrants and rock-solid evidence before they go in the field. I don't want any repeats of the Rampart One fiasco, Sergeant Major, or the robots get sent to the trash compactor, and you and Richter spend what's left of your military careers distributing deodorant in Djibouti. Get on it."

OFFICE OF THE PRESIDENT OF THE
UNITED MEXICAN STATES, PALACIO NACIONAL,
ZOCALO, MEXICO CITY
THAT SAME TIME

"He dared put the military on the border without consulting me—*twice!*" Mexican president Carmen Maravilloso said angrily, nearly tossing the phone on the floor in anger before her aide Pedro could collect it and safely put it out of reach. "How *dare* that *man* ignore me? I am the president of the United Mexican States!"

Women in general and especially women outside the home were never very highly regarded in Mexico, and female politicians even less so, but Maravilloso—her given surname was Tamez, but she changed it when she became a national news anchorwoman on Mexico's largest television network years earlier—fought to change that perception. Maravilloso's entire political life had been a struggle, and she used every trick in the book—personal, feminine tricks as well as political—to get an advantage.

After becoming one of Mexico's most popular and recognizable television personalities in both news and variety entertainment shows, she married a young, up-and-coming politician seven years her junior and helped him ascend from virtual political obscurity to become first the governor of Mexico's largest state, then president of the United Mexican States. Like Jacqueline Kennedy in the United States, Carmen Maravilloso was just as popular as her husband, not just in Mexico but around the world. She liked being around the rich and powerful and could hold her own in just about any forum anywhere in the world, from attending the Little League World Series in Taiwan with Fidel Castro, to a state dinner at the White House, to conducting a surprise guided tour of the presidential palace with one hundred astonished visitors.

The Mexican revolutionary constitution prohibited the president from running for reelection until six years after leaving office, and since that law had always been assumed to apply equally to the president's spouse, everyone believed Maravilloso would go back to being a television personality after her husband's six-year term ended. She had different ideas. Her surprise candidacy was immediately challenged by her political foes, and the question went all the way to the Mexican Supreme Court, where the twenty-five-judge court ruled against her in a hair-thin majority: in order to prevent the establishment of a nepotistic quasimonarchy, no member of a president's immediate family could run for president within one full term, six years, of the president leaving office.

But that didn't stop her either: Maravilloso requested and received an annulment of her marriage from the Roman Catholic Church, on the grounds that her husband defied the Church's wishes by not wanting children. It was widely thought that the situation was the reverse, but her husband did not contest the pleading—convinced not to do so, it was rumored, with a secret eight-figure tax-free divorce settlement.

In a country that had the fourth-lowest divorce rate in the world in which the Roman Catholic religion was recognized as the official state religion in the constitution, this shocked the Mexican people—but delighted most of the rest of the world, including women in the United States of America, who saw Maravilloso's candidacy as a boon to women's rights and a slap at the powerful male-dominated macho culture in most of the Third World. Although this development too was argued in front of the Mexican Supreme Court, popular opinion in favor of Maravilloso's courage and dedication was loud and insistent, and the court refused to consider the case. Maravilloso won her election in a landslide.

She was a woman who was accustomed to getting what she wanted, and no one—especially no *male,* not even the President of the United States—was going to deny her. Carmen Maravilloso was in her early fifties but looked younger by at least ten years, with long flowing black hair, dark eyes usually hidden behind designer sunglasses, and a slender, attractive figure. She was a tough, no-nonsense politician, known for occasionally lighting up a Cuban cigar and letting an expletive or two "slip" past her full red lips when the opportunity suited her.

"How *dare* he do this without consulting us?" Maravilloso screeched. She lit up a Cohiba Exquisito and wielded the thin cigar like a dagger, aiming it at everyone she spoke to. She aimed it first at the Minister of National Defense, General Alberto Rojas: "I want twice as many soldiers on the border as the Americans have. How many can we send there?"

"Madame President, they have as many troops just in the state of California as we do *in our entire army,*" the general said. "We cannot outgun them."

"They are only National Guard troops . . ."

"I am *talking* about the National Guard, madam," he said. "California is the most populous state in America and can field a vast number of paramilitary forces—even though heavily committed around the world, their national guard outnumbers even our regular military forces in every category. You do not want to escalate a military confrontation, señora."

"Then we will take our case to the United Nations Security Council and to the Organization of American States," Minister of Internal Affairs Felix Díaz said as he breezed through the doors to the president's office. "This situation is becoming an international crisis, Madam President, and we should respond accordingly."

"Minister Díaz!" Maravilloso exclaimed happily. "We were afraid you were dead after your stunt the other day, riding around in your helicopter and inciting riots."

"I thank you for your concern, Madam President," Díaz said, smiling and bowing. Tall, young, and impossibly handsome, he hailed from several generations of rich, powerful hacienda owners dating back to the original Mexican land grants from the royal court in Madrid, Spain. His family had managed to keep the majority of their lands by aligning with whichever side had more power at the time—the military, the Catholic Church, the revolutionaries, the Communists, the Spanish, the Bonapartists, even the Americans: whoever could benefit the Díaz family the most received their political and financial allegiance . . . until power shifted again.

Díaz was educated in the finest private schools in Mexico, attended the military academy at Chapultepec, went to undergraduate flight training in Arizona, then served four years in a variety of flying units in the Fuerza Aerea Mexicana, the Mexican Air Force, including one year as squadron commander of an air combat squadron of F-5A Freedom Fighter air defense jets and AT-33A propeller trainers modified for counterinsurgency missions.

While commanding the 202nd Air Combat Squadron in Santa Lucia, Díaz helped organize and conduct a series of exercises with the Cuban Air Force, where he flew his F-5s against several different models of MiG fighters and fighter-bombers. He received considerable attention from generals and defense ministers from around the world for his political as well as flying skills. He served out his military commitment as the Mexican air attaché to the Caribbean and Latin America, shuttling all over the hemisphere almost on a daily basis on behalf of the Mexican government.

Even though he spent eight successful years in the Mexican armed forces, Felix Díaz was destined for politics almost from birth. For most of the past eighty years, his family were loyal and high-ranking members of the Partido Revolucionario Institucional, or PRI. But Felix Díaz saw something happening that others failed to see: the emergence of a tremendous groundswell of support for a strong-willed, outgoing, hardworking, and hard-charging woman, Carmen Maravilloso, and her young husband. Mexican culture was slowly but surely changing, just as surely as its politics—Díaz knew he had to change with it, or be left behind.

He switched party allegiance to the Partido Accion Nacional just in time for the surprise ascension of Maravilloso's husband, bringing a considerable amount of money and national prestige along with him, and was offered several positions in the new government as a reward. His personal gamble paid off, as he knew from past generations it would. When Carmen took the office of president, Díaz was immediately appointed Minister of Internal Affairs, the third-highest-ranking position in the executive branch of the Mexican government.

"I like that idea—let us go before the Security Council," Maravilloso said. "Amassing those troops on the border is a clear provocation, meant to falsely imprison Mexican citizens and force unfair and oppressive economic and political terms on a peaceful neighbor. Very good suggestion, Minister Díaz." She turned to another one of her advisers in her office: "General Rojas?"

"I agree that a diplomatic response would be far better than a military one, Madam President," General Alberto Rojas, the silver-haired, grandfatherly-looking Mexican Minister of National Defense, said. "The more military forces the Americans

place on the border, the worse it looks for them. Since President
Conrad when asked did not tell you exactly why he placed all
those heavily armed troops on the border, we have every right to
demand that the UN and OAS get an answer. The UN General
Assembly will surely be open to—"

"No. We will *not* go to the General Assembly—we will go directly to the Security Council," Maravilloso said, taking a deep
drag on her cigar. "This is no mere water, cattle-grazing, or cultural exchange issue—with missile-launching vehicles and armed
helicopters flying dangerously close to our towns and villages,
threatening our people with death or imprisonment, this is certainly an urgent national security issue." The defense and foreign
affairs ministers looked at each other worriedly but said nothing.
"And I will address the Security Council myself."

"I do not believe that is wise, Madam President," Rojas said.
"Addresses to the Security Council should be on issues that
threaten peace and stability not just for the states involved, but for
the entire world community. This incident, although serious to be
sure, poses no imminent danger to the rest of the . . ."

"I do not care!" Maravilloso said. "I want this issue brought up
before the Security Council, and I wish to present it myself. Do not
tell *me* what reality for the world or for Mexico is. *¡Soy México!* I
am Mexico! Now make it happen! And get my speechwriters busy
drafting up my address to the Council! I want a draft on my desk
in four hours."

Rojas looked at Maravilloso and sighed with obvious exasperation. "I will do as you say, Madam President," he said with a defeated smile, "but I urge you not to use this situation for political
or personal *ventaja*. I know it is in your nature to do so, but let us
deal with this situation openly and honestly, not just to appeal to
the television cameras."

"What do you know of it, you old goat?" Maravilloso asked
with an alluring, disarming smile on her face. "You are a good and
wise fellow in international geopolitics, Alberto, but what you

know about public relations and how to get the world's attention for a worthy and noble cause wouldn't even fill a thimble."

"That may be so, Carmen." Rojas stepped over to the beautiful, fiery president of Mexico as she smoked her Cuban cigar and made notes to herself at her desk. "But in my opinion, Mexico will not be served by doing anything just for the publicity value. Mexico already has an international reputation for poverty, crime, and corruption. More and more of our people are leaving every year, and the workers that leave are sending back less and less of the money they earn. We are losing our best workers, and we get little in return. This is a legitimate concern for Mexico—let's *treat* it as such."

"Do not give so much credit to the United Nations or the Security Council, General Rojas," Felix Díaz said. "Do you expect them to do anything about our out-of-control émigré problem? Every industrialized country in the Western world has an immigration problem. The current rotating chairmanship of the Security Council is held by Australia, who has an illegal immigration problem ten times worse than the United States—they have illegal immigrants from most of Polynesia and half of Asia invading their shores every day. Do you think they will be sympathetic to us? You know as well as I that the United Nations Security Council is nothing but a collection of painted toy bobble-heads that respond only when rapped on the head—whoever raps hardest gets their nod."

Rojas remained silent, but inwardly he felt a twinge of concern as he looked at this young politician. Díaz was intelligent, but he was also impulsive—and Maravilloso was quite simply enamored with him. It was a dangerous—no, an *explosive*—combination.

"I have told you this many times before, Alberto—there are proper channels to follow to get things done, and then there are *my* channels," Maravilloso went on. "I wish to speak before the Security Council because I know my speech will be carried live by half the news outlets in the world. I will be on the covers of a hundred

magazines and several hundred newspapers around the world—
not just major outlets and political rags, but every kind of publi-
cation: fashion, teens, gossip, human rights, celebrity, even lesbian
publications, reaching hundreds of millions around the world.
With all your education and wisdom, my friend, and with all due
respect, do you think you have any chance in hell of getting that
kind of coverage?" She took another deep puff of her cigar, her
perfume mixing with the smooth, aromatic aroma of the cigar,
forming a musky, intoxicating potion. "I am not seeking action
from the United Nations, Alberto—I am looking for a reaction
from the *people,* Alberto."

"People? What people? The Mexican people? Perhaps one percent of our people read newspapers or watch television for hard
news stories. Who is your target audience? What is your message?"

"There are millions of wealthy Latinos in North America that
want to be told what to do for their motherland, General, and
President Maravilloso is the one who should tell them," Díaz said
confidently. "They, or their parents, a relative, or a close friend,
managed to escape the crushing poverty and creeping despair of
their homelands, and they all feel the guilt of abandoning their
motherland. Even if they gave up everything they owned, left
their wives and children, sat in a sweltering U-Haul truck or
cargo container for days or even weeks with three dozen other
refugees, walked across miles of scorching desert with nothing but
a jug of water, or floated for days in homemade rafts to reach
American shores, they feel the guilt of leaving their brothers and
sisters behind. The more money they make in the New World, the
guiltier they feel."

"They are the ones I will reach," Maravilloso chimed in. "They
are the ones who will help us."

"Help us? Help us . . . do *what?*" Rojas asked, almost begging.
"What is it you want to do, Madam President?"

"Induce the American Congress to pass a simple guest worker
program, one without onerous conditions, bureaucracy, and requirements," Díaz said. "The current program making its way

through Congress would require all Mexican citizens to return to Mexico first before applying. If even half of those that wished to comply did so, it would bankrupt this country! Can you imagine the chaos that would erupt if *ten million* men, women, and children returned to Mexico over the next five years?"

Rojas glared at Díaz, showing his displeasure at cutting off his conversation with Maravilloso. He was definitely being ganged up on here, and he didn't like it. "I agree, Minister, that it would place an enormous burden on our government . . ."

"And do you think for one minute that the American government will pay for any of it? No way." Maravilloso took another angry puff of her cigar.

"If the United States wants Mexican workers, they need to pass legislation that will allow them to apply for a guest worker program from wherever they are—which will be working away in farms, factories, kitchen, and laundry rooms all across America, doing the work the lazy, pretentious Americans will not do," Diaz said determinedly. "The government does not need to uproot families, destroy jobs, drain our economy, and create a tidal wave of economic and political refugees just to appease the far-right conservative neofascists in their country.

"And if they want to apply for American citizenship, they should be rewarded for their courage and service to America by receiving it automatically—no tests, no classes, no more paperwork. If they work for five years, keep their noses clean, pay their taxes, and learn the language, they should not have to do anything more than raise their right hand and swear loyalty to the United States—even though they have already *demonstrated* their loyalty by sacrificing all to live and work in America."

"I agree, Minister, I agree—we have had this discussion many times before," Rojas said patiently. "We and the citizen groups and human rights organizations we sponsor have been lobbying the American Congress for many years to pass meaningful, open, fair, and simple guest worker legislation. We cannot do more than what we are already doing."

"I do not believe that," Díaz said. "Even stuffy, old blowhard American politicians respond to issues that grab headlines and the public's attention."

"I know the American media," Maravilloso said. "I know how the people are riveted to the right controversy or the right personality."

"Well, you can certainly *be* that personality, Madam President," Rojas said. "But do you think the American people will listen to you now after one of your Council of Government ministers incited a riot in their detention facility?"

"You have seen the polls as well as I, General," Díaz said. "The polls indicate that most Americans thought that detention facility was illegal, evil, demeaning, and un-American . . ."

"But those same polls also said that you were wrong to call for those detainees to break free and riot, even though most did not like the sight of immigrants being penned-up like animals in the hot desert," Rojas pointed out. "A slight majority blame *you,* Madam President, for our people's deaths and for that soldier's suicide."

"I am not worried about slight majorities," Maravilloso said, waving her cigar dismissively. "The point is, Alberto, Americans are divided and unsure of what should happen. They are afraid of acts of terrorism, and they are certainly paranoid, bigoted, and xenophobic—even the blacks and other minorities who have suffered under white bigotry and hatred dislike the thought of Mexicans crossing the borders illegally and taking jobs. But then when the government actually *does* something about it, like build a detention facility or put even a very few troops on the border, they strongly condemn it."

"It is the politically correct thing to oppose any new government excess, especially when it involves imprisoning or even slightly affecting a weaker person's life . . ."

"This is much more than just political correctness—it is even more than trying to deal with racism and bigotry," Felix Díaz said. "I believe the American people want to be *led* on this issue. They want a person to step forward, speak to them, give them their thoughts and arguments plainly and simply, and have a plan to *do something* about the matter. Right now, all they have is the government and neofascist wackos like Bob O'Rourke preaching hate and fear to them. O'Rourke is a powerful personality—it will take someone equally as powerful to get our side of the argument across to the people. Preferably someone younger, smarter, and better-looking than he."

"That person will be difficult to find," Rojas said. He looked on nervously as he saw Maravilloso and Díaz silently gaze into each other's eyes. "What do you wish to do, Madam President?" he asked, trying to break the spell between them.

"Get out of here and get back to work, you old goat," Maravilloso yelled after him jovially. "I wish to speak with Minister Díaz for a few minutes. Have the chief of staff report to me then. And find a way to make the damned Americans back off, or I will have your *cojones* in a jar on my desk—if you still *have* any! *Now* you may leave." Before departing, Rojas shot her a warning glare, which he doubted she noticed.

"Ah, the smell of a good Cuban cigar," Díaz said, walking toward Maravilloso. "Your husband never smoked cigars except for photo opportunities, as I recall, and he would only smoke Mexican-made cigars, like a good nationalist. I am glad you are a true aficionado."

"Why do you bring him up, Minister Díaz?"

"The scent of your cigar reminded me that your husband chose never to be alone with you in the presidential office because he was afraid of what the people might think was going on," Díaz said, a mischievous smile on his face. "A woman of your beauty, your passion, your energy—he was afraid people might think you and he spent all your time fornicating on the president's desk. He was always so proper, so totally in control of everything—his environment, his image, his words, his emotions."

"So?"

Díaz stepped closer to the president of Mexico, slipped his arms around her waist, pulled her closer to him, and kissed her deeply. "*Ay,* I am so glad you are not like him," Díaz breathed after their lips parted. "I always feel your fire, your passion, your spirit whenever I walk into this room. I could never keep it contained."

"Felix, would you please just shut up and bring your hard Spanish *paro* over here, *now?*" she breathed, and pressed her body tightly against his as they kissed again.

They both explored, then used each other's bodies quickly, efficiently, tactically—they were in tune with each other's passion and could tell immediately how the other wanted it and knew exactly how best to get the other to that level. Maravilloso kept the shades drawn and her desk cleared off for exactly that reason. It was *polvo,* not lovemaking, but they both knew it and both accepted it because to do otherwise would not serve either of their desires or ambitions.

They shared what was left of her Cuban cigar afterward as they straightened their clothing and she fixed her makeup. "Did you tell Pedro to give us at least twenty minutes this time before he is to call, darling?" Díaz asked.

"Fifteen. You are quicker than you believe you are, *jodonton*."

"Get a decent sofa and a door that locks from the inside, and I'll be slower, *culito*." She smiled like a schoolgirl on her first date— he was the only man in the Federal District who ever had the nerve to swear and talk dirty in front of her, even before he learned how aroused she got by it. "So. Rojas is all worried about the California National Guard, eh? Tell him to stop worrying. The Americans will be gone from the border before you know it."

She was disturbed that he knew about her adviser's fears, as if he had been in the meeting with them just now. "The *Politicos* are not still bugging my office, are they, Felíx?" she asked, trying not to make it sound like an accusation.

"I told you I took all of the *Politico*'s bugs out months ago, my dear," Díaz said. "I do not need to bug the general's office to hear what he has to say—a few shots of tequila or glasses of cerveza in the afternoon and his deputies and aides blab like a housewife on her neighbor's fence. I pretend to be talking on my cell phone in his outer office and I can hear everything he says quite clearly."

Felix Díaz knew a lot about chatty members of the Mexican government. It was the duty of the Minister of Internal Affairs to protect the republic, constitution, government, and courts from threats from inside the country, a purposely broad and far-reaching responsibility. Along with overseeing the ministry itself, Díaz had control of several other important bureaus and agencies in the government, including the Federal District Police, Political Police, Border Police, and the Rural Defense Force. Felix Díaz had extraordinary powers of investigation and commanded a large and well-equipped paramilitary force that equaled, and in some areas exceeded, the power of the armed forces.

Numbering over five thousand agents, technicians, and support staff, the Political Police, or *Politicos*, investigated any possible threats to all Mexican political institutions, including the president, legislature, the judiciary, the treasury, the Council of Government, political parties, opposition groups, and insurgent or revolutionary groups. Within the Political Police was a clandestine unit of almost five hundred specially trained and equipped agents called the *Escuadrilla Especial De las Investigaciones,* but known by their nickname *Los Sombras*—the "Shadows"—their identities secret to all but Díaz and José Elvarez, Deputy Minster of Internal Affairs. The *Sombras* could seize any documents they deemed necessary, wiretap any phone, open any door or safe deposit box, access any record, and arrest any person for any reason whatsoever—or for no reason at all.

Of course, Carmen Maravilloso knew all this—which is why she first appointed him to the position of Minister of Internal Affairs, and then began sleeping with him. At best she could keep an eye on him and use her feminine charms on his postpubescent urges to keep him sympathetic and loyal to her, as much as any man could stay loyal to a woman; at worst, their affair might buy his silence, or at least cause a lot of distrust against him among others in the government. The culture of machismo still existed, even in the highest levels of Latino government—women, even power-ful and influential women working outside the home, were not to be taken advantage of. They could be subdued, embarrassed, even silenced. But a man's power over a woman was assumed to be ab-solute and universal, and it was in poor taste for a man to abuse his God-given sexual, physical, or anthropological power and author-ity against the weaker sex.

But it turned out that Felix Díaz was a good choice for the post, because he appeared to have no burning vendetta against any per-son or political party and didn't seem to have any sort of resent-ment against a woman being his superior. His extreme wealth, and his family's long-standing policy of siding with whoever was in power or soon to be in power, left him with few strong enemies. He had personal political aspirations, of course—it was no secret that he wanted to be president of Mexico, a position that no others in his family had ever attained. But, typically, politicians in Mex-ico tried to exploit the least little bit of power they attained, and at least as far as Maravilloso's trained eye could see, Felix Díaz was not acting like a typical Mexican politician.

Even so, she was careful to be forever watchful for any signs of a power grab by this man or any other man close to her. No politi-cian in Mexico could afford to be a nice guy, even nice guys like Felix Díaz. She had made a woman's mistake by letting him take sexual liberties in this, her base of power—that made her vulner-able. If he ever exhibited any desire whatsoever to take advantage of that vulnerability, she would have to squash it immediately.

Now it was time to challenge him, put him back on the defen-sive, before he had a chance to even pull up the fly on his pants: "How in hell do you know what the Americans will do, Felix?" she asked.

"One of my agents intercepted a message sent from Washing-ton for the American ambassador here in Mexico City," Díaz said. "The message stated that effective immediately their Operation Rampart was suspended and all of their Cybernetic Infantry De-vices were being withdrawn from the border."

"So? We already know they have replaced those robots with National Guard troops. They haven't withdrawn—if anything, they have increased and reinforced their presence."

"Our informants in Washington tell us that the American President has summoned the commander of those National Guard forces to the White House, as well as the Secretary of Defense and the Attorney General, and that he is not happy at all," Díaz said, wiping bright red lipstick from his neck and straightening his necktie. "The analysts say he will gradually pull forces back from the border so it will not look like a retreat. He does not want to be seen as backing down in the face of pressure from Mexico. But he *will* back down."

"Perhaps—until the next terrorist or smuggler decides to kill an American vigilante or Border Patrol agent," Maravilloso said bitterly. She looked at him carefully. "You insist these attacks are not being done by Mexicans, Felix, but then you give me reports of yet another videotape being distributed by this 'Comandante Veracruz' character, inciting the Mexican people to commit even more atrocities. How sure are you that these attacks are not being perpetuated by him?"

"I am not sure of much when it comes to Veracruz, Carmen."

Her stare intensified. "You seem to have very good, reliable contacts throughout the world, Felix," Maravilloso said suspiciously, "but I find it very strange that you cannot tell me very much about Veracruz. Why is that, Felix?"

"Because he is probably not Mexican," Diaz replied. "All of our internal investigations have come up empty so far, and most foreign governments will not share information on anyone who might have had specialized military or guerrilla training."

"Well, what *can* you tell me about him?"

"Just the basics. His name is Ernesto Fuerza, reported in a French newspaper interview a couple years ago but never independently verified. His nationality is unknown. He is in his late thirties or early forties, male, tall, and slender . . ."

"I mean some *real* information about him, Felix," she said irritably. "The whole world knows that trivia—I read all that last week in *People* magazine . . ."

"Next to the article on you, I noticed, the one on 'The New Faces of Mexico.' " She gave him a warning glare, and Díaz's tone turned serious: "The uniform he often wears looks American, English, or Canadian, and the headdress he wears looks very Middle Eastern—very confusing to analysts. His Spanish is good, but it sounds more South American, perhaps Brazilian or Venezuelan, more sophisticated, more European. He obviously has some military training, judging by the way he speaks and the way he holds a weapon . . ."

"How can you tell anything by how one holds a weapon?"

"A trained man will never put his finger on a trigger unless he is ready to shoot—he will lay his finger on the side of the trigger guard," Diaz said. "That is pounded into a soldier from the first moment he is given a gun."

"What else?"

"Everything is guesswork and speculation—it can hardly even be called 'analysis,' " Díaz admitted. "One thing is for certain: he is bound to slip up, try to cross the border once too often, or take a shot at the wrong target, and he will either be dead or captured. Revolutionaries do not have much of a shelf life these days, since the Americans started clamping down hard on anyone who might even remotely smell like a terrorist." Díaz fell silent for a moment. Then, "Maybe we should not be trying to hunt this man down," he said. "Maybe we should use him instead."

"Bad idea, Felix," Maravilloso said. "He is certainly popular all around the world. But the magazine articles state he was—perhaps still is—a drug smuggler. Why would I want to be associated with such a man?"

"I do not think it matters much," the Minister of Internal Affairs said. "As long as he is truly committed to helping the Mexican people who choose to work in the United States, I think our cause would be greatly helped. A slight imperfection might enhance his character a bit."

"There is no way on earth we can find that out for sure without a face-to-face meeting."

"I can make it happen, Carmen."

"A meeting with the infamous Comandante Veracruz?" Her face turned from serious to thoughtful. "You are the one person in the world who could pull off such a meeting, my dear." Maravilloso thought for a moment, then shook her head. "Collect more information on this man—hopefully even capture him so you can question him directly."

"Or kill him, if necessary, if he proves a threat to your administration's plans to work with the Americans and solve this immigration dilemma," Diaz said matter-of-factly.

Maravilloso smiled, stepped over to Díaz, put her arms around him, and kissed his lips. "Why, Felix, you almost sound as if you really care about what happens to me," she said.

He kissed her again, grasping her shoulders seriously. "I admitted to you from the first day we met that I aspired to the presidency, Carmen," he said. "We even would not talk about marriage for that very reason, although you know how much I love you and want to spend the rest of my life with you. But I am not your political rival, or just your lover. I am a member of your government, and I am a Mexican. Whether you believe it or not, I do care about what happens to our country—and yes, I care about this government too, if for no other reason than I will have less to clean up after assuming this office."

"Do not try to pretend that you care that much, Felix," Maravilloso said. She pushed away from him and looked at him with great concern. "Why that stunt with the helicopter, Felix? You embarrassed me on worldwide television. You provoked a riot while I was talking to the President of the United States!"

"Carmen, I was out there inspecting that base firsthand—I didn't go out there to incite a riot or embarrass you," Diaz said. "It just made me angry that our people were being herded around like that. I wanted to be sure they knew their government was there looking out for them."

"That is *my* job, Felix—yours is to inform me of developments like this Rampart One abomination and help me decide the best course of action," Maravilloso said. "We need to keep avenues of dialogue open with the Americans, not shut them down. Do you understand, Felix?"

"Of course, Madam President."

The phone on her desk rang. She kissed him again, then held his face between her hands. "What in hell am I going to do with you, Felix Díaz?" she asked, then released him and went to her desk and picked up the phone. "I told you not to disturb me," she said into the receiver. "I will kick you in the . . . what? *He what?* Bring it in here immediately!" She hung up the phone.

"Fifteen minutes, on the dot," Díaz said.

"This is the real thing, Felix—another videotape by that Vera-cruz character, released to the press, with a detailed account of the incident in Arizona and calling for a worldwide insurgency against America to avenge the killings."

"The man might be a genius," Díaz said. "Imagine the power one could have if she could sway *every Hispanic man and woman* in the United States, Carmen! Imagine the influence one could have if you could take one tenth of America's entire workforce and not only order them *not* to show up for work, but to *rise up* against their employers! The American government would be forced to make a just deal for worker amnesty!"

"This Fuerza guy is a complete unknown—worse than a loose cannon, he is a criminal with a popular following," Maravilloso said. "How can you trust someone like that?"

"I think it is worth a try," Díaz said. "I might be able to use my special investigators, the *Sombras*, to find this man."

Maravilloso was silent for a long moment, then: "This is some-thing I cannot support, Felix," she said finally. "This Fuerza is too dangerous. He could turn on his handlers in an instant, like a wild animal trainer surrounded by lions."

"You and he, together—it would certainly be a very powerful combination."

She looked at him with a knowing smile. "Or it could be a disaster, and you would certainly benefit from that, would you not, Felix?" He did not reply. "You are not ready to give up your chance at the presidency of Mexico . . . for me," she said. His smile dimmed, only for a moment, but she knew she had hit her target. She made a little show of acting disappointed, happy that she had uncovered a tiny bit of the man, the *real* man, before her; then, as her assistant came into the office after a very quiet knock, shrugged her shoulders. "Good day to you, Minister Díaz," she said icily. "Please come again." Her tense body language and hooded eyes told him the meeting was definitely over—perhaps for good—and he departed with a courteous bow and no words.

Díaz paid courtesy visits on several government officials in the Palacio Nacional, shook hands with visitors, and made a brief statement in the press office about the worsening situation on the U.S.-Mexican border but said that he was confident that all could be resolved peacefully. Then he headed to his waiting car. The Ministry of Internal Affairs was located on the other side of the Federal District from the Palacio Nacional, south of the president's residence on Constitution Avenue in the center of the Bosque de Chapultepec, so even with a police escort it would take a long time to make it back to his office.

Although Díaz had ready access to a helicopter—he could even fly it himself, and had done so many times—he preferred the relative peace and quiet of his specially outfitted armored Mercedes S600 sedan and its wide array of secure voice, data, and video communications equipment, specially installed himself and tied into the government communications net only one way—he could access all government systems and networks, but they could not access *his*. With a police escort, he could get back to his office relatively quickly. He donned his lightweight headset and called back to his office and was immediately connected to José Elvarez, deputy minister of Internal Affairs, director of operations of the Political Police and of the *Sombras,* or Special Investigations Unit. "Report, José," Díaz ordered.

"Follow-up report regarding the visit by TALON One and Two and FBI Director DeLaine in San Diego, sir," Elvarez said. The computer screen in the back of the sedan came to life. It showed a photograph, obviously taken from the ground at a street intersection, through the clear windshield of a dark government-looking armored Suburban. Four persons could clearly be seen in the photo, two men and two women, seated in the rear two forward-facing rows of the vehicle, plus a driver and woman sitting in the front passenger seat. "Subjects were photographed leaving the FBI field office yesterday. The second man has just been identified as Paul Purdy, one of the U.S. Border Patrol agents believed to have been killed near Blythe, California."

"*Mi Díos,*" Díaz breathed, studying the digital photo. Damn, a survivor, a *witness*—that could be a very significant development. "Where did they take him?"

"They first went to Montgomery Airport, where DeLaine, her female bodyguard, and TALON Two were dropped off at her jet, and then the others went to a charity store in downtown San Diego," Elvarez said. The *Sombras* had managed to plant tracking devices on most of the American official government vehicles, and although the bugs were usually discovered and deactivated within a few days, quite often they could still get a great amount of useful intelligence from them. "They purchased several bags of clothes."

"Clothes, eh? From a charity used-clothing store? Sounds like they are going undercover."

"After that, they went to a market and came out with several more bags of supplies, then got on Interstate 15 northbound. We lost GPS tracking a few minutes later and notified all of our southern California lookouts to watch for the vehicle."

"And did someone spot it?"

"Yes, sir. It was observed arriving at the U.S. Border Patrol sector field office in Indio, California."

Interesting, Díaz thought—the heart of the Coachella Valley, with a very large concentration of illegal immigrants and smugglers nearby. "And then?"

"After two hours, TALON One and Purdy were observed wearing civilian clothes and getting into an unmarked civilian-asset-seizure vehicle. We had this vehicle under both electronic and agent surveillance. The vehicle was heading south on Route 196. The agents we had following the vehicle terminated visual contact when they suspected Purdy was making some countersurveillance turns, so we lost visual contact, but we are still tracking it electronically."

"Interesting," Díaz commented. "This Border Patrol agent, Purdy, seems quite resourceful. He may require some . . . *diligencia especial.*"

"Understood, sir," Elvarez said. "The vehicle made several stops along Route 196 and Highway 111 before stopping last night at a motel south of Niland. We have not made direct visual contact with the subjects in the past few hours but we now have their vehicle under both visual and electronic surveillance."

"I need round-the-clock direct visual contact on the subjects, José," Díaz said. "Put your best men on this one. This Agent Purdy seems very well trained and experienced—unusual for a Border Patrol agent. He may be getting countersurveillance help from Richter and Vega, so tell your men to be extra careful, or they could be face-to-face with one of those robots."

"My best men in southern California are already on it, sir."

"Good. Now we need to find out what those three are up to."

"Unfortunately we do not have any listening devices in the FBI field office in San Diego," Elvarez said. "We can monitor comings and goings but cannot reliably tap their phone or data transmissions without risking discovery. The same is true for all of the high-level American government offices in southern California."

"But we *do* have some good human intelligence . . . the consular office in San Diego," Díaz said. "The consulate has excellent connections in the U.S. Attorney's office. I think it's time to send the consul back out there to see what he can find out. That will be all, José. Find those three Americans and try to determine why they are playing spymaster." He terminated the secure phone call.

A *survivor* of that attack near Blythe, Díaz thought ruefully—that could be real trouble. But even more trouble could develop with President Maravilloso's request to meet with Ernesto Fuerza. Hopefully it was just an idle demand, soon to be forgotten once the political dangers became clear . . .

. . . but with Carmen Maravilloso, anything could happen. He had to be ready to make Fuerza available to meet the president soon. It was a meeting he was certainly not looking forward to making happen.

CHAPTER 7

U.S. FEDERAL COURTHOUSE,
LOS ANGELES, CALIFORNIA
LATER THAT DAY

"I'm very glad to see you, Señor Ochoa," Annette Cass, the U.S. Attorney for the southern district of California, said. She had met the deputy consul general of the United Mexican States' consulate in San Diego, Armando Ochoa, just outside the security screening station at the federal courthouse in Los Angeles. She waved at the security guards at the X-ray machine and metal detector and breezed past them before they could remind her to follow their security precautions. "I hope we can come to an agreement on settling the questions before us."

"As do I, Miss Cass," Ochoa said. "My government and my office wish to see all of the unpleasantness we have experienced settled and forgotten as soon as possible."

Cass escorted the Mexican deputy consul to her office and had her assistant fetch him coffee. "As I said before, Mr. Ochoa, my office still has not resolved the jurisdictional questions related to border security and the treatment of detainees suspected of illegally crossing the U.S.-Mexico border," Cass said. "With the recent attacks by the Consortium, Congress successfully passing a war resolution against them, and the perceived similarity between the recent attacks on the border and activities by the Consortium, the military has a pretty strong hand in this debate."

"I understand, Miss Cass," Ochoa said. "I am confident this will soon be resolved so there will be no more hostilities between our countries."

"We're all hoping for the same thing, sir." Cass withdrew a folder from a drawer in her desk. "I have been authorized to offer you a settlement on your own claims against my government for your treatment, Mr. Ochoa: formal apologies from the Secretary of Defense, Brigadier General Lopez the man in charge of the military operation, and Major Jason Richter, who was the officer in charge at the scene at the time of the offense; a guarantee of full reimbursement for any medical bills you may incur for a period of five years from the date of the incident; and a lump sum cash award of twenty-five thousand dollars. All my government asks in return is a strict gag order on the terms of our settlement."

The deputy consul took the offer form and looked it over. "I myself believe that this is an exceedingly generous offer," Ochoa said, "but of course I must confer with the consul general first before I can accept."

"I understand. I'm sure all sides will be as fair and flexible as possible."

"Of course." Ochoa paused for a moment, then: "So Brigadier General Lopez is still in charge of the border security operations along the U.S.-Mexico border?"

"Yes, sir. As I'm sure you know, the dynamics have changed in response to the recent killings in Arizona, but I assure you that the whole face of the operation has been toned down considerably. According to my briefing, the National Guard units currently being deployed on the border are completely subordinate to the U.S. Border Patrol. The Guard's job is merely to assist the Border Patrol in conducting surveillance, nothing more. They are prohibited from making arrests and will not impede or interdict any person unless that person is actually observed committing a serious crime. I would be pleased if you would pass this information along to the Mexican embassy in Washington."

"But of course," Ochoa said. "But there are other serious concerns."

"Oh?"

"As troubling as the presence of heavily armed National Guard troops on the border is, Miss Cass, my government is extremely concerned about those robots, the TALON devices . . ."

Cass appeared greatly relieved. "TALON? They are no longer involved in Operation Rampart," Cass said, waving a hand. "They are back doing . . . well, whatever they were doing before, chasing down bad guys, *real* bad guys like the Consortium, not in any way bothering Mexican citizens."

"Ah." Ochoa put on his best pained expression. "Then may I please ask you to comment on a recent report I received, Miss Cass, from an immigrant advocacy agency in Indio, California, that claimed that Major Richter was recently spotted at the U.S. Border Patrol sector headquarters?"

Cass's eyes bulged, and her mouth opened and closed in confusion. "I . . . I don't know anything about this, Mr. Deputy Consul, nothing at all," she said. "I was assured by the FBI and the Department of Defense that Task Force TALON was no longer involved whatsoever in border security operations. Perhaps your informants were mistaken, or Richter and Vega were involved in some other task . . . ?"

"I am sure you are correct, Miss Cass," Ochoa said, "but it would be very unlikely for the consul general to approve a settlement with the U.S. Justice Department with this question still lingering. Perhaps there is some way to check, perhaps with the commander of the sector headquarters?"

"Of course," Cass said. She picked up the phone on her desk. "Get me the Border Patrol sector commander in Indio right away." She turned to Ochoa. "Please remember, Mr. Ochoa, that this conversation and this information are highly confidential."

"Of course, Miss Cass. You have my solemn assurance that I will divulge nothing of this conversation. The consul general need not know anything about this phone call, only of the results of my negotiations regarding the settlement offer."

"Thank you." She turned to the phone: "Yes, hello, this is U.S. Attorney Annette Cass, southern district of California in Los Angeles. Who is this . . . ? Special Agent Roberts, I'm conducting an investigation involving the recent incidents at the Rampart One border security facility . . . yes, that's it, that's the incident . . . no, I know no one from your sector was involved. The reason I'm calling is to follow up on a report I've received that claimed that Army Major Jason Richter had a meeting at your headquarters recently, perhaps as early as yesterday.

"I . . . say again . . . ? Yes . . . no, I understand. I'll be waiting." Cass hung up the receiver. "A routine security procedure," she said to Ochoa. "He'll call the office back in a few minutes to verify that he wasn't talking to the media or some other person. Shouldn't take more than a minute."

"Of course. A wise precaution."

The phone rang a couple minutes later: "This is Cass . . . yes, I'm expecting his call . . . this is Cass . . . Special Agent Roberts, thank you for calling back so fast. Okay, what do you have for me . . . he was there yesterday. I see. My reports were accurate then . . . you didn't? You didn't request a meeting with him? Then why were they . . . what? I see . . . that's incredible . . . well, that's good news, that's great news. But I still don't see how Richter and Purdy are involved. Any involvement on their part could be extremely serious to any legal or diplomatic initiatives with the Mexican government. Who authorized them to . . . oh. I see. No, I wasn't informed . . . I know, we're all supposed to be on the same team, but apparently it doesn't apply both ways between investigations and the prosecutors' office—or the White House, at least when TALON is involved. I shouldn't have to play phone tag to find out information from my own department . . . well, I appreciate your assistance, Mr. Roberts. Thank you." She hung up the phone with a disturbed expression.

"So it is true, Miss Cass?" Ochoa prompted her after a few silent moments. "My information was correct—TALON is still involved in some way with border security operations?"

"I wouldn't be too hasty to come to conclusions, Mr. Ochoa," Cass said with an edge in her voice. "Richter and Purdy definitely were at the Indio sector headquarters, but the purpose of their visit and their involvement with the Border Patrol is still unclear."

"Unclear? But did you not just speak with the man in charge . . ."

"The special agent in charge of the sector didn't know what was going on," Cass explained. "Apparently there are some witnesses who survived the shootings near Blythe, California a few weeks ago. I don't know why, but TALON was asked to assist in the search for other witnesses that may be in the area. They're out looking for them in the Indio sector now."

"Is that not a job for the FBI, Miss Cass?"

Cass looked pained, even embarrassed. "The FBI *is* involved—apparently the director of the FBI as well as the director of Customs and Border Protection contacted the special agent in charge and notified him of this activity, but there are very few other details. I will probably need to contact someone in Washington, perhaps the Secretary of Homeland Security himself, to get to the bottom of this."

"This is highly irregular, Miss Cass," Ochoa said. He could easily tell that Cass was lost in her own thoughts: he was quickly being dismissed from her attention and would be gone in moments if he didn't do something. "*¡Esto es absurdo!*" Ochoa barked. He shot to his feet and asked indignantly, "What is going on here, Miss Cass?" His sudden movement and shrill tone startled her—the first time he had ever seen this tough lady surprised. "I came here as a gesture of good will, seeking to put the past episodes of violence and mistrust behind us and start afresh, but instead I am being stonewalled and given misleading and evasive information. Exactly what is the meaning of this, señora?"

"Mr. Ochoa, I assure you, I would like to cooperate with you, but I'm in the dark as much as you are," Cass said, flustered and confused. "The U.S. Attorney for the appropriate district is usually notified of any ongoing federal investigations, especially if it involves multidepartment operations. I don't like being given only half the facts like this, and I'm going to get some answers." She stood, walked around her desk, and extended a hand apologetically. "Unfortunately, I won't have any answers for you this afternoon, Mr. Ochoa. I will be sure to notify you as soon as I've . . ."

"*¡Esto es indignante!* I have never been treated so disrespectfully since . . . since I was assaulted by those soldiers at Rampart One!" Ochoa said hotly. "You will be hearing from the consul general about this, and so will your State Department! Good day to you, madam!" He ignored her proffered hand, spun on his heel, and left the office.

Annette Cass stood in the center of her office with a blank expression on her face—but only for a moment. "Laura! Get me Director DeLaine on the phone! I want answers, and I want them *now!*"

It took several minutes, during which time Cass fired off several angry e-mails to the Attorney General, her assistant prosecutors, and several judges who might become involved in this case, complaining about what she had learned that afternoon. Finally: "This is Director DeLaine."

"Miss DeLaine, this is Annette Cass, U.S. Attorney for the southern California district."

"How are you, Annette?" Kelsey DeLaine said, her voice businesslike and neutral, not friendly but not yet confrontational.

"I'm angry, that's how I am, Miss Director. I just learned from the commander of the Border Patrol sector field office in Indio, California, that Richter was there. The indications were that the FBI is conducting an investigation regarding the shootings near Blythe. Why wasn't I informed of this?"

"It's an FBI investigation, Annette. You'll be brought in as soon as we need support from your office."

"Miss Director, I'm not sure if you're fully aware of how we do things out here, but it's customary to bring the U.S. Attorney's of-

fice in right away, at the *beginning* of any investigation, even if
there's no requirement or . . ."

"And I'm not sure if you're aware of how *I* do things, Miss
Cass," Kelsey interjected. "It's simple: when I need you, or if the
field office in San Diego who's coordinating this investigation
needs you, we'll call you." Cass was momentarily flustered into
silence—she was not accustomed to being blown off like that.
"Anything else for me, Annette?"

Cass quickly decided that confronting the director of the FBI
was not going to gain her anything at this point. "What is going on
out here, Miss Director?" Cass asked. "I'm asking for a little
heads-up, that's all. If there's anything I can contribute, I'd be
happy to do so, but I need a little background info first."

"You wouldn't happen to be annoyed because Richter is out
walking around free and clear and still in your district?"

Cass silently swore at DeLaine. "Of course, I'm *concerned*
about his activities, Miss Director," she admitted. "I've still got
U.S. marshals in the hospital with serious injuries, and no one is
being punished for that. It's still my opinion that Richter is part
of the problem, not the solution. But I also hate surprises; I'm
sure you do too. I have sixty prosecutors and a staff of five hundred standing ready to assist and support other local, state, and
federal agencies in their work, especially the FBI. I'm accustomed to being asked for support, that's all. I'm *trying* to help,
Miss Director."

There was a slight pause on the other end of the line; then: "All
I can tell you right now, Annette, is that we received information
that there are witnesses to the murders at Blythe."

"*Witnesses?* That's great! Who are they? Migrants? Border
Patrol?"

"One of the Border Patrol agents on the scene that we reported
as killed survived," Kelsey said, hesitant to talk too much and anxious to end this call. "We debriefed him at our office in San Diego.
He reported that there were not one, but two smugglers at the
scene of the shooting. The second one, a kid named Flores, is miss-

ing. Richter and the surviving agent are going down there to try to find him."

"Why the Border Patrol and TALON? Why not the FBI?"

DeLaine hesitated again, afraid she was talking too much, but hurried on: "The Border Patrol agent identified one of the men at the shooting scene near Blythe as possibly being Yegor Zakharov."

"*Zakharov!* The terrorist? *He's* back in the U.S. . . . ?"

"That's what we're looking into," Kelsey said. "The shooters at Blythe could have been Consortium. If it was Zakharov and the Consortium, Task Force TALON has the authority to go after them anywhere in the world."

"Well . . . yes . . . yes, I agree," Cass said, mollified. "This is all new information, Miss Director. Thank you for sharing it with me. My office will do anything we can to help. I hope they find Flores."

"Thank you, Miss Cass. I am the point of contact for all matters dealing with TALON. Don't hesitate to call if necessary."

"Yes, Miss Director."

"This is all confidential information, of course, Annette."

"Of course." The phone connection was broken . . .

. . . but another connection—a small listening device planted under the front edge of Cass's desk, directly opposite of where Ochoa had been seated—was still very much alive.

BAKERSFIELD, CALIFORNIA
A SHORT TIME LATER

The streetwalkers were so easy, especially the older ones who thought they knew how to handle their johns. Act macho and smooth during the initial exchange; change to acting indecisive and unsure during negotiations to reel the girl in; then act apprehensive and a little scared as each date began in the hotel room. A few drinks, some tense necking, some clumsy stripping and play-acting to get the john hard, and then let her get on top and have the reins so she might think this was going to be an easy "wham-bang-thank-you-ma'am" date.

Then, when she was ready to wrap it up and leave—turn the tables, quickly and violently. Make her fear for her safety within seconds, and then her life within a minute or two. Delight in watching her transform from an experienced pro to a quivering, whimpering, begging child. Anything goes at that point—she was ready to accept anything, agree to do any perversity or act, as long as she believed she had a chance to survive and get out of that room alive and relatively unhurt.

They were usually gone in the wink of an eye when he was finished, and they didn't stop for several blocks. They would notice that the money was fake then, but most wouldn't have the courage to go back for it. A few had their pimps and enforcers go back to try to collect—that's usually when he would pick up a new gun, maybe some nice jewelry, and some traveling cash before leaving that part of town, before the cops found the badly mutilated bodies he'd leave behind.

Yegor Zakharov had just finished one such encounter—his second of the evening—and was on his way back to the place he had left his car when his satellite phone rang. He read the decryption code on the display, looked up the unlock code on a card in his pocket, entered it, and waited until he heard the electronic chirps and beeps stop. "*¿Chto eto?*"

"Tell me your men did not enjoy it, Colonel," the voice of Ernesto Fuerza said.

"Fuck you. My men and I are not your wet-workers."

"But they *did* enjoy it, no?"

"What do you want?"

"The Americans are putting a thousand National Guard troops per week out on the border over the next few months," Fuerza said. "The Mexican government and the Hispanic community in America will explode long before that. The revolution is well underway, thanks to you."

"I am happy for you, *zalupa*."

"Within days the backlash will start," Fuerza went on. "The editorials in the liberal newspapers will start to moan about the cost and the ugliness of armed troops on the peaceful borders; the human rights groups will be at fever pitch within a week, filing lawsuits and making their case on every TV show in the world to protect the immigrants and condemn the neofascist government; and Hispanic people from all over the world will start to fight, with the radicals and revolutionaries leading the fight, soon to be joined by the common people, and soon after that by the politicians, headline-grabbers, and even actors. The American government will be on its guilt-ridden, confused, beleaguered knees in no time."

"What the fuck do you want?"

"To give you a reward, my friend. I have information that you might find very gratifying."

"How much is it going to cost me?"

"Not a penny, *tovarisch*."

"Another ambush, to be broadcast on the damned Internet?"

"You may do with the information as you wish, my friend—it is entirely up to you."

"So? What is this reward?"

"I know exactly where your friend Major Jason Richter is right now, Colonel."

"*What?* Where?"

"I knew you would be pleased," Fuerza said. "He is searching for you in the migrant community of the Imperial Valley, just a few hours south of you, with a Border Patrol agent by the name of Purdy. It is just the two of them, and they are not being supported by anyone, especially not the U.S. attorney in San Diego who would certainly throw anyone from Task Force TALON in prison if she could. They appear to be out on their own—they are no longer part of Task Force TALON, Operation Rampart, or any other organization I can discern." Fuerza gave him details of how and where they were to be spotted.

"This had better not be a setup, Fuerza," Zakharov warned, "or I'll spend the rest of my life hunting you down so I can take great pleasure in stripping the skin from your body, a bit at a time."

"Call my satellite phone number at any time and ask me for assistance, Colonel," Fuerza said. "I will be close by, and so will my men."

"Then let us take them together, you and I."

"I am not so foolish as to face this robot enemy of yours, Colonel—I will be happy to leave him all to you and those heavy weapons I sold to you," Fuerza said. "My target is much more vulnerable: a survivor of our rendezvous near Blythe. I wish to keep him from talking to the authorities, so I will be in the same area looking for him."

"I warn you again, Fuerza—you had better not double-cross me, or you had better pray that they kill me, because if you send me into a trap and I'm still alive afterward . . ."

"Do not worry, Colonel—I promise, this is not a setup," Fuerza insisted. "I wish to do business with you again many times in the future. And as you undoubtedly know, there is a price on my head as well, almost as great as yours—I will certainly never be allowed to keep any reward money."

NILAND, CALIFORNIA
TWO DAYS LATER

Maria Arevalo rose before daybreak every morning without the help of an alarm clock—the sound of trucks, buses, farm equipment, and sleepy men getting ready for another hard day at work was her only wake-up call. Careful not to disturb her three children, sleeping either in or around her bed, she tiptoed to the kitchen to put on a large pot of coffee and began making breakfast. Her husband had already left for the day's work; the children could sleep in another couple hours before they had to get ready.

She lived in a two-room shack in a remote corner of a relatively small two-thousand-acre lettuce and cilantro farm near the town of Niland in the Imperial Valley of southern California, just east of the southern tip of the Salton Sea. During most of the growing season, Maria worked the fields with her husband, but in the summer she made meals for the thirty or so migrant farmworkers here. It was hard, exhausting work alone in the tiny kitchen, but she preferred it to being in the blazing sun all day with the others, doing "stoop labor."

Breakfast was scrambled eggs with tomatoes, peppers, and scallions, potatoes, refried beans, beef and chicken tacos, gorditas, coffee, and water. Maria charged four dollars per man per day for breakfast and lunch; she gave 20 percent to the owner for the use of the shack, paid for the food, and kept the rest for herself and her family. The men ate well and it was easier, faster, cheaper, and safer than going home for meals; the owner and farm foreman liked it because the men stayed on the job site and they could keep an eye on them; and Maria liked it because she loved cooking and her only other option was to work in the fields herself.

By the time everything was cooked and loaded up into large pans for the trip out to the fields, it was time to get the children up and dressed. Fortunately Maria's older daughter, at age eight and a half, was more than capable of helping her younger brother get ready, while Maria handled the infant daughter. At seven-thirty a small rickety bus arrived to take the boy to the community day care center, and a few minutes later the older daughter caught a station wagon filled with kids to go to summer school to brush up on her English and math before beginning second grade in the fall in the Imperial County public elementary school. The infant stayed with Maria; she tried to give her as much attention as possible, but unfortunately the baby stayed strapped into her car seat for most of the day, with a little battery-powered fan to help keep her cool and to keep pesky flies and mosquitoes away.

About that same time a forty-year-old milk delivery truck pulled up to the shack, and an older gentleman wearing the ever-present green bib overalls and old crusty work boots greeted Maria. *"Buenos dias, señora. ¿Como esta?"*

"You are late, old man," she said irritably in Spanish.

"Perdon," the man said. He stepped out of the truck along with a younger man in tattered jeans, two layers of faded flannel shirts, sunglasses, thick horn-rimmed glasses, and ratty sneakers and began loading up the food, urns of water and coffee, and cardboard boxes of clean place-ware.

Maria was irked that the younger man took so long adjusting the lids to the water urns, but finally everything was secure and tightly strapped down for the bumpy ride into the fields. "Let us be off." Maria made sure the stove and oven were off, locked the door to the shack behind her, and climbed aboard the truck. She changed a diaper and fed the baby on the way to the fields.

Ten minutes after eight the truck rumbled to a stop on the side of the private dirt access road beside Highway 111, and Maria beeped the horn. The two men hurriedly set up two folding tables and started setting out the pans of food and the urns of coffee and water, with Maria busily behind them, stirring the pots and arranging everything just so. As they worked, the men started walking in from the lettuce field toward their waiting breakfast, wiping sweat from their faces and dirt from their hands—they had already been hard at work for hours, and everyone was ravenous. A few minutes later a worker on a tractor pulling a trailer full of boxes drove up, jumping off the tractor excitedly and chatting with the others in line as he waited for his turn.

The workers moved down the line quickly—the faster they got their food, the more time they had to rest. Maria and her helpers were constantly rearranging the pans and urns as the workers jostled their way through the line—the workers tried to help, but Maria's helpers politely but firmly reset things themselves, greeting each one and wishing them a good day.

"Usted parece fuerte," one of the workers said to the young helper standing behind the urn of water as he helped himself to a cup of water. *"Usted debe estar fuera allí de ayudarnos."* The helper

smiled and nodded. "*Venido. ¿Usted puede tomar mi lugar,* okay?"
The helper only nodded again, keeping his eyes averted. The
worker looked at him with some aggravation. "*¿O usted tiene gusto
quizá de trabajar en la cocina como una mujer?*" The helper only
nodded again, then headed back to the truck. "Hey. *¡Vete a hacer
punetas, amaricado!*"

"Watch your language, José," Maria scolded the worker. "Go
back and sit with the lettuce if you want to swear."

"Well, that asshole is just ignoring me," the worker named José
said. "What's his problem?"

"Maybe you're scaring him, you big bully," Maria said playfully.

"Where do you find these *pendejos*, Maria?" Jose asked. The
urn of water was almost empty, so José had to tip it forward to fill
his cup.

"I will gladly hire anyone willing to put up with the likes of
you, José. Now get out of here and finish your meal before you
make him cry."

"I would like to see him cry, Maria," the worker said, laughing.
The helper was just coming back from the truck with a full urn of
water, carrying the heavy seven-gallon metal jug with both hands.
"Maybe he would not do so well out in the field after all—looks
like he can barely carry that jug. You need some help, *pedo?*"

The worker wasn't paying attention to what he was doing, and
as he tipped the urn farther and farther, the lid slipped off. The
young helper noticed what was happening, and in a flash of motion dropped the urn of water he was carrying and lunged for the
lid. But it was too late. The lid fell, but was prevented from hitting
the table by some wires. José lifted the lid and examined it—and
that's when he noticed what looked like a tiny camera lens built
into the lid.

"Hey! What's this . . . ?" The young helper snatched the lid out
of José's hand. José glared angrily at the helper—and then realized
that he had *blue eyes,* something not often seen out in the fields.
"Who the hell are *you?*"

"*¿Problema, amigo?*" the older helper asked, stepping over to the younger man and pushing him toward the delivery truck. "You, pick up that water and stop being so damned clumsy." To the worker he said in Spanish, "Don't worry about him, amigo. He is my wife's cousin's boy." He tapped the side of his own head. "He is a little slow, you know what I mean?"

But as he spoke, he realized he recognized the worker named José . . . and at the same instant, José recognized him too. Paul Purdy closed his eyes, but it was too late. He could only mutter, "Oh, shit . . ." before the whole place erupted into sheer bedlam.

"Purdy . . . *puneta!* It's Purdy!" José turned toward the others squatting next to the road eating. *"¡La Migra! ¡La Migra! ¡Inmigración!"* Workers scattered in all directions, dashing through the cilantro and lettuce fields as fast as they could.

"Smart move, Purdy—the men can spot a *federale* a mile away, especially if he has blue eyes," Maria said with a smile and a shake of her head as she started to pack up her pans. "Why did you hire a gringo to go undercover with you in a migrant farm? Are you crazy?"

"I got the best help I could find, darlin'," Border Patrol Agent Paul Purdy replied with a smile as he began to unzip his overalls.

"You know, I'm never going to be able to work in this part of the county again, Purdy—everyone will think I work with the *federales* now," she said.

"I told you I'd make it good, Maria," Purdy said as he climbed out of his overalls and retrieved his utility belt, badge, bulletproof vest, police jacket, and sidearm from the truck. "I found a job for you out in Twentynine Palms . . ."

"Twentynine Palms? You mean, working at a military base? No way, Purdy!"

"I found schools for your kids and a job for your husband . . ."

"I said no way."

"Okay, Maria. Oh, did I mention . . . ?"

"What now?"

"It comes with a green card."

"¡Acepto!" Maria said immediately.

"I thought you might. My boys are taking your kids to the church right now, and they'll move you to a place up there and keep an eye on you until our operation is over. Trust me, will you? Have I ever steered you wrong, love?"

Maria smiled, shook her head, and waved her hand down the road. "Just go, will you? Unless you're going to leave your blue-eyed assistant with me to help clean up?"

"Sorry, sweetie. He's got work to do," Purdy said. He turned to Richter. "Any hits on that gadget of yours, Major?"

"Stand by," Jason Richter said, hopping into the milk truck. With Maria's baby daughter looking on with interest, Jason pulled out a small tablet PC computer and awakened the screen, which was flipping through pictures of each of the migrant workers who had come up to the tables for their morning meal. The DDICE, or digital distant identification and collection equipment system, digitally scanned every person who walked within thirty feet of the fine line scan digital imager on top of the water urn, measuring and cataloging hundreds of different physical parameters in a matter of seconds. The system then compared the collected information with a database of known suspects, and would alert the user if there was a match.

"C'mon, Major, we don't have all day," Purdy said anxiously, scanning the fields where all the workers had scattered. "In about two minutes they're all going to be gone."

"Still processing."

"Nuts to that," Purdy said. He continued scanning the fields until he found what he was looking for—one worker who wasn't running, hiding behind the front of the tractor, watching. "I got him, Major. Follow me." He turned on his walkie-talkie and ran out into the lettuce field. The young migrant worker looked confused. "Hold it, Victor! ¡Parada! It's me, Purdy! ¡Espera! Dammit!"

Jason looked over in amazement. "How did you know that was Flores? How did you know he wouldn't run?"

"I told you, he knows me—they *all* know me," Purdy said.

"They know I'm not out here to screw them." Thankfully Victor Flores stopped a few yards later—Purdy had run less than fifty yards but was already feeling winded. But then Flores starting looking around—not like he was searching for a better direction to run, but searching for something else. "Hold on, Victor. It's me, Purdy. I'm here to help you. Wait and I'll . . ."

Suddenly Flores turned and bolted down a row of lettuce—just as an immense geyser of mud and shattered lettuce erupted in the spot near where he was standing. *"Shots fired, shots fired!"* Purdy shouted into his walkie-talkie. "Get some help out here, Richter!" He drew his service automatic and flattened out on his stomach, with nothing but a row of lettuce to shield him. To Flores, he shouted, *"¡Consiga abajo!* Victor, get down!" Victor ran a few more yards before half-jumping, half-tripping face-first into a plowed furrow.

Back at the delivery truck, Jason keyed another handheld communicator: "Talon Two, this is One. We've got a sniper out here somewhere on Highway 111. Bring in the Condor and see if you can draw some fire."

"On the way, One," Ariadna Vega responded. She had not returned to Washington with Kelsey, but instead had returned to the Condor airship's control trailer parked at Montgomery Field to assist Richter and Purdy in the search for Flores.

Jason ran around to the back and opened the double doors. At the very bottom of a set of steel shelves along the right side of the truck, he pulled a rectangular container out of the back and let it fall to the ground. "CID One, deploy," he said. As Maria watched in surprise, the container began to move, and within a minute it had unfolded itself into a nine-foot-tall two-legged robot. "CID One, pilot up," Richter said, and the robot assumed a stance with one leg extended behind it, crouched down, and its two arms angled back to form a railing. Jason hopped up behind the robot and slid inside it. A few moments later, the robot with Richter inside got up out of its crouch and sped off with amazing speed into the lettuce field.

Jason reached Purdy in a flash, covering him as best he could from their unseen assailant. "Where's Flores?" Purdy shouted.

"I don't think we need him to find Zakharov anymore, Paul—looks like *he* found *us,*" Jason said. He activated the robot's on-board radar sensor, which picked up every object within a two-mile radius. There were several trucks parked on another dirt road on the other side of the highway, plus a few dozen workers in the fields beyond and the fleeing workers behind him. There was one person running away closest to them—he assumed it was Flores. "I've got Flores. I need to find where that . . ."

At that instant the radar tracking computer issued a warning—it had picked up a high-speed projectile fired from the highway directly at Flores. The tracking radar pinpointed the origin of the bullet as well as its unfortunate terminus. "I've got the shooter," Jason said. "Flores went down. Wait until I reach the truck, then help Flores." He ran off again.

The target truck, a three-quarter-ton pickup with a large camper on the bed, was about a hundred yards away, parked on the side of the highway instead of on the dirt road like the other nearby trucks. The robot's magnifying visual sensors picked up a man with a sniper rifle propped on the hood of the truck—a *Russian* sniper rifle. It could only be Yegor Zakharov.

"Richter!" Purdy shouted, gesturing at the man crossing the highway. "It's Zakharov! Get that bastard!" Richter started to run at the vehicle—once he picked up full speed, he would reach it in seconds.

But at that moment, the back doors of the camper flew open, and two men with what looked like guided missile launchers leaped out, arrayed themselves on either side of the pickup, aimed, and fired almost simultaneously.

The first round hit squarely on the left side of the robot's chest, and the force of the blast of the missile's three-pound warhead spun Jason around and up into the air like a child throwing a rag doll out of a speeding car. The second missile missed by less than a foot, but its proximity fuse detected the miss and detonated the warhead a few yards behind Jason, adding a second tremendous concussion to the first. The robot flew several yards in the air, spinning and cartwheeling madly within the cloud of fire and smoke of the double blasts, before coming to a smoldering stop on the side of the highway.

"Oh, *man!*" Purdy gasped. The robot was lying in a heap on the side of the highway, blackened and still smoking. He got up and started running toward Richter, but soon realized he had his own problems here: the two soldiers had run back to the camper and were retrieving two more antitank missiles; Zakharov started to walk across the highway toward the robot with a large sniper rifle in his hands. He crouched down on one knee, leveled his pistol, and took aim.

But in a flash Zakharov fired the rifle without even raising the sights to his eye, firing from his hip. Purdy felt the air gush out of his lungs in an explosive "*Whufff!*" His vision exploded in a cloud of stars, his head spun, the pain radiated through his chest and across his entire body, and he pitched over backward into a row of lettuce.

"You must be Border Patrol Agent Purdy, the clever and enter-prising veteran I have heard so much about," he heard Zakharov say a few moments later. "I am pleased to meet you."

"Yeah?" Purdy grunted, barely able to speak. "Now you can do me a big favor and kiss my ass, Zakharov."

"I have a much more productive use for your ass, Agent Purdy." Zakharov pulled Purdy to his feet, helped by his two missileers, and together they dragged him about thirty feet in front of the stricken CID unit. Two more soldiers appeared from the camper, automatic rifles at the ready. Richter was slowly getting to his feet—he was obviously struggling through some internal damage, but he still appeared to be operational. "Is that you in there, Major Richter?" Zakharov shouted. He slung his Dragunov rifle over a shoulder, pulled out an automatic pistol, and pointed it at Purdy's head. "I have a proposition for you, my friend. Come out of there."

Richter was now on his hands and knees, trying unsuccessfully to put his armored feet under him, but he was able to look up. "Either shoot me or run, Zakharov," he said, "because if you're still standing there yakking in fifteen seconds, I'm going to tear you into tiny little pieces."

Zakharov shouted an order in Russian, and immediately the two soldiers with the antitank missiles activated and pointed them at Richter. "I am going to ask you one question, Richter," the Russian said. "My demand is simple: get out of the robot and collapse it for transport, and I promise you and Purdy will live. Refuse, and you die. The next word you utter will determine whether you live or die. You have five seconds to respond."

"*Don't do it, Richter!*" Purdy shouted. "He'll kill us anyway!"

"Okay, Zakharov, I agree," Richter said immediately. "Put the guns and missiles on the ground and let Purdy go."

"No conditions, Richter," Zakharov said. "Do as I tell you, or die."

"You want the CID unit in one piece, Zakharov? You put your weapons down. Otherwise go ahead and fire those missiles."

Zakharov hesitated, then smiled, nodded, and barked an order to his men, who disbelievingly safed and lowered their weapons and laid them on the ground. Zakharov was the last to relinquish his.

The soldiers released Purdy, who painfully hobbled across the road. "*Now get up and nail him, Richter!*" Purdy screamed. "Get him, or we're dead!" But moments later the CID unit assumed its load stance, the hatch on the robot's back popped open, and Jason Richter climbed out. "Oh, shit . . ." Purdy retrieved his pistol from the field and aimed it at Zakharov; as he did so, the soldiers retrieved their rifles as well. "You're under arrest, Zakharov!" Zakharov merely smiled, casually picked up his pistol and Dragunov rifle, holstered the pistol, and slung the rifle over his shoulder. "Don't move!"

"Don't, Paul," Jason said. "He won't go far with it, and he's too stupid to figure out how to operate it."

"Stop, Richter!" Purdy shouted. "I'm warning you, he's not just after the robot!"

"We got no choice, Paul."

"Richter, *don't* . . . *!*"

But Jason jumped off the robot, then ordered, "CID One, stow." The robot began to collapse, intricately folding itself down to the size of a large steamer trunk.

"Wise move, Major," Zakharov said. He picked up the antitank missile canisters, ordered two of his men to pick up the stowed CID unit, then pulled his pistol from his holster and aimed it at Richter. "But I have decided that I need both of you to come with me now. Drop your weapons."

"Screw you, Zakharov!" Purdy screamed, and he started shooting and at the same time diving for cover into the shallow ditch at the side of the road.

Jason ducked, ran backward, and reached down to the remote CID control unit on his wrist to enter auto-defense commands to the robot, but Zakharov was too fast. A bullet caught Jason in the right thigh, and he went down. "Grab him and the robot and let's get out of here!" Zakharov shouted in Russian. *"Move!"* He fired a shot in Purdy's direction as his soldiers scooped up Richter and dragged the folded CID unit toward their camper.

A sudden unexpected movement caught Zakharov's eye, and he looked up into the morning sky—at the sight of an immense bird zooming down at him! "What in hell is *that?*" Swooping down toward the melee, still several hundred feet in the sky but moving in with breathtaking speed, was a massive aircraft with long, gracefully sweeping wings and a bulbous fuselage. It was one of the Condor unmanned reconnaissance airships, barreling almost straight down at them like an eagle about to capture its prey.

"Don't stop! Get them into the truck!" Zakharov shouted. "I will take care of this thing!" Zakharov began firing his rifle at the airship, but it kept on coming at them. He reloaded a fresh magazine of shells and took aim again. The airship started to wobble, slightly at first and then more wildly as more and more helium escaped from chambers throughout its structure.

At that moment he felt a bullet whiz just centimeters past his head. He didn't even have to look to know who fired that shot. "I have had enough of you, Agent Purdy," Zakharov said. "Time to end your tired old existence." He unslung his rifle from his shoulder, raised, aimed, and . . .

. . . at that moment another motion caught his eye, and he turned to see a wounded Victor Flores driving the farm tractor right at him! It looked like most of Flores's right shoulder was gone and blood covered almost his entire torso, but he was still conscious and shouting epithets as he barreled toward the Russian. He dodged as fast as he could and swung the Dragunov around, but the large right tire clipped him, nearly running him over.

"A brave move, young man," Zakharov said. He swung his rifle around and fired at the passing tractor. A cloud of red gore exploded out of Victor Flores's chest, and he slumped forward, dead before he hit the steering wheel. The tractor continued on across the highway, overturning into a ditch on the other side.

Zakharov's right hip was throbbing, and he was angry enough to chew nails. "*¡Pidar!*" he swore. He was seriously hurt, and he realized he had to get out of there before the police showed up. He started hobbling toward the camper, holding his side . . .

. . . when he saw something that surprised him—the farmworkers running out of the fields, carrying shovels, picking tools, rakes, and anything else they could use as a weapon. "*¡Consígalo! ¡Mátelo!*" they shouted, raising their tools and fists into the air. "You kill Victor Flores—now we kill *you!*" Farther down the road, Zakharov could see several other farmworkers rushing his pickup truck.

"Let's get out of here, Colonel!" one of the commandos shouted. He turned his submachine gun toward the farmworkers and fired a burst. They took cover behind the camper, then started rocking it, threatening to overturn it in moments. Gunshots erupted from inside the cab as the driver fired at the crowd from inside the truck, but before he could fire again one of the workers poked him in the face with a shovel, knocking the gun out of his hand, and then the others were on him.

Zakharov drew his pistol and fired. Three farmworkers went down, and the rest turned and fled into the fields for cover. Zakharov scared the others off with shots from his sidearm, got into the camper, and he and the last three commandos sped south down Highway 111.

Back in the lettuce field, a small crowd of farmworkers along with Maria Arevalo slowly approached Purdy. The Border Patrol agent was awake but lying down, grimacing in pain as he smoked a cigarette. "You okay, Purdy?" she asked.

"The bastard broke my damned sternum, I think," Purdy said, "but I'm still alive. I remembered the shock plate this time. Something to tell the grandkids when they get older, I guess—Grandpa was shot by the world-famous terrorist mastermind Colonel Yegor Zakharov, and survived. I hope." He reached up and grasped Maria's hand. "How about granting a dying man's one last wish, eh, gorgeous?"

"You must be hallucinating, old man," Arevalo said with a smile, dropping his hand in mock disgust. "Or should I ask my husband what he thinks of your request?"

"You broke my heart again with the 'H' word, baby," Purdy said. "Where's that Russian?"

"Got away," Maria said.

"Dammit, Richter deserves to get tortured for tryin' to make a deal with that snake," Purdy muttered. He pulled out a cellular phone, praying he could get a signal out here and relieved when he got one.

"DeLaine."

"Miss Director, this is Purdy."

"What's happened, Purdy? You don't sound good."

"I got real bad news. We ran into Zakharov, and he was ready for us. He got Richter and his robot."

"He *what?* Where's he headed?"

"DeLaine, you need to get the Border Patrol, the California Highway Patrol, the Imperial County Sheriff's Department, and every soldier, sailor, airman, and Marine from El Centro to help you cover all the routes between Niland, California, and the border—you'll need everyone you can scrape up," Purdy said. "They were heading south on Highway 111 toward Brawley and El Centro. My guess is Zakharov is headed for the border. He's got three guys and some heavy weapons with him. Get the Highway Patrol with infrared scanners to look in the fields and orchards, and have them seal off Highway 98 and Interstate 8 tight."

"I'm on it, Purdy."

Purdy ended his call, then painfully walked over to the tractor across the road. A small group of workers had pulled the body of Victor Flores out of the wreckage and onto the ground. His bullet-torn body made him look even younger than he was. If he ever had a son, Purdy thought, he hoped he would have half the courage of this young man.

He knelt beside him and brushed his hair and cheeks, hoping that he could see some sign of life, but his wounds were simply too massive. "Zakharov, you are one cold son of a bitch to shoot an innocent kid like this," he said angrily. "If it's the last thing I do, you are going *down*."

"*¿Qué dijo usted,* Purdy?" one of the workers asked him.

Purdy shook his head—it was between him, Victor Flores, and God, he thought. "*Una promesa a Victor, señor,*" he said. He gave the young man another pat on the cheek. "*Gracias por salvar mi vida, amigo,*" he said. "Thanks for saving my hide, buddy. Don't worry about Zakharov—I'll get the bastard for you."

Zakharov ditched the camper at a rest stop on Route S30 near Calipatria for a Dodge Caravan minivan driven by an older retired couple, and they headed east toward the Coachella Canal through endless fields of crops in the fertile Imperial Valley. At the intersection of Routes S33 and 78, fearing that the elderly owners of the minivan would have had time to report the theft, they transferred all of their remaining weapons and equipment to a battered farmer's pickup truck that had the keys left in it, ditched the Caravan, and continued south.

As they drove away, Zakharov snapped off the satellite phone. "Dammit, I am not sure if I'm getting through to anyone—there's a connection, but no response," he said. "Fuerza had better answer me, or I hunt him down *next*. We are only twenty miles or so from the border, but they will certainly have shut down the highways and border crossing points."

"There is a steel fence on the border twenty miles either side of Calexico—they will certainly deploy every Border Patrol agent in this sector there," one of the commandos said.

"We go east around the fence," Zakharov said. "We will make better time on the highway than in the fields, and we will get off and cross the border as soon as we are clear of the fence."

Instead of getting on Interstate 8 near Holtville, they took the Evan Hewes Highway, which paralleled the freeway, being very careful not to go too fast or do anything to attract attention; Zakharov slumped down in his seat so he wouldn't be recognized. Soon they saw one, then two, then several California Highway Patrol interceptors, lights and sirens flashing, cruising both sides of the interstate highway. A few minutes later, they saw a gray military helicopter fly overhead. "A Navy helicopter, probably from El Centro," Zakharov said. "They want us very badly, I think."

It appeared they made the right decision by going east instead of straight south, because most of the police action seemed to center near Bonds Corner and Highway 98, close to the border. But Zakharov's military-trained sixth sense told him that even this dusty highway was no place to be for very much longer. "We need to get off this road," he said, after trying for the umpteenth time to make a connection with his satellite phone. "We are violating all the rules of tactical evasion. The police will have the highways closed off soon. We will hide this truck and go to ground until nightfall, then find a way across the border."

The highway was so straight and flat that it was easy to see several miles ahead, and soon Zakharov saw what he had feared: a roadblock set up ahead, both on the interstate and frontage road. They turned north off the highway at a farm access road and stopped at a portable restroom set up at the edge of a field. The men began arming themselves, preparing at any moment to jump out of the truck and fight if necessary. They were surrounded by fields of durum wheat and alfalfa, which would provide cover from ground searches but no cover at all from the air. "Our only option is to try to escape in the fields," Zakharov said. "We have perhaps an hour or less before the roadblocks are set up on the highways and the searches can extend into the . . ."

But at that moment they heard the sound of a helicopter approaching. They took cover inside the truck. A gray HH-1N Huey helicopter with the words "U.S. NAVY" on the side could be seen flying at a moderate speed down Evan Hewes Highway, in the same direction they had been traveling. The noise from the Huey search and rescue chopper got steadily quieter . . . before becoming louder again. They did not need to get out and look to know the helicopter was coming toward them.

On Zakharov's orders, one of the commandos unpacked the long green fiberglass box in the back of the pickup and hurriedly got the weapon ready to fire. It took less than a minute, and soon he had the SA-14 Strela antiaircraft missile launcher ready and was hiding with the Porta-Potty between him and the oncoming helicopter. Zakharov made sure the commando had the weapon powered up and steered him south and east toward the sound of the helicopter's rotors, then stepped out onto the dirt road with his sniper rifle in his hands. *"Zhdat',"* Zakharov said. "We do not want that thing crashing down on top of us. Be patient. He will try to get away. That is when you nail him."

Seconds later, the Navy helicopter appeared, just a few hundred yards away. It had descended to just a hundred feet over the fields. As soon as he clearly saw the pilot's white helmet, he raised his pistol and fired a round into the helicopter's windscreen. He had aimed it quickly and didn't expect to hit anything, but he must've hit the pilot because the helicopter veered sharply backward, wobbled from side to side, spun almost an entire revolution, and dove almost to the ground before the copilot managed to take the controls.

Zakharov raised a fist at the commando, hoping he knew that it was the signal to stop and that he would not waste a missile on the stricken chopper. They piled aboard the pickup truck, with Zakharov driving, one commando in the cab with Richter, and the other commandos in the back with the SA-14 MANPADS, and raced down the dirt road north. A few minutes later, a commando pounded on the roof, and Zakharov came to a stop. The missileer dropped down off the cargo bed, crouched below the front of the truck to conceal himself the best he could, and took aim on another helicopter coming toward them.

"If you get a clear shot at the engine exhaust, shoot," Zakharov ordered, and he began jogging back down the road away from the truck.

This time it was a U.S. Marine Corps AH-1W Super Cobra attack helicopter chasing them. Zakharov could see its twenty-millimeter cannon sweeping back and forth along the fields as the crew looked for targets—but he was relieved to notice that the four weapon pylons were empty. He had to take a chance that they hadn't had a chance to load an ammunition canister for the cannon either. Zakharov aimed and fired a round from his pistol at the helicopter. He didn't expect any damage, nor did he get any indication of it, so he started trotting back south along the dirt road toward the helicopter.

As he surmised, the helicopter merely tracked him, but did not attack—it had no ammo. When he walked underneath the helicopter, it slowly pedal-turned around and began to descend, preparing to "dust" him—inundate him with sufficient prop wash that would stir up enough dust and dirt to make it impossible to move or see.

Zakharov could sense his man ready to fire, so before the swirling, blinding dust and dirt got any worse, he started running faster toward the highway—and as he did there was a brilliant flash of light behind him, followed by an incredibly thunderous *boooom!* and a gush of heat. Zakharov ran until he could run no more, then dove to the ground. The Super Cobra, hit point-blank by the SA-14 missile, careened to the east of the dirt road in a death's spin and crashed-landed into the alfalfa field beyond.

Zakharov jogged back toward his truck, dispatching the Super Cobra's pilot with a shot to his chest as he tried to climb out of the cockpit. In moments his commandos had picked him up, and they raced northward along the dirt road deeper into the fields.

But soon the dirt road ended. Not daring to head west toward Brawley and Naval Air Facility El Centro, they headed east through the fields until they were stopped by the Coachella Canal. They turned north toward the nearest bridge they could see, about a half-mile away. Just as they began heading toward it, however, two more helicopters could be seen rolling in on their position from the south and southeast, another gray Marine Corps Super Cobra and a blue, white, and yellow California Highway Patrol H20 Aerostar patrol helicopter.

"What weapons are left?" Zakharov asked.

"None, except a couple grenades and our personal weapons," one of the commandos said. Zakharov nodded grimly. They'd brought all the weapons they could gather on short notice and could carry, knowing they would have to fight the TALON robots—they did not expect to take on U.S. Marine Corps helicopters too. "What should we do, sir?"

"We stay together and fight," Zakharov said finally, checking the ammo supply for his pistol: three rounds left in the magazine, plus two more ten-round magazines—not much at all, but perhaps enough. "They are not going to take us alive." He motioned to the smoke and fire caused by the destroyed Super Cobra. "I am betting none of their helicopters are armed, so that is our chance. I will try to bring another helicopter down—the smoke and fires will intensify, and the confusion will grow as the authorities try to guess what weapons we have. We can jump across to . . ."

"*You two on the road, drop your weapons, raise you hands in the air, turn around, and kneel down!*" they heard from a loudspeaker on the CHP helicopter. "You will receive no more warnings!" The message was repeated in Spanish.

"Come and get us, filthy Americans!" one of the commandos shouted, and he pulled a grenade from a pocket and threw it toward the helicopters. But milliseconds later, the commando disappeared in an incredible cloud of red gore—and then Zakharov heard the loud, chilling *brrraaappp!* sound of the Chain Gun firing, sending fifty twenty-millimeter shells dead on target in one second. There was nothing left of the commando but bits of his boots.

The grenade sailed in front of the CHP helicopter, missing it by several dozen yards, but the mid-air explosion had the desired effect—Zakharov could hear the helicopter's engine whine louder and louder as shrapnel was sucked into the turbine and started to shred the compressor blades; the helicopter spun, then dipped, then smacked hard into the alfalfa field.

"Forget the robot!" Zakharov shouted. "Grab Richter! We'll use him as a human shield!" Zakharov turned and started running toward the bridge across the Coachella Canal, but he hadn't gone more than a few steps when he heard the Super Cobra's cannon fire again. He waited for the slugs to pierce his body . . . but they were just a warning shot, the shells impacting the ground behind him where he had stood just seconds earlier, hitting so close that he could feel the ground shake. He froze, his pistol out of sight in front of him. He had one grenade in his coat pocket and if he could get a lucky shot off with the pistol . . .

Just then there was another warning burst of fire, just a meter to his left, the shells whizzing by so close that he felt as if he was being sharply patted down by a police officer. He had no choice: he slowly lifted his hands, the pistol still in his right hand. The cannon roared again, this time close enough to his right arm to blacken his sleeve. Zakharov screamed, and he sank to his knees, clutching his thankfully uninjured right hand, his arms and legs shaking so violently that he thought he would pass out if he didn't fall down first. Off in the distance he could hear sirens—the police, moving in for the arrest.

It was over. Well, he had managed to avoid capture for many months; he had attacked the U.S. government in its own capital; he had caused untold thousands of deaths and trillions of dollars in damage—and it had finally taken no less than a U.S. Marine Corps Super Cobra gunship to stop him. Even Task Force TALON's high-tech robots couldn't . . .

Suddenly there was a bright flash of red and yellow light behind him, and moments later he was knocked onto his face by a tremendous blast of superheated air and a concussion shock wave. He thought that maybe the Super Cobra pilot had received orders to just kill him and not waste time and money on a trial—but he was still alive. Amid a series of explosions and the sounds of crunching metal and jet fuel–fed fires, Zakharov fumbled for the grenade in his coat pocket, then rolled onto his back, ready to toss the grenade at the approaching police cars . . .

. . . when he realized he was lying in the midst of an inferno. The Super Cobra helicopter had been blown from the sky—it had been completely *obliterated* in mid-air. The whole field around him seemed to be on fire . . .

. . . and at that moment he saw two jets flying overhead, less than a thousand feet aboveground, both Northrop F-5 Freedom Fighter air defense fighters. Both were in green, brown, and gray jungle camouflage colors; the leader had one air-to-air missile missing from its wingtip pylon, while the wingman still had both of his missiles, which appeared to be AIM-9L Sidewinder heat-seeking missiles. Had those American jets accidentally fired on a Marine Corps helicopter? He knew the U.S. Air Force and Navy

flew the F-5 as an "adversary" fighter, its pilot trained to mimic
air-to-air engagement tactics of various enemy air forces; certainly
the Navy base at El Centro had several F-5s in its "Aggressor"
squadron. But it was incredible that it would accidentally shoot
down one of its own aircraft! Zakharov's head was swimming in
confusion. What was going on . . . ?

No, they weren't American jets, he realized—they were *Mexican* jets! The Mexican Air Force flew two squadrons of F-5E
Freedom Fighter jets as air defense interceptors, one squadron in
the south and one over the capital. What in the world were they
doing here, firing missiles at *American* helicopters in *American* airspace?

Through the smoke and fires raging all around him, four more
helicopters arrived—small single-pilot McDonnell-Douglas
MD530 light counterinsurgency attack helicopters, their official
markings blacked out on the sides of the fuselage, each fitted with
rocket launchers and machine guns on their landing skids. While
three of the helicopters hovered nearby on patrol, pedal-turning in
all directions on guard for any pursuit, one set down on a road intersection across the canal. Zakharov didn't hesitate—he ran as
fast as he could across the bridge. The right side door to the helicopter had been removed, making it easy for him to climb aboard.

"*Coronel Zakharov?*" the pilot shouted in Spanish when the
Russian climbed inside.

"*Sí!*" Zakharov shouted. The pilot's face was obscured by the
helmet's smoked visor. "Who are you?"

"A friend. Get in, quickly!"

Zakharov pulled his sidearm and aimed it at the pilot. "I said,
who are you?"

"*¿Usted no me cree, Coronel?*" the pilot asked in good Spanish,
smiling. "If I'm an American agent, perhaps you are captured—
but if I leave you here in this burning wheat field, in five minutes
you are *definitely* captured."

"Answer me!"

The pilot smiled again, then lifted the dark visor. "Believe me

now, Colonel? Now get in, sir." Zakharov smiled broadly, then
scrambled inside and hurriedly pulled on shoulder straps. The
helicopter lifted off and stood guard. One by one the other helicopters alighted. The CID unit was strapped onto the landing
skids of one helicopter; Richter and the Russian commando
boarded the other two helicopters, and soon all four Mexican helicopters were speeding southward at treetop level, crossing the border into safety just moments later.

HENDERSON, NEVADA
A SHORT TIME LATER

The recorded commercial message abruptly cut off, and Bob
O'Rourke's voice, shaking and unusually muted, came on moments later: "This flash message has just been handed to me, ladies
and gentlemen, from the news wire services. Just minutes ago,
down near the California-Mexico border near El Centro, a U.S.
Marine Corps helicopter was shot down by a Mexican Air Force
fighter jet. The two crew members were killed instantly. Yes, you
heard me correctly: reports are that a U.S. military helicopter was
shot down by the armed forces of the republic of Mexico, just moments ago."

O'Rourke paused briefly, making no attempt at all to muffle his
labored breathing. He had bandages on the left side of his face
from the incident in the Arizona mountains with the American
Watchdog Project, along with elastic bandages securing a broken
rib, from when Georgie Wayne jumped on top of him; his left arm
was in an elastic bandage too from a strain, which he always put
in a sling whenever he knew he was going to be photographed. He
looked every inch the combat veteran he wanted to appear to be.
"Eyewitness accounts made by the Imperial County Sheriff's Department and the U.S. Navy report that law enforcement agencies,
assisted by military search teams from Naval Air Facility El Cen-

tro, were searching for terrorists discovered farther north near Niland, California, who were trying to escape across the border into Mexico. The terrorists were armed with sophisticated weapons including shoulder-fired antiaircraft weapons and sniper rifles, and they had apparently attacked other law enforcement pursuers with these weapons. But when an armed Marine Corps Super Cobra helicopter gunship tried to corner the terrorists just a few miles north of the border, it was shot down by an air-to-air missile fired from a Mexican Air Force F-5 Freedom Fighter jet, made in the U.S. and sold to Mexico for air defense purposes. One, perhaps two terrorists are believed to have escaped across the border.

"The death toll—the *American* death toll—in this whole incredible bloody ordeal is five, with two California Highway Patrol officers killed and one seriously injured when their helicopter was shot down by the terrorists, and three U.S. Marine Corps officers killed and one slightly injured when their choppers were downed, one by the terrorists and one—I still can't believe this has happened, folks—one by a Mexican Air Force fighter jet. One terrorist was killed by the Marine Corps after he attacked the CHP helicopter; the other terrorist, as I said, escaped in the carnage and confusion.

"This horrible incident follows the initial discovery of the terrorists in Niland, California, a farming community about forty miles from the border in the Imperial Valley agricultural region. Four armed terrorists opened fire on Border Patrol agents, injuring two. The terrorists also attacked several farmworkers, killing seven. The farmworkers killed two of the terrorists with farm tools before the others escaped. The terrorists stole two vehicles as they made their way toward the Mexican border."

O'Rourke paused briefly, taking another deep, audible breath, before continuing: "We don't yet know who the terrorists were—what nationality, what religious persuasion, what group or cell they belong to. They could be home-grown terrorists, or they could be Mexican, or they could be the return of the Consortium that created so much death and destruction in this country last year. But in the end it doesn't matter. The threat is real, it exists, and we need to deal with *now*.

"Is there any doubt in your minds now, my friends, that America is in a real shooting war with terrorists—and that the Mexican border is now their primary avenue of infiltration and escape? Is there any doubt of the Mexican government's duplicity, if not their complete and total *involvement,* in terror attacks against American law enforcement, attempting to coerce our lawmakers into enacting more open immigration legislation? A more important question here is: how should the United States respond to this horrible, bloody attack?

"There is no question in *my* mind, ladies and gentlemen, that the U.S.-Mexico border should be considered hostile territory, and any persons found crossing the border or even approaching the frontier should be considered hostile enemy combatants, not just illegal migrants. Every one of those one million illegal immigrants who make it into this country every year should be considered threats to American peace and security and possible terrorists and insurgents. If the intruders are wearing uniforms, they should be stopped by all means necessary, including use of deadly force, and if captured they should be treated as prisoners of war under the Geneva Conventions. If they are not wearing uniforms, they should be imprisoned and treated as spies and saboteurs, not subject to the Geneva Conventions; and if found guilty of any crime against the United States, they should be *executed*. No exceptions!

"I call on President Samuel Conrad to declare a federal state of emergency in all of the border states, and to immediately dispatch the National Guard to seal off the borders and use all means necessary, including deadly force, to repel anyone approaching the border. Full air defense measures should be instituted, including round-the-clock air patrols and Patriot air defense weapons, to prevent any more incursions into U.S. airspace."

O'Rourke paused once more, and his producer Fand Kent saw something in his face that made her skin crawl. She hit the intercom button: "Bob, what are you going to say now?"

"You know what I'm going to say, Fonda," he said darkly.

"I'm going to commercial. Let's talk about it first."

"No."

"Bob, take a deep breath, and send us over to commercial," she said, quickly cueing up two minutes of recordings. "I've got two minutes in the computer right now, and then we can go to news a little early and put in another ninety seconds . . ."

"I said no."

"Bob, we need to discuss this first," Kent insisted. She picked up the phone. "I'm calling the general manager." But there was no need—he was already in the booth with O'Rourke moments later. He had cut off the intercom, so she could barely hear. Their voices got louder and louder very quickly, and soon O'Rourke pushed the GM away, yelling at him to get out. The GM turned to Kent, said and indicated nothing, then left.

Bob O'Rourke readjusted his headphones and microphone, and when he resumed, his voice was shaking even more: "Ladies and gentlemen, this is Bob O'Rourke, and you're listening to *The Bottom Line*. I am reacting to the recent news of an attack on U.S. military and law enforcement by unknown terrorists and by the Mexican Air Force. I . . . I am trying to remain calm and think rationally, but frankly I think the time for thought and introspection is over, don't you? America has been attacked, *again,* and this time it has come not from some shadowy underworld figure from Russia, but from our neighbors to the south. America is under siege, and the enemy is *Mexico.*"

O'Rourke grabbed the microphone and rose out of his seat, his voice quickly rising in intensity. "You know something, my friends? Do you want to know what I think? Do you want to know the truth? The truth is I don't believe President Conrad is going to do a damned thing about this brutal attack. He will call for investigations, maybe put a few more Border Patrol agents or troops on the border to try to show how tough he is, but in the end it'll be business as usual. President Carmen Maravilloso of Mexico will claim it was all a horrible mistake, beg forgiveness, blame the

United States for increasing tensions on the border with Task Force TALON and the National Guard, and maybe fire or imprison some low-level bureaucrat or general. After a week or two, it'll be over and forgotten—except of course by the grieving families of those officers and Marines slaughtered by the terrorists and the government of Mexico. In short, my friends, Mexico will get away with murder, and again our government will prove that it is either unable or unwilling to protect its citizens and its borders in the name of political correctness and expediency.

"I therefore urge my fellow Americans to do everything you can to protect yourself, your families, your community, and your place of business," O'Rourke went on. "You have to do more than just be aware of your surroundings—you have to *act* to defend yourselves and your property. There are enemies in our midst, my friends, dangerous criminals and murderous terrorists that will do anything, especially steal and kill, to escape justice or carry out their plans of destruction. They have sneaked in across our borders with ease by the millions because our government has refused to seal the borders, American employers have skirted the law simply to increase their profits, and the Mexican government wants the money the illegals bring back into their country and they don't want the burden of finding jobs and creating a better life for their own people. The result of this conspiracy of neglect, greed, and corruption is death in our own backyards, with no end and no solution in sight."

"No, Bob," Fand Kent spoke into the intercom. "That's far enough. Don't go any farther . . ."

"I urge my fellow Americans to do everything in their legal and Constitutional powers to help law enforcement track down, capture, and bring to justice anyone who might be in this country illegally," O'Rourke went on, ignoring his producer's pleas. "If you are legally allowed to bear arms, I urge you to do so—you might be the *only* person who stops a terrorist or illegal from stealing your possessions or committing murder and mayhem in your schools, churches, and the places you frequent such as restaurants and supermarkets.

"I also strongly urge my fellow citizens, everyone concerned about terrorism and the out-of-control rise in illegal immigration in the United States, to report anyone you might think is an illegal alien to U.S. Immigration and Customs Enforcement," O'Rourke went on, shaking his head at his producer. He gave ICE's toll-free telephone number and Web site address. "You can anonymously report anyone you feel might be in the country illegally, but I will tell you now that if you make an anonymous report, the government will put your report at the bottom of a very large stack of reports, which means it will probably never be investigated. That's because anonymous reports are always considered retaliations by *other* illegals, most often warring gangs or families. Don't be afraid to give ICE your personal information—that way, your tip will much more likely be acted on. If you have any doubts or questions, contact my producer Fand by e-mail or phone and I'll help you get it straightened out.

"One more point: do not, I repeat, do *not* waste your time trying to contact local law enforcement about illegals living or working in your neighborhood. Ninety-nine percent of local law enforcement agencies in the United States will not do anything with the information you give, citing such nonsense such as states' rights, localities not required to enforce federal law, lack of resources, fear of civil rights lawsuits, and similar cowardly dodges. States and municipalities are required to care, educate, feed, provide medical, welfare, and legal services to all their residents, but for some bizarre reason they will not ask for *proof* of citizenship or residency; and unless the illegal person has committed a crime, they will not call Immigration and Customs Enforcement to have the person deported. There's something twisted and backward about that policy, and we'll discuss that on a future show.

"If you feel these persons are a threat to you, your family, or your community, then by all means dial 911 and report it," he went on, "but your responsibility is to protect your life, the lives of your family, and your property, so I urge you to do so to the utmost extent your state and local laws allow. You are making a big mistake if you expect the government to protect you. We have the right in this country to keep and bear arms, guaranteed to us by the Second Amendment to the Constitution, and if you do not take advantage of this right, at best you may someday lose this right—and at worst, you could lose your *life* to someone who values neither your rights nor your life. Don't be stupid, naïve, passive, or impartial. Do what you must to protect yourselves and the ones you love, *right now*. This is a war, ladies and gentlemen, and it's about time we started taking the fight to *them*.

"Of course, I predict the government will whine and cry that my message this morning has resulted in a flood of bogus and paranoid-fueled reports that they are completely unable to contend with—and it'll be all *my* fault," O'Rourke went on. "That excuse is *unacceptable*. If the alphabet-soup list of civil agencies we have to secure our borders, control immigration, and combat terrorism can't deal with the problem, we need to make sure that the government does whatever is necessary to deal with it, or we need to take matters into our own hands. I don't care if they call in the National Guard and have soldiers link arms and create a human wall of protection on the border—they need to do something about the illegal immigration problem, *now*. No more excuses, no more deaths, no more political correctness! President Conrad needs to get off his backside and get some troops out here *immediately* to secure our borders and hunt down these terrorists, or the American people *will!*

"The *Bottom Line*, my friends: the time to start taking back our country and securing our families, homes, and neighborhoods is *now*. You may think that what has happened this morning is thousands of miles away from where you live and work, and that it will never affect you because you live in Iowa or Connecticut and you don't live on the Mexican border, but you're wrong. Illegal immigration hurts all of us, no matter where you live, and sooner or later the violence that we saw in the Imperial Valley of southern California will spread all across our country, wherever illegal immigrants live and work, and then you'll realize how long the violence and trespass has been with us, and how badly it affects our lives every day."

"I'll have more about this deadly, bloody morning in the great United States, the latest acts of terrorism on our own soil, right after these messages. Stay tuned, we'll be right back."

CHAPTER 8

The past hour had been a complete whirlwind of confusion, reminiscent of the Consortium attacks last year. The President would have thought that his government and the first responders would be accustomed to leaping into action after another terrorist event, but it was every bit the same semicontrolled madhouse they had experienced before.

When the news of the shoot-down near El Centro came in, President Samuel Conrad had been immediately whisked away from a breakfast meeting, tour, and speech at the National Cancer Institute at Fort Detrick, near Frederick, Maryland, and quickly escorted to his waiting helicopter at the Army base for the short flight back to Washington. Initial reports indicated it might be another Consortium terror attack, so the government had been sent into crisis mode, with the vice president and other key members of the administration and Congress sent to alternate emergency command centers. The alert had been canceled quickly, but like a locomotive or aircraft carrier going at full speed, it was hard to stop the government crisis juggernaut once it got going.

Things were fairly quiet and relatively calm back at the White House. The President strode quickly into the White House Situation Room. "Seats," he said as soon as he stepped to his chair at the head of the conference table. His advisers shuffled to their chairs. "Okay, let's get started. Tom?"

"The vice president is in Washington State this morning, and is now airborne and on his way to the western alternate command center in St. George, Utah," the Chief of Staff said. He ran down the locations and status of all the other cabinet officers, the leadership of Congress, and the members of the Supreme Court. "The Homeland Security Threat Assessment team met a short time ago. As you know, sir, following the incident in Arizona and the other attacks on Border Patrol personnel, the Homeland Security Threat Advisory level was already at 'orange,' or 'High.' Following the attack on the Marine Corps and CHP helicopters near El Centro, the assessment team recommends raising the threat level to 'red,' or 'Extreme.' They gave me a call and I told them I'd ask your advice."

"Sergeant Major?"

"I recommend going ahead and raising the threat level to 'red,' sir," National Security Adviser Ray Jefferson replied immediately.

President Conrad sat back in his seat, physically and emotionally drained and exhausted. This would be the first time since the Consortium attacks that the nation had been back on "Extreme," something that he had dearly hoped to avoid. The Homeland Security Threat Assessment Team, composed of the Attorney General, the President's Homeland Security Adviser, the Director of National Intelligence, and the commander of U.S. Northern Command, were in charge of setting the Homeland Security Threat Advisory level and determined the recommended "Protective Measure" response, which varied by agency and state depending on the location, severity, and gravity of the threat. It was not required by law, but before publicly announcing their decision, the Threat Assessment Team always made a courtesy call to the White House to advise the President of their recommended response.

"Sergeant Major, I think the American people are exhausted," the President said, "and if we raise the threat level to 'red' again, they're not going to react at all when we *really* need them to do so. Is the Threat Assessment Team *absolutely* sure that this incident rises to the level of a *terrorist* action against the United States? In my mind, it does not. It *could* have been an accident."

"We're suspicious about the tasking of those Mexican Air Force jets, sir," Air Force General Gordon Joelson, commander of U.S. Northern Command, the unified military command in charge of the defense of the continental United States, interjected. "We're trying to precisely nail down the timeline, but it appears that those jets launched from their base near Mexico City moments after the battle with Task Force TALON farther north."

"I'm in the dark," the President said. He looked perturbedly at Jefferson. "What battle? TALON was in a battle?"

"Yes, sir, about ninety minutes ago," Jefferson said. "FBI Director DeLaine's joint task force group, sent out to track down the survivor of the first terrorist attack near Blythe, had a shootout with terrorists, one of whom was identified by Major Richter as Yegor Zakharov."

"Oh, *shit . . . !*"

"Zakharov had several heavy weapons with him and was obviously expecting an encounter with the CID robots," Jefferson went on. "He escaped, after killing several civilians, injuring a Border Patrol agent, and . . . and capturing the CID unit and Major Richter."

"He *what?*" the President shouted. The room exploded in sheer pandemonium. *"Zakharov has Richter and one of the robots?"*

"I'm afraid so, sir," Jefferson said. "We're tracking Zakharov down as we speak. TALON's reconnaissance airship detected several encrypted satellite phone transmissions from the area, which we believe Zakharov made himself—they could not unscramble the message, but the transmissions came from a vehicle that turned out to be stolen, heading for the Mexico border at high speed. Minutes after the first few calls, the jets launched."

"That could be a coincidence."

"It would have been, sir, if the jets went on a normal patrol or went to a practice area," Joelson said. "But we tracked the planes using OTH-B radar almost from liftoff, and it does not appear to have been a normal flight profile at all." OTH-B, or over-the-horizon-backscatter, was an ultralong-range radar system that bounced radar energy off the ionosphere, allowing radar operators to detect and track aircraft as far as five thousand miles away. The system, based in Maine and originally designed to detect attacking Soviet bombers from the north, had been steered to look south to detect drug smugglers flying from South America. "Those F-5s made a beeline toward El Centro, even flying supersonic for a short period of time. My guess is that they were summoned to respond to the area that Zakharov was going to use for his escape route."

"You actually think Yegor Zakharov or the Consortium has allies so deep and so high up in the Mexican government that he can order fighter jets to launch on a moment's notice like that?" the President asked, although he didn't dare believe it was so crazy as to totally discount it.

"I don't know, sir," Joelson said. "It doesn't seem likely—the Mexican government is corrupt, but they'd be stone-cold insane to make any kind of deal with Yegor Zakharov so soon after the Consortium attacks against the United States. But there's no doubt in my mind that those jets headed *directly* for the exact location where Zakharov was heading. I believe they were *dispatched*."

"What about those helicopters?" the President asked. "Where did they come from, and where did they go?"

"OTH-B can't see close to the U.S. border, and civil or military radars didn't pick up anything until the incident was over because they flew so low, but we think the three helicopters involved in the incident came from Rodolfo Sanchez Taboada Airport near Mexicali, which also has air force and Ministry of Internal Affairs aircraft based there as well," Joelson said. "Based on the range of those helicopters, they could have flown as far south as Hermosillo. The jets didn't fly all the way back to Mexico City, so they probably landed and refueled nearby, possibly at Hermosillo as well."

"My God, they got away with kidnapping and murder—and now Zakharov has a robot," the President muttered. "Jesus, Jefferson, this is a massive screw-up."

"The CID unit has several telemetry and tracking systems onboard," Jefferson said. "If Zakharov tried to activate it, we'll have it pinpointed in seconds. We'll get it back. Zakharov will never get a chance to use it. But we need Mexico's cooperation to track down Zakharov and get Richter and the robot back."

"Maravilloso will never cooperate," the President said. "Zakharov will either bribe or threaten her enough to convince her to stonewall us until he has a chance to figure out how to use the robot. What in hell are we supposed to do?"

"Mr. President, our path is clear," Ray Jefferson said. "By executive order, Task Force TALON has the authority to pursue Yegor Zakharov and the Consortium anywhere on the planet—and that includes Mexico. We should reactivate them immediately."

"I strongly disagree with the sergeant major, sir," Kinsly said. "My opinion at this moment is that this incident was horrendous and ill-timed but an unfortunate accident."

"Hold it, everyone, just *hold* it," the President said. "I'm not going to send anyone until I find out what happened from Maravilloso herself." He picked up the phone by his right elbow and waited until after the familiar "Yes, Mr. President?" query from the operator. "Get me the president of Mexico, immediately," Conrad ordered. "Tell her it's urgent."

PALACIAO NACIONAL, MEXICO CITY, MEXICO
THAT SAME TIME

"Where in hell is Díaz?" United Mexican States President Carmen Maravilloso shouted. "I called for him almost an hour ago!"

"He is on his way, Madam President," her assistant said. "He phoned and said his helicopter was damaged, so he must travel by car. He may not be here for another thirty minutes at best."

"*¡Hideputa!*" Maravilloso swore. "The President of the United States is going to call me any minute now, and the only explanation I have is this sorry-assed fairy tale! I want to talk with Díaz on a secure line, and I want it *now!*"

"Madam President, this is an absolute outrage," Minister of Defense Alberto Rojas said hotly. "I never authorized those jets to fly near the border! *Never!* We have very specific rules about military flights near the border, and they all require . . ."

"I heard you the first time, General, I heard you," Maravilloso said. "I am going to get to the bottom of this. Pedro!" At that moment her assistant walked in. "Get Díaz in here in the next two minutes or I'll . . . !"

"The President of the United States is calling, Madam," her assistant said.

Maravilloso stopped, took a deep breath, and nodded. "Get Díaz in here . . ."

"He will be here within minutes, Madam President," Pedro said, and quickly retreated.

Maravilloso took another deep breath, resignedly shook her head, and picked up the phone. "This is the president. Go ahead."

"Madame President, this is Samuel Conrad."

"Yes, Mr. President, thank you for the call," she said. "I send my sincerest condolences to you and your citizens for this tragedy."

"Can you tell me what happened, Madam President?"

"A tragic but completely innocent error." She made a quick report of what she had been told about the incident. "Our investigation is under way, but I can assure you, this will be scrupulously examined. I deeply and sincerely apologize for the tragic loss of life, but it was nothing more than an unfortunate accident. The military received a request for support from the Minister of Internal Affairs and the Attorney General, stating that rival drug gangs from Mexicali, who had been involved in several murders, kidnappings, and bank robberies, were attempting to flee justice. Military jets and helicopters were immediately dispatched to assist local police and Internal Affairs investigators . . ."

"*Jets?* Do you regularly dispatch *armed jet fighters* to chase down drug smugglers?"

"We had heard that the gang members had heavy military weapons, including rocket-propelled grenades, which as you know they did indeed have such weapons. We decided to take no chances—better to bring too much firepower than not enough. They found the gang members in a very short period of time. The criminals fired what appeared to be a shoulder-fired missile, so our aircraft returned fire in self-defense . . ."

"So are you trying to say that your jets fired a missile and it strayed off course and accidentally hit the helicopter?"

"I am telling you what has happened, Mr. Conrad—I have no explanations yet," Maravilloso said. "I am told that the attacks on the criminals were initiated over *Mexican* territory, not American airspace. It was only after the attack commenced that they realized they had overflown U.S. airspace, and they immediately withdrew without firing any more shots."

"Why didn't you notify any U.S. agencies that you were flying military aircraft in the vicinity of the border?" the President asked. "The danger of high-speed jets flying so close to civilian and military airfields without prior notification is obvious . . ."

"Our pilots never had authorization to fly into U.S, airspace, sir—it was a mistake, one for which they will be punished, following our own military investigation," Maravilloso said. "The commanders on the scene did not believe any danger existed. Obviously they did not anticipate the accidental overflight and what

might happen if innocent American aircraft were in the same
area. Unfortunately the worst happened . . ."

"A courtesy call still would have been appropriate."

"Oh? I do not recall getting a 'courtesy call' when you set up
Rampart One, or when you moved National Guard troops to the
border, sir," Maravilloso said. "Courtesy works both ways, Mr.
Conrad, does it not?"

"The difference is, Madam President, that our forces were
merely guarding our *own* borders and did not run the danger of
crossing Mexico's border . . ."

"Oh, really? I think the danger was *very* clear."

". . . and there is no duty to inform you of actions we take that
affect only *our* territory," Conrad said. "If you thought the gang
members might try to cross the border, on the other hand, a call
to American state and federal law enforcement agencies, for
proper notification or assistance, would have been desirable and
appropriate."

"Do not lecture me on what is 'appropriate,' Mr. Conrad, after
what the United States has done over the past few days!" Maravilloso snapped. "You are certainly in no such position!"

"Madam President, we have information that one of our Cybernetic Infantry Devices—the man-piloted robot—and the commander of Task Force TALON, Jason Richter, were taken at the
same time," the President said. "Obviously the danger in having
one of those robots in the hands of a terrorist mastermind like
Yegor Zakharov is clear. We request . . ."

"Zakharov? *Yegor Zakharov?*" Maravilloso looked in shock at
the others in her office. "I know nothing of Zakharov being involved in this! This is . . . this is not possible . . . !"

"Madam President, there's no time to waste," the President said.
"We request immediate assistance from the Mexican government
and military to recover Major Richter and the CID unit, and to
help bring the terrorists involved to justice."

Minister of Internal Affairs Felix Díaz entered the president's
office and stood before her desk, his hands calmly folded in front

of him, smiling slightly—a smile which completely enraged her. She took a deep breath, paused, then went on: "I agree, our commanders should have foreseen this and made the proper notifications. At this time, Mr. President, I can offer nothing more than my sincerest apologies and my offer to do whatever I must to discover the truth."

"In light of our recent terrorist attacks and the continued threat posed to military and civil locations, the United States requests that the Federal Bureau of Investigation and the Navy Judge Advocate General take the lead in this investigation," President Conrad said. "We are ready to provide the best forensic and investigative tools available to assist your investigators."

"Very well, Mr. President," Maravilloso said after a slight pause. She looked at the faces of her advisers in the office with her. "Mexico stands ready to receive your investigation teams, and we will cooperate to the fullest extent possible. Again, sir, I deeply apologize for this terrible incident."

She hung up the phone, then pulled a cigar from a humidor on her desk but tossed it back impatiently—she wasn't going to waste a good cigar now. "All right," she said finally to the advisers with her in her office after rubbing her eyes and temples wearily, "someone explain to me what in hell *really* happened this morning!"

"It was as I already reported, Madam President," Alberto Rojas said. "I received an urgent request from Minister Díaz to help locate and interdict a group of warring drug gang members who were driving eastbound on Federal Highway 2 from Mexicali. He said they had sophisticated military weapons with them and requested counterinsurgency aircraft, including jet fighters."

"Jet fighters—against drug smugglers, Minister Díaz?"

"I admit I may have reacted instinctively, as a former Air Force officer, Madam President," Minister of Internal Affairs Felix Díaz said, "but I felt time was of the essence, and I believed a strong show of force might take the fight out of the gangsters. The helicopters might have been sufficient, and certainly should have avoided overflying U.S. territory, but I made a judgment call. It turns out the jets were needed—the gangsters did indeed have antiaircraft weapons and were lying in wait for whoever might pursue them."

"I want it made perfectly clear that the Ministry of National Defense bears no responsibility for this incident," Rojas said hotly. "On his urgent request, and against my better judgment, I made the decision to turn over tactical control of the engagement to Minister Díaz, and he accepted."

"Minister?"

"It is true, Madam President," Díaz said, "and I accept full responsibility for what has occurred. The downing of that Marine Corps helicopter was an unfortunate error, an accident. In retrospect, the Ministry of Internal Affairs' helicopters from Mexicali probably would have been sufficient for the job, but it was unsure if they could have arrived on time to catch the gangsters before they escaped, or withstand their attack if they did. I made a decision, and I stand by it."

"You were afraid that helicopters just a few miles away wouldn't have arrived in time," Rojas pointed out in confusion, "so you requested help from fighter jets based almost *five hundred* miles away? That doesn't make sense!"

"Thank you for taking advantage of twenty-twenty hindsight and criticizing a last-second decision I made to safeguard lives and property, General," Díaz shot back. "My staff discussed all options for dealing with these criminals and decided to call on the jets from Mexico City. I never thought we would actually *use* them. But when the helicopters failed to respond in time, we had no choice but to use the first assets available. If I had tanks and armored vehicles, I would have used them too."

Maravilloso studied Díaz's face for a moment, nodded, then glanced at Sotelo and then at Alberto Rojas. "Are you satisfied, General Rojas?" He nodded, glaring at Díaz, who ignored him. "Very well then. I assure you that the Ministry of National Defense will be absolved of any responsibility in this matter. Please stay for a moment, General Rojas. I would like your advice."

"Gladly, Madam President."

Maravilloso stood behind her desk and affixed an angry gaze at Díaz. "This had better be good, Felix," she said seriously, "because you have just made up for everything the Americans have done to us over the past several days, and much more. It looks like a retaliation, plain and simple, and now the Ministry of Internal Affairs has taken full responsibility for it. What is the *real* reason for the overflight? What in hell is going on?"

"Are you sure you want to know, Carmen?" Díaz asked.

"What do you mean, Felix?" she demanded. That was the first time, Maravilloso thought, that anything Felix Díaz said ever scared her. She had always assumed that this handsome, wealthy, and very powerful man had his own personal, business, and political agendas, but he had never before given any indication of what they were, or that they might be contrary to *hers*. For the first time, she felt a shiver of vulnerability in her own office. Even Rojas's face fell in surprise at Díaz's simple question. "What is going on here?" Díaz hesitated again. "Tell me, Felix. *¡Ahora!*"

Díaz glanced once at Rojas, silently asking Maravilloso if she was sure she wanted the Minister of Defense to hear what he was about to say; when she remained silent, he said, "We found out that Task Force TALON had found Ernesto Fuerza—'Comandante Veracruz.' "

"*¡Mi Díos!*" Maravilloso gasped. "Fuerza was in the United States?"

"He was organizing workers up in the Imperial Valley of California—building a resistance force, raising money, recruiting supporters, even gathering weapons," Díaz said. "TALON was going to capture him at any moment, and I seriously doubt if the Americans would have notified us of the capture for a long time. I made a decision to snatch him before TALON could close in on him, and I dispatched the *Sombras* . . ."

"The *Sombras* . . . inside the United States . . . ?" Rojas gasped.

"The *Sombras* have operated many times inside the United States on officially sanctioned clandestine missions, Alberto—you know it as well as I," Díaz said. To Maravilloso, he continued: "When I found out that TALON was involved, and they had called in U.S. Marines from El Centro Naval Air Facility to assist, I called in the jets."

"You requested our fighter jets to attack U.S. military aircraft to rescue a *drug smuggler*? Why?"

"I was hoping the jets would create enough confusion and allow helicopters to come in and snatch Fuerza," Díaz said. "Fuerza himself destroyed two helicopters, but that only succeeded in bringing more and better-armed helicopters—they weren't going to be chased away. I ordered the pilots to attack."

"This is incredible!" Maravilloso retorted. "This is a disaster!" She sank into her chair behind her desk as if all of her muscles had gone weak at once. "My God, Felix, what have you done?" she muttered, shaking her head. "At the very least, that's an international incident of the most serious order—at worst, it is an act of *war*. And Conrad says that Yegor Zakharov was somehow involved, and that Zakharov has one of Task Force TALON's robots and its commander captive."

"I know nothing of any of this," Díaz snapped. "It sounds to me as if Conrad is threatening to enflame American and world public opinion against us by yet again mentioning Zakharov's involvement. This is nothing but a fairy tale. I have Fuerza—that's all."

Maravilloso remained silent . . . but only for a moment before finally asking, "So, is he . . . ?"

"Vivo," Díaz said proudly. "He is in a safe house in Hermosillo getting medical treatment, and then I will bring him here to meet with you."

"Is he . . . is he badly hurt?"

"It appears TALON and the Border Patrol tried to torture him to reveal information," Díaz said. "He is injured, but he will make a full recovery."

Carmen Maravilloso momentarily forgot about the border incursion and attack, thinking only of meeting Fuerza. "It was even better that TALON and the Border Patrol were involved, since they are the spearhead of this new anti-immigrant *pogrom*." She looked at Díaz seriously. "But there is the question of explaining the initial story about the incident, especially to the Council of Government . . ."

"Just tell the council exactly what I have already told you, Carmen," Díaz said. "We can show plenty of pictures of dangerous drug dealers and explain how we are doing everything in our power to stop them, even if it means crossing the border. Let me get together with the Ministry of Information and present you with a plan on how we should deal with the press."

Rojas looked at Díaz suspiciously, but nodded. "You may have to submit to questioning by the Supreme Court, perhaps even resign your post," Rojas said.

"I will not resign my post, General Rojas," Díaz said. "I was acting in my capacity as Minister of Internal Affairs and as chief border security and anti-drug officer of the Mexican government. The president expressed her desire to meet with Fuerza, which would have been impossible if he was captured or killed. Need I remind you that the man is wanted in Mexico for drug dealing and gun smuggling as well?"

"The American government will want to question you," Rojas said, "and they will not like it if we refuse."

"I've got plenty of bodies of dead drug smugglers to show the Americans—and if I don't have enough, I'll get some more," Diaz said. "I can handle the Americans. They like Mexicans who are tough on crime and drugs. If necessary, I will apologize profusely and offer my resignation." He looked at Maravilloso and added, "It will be refused, of course."

"Of course it will, Felix," Maravilloso said. "But what about Fuerza? What should we do with him? After what has just happened, can he help us convince the American Congress to address the immigration problem without causing a deluge of refugees back to Mexico?"

"He is a complete unknown, Carmen," Rojas said. "We know of him only by rumor and legend, and most of the legend is not favorable. A drug smuggler turned so-called nationalist and self-proclaimed 'patriotic freedom-fighter' is still a drug smuggler. He is damaged goods, Carmen. If he is wanted in Mexico for any crimes, he should stand trial for them. Otherwise, he should be sent to a remote part of the country and placed under close scrutiny, perhaps even house arrest, to be sure he doesn't make any more of those ridiculous videotapes and stir up the people . . ."

"The people *listen* to him, Alberto," Maravilloso said. "They *like* him. He is dashing, energetic, inspirational—"

"You are too obsessed with the media image, Carmen—that may not be the real man at all," Rojas said. "You are a much more influential person than he. Do not be sucked in by his cult of personality. Send him to a prison in Durango or San Luis Potosí state and make sure he never leaves." Maravilloso fell silent, trying but failing to come up with a better argument than her most trusted adviser's.

"Fuerza's power lies in his popularity," Díaz interjected in the silence. "His message has attracted the attention of many progressives around the world." He noticed Rojas's warning expression and said: "If the people of the world are attracted to Fuerza, perhaps we should take advantage of that." He looked at the president of Mexico carefully. "You two, *together*—you form a very powerful, very direct, and—to use your own emphasis—very photogenic duo."

The Minister of National Defense looked at Díaz as if he was going to tell him that he had no right to speak. "The president of Mexico *will not* appear in the electronic media with this man, this . . . this *criminal!*" Rojas retorted.

"We do not know who he is, Alberto—we know only what the media says about him," Maravilloso said.

"That is very often enough—you have said so yourself many times, Carmen," Rojas pointed out. "The people know what the media tell them, is it not so?"

"I want to meet him," Maravilloso insisted. "I want to see if this man can provide the spark to ignite a revolution in border and émigré matters between our country and the United States."

"Carmen, I think it would be a grave mistake," Rojas said. "If you align yourself with such a man, you may never be taken seriously again by any nation. It could ruin relations with the United States for a generation . . ."

"Relations have *already* been ruined, Alberto, but not by me," Maravilloso said. "I will not allow the immigration debate to be steered by men like Bob O'Rourke. My position as president of Mexico prohibits me from doing much to stir the debate . . . but this Comandante Veracruz may be able to do what I cannot."

She turned to Díaz. "Felix, do not worry: I will keep to your initial story—be sure you do everything you need to do to procure as much evidence as you can to back your story up. Mexico will shield you from prosecution for abuse of power . . . *this* time. Next time, inform this office before you pull such stunts again, or I can guarantee you no such protection." Maravilloso thought Díaz was going to argue with her—she saw a brief flare of defiance and untold strength in his features—but instead he lowered his eyes and nodded. "And I want to meet with this Ernesto Fuerza. Set it up right away. You are dismissed."

As Díaz headed to the door, Alberto Rojas held up a hand to stop him. "You did not mention, Minister Díaz, how you discovered Ernesto Fuerza was in the United States, where he was headed, and how you managed to steer three military aircraft so precisely in his vicinity that they could effect a rescue."

"It is my job to know these things, General," Díaz replied.

Rojas nodded. "I see. So you knew where Fuerza was all the time, and your *Sombras* could have scooped him up any time you wished, eh? Strange you waited until he was being chased by Task Force TALON before doing so." Díaz said nothing, but turned and walked away.

After Díaz departed, Rojas said, "You may still have to fire Díaz, Carmen, even if you give him blanket immunity. And forget this insane idea to meet with Fuerza. He can do nothing but hurt you."

"You still do not understand, do you, Alberto?" Maravilloso asked. "Are you blind, or have you been in the Federal District too long? Do you not have any notion of what the American people will do once details of this incident are released in the press? There will be a tremendous backlash of anger against all Mexicans that will set relations between our countries and the hopes for a peaceful solution to our immigration issues back a *generation*."

"I do indeed fear this, Madam," Rojas said, "but I do not understand how this 'Comandante Veracruz' can help. What magic do you expect him to perform for you?"

"I do not know, Alberto—that is why I need to meet with him," Maravilloso said. "But we need to find some message to tell the world that Mexico is the aggrieved party in this conflict, not the United States. I am hoping Fuerza has this message. If he does, we could possibly come to terms with the Americans and end this feud. If he does not, we will be struggling with the Americans— and perhaps even our own people—for years and years to come."

"The Council of Government will not support you," Rojas said.

"You mean, *you* will not support me."

"Carmen, forget this insane idea," Rojas pleaded. "I know it is your nature to be unconventional and bold, but I do not believe this is the time." He paused, then said, "You must issue the statement about Díaz's involvement immediately to the Ministry of Foreign Affairs and have the message sent out to all foreign embassies immediately—starting with the American embassy, of course."

"Do you think Díaz is telling the truth, Alberto?"

"I do not know, Carmen," Rojas said. "This I *do* know: we are involved in some sort of game in which we do not know all the rules or the players. We must play along for now because we have no other choice. But we must find a way to take control of this situation, or we will quickly find ourselves rendered . . . inconsequential."

THE SITUATION ROOM, THE WHITE HOUSE,
WASHINGTON, D.C.
THAT SAME TIME

"I'm surprised, Mr. President," Attorney General George Wentworth said as the President hung up the dead telephone. "I never
would have expected her to agree to assist us."

"But she did—that's the best news I've heard in weeks," the
President said. He turned to the Secretary of State. "Chris, you
and George will be leading the investigation team—push this
thing for all it's worth. We need to take advantage of this sudden
largesse when we can. Get down to Mexico City right away and
interview as many of their military commanders, the Interior
Ministry higher-ups—everyone we can get our hands on."

"Yes, Mr. President."

"A flash message coming over the wire services, Mr. President,"
the Chief of Staff, reading from his computer monitor, said.
"They're reporting that Bob O'Rourke on his morning radio show
called for Americans to take up arms in defense of their neighborhoods and to report all illegal aliens to the government."

"He did *what?*" the President moaned. "For God's sake, he's
going to create a damned panic!"

"The word's gotten out already," Attorney General George
Wentworth said. "We should notify every state and local law enforcement agency in the country to expect trouble. Every Hispanic
in the U.S. could become a target."

"Do it, George," the President said. To his Chief of Staff, he ordered, "Tom, set up a press conference at noon so I can respond to
this. And get O'Rourke on the phone. Tell him to tone down the
rhetoric or the FCC will pull the plug on him."

"Yes, Mr. President," Kinsly said. As Kinsly picked up the
phone to call his staff, his computer terminal beeped again. "A
flash message from the embassy in Mexico City, Mr. President:
President Maravilloso has assumed full responsibility for the acci-

dental downing of the American aircraft, and sincerely apologizes to the people and government of the United States." He turned, a satisfied expression on his face. "There we have it. She's coming clean."

"No mention of Zakharov or the captured CID unit, though," Jefferson pointed out.

"We have no evidence that these incidents were connected," Kinsly said. To the President, he said, "I think we may want to make a statement or gesture to show that we acknowledge Maravilloso's effort to reveal those involved in this incident, sir. Perhaps removing a few more military units away from the border?"

"I was thinking the same thing, Tom," the President said. To Ray Jefferson, he ordered, "Tell General Lopez to pull a few Guard units back, stop the deployment of any more Guard units to the border, and accelerate the removal of those antitank weapons." He shook his head. "Hell, if worse comes to worse, the states might need their Guard units to keep the peace on the streets if citizens start targeting Mexicans."

"I request permission for Task Force TALON to deploy wherever necessary to follow any leads on the whereabouts of Major Richter and the stolen CID unit," Jefferson said.

"We don't want TALON in Mexico before the FBI," Kinsly said immediately. "Maravilloso gave us excellent access and we shouldn't screw up this opportunity. Those robots have killed Mexican citizens . . ."

"One of our men is missing and a CID unit might be in the hands of the world's most notorious terrorist," Jefferson said. "We need to move quickly or we'll lose the trail . . ."

"Disapproved . . . for now," the President said. "I want the staff and the FBI briefed on CID's capabilities and potential threats to American targets, and the possibility of Zakharov being able to figure out how to utilize that thing. But no TALON units go outside the U.S. for now."

Jefferson's eyes blazed, but he held himself in check—barely. "Yes, sir," he growled, glaring at Kinsly. He knew the Chief of

Staff wasn't completely to blame: the President looked and sounded exhausted, and he was clinging to any possible relief.

"George, I'd like twice-daily briefings on the investigation into the incident near El Centro," the President said. "Russ, let Tom know when the memorials will be for the pilots killed out there. I want to be there." Both advisers, obviously anxious to move on as well, responded immediately and affirmatively. The President shook his head wearily. "I really want things to start returning to normal, folks," he said. "No more surprises."

"Sir, any comment on the Homeland Security Advisory threat level?" Jefferson reminded the President.

"Yes—ask them to reconsider leaving it at orange," the President replied. "I'll defer to their judgment, but if at all possible, I'd like to keep it where it is right now."

"In light of the loss of the CID unit, sir, perhaps we should consider . . ."

"I'd like to keep that quiet for now, Sergeant Major," the President said. "I realize how powerful those things are, but I don't think just one poses a serious threat to this country. Work with the FBI to find that thing right away."

"Sir, I strongly suggest . . ."

"That's all for now, Sergeant Major," the President insisted. "If you have any more concrete evidence that Zakharov has the robot and that it poses a significant threat, advise me immediately. Otherwise, I want the border situation to calm the hell down before anyone else gets killed—'accidentally' or otherwise." He stood, and everyone else got to their feet. "Thanks, everyone," he said brusquely as he strode out of the Situation Room, followed closely by the Chief of Staff. The rest of the National Security Staff departed right behind them.

Alone in the Situation Room, Ray Jefferson sat and thought about the meeting for a few minutes, then picked up a secure phone and dialed a number. "Yes, Sergeant Major?" Brigadier General Lopez responded a few moments later.

"Any news on your end since the incident in El Centro this morning, sir?"

"No, Sergeant Major, everything is quiet for the time being. My units have made a few dozen illegal immigrant intercepts over the past forty-eight hours, down slightly from normal. No trouble. We have a few volunteer border watch groups out east of Rampart One on private land, maybe three camps with a couple dozen folks, mostly elderly local ranchers. We're keeping an eye on them."

"The president of Mexico has assumed responsibility for the El Centro attack, sir," Jefferson said. "She claims she authorized the aircraft to fly across the border but denies giving any orders for the jets to attack American aircraft."

"You buy that, Sergeant Major?"

"No, sir, but the President does, and he wants to drop Maravilloso a kudo. He wants to remove the TOW missiles from the border immediately, stop all further Guard deployments, and pull some Guard units off the border."

"No problem. The guys don't like being out there, I can tell you."

"Sir?"

"No official reports from any units out there, Sergeant Major, just the buzz I'm picking up—it may sound like typical soldier bellyaching, but I'm picking up a definite read on these guys out there, and it's not favorable," Lopez said uneasily. "They're staying pretty busy despite the tension and the presence of troops on both sides. Weather conditions are uncomfortable, very much like Iraq . . ."

"I would've thought the southwestern Guard guys are used to working in the heat."

"Again, Sergeant Major, I categorize a lot of this as typical soldier moaning and groaning," Lopez said, "but there is an undercurrent of uneasiness. Hours and hours sweating away in the heat or freezing at night, and all they come up with is a handful of thirsty, starving, desperate Mexicans who just want to go to work. The units that find dead migrants are especially hard-hit—dying of thirst is a tough way to go, and a lot of the guys aren't accustomed to seeing death like that. They've found . . . I believe over sixty-five dead migrants during their patrols, including children. It hits them hard."

"Yes, sir."

"It's tough on them, that's all," Lopez said. Jefferson detected a hint of frustration in the general's voice, as if he expected a bit more empathy from the National Security Adviser and was disappointed he didn't get it. "Which units do you want gone, specifically, Sergeant Major?" he asked perturbedly.

"Choose TOW missile units, units in high-visibility locations with lots of press around, and units that have been in the field the longest, in that order, sir," Jefferson said. "I want it to look like a reduction but I don't want it to be an open invitation for smugglers to resume travel through those areas. Limit the reductions to around ten percent until we get further guidance. I'll send a written copy of the order to your headquarters."

"Okay, Sergeant Major."

"Thank you, sir. Jefferson out." His next phone call was to Ariadna Vega and FBI Director Kelsey DeLaine, teleconferenced in together. "Have you been briefed, Miss Director?" he asked.

"Dr. Vega briefed me moments ago," Kelsey replied, "and the Attorney General just called and scheduled a meeting in fifteen minutes."

"What's the word, Sergeant Major?" Ariadna asked impatiently. "Are we going into Mexico with the FBI, or is TALON going in by itself? We're standing by."

"Neither, Doctor," Jefferson replied.

"*What?* And let Zakharov get away? Are they *crazy?*"

"The President wants you to stand down until we see what shakes out in Mexico."

"We're not even going to ask Mexico to apprehend whoever was in those helicopters so we can question them?" DeLaine asked.

"Your job is to make contact with the Mexican government and demand anything and everything you can think of to do this investigation, Miss Director," Jefferson said. He paused for a mo-

ment; then: " I'll brief the Attorney General and get some warrants issued, but I want to operate under the assumption that the
FBI will learn information as to the major's or Zakharov's whereabouts, but the Mexican government will balk rather than give us
carte blanche to go in and get them. Ariadna, I want a plan drawn
up to go into Mexico to get the major, the CID unit, and Zakharov,
and I want you guys standing by."

"You got it, Sergeant Major."

"Work closely with Director DeLaine and get ready to act on
whatever intelligence information you receive," Jefferson said. "I
want a plan from you to covertly send TALON to Mexico if we
don't get cooperation, but TALON stays out of the country until I
give the word. Miss Director, who is your contact person for
TALON now?"

"I'm assigning my deputy assistant director for counterterrorism, Bruno Watts, to head up TALON," Kelsey replied. "Bruno's
an ex–Navy SEAL, and he's been pestering me for more info on
TALON and to let him go back out into the field, so I just
dumped all the TALON files on his desk and now he's as happy
as a pig in shit. His staff has been drawing up some plans if we
need to go in on short notice to hunt for Zakharov, and I'll shoot
them over to you after I've gotten the briefing. What assets can we
count on?"

"For now, anything in the Mexican MOU that we don't need
permission to bring into the country."

"That's not much, Sergeant Major," DeLaine said. "Standard
law enforcement equipment, vehicles, and aircraft—no weapons,
no armored vehicles, no attack or covert ops aircraft, no unmanned aircraft, no surveillance equipment beyond ordinary
cameras and voice recorders. Anything beyond that requires permission, and that takes time and a lot more political juice than I
will ever possess."

"Unless Maravilloso and the Internal Affairs Ministry suddenly
has a complete personality makeover, I definitely wouldn't count
on any special consideration here at all," Jefferson concluded. He

paused for a few moments, then: "I believe I read somewhere that the 58th Special Operations Wing at Kirtland Air Force Base near Albuquerque wanted to do some training out at the Pecos East training ranges near TALON's home base," he said. "They're bringing a CV-22 Osprey tilt-rotor, an HC-130 aerial refueler, and maybe an MC-130 Combat Shadow transport to practice some covert insertion procedures, possibly with ground and air enemy pursuing forces."

"Is that right?" Ari asked inquisitively. "I don't recall being notified of any special ops guys wanting to use our ranges."

"I think if you check your recollection, *ma'am,* that they'll be out that way later on today," Jefferson deadpanned. He quickly typed out a message to his assistant on the computer terminal in front of him to get the commander of the 58th SOW on the telephone for him. "That might be a good time to get together with them and plan some joint training exercises with TALON and Director DeLaine's Hostage Rescue Teams."

"What a great idea, Sergeant Major," Ariadna said happily. "In all the confusion, I must've missed it in my scheduler. We'll be waiting for them."

SOUTH OF THE U.S.-MEXICO BORDER,
NEAR RAMPART ONE, BOULEVARD, CALIFORNIA
EARLY THE NEXT MORNING

Sergeant Ed Herlihey finished his cup of coffee before it got cold, picked up his binocular night vision device, and carefully scanned the desert landscape to the south from just outside the front passenger seat of his Humvee. He saw nothing but a lone coyote, on the hunt just before bedding down for the day. That chap was safer out here than any other animals prowling the night, he thought.

Things had been fairly quiet lately out on this stretch of desert east of Rampart One, the first dedicated border security base established by the U.S. military. He had seen fewer migrants out this way, although he knew that the National Guard presence had simply forced the migrants farther out into the remote desert sections of Arizona and New Mexico. But if he never ran into another poor migrant out here, half-dead from walking across the scorching desert to make it to his job in the United States, he would be very happy.

"Flatbush Seven, Flatbush," his radio crackled.

Herlihey turned up the volume again and picked up the microphone. His driver, Private First Class Henry Stargell, briefly awoke but drifted quickly back to sleep. It was almost time for them to move to a different observation point anyway. Although he knew it was against the regs, Herlihey let Stargell nap so he would stay as sharp and alert as possible. This assignment was tough enough without having punchy soldiers driving expensive rigs out in the desert. He keyed the mike button: "Seven, go."

"The bird has a possible sighting east of your position, heading in your direction." Herlihey copied down the grid coordinates of the contact as it was read to him. The "bird" referred to their unmanned aerial vehicle, an unarmed Predator drone being used for aerial reconnaissance. "Multiple individuals. No weapons observed."

"Copy all. On our way." Herlihey punched in the grid coordinates of the contact into his GPS navigation computer and studied the high-resolution terrain contour map. "Okay, Hank, fire her up." The young private could wake up and swing into action even faster than he could drop off to sleep, and within moments he had his night vision gear on and was following the navigation prompts. The Humvee was equipped with infrared headlights and an infrared searchlight that could illuminate the terrain for almost a mile but was invisible to anyone not wearing night vision equipment, so driving across the desert was fairly safe and easy.

After about two miles, very close to the target coordinates, they came on a body lying in the desert. "Oh, shit, not another one," Herhiley moaned. "That's the second one on this shift alone."

"I'll take care of it, Sarge," Stargell said. "You got the last one."

"No, I'll do it," Herlihey said. "Radio it in and send the bird on its way."

"Roger. Holler if you need any help." Stargell picked up the microphone: "Flatbush, Seven, made contact with one individual at the target coordinates, looks like a DOA. Secure the bird and send a wagon."

"Wilco, Seven," the company radio operator responded.

Meanwhile, Herlihey went to the back of the Humvee and brought a duffel bag with the necessary items in it, first and foremost of which was a digital camera. Using a regular flashlight, he approached the body, snapping pictures every few paces. Stargell watched him from the cab of the Humvee for a few moments until Herlihey reached the body, then drifted off to sleep.

He wasn't sure exactly how long it was, but it seemed like only moments later when the radio blared to life again: "Flatbush Seven, Flatbush, how copy?"

Stargell picked up the microphone: "Loud and clear, Flatbush. Go ahead."

"The Bravo wagon is on its way, ETE five mike." Bravo was the National Guard's shorthand for the Border Patrol. "Have you secured the scene yet?"

"Stand by, Flatbush, and I'll check with the sarge." He stepped out of the Humvee and started toward where they had found the body. Herlihey was stooped over the body, which appeared to be that of a Hispanic woman. "Hey, Sarge, Control says the wagon is a couple minutes out and they want to . . ."

Stargell froze in absolute horror. Herlihey was not stooped over the woman—he was *on top* of her, between her legs, with his BDU pants down around his knees. The woman was struggling to free herself. She had a rock in her left hand. Blood was streaming from the right side of Herlihey's face, and he appeared to be unconscious. *"Sarge!"* he shouted. "What in hell did you do?"

"¡Ayúdeme! ¡Este hombre trató de violarme!" the woman shouted when she heard Stargell. *"¡Socorro!"*

"Jesus Christ!" Stargell exclaimed. He rushed over, grabbed Herlihey, and pulled him off the woman. Her dress was pulled up to her chest, the top of her dress was ripped apart, her panties were ripped off on one side, and her breasts exposed. The woman immediately tried to get to her feet, but she was too weak and scared to get up, so she tried crawling away. Stargell felt for a pulse and found one. "Sarge? Can you hear me? Are you okay?" He heard a moan and felt relieved.

At that moment he saw a set of bouncing headlight beams coming toward them. The Border Patrol unit from Rampart One had arrived, bouncing quickly across the desert. Soon flashlight beams were heading in their direction. "Oh my God," Stargell heard someone exclaim.

"The sarge was clobbered over the head."

"What the fuck? Did he *rape* that woman?"

"No . . . I mean, I didn't see anything . . ."

"God *damn,* Private, what the hell do you mean, you didn't see anything?" the Border Patrol agent said angrily. "Your partner is out here in the desert right in front of your face and you didn't see a thing?" He keyed a microphone clipped to his jacket. "Control, Unit Ten, I need a supervisor out here, and I need one *now.*"

"What is your situation, Ten?" the duty officer responded.

"I have a code ten-one-oh-six, signal thirty-five. Get a supervisor out here."

There was a short silence; then: "Say again, Ten? You have a signal thirty-five? Aren't you foxtrot-one-one with a Rampart unit?"

"Dammit, Control, just get a supervisor out here, *right now.* And stay off the air until we get this scene cleaned up. Out."

CHAPTER 9

THE FEDERAL DISTRICT, MEXICO CITY,
MEXICO
LATER THAT DAY

"My fellow citizens of Mexico, I bid you peace and happiness," the broadcast began. "My name is Ernesto Fuerza, but you know me by my *nom de guerre,* Comandante Veracruz. This message is being relayed to you through the broadcast studios of TV Azteca in Mexico City, courtesy of the owners and general manager of this station. I realize that they may be under some considerable danger from the government by allowing me to broadcast this message, but they have graciously given their consent to do so as long as possible, and I applaud their courage."

Fuerza shifted slightly, lowered his head, and touched the bandages covering the left side of his face, as if trying to ward off a sudden shiver of pain. He still wore his sunglasses and the bandanna on his head, but he was not wearing the bandanna normally covering his face, revealing a longer goatee than normal and a considerable darkening of the right side of his face as if caused by exposure to fire or intense heat. He wore desert camouflage fatigues similar to the U.S. Army's standard day desert battle dress uniform, a tan undershirt, a tan web belt with a sidearm, and even a pouch resembling a carrier for night vision goggles or a gas mask.

"Exactly what we have feared for so long has come true," he said after a momentary pause. The pause was only a few seconds, but it spoke volumes on his condition—and it was of course all carefully caught on tape. "As a result of the warlike stance of the government of the United States and yesterday's public call for armed aggression against the Mexican people by American right-wing radio personality Bob O'Rourke, a hideous and bloodthirsty crime was committed. Today, in the early morning hours, a California National Guard soldier brutally attacked and sexually assaulted a Mexican woman in the desert east of the illegal border patrol base known as Rampart One. This action was obviously in retaliation for the accidental downing of an American helicopter yesterday.

"As of this moment, the Americans have not released the woman or have even acknowledged that this crime took place," Fuerza went on. "However, we have obtained radio scanner recordings of the incident that I will play for you now." The recording was very short . . . and remarkably clear. "The Border Patrol agents use what are called 'ten codes' to confuse and disguise their messages, but fortunately they also publish the meanings of these codes on the Internet, which anyone can look up," Fuerza explained. "A code 'ten-one-oh-six' is an officer involved in an incident; a 'signal three-five' is a rape or sexual assault; and a 'foxtrot-one-one' means providing assistance to an outside agency. The Americans cannot hide their crimes any longer—they have admitted their guilt with their own lips. You can obviously discern the disgust and horror of the Border Patrol agent's voice as he reports what he has seen.

"To my fellow Mexicans all around the world, but especially those living and working in the United States of America, I say to you today, this must not be allowed to stand," Fuerza went on. "That poor woman, raped by American soldiers in the desert, was simply trying to go to her place of work, where she probably earns less than a fourth of what other workers earn simply because she is undocumented. She did not deserve to be attacked like this. She deserved respect, a decent wage, and protections guaranteed to any other person living in the United States, protections that are a God-given right as well as guaranteed by the Constitution of the United States.

"I call on every Mexican person in the United States who is working without documentation to leave your place of work right now. Yes, you have heard me correctly: I want you to leave your place of work immediately. Why give the Americans the fruits of your labor and then be treated no better than a cheap whore? Why slave fourteen to eighteen hours a day in their fields for pennies, and then be afraid for your lives and your family's welfare every other hour of the day?

"I understand that you are afraid of deportation and losing your jobs, but I am here to tell you, my brothers and sisters, that when enough of you abandon the fields, workplaces, homes, and slums of America, and ordinary Americans must pick up your tools and clean their own homes and pick their own crops, the Americans will *beg* for you to return. America has stood on your backs long enough—it is time for them to realize exactly how important you are to their economy and their way of life.

"I know you will be in fear of retribution for your act of defiance. Many spiteful Americans will lash out at you just because they are powerless to do anything about what you will do. You must protect yourself and your family at all times. Do not fight with the government authorities or police, but use every means at your disposal to defend yourself from vigilantes, criminals, and angry citizens.

"Soon, the authorities will be unable to handle the sheer vastness of your numbers. They will not be able to merely pile you into a bus and drive you across the border; you will not be inhumanely 'processed' as before because there will be too many for them to handle. But more important, they will soon learn that their economy, their industry, and their way of life cannot continue without you. They will soon realize that the best way to deal with the loss of your valuable labor is to formulate a fair foreign worker policy that guarantees you all legal rights, a fair wage, education and health care for your children, and eventually citizenship for those who desire it. Not only will they be unable to stop you—they will be unable to deal with you, except as the valuable, indispensable, vital human beings you are. They will quickly realize that their only recourse will be to offer you more than what you receive now. It will certainly not be more than you deserve.

"I promise you, the Mexican government will do everything it can possibly do to guarantee your safety while you are in the United States, and will make you as secure and comfortable as possible upon your return to Mexico. I ask that you report to the nearest *futbol* stadium upon your return to Mexico. There, the Ministry of Internal Affairs will take down your personal information, conduct a medical examination, arrange for temporary shelter for transportation home.

"My friends and fellow Mexicans, I know you chose to leave your homeland to try to find a better life for yourselves and your family—that is the way of all hardworking Mexicans," Fuerza said. "But after over a hundred years of hard work and struggle, is your life any better now than it was for your father or grandfather? Hispanics make up the majority of residents in California, but do we have any more rights than we did as mere aliens, migrants, or Chicanos? Our lives have not changed because we are treated the same as our forefathers were treated decades ago: at best as underpaid workers who should feel privileged to be allowed to work like virtual slaves; at worst as criminal trespassers who should be rounded up like cattle and dumped back across the border, no matter how hard we work.

"My brothers and sisters, I do not know what will happen to us when you leave your place of work and try to make your way back to Mexico," Fuerza concluded. "But what I do know is that if we do nothing as a people to correct the injustices against us, our lot in life will never change. I want something better for my children and my future than to live in perpetual servitude to an ungrateful, uncaring, and increasingly hostile nation such as the United States of America has become. We cannot wait any longer for the Anglo politicians to act. We have the power to do something; we always have had it. Our labor has value, *real* value, not what the greedy slave labor capitalists give us. It is time the people of the United States of America realize this.

"I will continue to monitor both our government and the American government and media and report to you the progress we make during this historic movement, and I will do everything I can to make this transition as safe and as hopeful as possible. There will be sacrifice, let there be no doubt. But your sacrifice will be rewarded with a better life for you and a better future for your children. God bless the people, and God bless the United Mexican States."

A few minutes after checking that the message had been successfully uplinked to TV Azteca studios in Mexico City, Fuerza sat silently, cueing up the digital recording of his message almost to the beginning. As he did so, he heard a commotion outside, and he unfastened the holster's safety catch, but did not get up. Moments later a security guard opened the door to the office . . .

. . . and behind him walked the president of Mexico, Carmen Maravilloso. The president stopped dead in her tracks, shocked and surprised at what she saw—so shocked that she did not even notice Ministry of Internal Affairs deputy minister José Elvarez and two of his men already inside the room, all carrying small submachine guns under their suit jackets, along with a tall, large, imposing man in a long black leather overcoat, boots, and sunglasses seated in a corner of the office. Once inside, two agents departed while Elvarez stayed inside the office and guarded the door.

"You!" she exclaimed. She was so shocked at seeing the infamous Comandante Veracruz before her that she hardly noticed herself being led into the room, the door closed and locked behind her. Her voice was not angry or upset, just surprised—in fact,

rather *pleasantly* surprised. She heard herself say, "I have wanted to meet you for some time, señor, but it is not yet safe for you. What are you doing here?"

"Issuing more instructions to the faithful patriots of Mexico, Madam President," Fuerza said. He started the recording and let her listen to it; when he saw that she was getting ready to explode with indignation and anger, he stopped the tape. "You agree with my sentiments, do you not, Madam President?"

"You have no right to speak for the government, señor," Maravilloso said worriedly. "What kind of plan is this? Tell our people to just *leave?* Thousands, perhaps *millions* of people will be homeless and penniless. They will be targets of racists and xenophobes, not to mention the American immigration authorities, who will round up and detain everyone heading south."

"I am hoping that is *exactly* what they try to do," Fuerza said. "They will quickly be overwhelmed and will commence mass deportations . . ."

"Which *we* will then have to absorb," Maravilloso said. "Once they are no longer America's problem, the issue will evaporate."

"Except for the thousands of American employers, farmers, and households who will be screaming for the return of their cheap laborers," Fuerza said. "Trust me, Madam President: the American government will be calling you in no time, wishing to issue a joint statement promising immigration simplification, a relaxation of immigrant worker rules, greatly increased allocations of work visas, better pay for immigrant workers, and a host of other reforms."

"You sound very well informed and very sure of yourself—for a drug and weapon smuggler," Maravilloso said. She stepped closer to Fuerza, studying him carefully. "Who are you really, señor?" she asked. "Obviously you wear a disguise, and I would even guess that you are not injured and your bandages are *part* of your disguise."

Fuerza stood and approached the president. She did not want to show any fear, but she glanced over to be sure the men of the

Political Police were nearby and ready to protect her. "You are indeed a very beautiful woman, Madam President," he said.

"Gracias, Comandante," she responded. She looked deeply into Fuerza's uncovered eye, shaking from both fear and delight at the same time. "I . . . I think you are a great man, a true inspiration to the people of Mexico. But your words are dangerous, señor. Won't you consider changing that recording?"

"I can deny you nothing, Madam President . . ."

"Carmen. Please call me Carmen, señor."

"Carmen. Your name is as beautiful and as powerful as the woman herself." He stepped closer. His first touch was electrifying, but his kiss was a million-volt charge running up and down her spine. The fear was still there, but his passion, his fire, was like a narcotic, rushing through her . . .

And then she froze, opened her eyes, and saw Fuerza smiling at her, and he saw the realization dawn in her eyes—she knew that she had willingly fallen into a trap she had suspected was there all along. Her lips curled into a snarl, her eyes blazed with white-hot anger, and her fingers became claws, tearing away at the bandages covering his face.

"This is why I love you so much, Carmen," Minister of Internal Affairs Felix Díaz said, grasping her wrists. "You are so fiery, so passionate—and so damned predictable." He pushed her away roughly, right into the arms of two Political Police *Sombras* agents behind her, who held her arms tightly. Díaz removed his bandanna and started to undo the bandages on his face. "You made it so easy for me to execute my plan."

"I *knew* it, Díaz," she snapped, struggling to regain her composure and regain the upper hand here. "I always knew it! You were too nice to be a politician, and I was too blind or too stupid to notice."

"You were too busy posing for *Paris Match* and *People* magazine and screwing me on your desk, Carmen."

"Bastard!" She jerked her arms free of the agents holding her,

then reached down to her wristwatch and pressed the hidden alert button on the back.

"The alarm works, Carmen," Díaz said casually, "but only my men are stationed outside—and do not forget that it is *my* men that protect the Federal District. No one will respond here unless I authorize it."

"*Puto!*" Maravilloso screamed. "I suspected from the day we first met that you were not just some milquetoast rich boy with delusions of grandeur. I should have seen through the disguise long ago." She looked around the room, hoping that one of the agents would come to her rescue, but knowing that was never going to happen. Her attention was drawn to a man in a seat in the corner, watching all that transpired with an amused smile on his face. "Who is that man?"

"*Perdón mis maneras pobres, Madam Presidente,*" the man said, standing and bowing slightly. "*Mi nombre es Coronel Yegor Viktorvich Zakharov.*"

"*Zakharov!*" Maravilloso exclaimed. "My God . . . Díaz, *you* are working with Colonel Yegor Zakharov, the world's number one most-wanted criminal? There are a dozen countries that would throw you in prison for twenty years just for being *associated* with him!" She glared at him in total confusion. "Is he the puppet master, pulling all the strings in this marionette show of yours?"

"I have my own agenda, Madam President, and I guarantee you, it does not include anything concerning the government of Mexico," Yegor Zakharov said. "I need 'Comandante Veracruz' and the *Sombras* in order to complete my mission in the United States. Once both our objectives are reached, with all of our mutual assurances, I will be out of your lives forever." Zakharov stepped closer to Maravilloso and removed his sunglasses, letting her see his empty eye socket for the first time. He ran a hand across her cheek, then down her neck to her breasts and belly. "You truly are beautiful, Madam President."

"Screw you, *pija,*" Maravilloso spat, slapping Zakharov's hand away. "You don't scare me with this boogeyman act of yours. I know lots of Mexican grandmothers with more horrifying faces than yours." She turned to Díaz, hoping—no, *praying*—that every second she could delay the inevitable meant one more chance for her to survive. "What is the meaning of all this, Felix? Who *are* you? Are you the lapdog of a Russian terrorist, or are you the true Mexican revolutionary patriot I had always wanted 'Comandante Veracruz' to be?"

"I am the patriot who just heard the president of Mexico agree to kiss the ass of the American president and allow an army of imperialist assassins to come into our country," Díaz said. "I had hoped the fire still burned in your belly, but it clearly has gone out. It is time to start the insurgency, the *real* revolution. It is time for the Mexican people to come out of the shadows and take their rightful place in society. It is time for the rights and welfare of hardworking Mexicans to be part of our foreign policy, not work in opposition to it. I hoped that you and I could lead this fight together, but like all the others, you sold out. You never truly believed that the people of Mexico could be anything else but third-rate citizens of a third-rate nation. The revolution means nothing to you."

"Then teach me, Felix," Maravilloso said softly, earnestly. "I am a woman and an entertainer. I do not have your vision. But I love you, and I have always thought you would make a great president. I wished for nothing except to be by your side, as your adviser as well as your lover." She stepped closer to him, then placed her hands on his chest. "Take me, Felix," she implored, looking deeply into his eyes, pressing herself against him. "Take my hand, take my heart, take my soul. I am ready to believe you. Tell me your vision for our country, and I will use all my powers to help you achieve it."

Felix Díaz nodded, closed his eyes, and placed his hands in hers, holding her closely. "Very well, Carmen. This is my vision, my love."

That was the last thing she would ever hear, except for the sudden roaring in her ears and the sound of her own muffled screams as the towel soaked with ketamine, a fast-acting veterinary anesthetic used to euthanize animals, was pressed over her nose and mouth. In seconds Maravilloso lost control of her voluntary muscles, so she was unable to struggle with José Elvarez, her assailant; in less than thirty seconds she was unconscious; and in less than a minute she was dead.

"Too bad she had to be eliminated—she was an extraordinarily beautiful woman," Yegor Zakharov said idly as he watched four *Sombras* carry the body out of the office. "I trust you have a foolproof cover story prepared for her untimely death?"

"I have been working for months to plant incriminating evidence in her homes, her prior places of employment, her ex-husband's and parents' home, and her office," Diaz said. "An investigation would eventually turn up enough long-standing corroborating evidence to make even General Alberto Rojas believe she did away with herself with a drug overdose. Distraught and under pressure from the disasters on the border, plus her earlier transgressions such as looting the treasury and establishing foreign bank accounts, she overdosed on heroin. Her medical records even hint at a possible heroin addiction when she was on TV. There is evidence of payoffs to a jealous homosexual lover for any really dedicated investigative journalists to discover. The ketamine will dissolve in less than an hour—there will be no trace of it to discover if there is an autopsy."

"It seems you have done your homework, Díaz—I hope you know what you're doing," Zakharov said. "What about the rest of the Council of Government?"

"I get reports every half hour on their exact whereabouts," Díaz said. "I have already targeted a few for elimination, such as General Rojas, if they become troublesome. I am not too concerned with the others. They care about their jobs, pensions, and girlfriends more than who is running the government. They have their escape plans ready."

"I congratulate you, sir—it appears to be a fairly well-organized coup," Zakharov said. "I thank you for rescuing me, but I must depart immediately. I have unfinished business in the United States."

"With the robot and the American officer?" Díaz asked. "Have you been able to figure out how the thing works?"

"It responds to voice commands—that is all I know," Zakharov admitted. "But there must be a way that a new user can employ the device without extensive training."

"So you must convince Richter to reprogram the device to allow anyone to pilot it? Do you think that will be difficult?"

"Richter is a U.S. Army officer, but he was trained as an engineer, not a field combat officer," Zakharov said. "My guess is that he will crack fairly easily under interrogation. But I will probably use drugs anyway to speed the process. Once we have control of the robot, he can be eliminated."

"The Ministry of Internal Affairs has an extensive medical facility and interrogation centers set up to do exactly as you wish," Díaz said. "We can transfer him here and begin immediately."

"I prefer to do my own interrogation, Díaz."

"Of course. But why not enjoy some Mexican hospitality for a while, *polkovnik*?"

"My mission is still incomplete."

"Your mysterious task in Amarillo, Texas?" Zakharov said nothing, but looked suspiciously at Díaz. "There are not many military-significant targets in that part of Texas, Colonel, so I have taken the liberty of having my operations staff draw up some general plans for an assault on some of the facilities they believe would make useful targets." Now Zakharov looked plainly worried—he didn't like outsiders horning in on his operations. "If you tell me your specific objective, I can arrange to have well-trained, well-equipped, and experienced scouts, intelligence agents, workers on the inside, and saboteurs in place well in time for you, your men, and the robot to begin your operation."

"I can handle all that myself, Díaz," Zakharov said. "Our original deal was to get my men and me to Amarillo. If you can get us there immediately with Richter and the robot, our business will be completed and you can carry on with your plan to take over the government."

"But you agreed to help train my men and provide security for . . ."

"That deal is terminated, Díaz," Zakharov said. "You are on the threshold of taking control of the entire Mexican government. You don't need me anymore."

"Alliances and loyalties change at the drop of a hat around here, Colonel. I need someone who will fight for *me*, not for the highest bidder. And with you in control of the robot, our power will be unquestioned." Zakharov was unmoved by that argument. "I'll double your pay and pay double *that* for use of the robot, plus another one hundred thousand dollars to sign with me for just sixty days."

"Not interested, Díaz."

"*Thirty* days, then, and I'll pay two hundred and fifty thousand dollars as a bonus."

"Not interested."

A flash of anger flashed across Díaz's face, and for a moment Zakharov was certain he was going to explode and order his men to try something; instead, Díaz smiled confidently. "Then I have an interesting tidbit of information to pass along in exchange for one more operation by your men inside the United States for me."

"I know now why your information is always so accurate, 'Comandante Minister,' " Zakharov acknowledged. "What this time?"

"I did some checking on one of your friends, the lovely Dr. Ariadna Vega."

"So?"

"As it so happens, Colonel, she is an illegal émigré from Mexico."

"*What?*"

"I found her Mexican birth certificate and those of her parents," Díaz said. "Her father is a university engineering professor in southern California; her mother works in her husband's office.

They are all illegals, overstaying the father's educational visa obtained over thirty years ago to attend the University of Southern California. She obtained false birth records that allowed her to be accepted into classified government research programs."

"So not only illegal—but *criminal?*" Zakharov exclaimed. "How perfect! How ironic . . . the deputy commander of America's military task force charged with border security to be from a family of illegal aliens? I would like to pay a visit to Dr. Vega's family."

"Now who is taking chances here, *tovarisch polkovnik?*"

"You worry about yourself and forget about me, Veracruz . . . Fuerza . . . Díaz, whatever the hell your name is now," Zakharov warned.

"Very well, Colonel," Díaz said, smiling casually. "You shall have support from the Internal Affairs Ministry to get you back to the United States together with your men and equipment."

"*Gracias, Díaz,*" Zakharov said. "But I warn you: if I even sniff the faintest whiff of a double-cross, you will be the *next* illegal immigrant casualty–turned buzzard food rotting in the California desert."

It wasn't until Zakharov was escorted out by Díaz's *Sombras* that Díaz's deputy, José Elvarez, fastened the holster strap over his pistol at his side and buttoned his suit jacket again. "The quicker we get rid of him, the better I'll feel, sir," he said.

"I as well, José," Díaz said. "But not before we get our hands on that robot he stole. That thing could be more valuable than any mercenary army he could ever raise in a *lifetime.*"

"Then why do we not simply eliminate him right now and take his prisoner and that machine?" Elvarez asked. "His men are good, and their security is strong, but they cannot withstand an attack by the entire ministry."

"Because he has one more important function to serve for us, and then we will let the Americans deal with him," Díaz said. "I need to know precisely when he begins to move against Vega's family. It might be right away."

"Do you believe he will risk discovery by going after the family, sir?"

"He is obsessed with revenge so strong that it overrides any common sense or tactical advantage the man possesses—almost to the point where he might forget this suicide plan in Amarillo, Texas," Díaz said. "We need to be close to him in case he asks us for our help in Texas. But he really wants revenge on the ones who defeated him the first time. He'll do it, I'm positive—and we need to be ready when he does."

SUMMERLIN, NEAR LAS VEGAS, NEVADA
EARLY THE NEXT MORNING

"Did you hear Veracruz's last message, Bob?" Fand Kent said excitedly.

"Yes, of course I heard it," Bob O'Rourke said on his cellular phone as he took a sip of coffee in the kitchen of his five-thousand-square-foot luxury home in an exclusive gated community west of Las Vegas. "So what? It's just another one of his rantings."

"I don't think so, Bob. This one was broadcast live all over the world on Mexico's largest radio network, streamed live on the Internet, and broadcast by shortwave—it wasn't secretly taped and delivered anonymously to a few news outlets like the other messages. I think the government is somehow supporting Veracruz now. What if folks start to do what he tells them to do?"

"What—leave here and start heading back toward Mexico?" he asked incredulously. "First of all, if they want to leave, fine—it'll save us the trouble and expense of deporting them. But they *won't* leave. As much as they may not like living the life of an illegal alien, that life is a million times better than life in Mexico. Wages are ten times higher here than in Mexico, even for undocumented aliens, and that's *if* they can find a job down there. Here there's work, and if they keep their noses clean and stay out of trouble, they can have a good life. Heck, some states give them every benefit and entitlement citizens receive—they have everything but citizenship. They get all the perks but none of the responsibilities."

"I'm not talking about all that, Bob. I'm talking about what might happen if the people *do* listen to Veracruz and start leaving," Kent argued. "Latest numbers are that there are almost two hundred thousand illegals in Clark County alone. If half of those are of working age, and only ten percent of them do what Veracruz says, that's *ten thousand* workers walking off the job! What do you think that would do to Las Vegas?"

"Granted, it would be inconvenient and chaotic right off," O'Rourke said dismissively, "but eventually the system would adjust. The casinos, restaurants, and hotels would immediately start hiring; wages would go up to attract more workers; things would eventually return to normal—except the prices, of course, which would stay high after folks got accustomed to paying them."

"Do you really think everything would just go back to normal? I think . . ."

"Listen, Fand, we can discuss all this at the station, when I can take some notes and we can get our facts and figures carefully researched," O'Rourke interrupted, finishing his coffee and grabbing his car keys. "I gotta talk to Lana and tell her to do the shopping after she gets done cleaning, and my tux is still at the cleaners; she has to pick it up before the Friday night fund-raiser thing. Talk at you later."

O'Rourke was taking his cowboy hat, leather jacket, and sunglasses out of the closet when he heard the sound of something metallic hit the front door. He immediately unlocked and whipped the door open . . . to find his housekeeper, Lana—he didn't even know her last name—walking quickly down the front sidewalk toward her Dodge Durango SUV. He looked down at his doorstep and saw a bundle of keys lying on his doormat. "Lana?" She didn't respond. "Lana! Hey, I'm talking to you! *¿Cómo está usted hoy?*" That was just about the only Spanish he knew except for *Otra cerveza, por favor.* "It's time to go to work."

Lana turned, clutching her purse protectively in front of her, but said nothing, looking down at the ground in front of her. "What's going on? Why are my house keys lying here?"

"I am leaving you now, Mr. O'Rourke."

"Leaving? What for?"

"I am no longer welcome in this country. I go back to Mexico."

"What do you mean, 'not welcome'? You have a good job, a nice car, a place to live." Actually he didn't know where or how she lived, but he figured with all the money he was paying her, she had to live somewhere decent. "You're not leaving because that Veracruz guy told you to leave, are you?"

"We leave because we are not welcome," she repeated. O'Rourke looked past Lana and saw that her Durango was filled with women, and the rear cargo area crammed with luggage. "We go back to Mexico until America wants us to return."

"Now wait a minute . . . that's nonsense," O'Rourke stammered. He trotted down the walkway toward Lana's SUV. "Don't believe that militant propaganda crap Veracruz is feeding you people. He wants to stir things up for his own reasons. He doesn't know you people and doesn't care about you one bit."

"No. We go."

"Wait a minute!" O'Rourke said, raising his voice perhaps a bit louder than he intended. "You can't just leave! I've got a whole list of stuff for you to do today." Lana ignored him. He lunged at her, grasping her left arm. She twisted her arm free with ease. "Listen, you, if you leave without thirty days' notice, I'm not paying you for last week." She kept on walking. He didn't see one of the other ladies step out of the SUV. "I'm going to have that Durango repossessed. You still owe me four grand on it, after I was nice enough to lend you the money at below-market interest rates!"

"No . . . !"

"You'd better stay!" O'Rourke shouted. "You've still got my garage door opener . . . wait, you've got to tell me where to pick up the damned dry cleaning! I just paid for an entire year's membership for you and your husband at Costco, you ungrateful *bitch . . . !*"

Suddenly he heard a woman shout, "*¡Déjela en paz, cagon!*" The woman who had gotten out of the Durango hit O'Rourke right in the face with a long, full shot of pepper spray. He went down to his knees, completely blinded and disoriented. The women got into the Durango and sped away.

O'Rourke found himself on his hands and knees on his front lawn trying but failing to blink away the pain and burning. He finally half-crawled, half-stumbled back inside his house, found his way back into his kitchen, and directed cold water from his sink sprayer onto his face for several minutes. It took almost fifteen minutes before he could see again. He almost contaminated himself again trying to take off his jacket, but finally he managed to change clothes. He dialed his office as soon as he was ready to go again. "Fand . . ."

"Bob! Where are you?"

"Still at home. You wouldn't believe it—that crazy bitch housekeeper of mine left, and one of her friends shot me with pepper spray! I think it was the Lewis's housekeeper! I just barely . . . !"

"Bob, whatever you do, *stay home,*" Fand said. "A couple of the cars in the front lot just got spray-painted, and there's a large group of people on the street. Looks like they're going to picket the station! There are cops and TV trucks everywhere! It's not safe."

He heard her talking, but only the words "TV trucks" got his attention. "Well, what the hell is going on, Fand? You're a reporter—tell me what's happening."

"I think it's that Veracruz radio message, Bob." She didn't mention the bombastic radio show he gave earlier, in effect telling all of America to start hunting down Mexicans. "I think the Mexicans are leaving, and they're going to stage protests and demonstrations on the way out."

"What do you mean, 'leaving'?" But he knew exactly what she meant—had in fact seen it with his own eyes, in front of his own home. "Never mind. I'll be there right away. Keep me advised if anything else happens." Fand started to warn him again, but he hung up before she could finish.

O'Rourke was heading out the door, but thinking about Fand's last warning made him stop, then head upstairs to the safe built into the nightstand next to the massive oak sleigh bed in his bedroom. There was no combination lock to the safe—instead, he pressed a code into a recessed rubberized keypad on top of the safe, and the heavy steel door popped open with ease, revealing several handguns in ready-to-draw position.

One cool thing about living in the great state of Nevada was how easy it was to get a concealed weapon permit: one day in mildly boring classes watching videotapes, listening to lectures, and seeing a few demonstrations; a half-day in an indoor shooting range; an hour or so getting photographed, fingerprinted, and filling out forms for a background check; and then a couple hours actually shopping for a suitable gun, ammunition, and accessories like holsters, cleaning equipment, and car safes. Three months later, he was proudly carrying a pearl-handled .45 caliber Smith & Wesson automatic in a shoulder rig, very aware of the fact that most everyone could see the bulge in his jacket and knew he was packing heat.

He had learned in his semiprivate concealed-carry classes that you couldn't carry a gun everywhere in Nevada—most casinos didn't allow it, although he had written permission from most of the casino managers to do so; most government offices like the DMV didn't allow guns inside, although he avoided all such offices as much as possible; guns within the Las Vegas city limits had to be unloaded (and even he couldn't get a permit from the chief of police to get around that one); and concealed weapons in Clark County could be loaded but couldn't have a round in the chamber. But he pretty much ignored those few restrictions. O'Rourke believed in the old saying: "Better to be judged by twelve than carried by six." If he was going to be the target of a kidnapping or robbery, he was going to fight.

Like one of his TV heroes, Sonny Crockett from *Miami Vice,*
O'Rourke preferred a brown leather shoulder holster for his .45,
even though he proved over and over in his concealed firearm permit classes that the big .45 was the clunkiest and most unwieldy
weapon to carry concealed, and he barely qualified with it on the
range because of its heft and recoil force. But the instructor said it
had plenty of "stopping power," unlike the nine-millimeters, the
.380, and the .38 calibers. "Stopping power"—O'Rourke liked that
notion. The .45 was heavy, hard to hold, hard to take care of,
bulky, and dug into his ribs all the time, but it had "stopping
power"—and wasn't that why one carried a piece in the first
place?

O'Rourke climbed into his big Ford Excursion SUV and
headed to the radio studio, located about thirty minutes away on
the other side of Las Vegas in Henderson. He quickly saw more
evidence that something big was underway even before he left the
carefully manicured lawns of his exclusive gated subdivision west
of The Strip in Las Vegas. Garbage cans once full of leaves and
grass clippings were strewn around the sidewalks and streets;
service trucks were parked haphazardly in front of driveways
and in the middle of intersections; and there were security vehicles racing up and down the streets. At the front gate, a long line
of Hispanic men and women were filing out on foot, throwing ID
cards and keys at the gatehouse. It was a confusing, scary, surre-
alistic scene: a woman was pleading with a departing Hispanic
nanny, while two crying children wailed in the minivan behind
her; not far away another man was shouting at a group of Hispanics about something, and the Hispanics shouted epithets in
Spanish in return.

The scene was repeated many times as he drove down Route
215 toward where the highway became the southern bypass freeway around the city—long lines of Hispanics walking down both
sides of the street, getting longer and longer by the moment, while
either law enforcement or cars followed them with either angry,

sad, or confused white citizens in them, words being exchanged through rolled-down windows.

His phone rang. "Bob, it's nuts down here," Fand warned once more. "Where are you?"

"Almost on the freeway—where else?"

"You see anything happening out there?"

"Lots of Hispanics on the street heading toward the freeway too, but . . ."

"You may not want to take North Pecos, Bob," Fand said. "Traffic is really backed up—there are masses of people everywhere pouring onto the streets. Stay on the freeway to Windsong and try Pebble Road."

He didn't usually take anyone's driving advice, but after the traffic on the freeway began getting heavier and heavier as he approached the Green Valley area, he decided to heed her advice. From the freeway he could see his usual exit, North Pecos Road, was backed up for about a half-mile, with police lights and sirens evident, so he was thankful for Fand's warning. But the east side of the Green Valley hotel and resort area was no better. This was complete insanity: just what were these people trying to accomplish here?

O'Rourke exited on Windsong Road and then, frustrated by the backed-up northbound traffic, exited at the entrance to a private residential golf club. He was instantly recognized by the gate guard, which he fully expected, and asked for directions. The guard was more than overjoyed to get into an electric golf cart and escort him to the western side of the complex to Pebble Road, just a few blocks from his office complex.

When he reached the wide intersection across from his office building, he saw huge clusters of Hispanics crowding the intersections on all four corners—they didn't seem violent, just loud—and their numbers, which seemed to grow by the minute, made them seem more intimidating. It took six light cycles to get through the largest group of people near the Green Valley Resort.

Another cell phone call: "Bob . . . ?"

"I'm almost at the studio, Fand," he said. "I don't think I'll have any trouble getting in. Looks like things are clearing out." But as he approached the studio, located in a new office complex over-looking Green Valley, it was clear that Fand was not exaggerating and that things were not clearing out. A crowd of about two hun-dred people, mostly Hispanic but with a good number of non-Hispanics mixed in, chanted and shouted in front of the office building's entrance, carrying picket signs and creating a loud din with a variety of noisemakers. There was a thin circle of police of-ficers surrounding the crowd, and across the street were several TV station satellite trucks—O'Rourke recognized every local news station and a couple from as far away as Los Angeles and Phoenix.

He briefly considered going around back and parking in the fenced-off secure employee parking area, but there were only a dozen VIP parking areas in front, and his was one of them—he was not going to be denied the coveted spot. Besides, if he sneaked in the back way, none of these reporters and cameramen would know he was here—they might assume he was just going to play a prerecorded or repeat broadcast, and that would show he was afraid. Nuts to that. He headed for the entrance, which was ob-scured by protesters and a few police officers, trusting the sheer size of his big SUV would cause the protesters to let him pass.

He was stopped immediately by a City of Henderson police of-ficer, wearing a motorcycle officer's hard helmet, leather gloves, and knee-high black leather boots, plus a bulletproof vest under his uniform shirt. "Hello, Mr. O'Rourke. I wouldn't recommend parking in front today, sir. The crowd's testy and getting bigger by the minute."

"I can see that, Sergeant," O'Rourke said loudly. "If it's not safe out here, I suggest you do something about that."

It was obvious that the officer didn't like being told what to do by a civilian, even a famous one. He leaned forward, putting his face closer to O'Rourke's. "We're in the process of clearing this crowd, *sir,*" he said, spitting out the word "sir" for emphasis, "but in the meantime, so you won't be delayed in getting inside, I *strongly* recommend you park somewhere else. Better yet, consider doing your broadcast from somewhere else entirely today. Sir."

"I'm *not* leaving just because of these . . . these *nutcases,*" O'Rourke said indignantly. "This is private property. Unless these people were invited here by the building owners—which I seriously doubt, because I am one of them—they are trespassing."

"We're trying to avoid an impromptu protest turning into a serious incident here, Mr. O'Rourke," the officer said. "The sooner I can get this situation under control, the faster things will return to normal."

"How do you propose to do that, Sergeant?"

"Once we identify the organizers, talk to them, and try to find out how long they plan on being out here . . ."

"You plan on *talking* to them all afternoon?"

"No, sir. But talking first gives me an opportunity to collect intelligence data, plan a response, and start moving our men and equipment to this location, Mr. O'Rourke. It takes time to decide which crowd control forces to bring in—more officers, mounted units, full riot control, or SWAT—and then get them moving out here. My job is to talk with the organizers, provide an initial assessment of the situation, and make a recommendation to the special operations commander. That's what I was trying to do before you showed up. The more time we can buy without letting the situation get worse, the better these things usually turn out. But if you insist on proceeding into that crowd with your vehicle, it could very easily escalate this situation into violence . . ."

"So let me get this straight, Sergeant: I'm escalating 'this situation into violence' by trying to park in my *own* parking space, while these trespassers are just exercising their constitutional rights of free speech and freedom of assembly? Is that how you want me to characterize this situation on my show this morning, Sergeant"—he read the officer's brass nameplate on his uniform— "Wilcox, is it?"

"Mr. O'Rourke, you know as well as I do that these protesters are probably here because of your—shall we say *bombastic* statements on the air yesterday," Wilcox said. "Don't play innocent with me, sir, by claiming you don't understand that the crowd is here because this is where you broadcast your show from; that your actual presence here is riling them up even more; and that you are insisting on parking right in the middle of the protesters in order to take advantage of this dangerous situation and get your face on TV."

"I resent that implication, Wilcox . . . !"

"Mr. O'Rourke, I can order you to back this thing up and move, for your own safety . . ."

"Sergeant, I'm not going to run and hide like a damned coward. If you think this situation is unsafe, I think you should do everything in your power to *make* it safe. If you don't, I, the people of Henderson and Las Vegas, and my listeners all around the world will hold you and your department responsible.

"In the meantime, I'm going to work. You can arrest me in front of all these TV cameras, so the only peaceful individual out here at the moment will be the one in handcuffs. But if you do, I guarantee you'll make yourself an enemy to all law-abiding citizens of this country. Or you can do your job and protect me while I go into my building. Take your pick."

The officer took a deep, exasperated breath and affixed the nationally syndicated radio host with a dead stare, quickly thinking about his options. Finally he looked over the Excursion's large hood and said to the officer on the other side, "Paul, get the crowd back and let Mr. O'Rourke's vehicle pass. Then form up and let's get him inside the building." The other officer hesitated for a moment, silently asking if that was a good idea, and then faced the crowd head-on, arms outstretched, trying to cut the line of demonstrators in half and move his half off to the side of the driveway. A couple more officers were called in to help. The crowd kept on shouting, but they seemed satisfied to be led back by the police.

It didn't take long for the media to notice what was happening, and soon they were surrounded by reporters and cameramen. "Bob! Mr. O'Rourke!" one well-known female correspondent for a cable TV news channel shouted. He didn't look in her direction until she called him "Mr. O'Rourke." "What are you going to do?"

O'Rourke rolled the window of his big SUV down, revved the engine, then put it into gear. "I'm going to work, that's what I'm doing."

"Will the police do anything to help you?"

"We'll see, won't we?" he replied, loud enough for Wilcox and the other officers to hear him. "It's totally up to them. They can protect me, or they can stand by and watch a law-abiding citizen of the United States be assaulted and threatened with bodily harm right in front of them."

"Do you feel any sense of responsibility for this demonstration outside your studios today?"

"Responsibility? I have nothing to do with any of this!" he shouted from inside his car. "If you don't want to blame the actual *people* who are out here disrupting free movement in this place of business, blame that Comandante Veracruz character for inciting the crowd like this! He's the one who should be thrown in jail for organizing this! I'm not going to be inconvenienced because some gangster from a corrupt third-world banana republic wants his name on the news!"

"Do you think it's wise to drive in there like that, Mr. O'Rourke? Don't you think it's dangerous?"

"I trust the Henderson Police Department to maintain order," O'Rourke said. "If they can't do it, the mayor needs to call in the Highway Patrol or even the National Guard to help restore order."

The police found it relatively easy to move the crowd aside, probably because the protesters quickly noticed that they would have O'Rourke's vehicle surrounded once it got inside the private parking lot. O'Rourke's car was hit repeatedly by rocks, bottles, empty cans, and picket signs. He laid on the horn several times to try to move the protesters away. He had to rev the engine several times and creep forward slowly to avoid running anyone over, but soon he was in his parking spot, surrounded by two police officers.

O'Rourke got out of his car and stood on the steel running board of his Excursion, making sure he would stay above the cameramen so he wouldn't look any shorter on TV, and he surveyed the crowd as calmly as he could. The TV reporters were being jostled a bit, sandwiched in between the crowds behind them and the police in front. Many in the crowd wanted to get on TV just as badly as Bob O'Rourke, while others wanted to get within spitting or yelling range of the famous radio personality. So far the protesters were obeying police instructions and staying behind the invisible line projecting from their outstretched arms. A stray banana peel sailed past O'Rourke's head—he tried to pretend it didn't bother him.

"Mr. O'Rourke," one of the female reporters asked, thrusting her microphone up toward him, "are you determined to go to your studio and do your morning broadcast as usual, despite this demonstration?"

"This is not a 'demonstration'—this is a near-riot, bordering on complete anarchy!" O'Rourke shouted. "But I am not going to be scared away by a bunch of rabble-rousers! I've got a job to do."

"Don't you think you should talk to the organizers of this rally?"

"You call this a 'rally'? I wouldn't dignify this insane act of criminal trespass, assault, hate crime, intimidation, and conspiracy as a 'rally.' And I do my talking on the air, for the rest of the free world to hear—and that's what I intend to do right now. If you want to hear what I think of these hatemongers, listen to my show, *The Bottom Line,* on your local radio, satellite radio, or on the Internet. Excuse me, but I have work to do."

He hated jumping off the tall running board, but there was no way else to get inside. Fortunately few in the crowd around them were taller than he was, and the protesters created such confusion that he hoped no one would notice how short he really was.

Wilcox and two other motorcycle patrol officers began clearing a path for him toward the office building, using nothing but their gloved hands to carefully but firmly push the crowd back as he approached the short set of stairs leading up to the semicircular drive and main entranceway. O'Rourke could see several workers at the entrance and waved to them. Just fifty feet more, he thought, and I'll be free and clear . . .

But as he reached the drive, the crowd suddenly seemed to surge forward. Both police officers on either side of O'Rourke were squeezed against him, and he pushed them away toward the crowd. The push seemed to anger many of the protesters, who pushed back even harder. A can bounced off one officer's helmet; a raw egg hit O'Rourke on the shoulder. Forty feet more . . .

The crowd started to chant, "RA-CIST! RA-CIST! RA-CIST!" Before long, the chanting turned to shouting, and then to screaming, and soon the words had changed to "¡CA-GU-E-TAS! ¡CA-GU-E-TAS!" which O'Rourke knew meant one of two things in Spanish—"little child" or "coward."

"Hey, why don't you just keep on walking home to Mexico or wherever you came from!" O'Rourke shouted in return. "We don't want you! We don't *need* you! Come back like real people and not burglars!"

More eggs and vegetables were thrown at him. "Mr. O'Rourke," Wilcox shouted behind him as he led the way toward the studios, "I'm ordering you right now to *shut up*. You want to address the crowd—do it on your radio show. Now is not the time!" O'Rourke swallowed nervously and fell quiet. Thirty feet . . .

Suddenly from his left, a large brown malt liquor bottle flew over the crowd, hitting another Henderson police officer squarely on his left temple at full force, and he went down. The protesters surged forward once more, now close enough to grasp O'Rourke's jacket, pull off his cowboy hat, and spin him around. Now O'Rourke couldn't see which way to go. Several sets of hands were grabbing him, threatening to rip his jacket right off his back, threatening to . . .

The gun! He had almost forgotten about the pistol in his shoulder holster! Even now he felt little dark fingers reaching for his weapon. If he let anyone grab that gun, there would be a bloodbath—he, then the cops, would certainly be the first ones to die . . .

He didn't actually remember doing so, but before he knew it, the big .45 was in his hand. He raised it up over his head and pulled the trigger, startled that it seemed to require hardly any effort at all to do so—and equally surprised that the second, third, and fourth pulls required even less. The crowd jerked down and away as if pulled by innumerable invisible ropes from behind. Women and men alike screamed hysterically. Most of the crowd turned and bolted away, trampling those too slow to get out of the way.

Except for two persons lying on the driveway, the path suddenly seemed to open up in front of him as if two giant hands had parted the crowd, and O'Rourke ran for his office building. Witnesses standing on the steps and in the lobby ran for cover when they saw O'Rourke with the smoking gun still in his fist heading for them. He ran inside the front doors, his thin chest heaving. "My . . . God, they . . . they tried to kill me!" he panted. He couldn't control his breathing, and he leaned forward, hands on his knees, trying to catch his . . .

"Police! Freeze! Drop the gun, now!" he heard. He didn't think they were talking to him, but someone else behind him in the crowd with a gun, so he stayed bent over until he was finally able to . . .

Wilcox and another Henderson Police Department officer tackled O'Rourke from behind, running at full force. O'Rourke's face was mashed into the tile floor, his arms pinned painfully behind his back, and the gun wrenched out of his right hand by breaking his index finger.

"This is Mike One-Seven, inside the Green Valley Business Plaza, shots fired, one suspect in custody—it's fucking Bob

O'Rourke," Wilcox said into his shoulder-mounted radio micro-phone after he and the other officer wrestled the gun out of O'Rourke's hand, twisted his arms behind him, and handcuffed his wrists together. "I'm declaring a code ten-ninety-nine at this location, approximately two hundred individuals. I want them cleared out *now* before someone else decides to bring a gun out here. Over."

CHAPTER 10

As expected, the streets surrounding the U.S. embassy on the Paseo de la Reforma in Mexico City were jammed with thousands of angry protesters. Two separate groups converged on the embassy from the east and west, one carrying signs in Spanish, the other in English. There were only the usual half-dozen Federal District Police stationed at the main and employee entrances of the embassy, none wearing riot gear. By the time the police realized what was happening, the crowds kept reinforcements from being brought in. They were in control.

The U.S. embassy in Mexico City is the largest American embassy in the Western Hemisphere and has one of the largest staffs of any in the world. As befitting a "friendly neighbor" embassy, the eight-story U.S. embassy complex in Mexico City was an "urban" model, situated in the heart of the city and set up to make it as accessible as possible without hampering security. It occupied an entire city block, but it was not centered in the block so it did not have a tightly controlled perimeter on all sides. There was an ornate twelve-foot-high spade-topped wrought-iron fence surrounding the entire complex, but in spots the fence was still very

close to the building, offering little actual protection. The north
and east sides bordered an open area with gardens and a small am-
phitheater, and there was a high wall protecting those sides with
trees screening out most of the interior yards.

The main and staff entrances were very close to major
thoroughfares—the building itself on the south and west sides
was less than five yards away from the sidewalk. Massive concrete
planters were placed on the streets beside the curbs to prevent anyone from parking near the building or driving directly into the entrances, but they were designed to stop vehicles, not protesters on
foot. The wrought-iron fence had been erected at the edge of the
sidewalk, outside of which the Mexican Federal District Police
were stationed every few yards. There was a U.S. Marine guard
post on one side of the public entrance and a U.S. Embassy Diplomatic Security Service officer and processing agent's kiosk on the
other side. Both were vacant now, with an egg- and feces-covered
sign in both English and Spanish proclaiming that the embassy
was closed due to "public demonstration activity."

"Where are the damned *federales?*" the U.S. ambassador to the
United Mexican States, Leon Poindexter, growled as he watched
a feed from the embassy's security cameras on the monitors in his
office.

"The crowds are preventing any more police from moving in,"
Poindexter's chief of the embassy's one-hundred-and-twenty-
person Diplomatic Security Service detachment, ex–U.S. Army
Lieutenant Colonel Richard Sorensen, said. "They'll probably
have to turn out their riot squads to see if they can disperse the
crowd."

The ambassador ran a hand nervously over his bald head, loosened his tie with an exasperated snap, and stood up and began to
pace the office. "Well, if the Foreign Minister wants to meet with
me in the Palacio Nacional, he's going to have to do a better job
calling out the *federales* to protect me."

"The motorcade is ready for you, Mr. Ambassador," the outer
office secretary said from the doorway.

"No way, Marne," Poindexter said. "I'm not moving from this office until the streets are clear—with the Mexican Army, not just the Federal District Police. I want those streets *clear!*"

"Sir, there is going to be some sort of major announcement on nationwide TV in less than two hours," his chief of staff said. "It would be advisable to confer with the president before she drafts her speech . . ."

"Why? It won't make any difference. She'll say whatever she wants to say. Hell, anything I tell her will be used *against* me in any speech she gives!"

"Sir . . ."

"All right, all right," Poindexter said irritably. "Get the Foreign Affairs Ministry on the phone, and as soon as the Federal District Police or the military gets here, we'll go over to the . . ."

"Here they come now, sir," the ambassador's assistant said. They looked outside. A large blue school bus with flashing blue, red, and yellow lights moved slowly down the Paseo de la Reforma, with a half-dozen men in green fatigues and white riot helmets with clear face shields, carrying M-16 rifles, jogged on either side of the bus. Behind the bus was a dark blue armored Suburban belonging to the Federal District Police, with gun ports visible on three sides.

Poindexter turned to his aide. "What about the evacuation route . . . ?"

"All set up, sir," she assured him. "There are DSS units stationed every couple blocks along your travel route, and four locations north and south of the route where they can set a helicopter down if necessary. Medical teams are standing by."

"This is a damned nightmare," he muttered. "Why won't the Internal Affairs Ministry allow us to fly our helicopter in here?"

"They said once the Federal District Police are able to control the central flight corridors in the district, they can't guarantee safety for any helicopters, and they don't want to have to deal with a chopper going down in the city," his aide said. "It could take days for them to secure the Federal District."

"Jesus," Poindexter groaned. He looked around at the nervous faces around him. "It'll be okay, folks," he said, smiling gamely, trying to be as reassuring as possible. "The *federales* are here, and hopefully they'll have the crowds under control by the time we're ready to roll. The best news is that we have sixty DSS agents arrayed along our route waiting for us. Let's go."

As they headed downstairs to the parking garage, Sorensen came up to the ambassador. "Excuse me, sir, but I'm recommending we delay this convoy awhile—perhaps an hour."

"An *hour?* That's no good, Rick. I need to try to get in to see Maravilloso before she starts throwing more firebombs on TV."

"As far as I can ascertain, sir, only half the normal contingent of Federal District Police are outside," Sorensen said. "I called the Internal Affairs Ministry and they said the rest are clearing the first several blocks of the route."

"Sounds normal to me."

"The usual procedure is to have one platoon of police outside the embassy to surround the convoy as it leaves the compound. They deploy motorcycles or Jeeps to secure the route ahead of the convoy only after we've formed up. We've only got half the detail here now—and I can actually see only six. Besides, we don't have any air support clearance yet."

"But our choppers are standing by . . . ?"

"Yes, sir, and they'll launch with or without clearance," Sorensen assured him. "But it's damned irregular for the president to ask for a meeting and at the same time the Internal Affairs Ministry keeps us grounded. The left hand is not talking to the right."

"After Maravilloso publicly admonished Díaz for that shoot down near El Centro, I'd be surprised if they even *look* at each other anymore, let alone talk."

"That kind of friction only makes the situation worse, sir."

"Rick, I need to get to the Palacio Nacional, ASAP," Poindexter said. "I don't like it any more than you do, but Washington is hoping that having the U.S. ambassador camped out in her outer office while she addresses the nation will coerce Maravilloso to say something to calm this situation down. Now, is there any action-able intel that you've received that leads you to believe we'd be in danger if we set out immediately?"

Sorensen hesitated, then shook his head. "No, sir. Just a hunch—that creepy feeling I get when things don't look quite right. But I have no information on any specific action against us—other than the normal level of threats of violence, of course."

"Then we go," Poindexter said. He tapped the bulletproof vest under his shirt. "Wonder if we'll ever get to the point where we won't have to wear this shit whenever we go outside the embassy here, Rick."

"I wouldn't count on it, sir."

Poindexter sighed, then clasped the DSS chief on the shoulder. " 'I only regret I have but one life to lose in the service of my country,' eh, Rick? Nathan Hale."

"Hale was sold out by a friend, captured by the British, refused a Bible while in custody, tortured, had all of the letters he wrote to his family burned, and was hanged without a trial, sir."

"You didn't need to remind me of all that, Rick. Let's roll."

The ambassador's convoy was three armored Suburbans, one in front and one in back of the ambassador's car. Each Suburban had four heavily armed Diplomatic Security Service agents in it, wear-ing bulletproof vests and armed with Heckler & Koch MP5 sub-machine guns and SIG Sauer P226 sidearms. A GPS tracking system recorded every vehicle's exact position and would immedi-ately notify the other DSS units along the route of any problems.

As soon as the convoy was formed up inside the parking garage, DSS notified the Federal District Police protective unit outside. The bus moved forward until it was past the gated garage en-trance. Once in position, Rick Sorensen stepped outside the steel gate, his jacket unbuttoned so he could have fast access to the MP5 submachine gun underneath. He carefully scanned both sides of the block. The street was cordoned off by Federal District Police in riot gear in both directions, and the street was empty. The po-lice had pushed the crowds back all the way across the intersection to the other side and blocked off the streets, leaving plenty of warning space. The windows and rooftops within sight appeared clear.

Everything looked okay—so far. Sorensen lifted his left sleeve microphone to his lips: "Bulldog, Tomcat, report." All of the Marine Corps guards and DSS security agents reported in, followed by the controllers monitoring the fourteen security cameras outside the complex. When everyone reported clear, Sorensen waved to the Federal District Police bus driver to move out, then motioned for the ambassador's motorcade to follow. He made one more visual sweep of the block. Everything looked good. The crowds were back, *way* back . . . good. No one in the windows, no one in the park across the plaza, no one . . .

It was then that Sorensen realized that the Federal District Police bus had not moved. The first Suburban was out of the compound and the ambassador's car was following right behind, not yet clear of the steel gate—that was another mistake. Either the car was all the way *in* or all the way *out,* never in between. Sorensen glanced at the bus driver's mirror . . .

. . . and noticed there was no one in the driver's seat.

He immediately lifted his microphone: *"Code red, code red!"* he shouted. *"Contain! Contain!"*

The first Suburban, which had cleared the steel gate, stopped in position to guard the entrance, its gun ports immediately open. The driver of the ambassador's Suburban jammed the transmission into reverse. But just before he cleared the gate he rammed into the Suburban behind him, which was following too close behind. Both vehicles stalled . . .

. . . and at the same time the heavy gauge steel car gates, propelled by small howitzer shells to ensure the gates could be closed even without electricity, slammed shut—crushing the ambassador's SUV's engine compartment, trapping it between the gates . . .

. . . and at the same moment, two hundred kilos of TNT hidden underneath the bus detonated. Sorensen and the Suburban outside the gate were immediately obliterated by the explosion. The engine compartment of the Suburban stuck in the gates exploded, propelling the SUV backward into the embassy compound and flipping it up and over the third security vehicle.

Major Gerardo Azueta was awakened by that unexplainable soldier's sixth sense of impending danger. He quickly swung out of his cot, pulled on his uniform, and slipped into his body armor vest and web gear. He grabbed his M-16 rifle, donned his Kevlar helmet, and hurried outside. He was on his way to the command vehicle, but saw Lieutenant Ignacio Salinas, the duty officer and second in command, speaking with a noncommissioned officer and went over to them instead. It was probably an hour or so before dawn, with just a hint of daylight to the east, but even in the darkness he could tell there was trouble. "Report, Lieutenant."

"Sir, report from Scout Seven, about ten minutes ago," Salinas reported. That scout unit, riding U.S. military surplus Humvees, was about thirteen kilometers to the east. "They saw a group of about fifteen migrants captured by what appears to be a civilian border patrol group."

"Those Watchdogs again?"

"Yes, sir, I think so," Salinas said. "About six heavily armed individuals in military gear, but they were not National Guard."

"Status of the California National Guard units in the area?"

"Slight decrease in numbers, sir, especially the TOW-equipped Humvees," Salinas said. "They were pulled out yesterday evening. Still several active patrols out there, but fewer in number and firepower."

"Damned renegade vigilantes," Azueta murmured. "Did you observe anyone getting badly hurt?"

"Yes, sir. Our scouts report some of the men were being beaten and physically restrained, and one woman was being pulled into the back of a truck with several Americans with her—no one else. It appeared as if she was resisting."

"Sir, we have to do something!" the noncommissioned officer in charge, Master Sergeant Jorge Castillo, interjected hotly. "This is in retaliation for the *accident* near El Centro and the embassy bombing. Are we going to stand by and watch as our women are raped by these *meados . . . !*"

"Sir, we know which camp they took them to," Salinas said. "It's only three kilometers north of the border. We will outnumber them with an extra patrol unit. Request permission to . . ."

"Denied," Azueta said. "I will report this incident to regimental headquarters and await instructions." But as soon as he said those words, he knew he had to reconsider them: even the young lieutenant was itching to get into action. "What's your plan, Lieutenant—or haven't you thought of one yet?" Azueta challenged him.

"The master sergeant recommends flanking the camp with two patrol units," Salinas replied. "We will come in from the east and southeast and sweep in, with one patrol unit attacking the camp and the other guarding the road to the west to cut off any response from the nearest National Guard patrol units."

"That's your plan, Lieutenant? What resistance do you expect? What weapons? What reserves do you plan to bring? What will you do if the California National Guard responds? Do you even have any idea who those people are and why they were being taken . . . ?"

"Sir, we are wasting time," Castillo said. "The scouts say they outnumber the Watchdogs right now. We have only observed *fewer* National Guard forces out there, not *more*. We may never get another opportunity to help those people. I respectfully recommend we proceed, sir."

" 'Respectfully recommend,' eh, Master Sergeant?" Azuerta mocked. "Your 'recommendation,' no matter how respectful, will not soothe my agony when I stand over your dead bodies, nor soothe my wife and children when I am thrown into prison for approving this insane idea."

"Sir, they are only civilians—they have probably been drinking all night, they are tired, and they are too busy *abusing our people* to expect a counterattack," Castillo said. "We should . . ."

"Hold your tongue, Master Sergeant, or I'll put you in irons myself!" Azueta said angrily. "You are just as crazed on vengeance as those Americans." But he looked at their excited, energized faces, thought for a moment, then nodded. "But we're out here to protect Mexico and its people, and that includes those who want to work in the United States." Castillo slapped a fist into his hand in glee. "Very well, Lieutenant. Get two more scout units moving toward that location to cover your withdrawal, and advise me when the two scouts are in position and ready to go in. If there is any observed change in opposition force deployment or numbers, terminate the mission and return to your patrol positions—don't ask for reinforcements, because you won't get them." Salinas immediately picked up his portable radio to issue the orders.

It took less than fifteen minutes for Azueta to get the message that the team was in position—Salinas and Castillo must've set a land speed record for driving a Humvee cross-country. They took command of the strike team, with one of the patrol units on the border withdrawing to a defensive position to the southwest, ready to cut off any pursuit from a California National Guard patrol whose last known position was only two kilometers from the Watchdog Project's camp.

That proved the National Guard's duplicity in this horrible action, Major Azueta thought: there was no way they would not know what the Watchdogs had done. Azueta knew the National Guard was out there to watch the Watchdogs as well as look for migrants. That made it much easier for him to issue the order to proceed across the border. When the last patrol unit was in position, Azueta ordered Salinas to go.

"We go," Salinas said to his men. "Now listen to me carefully. Our mission is to rescue as many of our people as we can. We are not here to engage the Watchdogs or the California National Guard except as necessary to accomplish our mission." He touched Castillo's sleeve. "Specifically, we *are not* here for revenge, Master Sergeant, is that clear?"

"*Entendido, Teniente.*"

"We go in, rescue the woman and as many men as we can, and get out, with a minimum of bloodshed," Salinas went on. "Fire only if fired upon, understood? We have watched these people for days: most of them are old and frail, and they will have been outdoors all night and are probably sleepy and cold. We use that to our advantage. Be smart, be safe. *Paseo rápido y duro, amigos.* Mount up."

On Master Sergeant Castillo's suggestion, the two Humvees went in with headlights shuttered, at full speed, and with an American flag attached to their radio antenna. They angled in from the east, trying to avoid the last known location of the Watchdog's lookouts and to put the rising sun at their backs to screen themselves, but it was almost dawn so they had no more time to be stealthy. Three hundred meters from the camp, they dropped off two soldiers, who would proceed in on foot to set up an overlook position and warn of any responders. At the last moment, Salinas ordered a third Humvee to drive north with only the driver on board to pick up as many captives as it could hold, and the fourth Humvee was standing by with soldiers ready to repel any pursuers.

Just thirty meters from the camp, they spotted the first lookout—he appeared to be an older man in cold-weather camouflaged hunting gear, lying on an aluminum and vinyl-webbed beach lounge chair, with a thermos of coffee beside him, a monocular night vision device hanging from a lanyard around his neck, and a walkie-talkie on a strap around the arm of the lounge chair. The man looked up, tipped his hat back to get a better look, then appeared to wave as the Humvee raced past. Salinas waved to the man, then ordered Castillo to radio his position to the dismounts. "One lookout, no weapon observed. Avoid him if you can."

They encountered a group of ten or eleven migrants just a few meters farther, sitting and lying on the cold desert ground about ten meters outside the large eight-person tent that was the American Watchdog Project's base camp. Salinas pulled up between the migrants and the tent. The men slowly shuffled to their feet as if they were drugged or injured, some helping others up. *"Vamos, amigos,"* Castillo said. He radioed for the third Humvee to come in, then quickly assessed the men. He picked two of the healthiest-looking ones. "There is one lookout down the road—secure him and make sure he doesn't report in."

"¿Quiénes son usted, señor?"

"Master Sergeant Castillo, Army of the United Mexican States," Castillo replied. "We're here to take you home." The men stood around, looking at each other in confusion. Castillo motioned to his Humvee. "Put your injured inside—the rest will have to ride outside the vehicle. We have more vehicles on the way. Where's the woman?" The migrant pointed at the tent, his finger shaking, and Castillo jabbed a finger at the tent.

Lieutenant Salinas led the way, his M-16 rifle at the ready. They took only a few steps before they heard screams coming from inside. Castillo bolted for the front of the tent before Salinas could tell him to wait. Castillo stooped down low, then using the muzzle of his M-16, he opened one of the door flaps. He saw four men standing around a camp table, one man on a stool in front of the table . . . and a woman lying on her back on the table, her dress pulled up around her neck, screaming in agony as the men watched. Two battery-powered lanterns brightly illuminated the scene. Most all of them wore camouflage gear, with a few sporting bright orange hunter's vests. The man on the stool had close-cropped hair, while the others had longer hair and beards. Some were grimacing, but a few were smiling and joking with one another despite the poor woman's screams . . .

. . . and at that moment, one of the bearded men looked up and noticed Castillo kneeling in the doorway with his M-16 aimed at him. *"Hey!"* the guy shouted. *What the fuck? Who the hell are you?"*

Something exploded in the veteran Mexican soldier's brain. *"¡Muerte a América!"* he shouted, and he started pulling the trigger. He surprised himself at how calmly he operated: with incredible control and accuracy, he picked off the four standing men. His targets were very close—centimeters away, close enough for the muzzle flash to hit the closer targets—but he kept himself steady, his weapon on single-shot, and his breathing perfectly measured.

Four targets, four trigger pulls, four down.

"¡Pare el tirar! Cease fire! Cease fire!" Salinas shouted. He threw open the tent flaps and swept the interior with his .45 caliber automatic, finally aiming at the only American alive inside. The soldier—a U.S. Army officer—that had been seated in front of the table had curled up into a ball and dropped under the table when the shots rang out, cowering in fear from the muzzle blasts thundering around him. Now he was on his back halfway under the table, his knees folded up against his obese belly, his hands covering his ears, his eyes behind his thick horn-rimmed spectacles bugging out wider than Salinas had ever seen before. His entire body was trembling so bad that his teeth rattled . . .

. . . and to Salinas's horror, he noticed that the soldier's hands and the front of his fatigues were covered with blood. Blood dripped from the table, huge pools of blood were on the floor—it was the most horrendous sight he had ever seen.

"Who . . . who are you?" the soldier screamed, his voice screeching and uncontrolled. Through the smell of cordite hanging thickly in the air, Salinas could smell feces and urine—the smell of fear, the smell when the guilty knew they were about to meet their just punishment.

"Su repartidor," Salinas said. "Her avenger." He pulled the trig-

ger on his .45 Colt and kept on pulling until the magazine was empty.

"Sir." Salinas couldn't hear anything through the roaring of blood pounding in his ears for several moments. *"Sir."* Salinas looked up at Master Sergeant Castillo, who motioned at the woman on the table. After several long moments, Salinas holstered his pistol and looked . . . and his throat instantly turned dry as the desert, and his mouth dropped open in complete shock. *"Mi Díos, Teniente . . . !"*

"Get . . . get everyone loaded up and out of here, *now,*" Salinas ordered. "Get some men in here and help her up, *carefully.*" He turned to the sergeant major and said, "Have the dismounts meet up here on the double." Their eyes locked, and Castillo nodded, signifying that he understood the unspoken orders.

Castillo directed four men to help the women into his Humvee, then issued orders to the dismounts when they came over to meet up with the team minutes later. Salinas slipped behind the wheel of the Humvee, waiting for the camp to be evacuated. Two shots rang out from outside the tent, but Salinas was too stunned, too horrified to notice. Within minutes, the Mexican patrols were on their way, and less than five minutes later, they were safely across the border with their precious cargo.

FARM TO MARKET (FM) ROAD 293,
JUST WEST OF PANHANDLE, TEXAS
LATER THAT NIGHT

"Rise and shine, Major."

Jason Richter found his vision blurry, his eyelids oily, his throat dry as dust. Cold rough hands grasped his shirt and pulled him to a sitting position, which made his head spin, then throb with pain. He ran the backs of his hands across his eyes to clear the grit and dirt away, then blinked to try to focus his eyes. When he could see again . . .

. . . he was looking right into the face of Yegor Zakharov himself. "Welcome back to the land of the living, Major. I trust you had a good nap."

"Screw you, Zakharov," Jason murmured. He could tell he was in a moving vehicle—it looked like a passenger van, although it was too dark to tell for sure. He was seated on the bench seat behind the driver, with several other persons seated very close to him.

Zakharov motioned to one of the men, retrieved a plastic bottle of water, and tossed some water into Jason's face; he lapped the welcome moisture up as fast as he could. The Russian terrorist was kneeling between the driver and front passenger seat, his sunglasses off, streaks of reddish-brown fluid dripping out of the empty eye socket and down his cheek. "Do not be cross with me, Jason. You are still alive, thanks to me."

"What did you do to me, Zakharov?"

"Tiny amounts of thiopental sodium administered over the past several hours," Zakharov said, smiling. "We have had several interesting and entertaining conversations about your Cybernetic Infantry Device. I have also learned much more than I ever wanted to know about your childhood, National Security Adviser Jefferson, your Oedipal conflict with one of your aunts, and your rather perverted sexual fantasies about Ariadna Vega."

"Fuck you."

"Let us get down to business, Major," Zakharov said, his smile gone. "We know all of the commands to use with the device except the most important one: the activation command. Apparently this is the only command that only the authorized pilot can give—according to you, anyone can pilot the robot once it is activated. That is why you are still alive. You will give the activation code once we are in position."

"I'm not giving you shit, Zakharov."

"You may want to reconsider, Major." Zakharov reached over and grasped the face of the person sitting next to him, pulling her into Jason's view. "Major, meet Marta. We found Marta playing in her front yard a few towns away, and we decided to bring her with us. She is ten or eleven years old, I do not really know. We also found a few others like Marta, another girl and a boy, who we also decided to bring along with us."

"You sick fucking bastard. Go to hell."

"Cooperate with me, Major, and you and the children will live," Zakharov said. "Refuse me, and you will all die. It is as simple as that."

"There is no way I'm going to help you do anything."

"Then you will be responsible for their deaths," Zakharov said matter-of-factly. "Do not try to be a hero now, Richter. You have no weapons, no robots, and no support. I have your robot and the hostages. You have lost this round, plain and simple—admit it and live. I am not a child killer, but I will slaughter them if you do not cooperate with me." Jason did not reply. "Have a little faith in the system, Richter. You are only one man. You can save the lives of these children by giving me access to the robot. My men and I will be gone, and you can return these children to their homes and families—but more important, you will live to fight another day."

"How do I know you won't kill us all after I give you control of the CID unit?"

"My fight is against you and your government, Richter, not these children," Zakharov said. "As I told you, I am not a child killer, but I am a soldier, and I will do whatever it takes to complete the mission. All I offer is my word, soldier to soldier. Give me access to the robot, and I will let you take these children home. Once they are safe, our battle resumes; but I promise you your life, and theirs, until then." He exchanged words with the driver. "You have thirty seconds to decide, Richter, and then I will order the driver to pull over into a field, and I will start killing these children in front of you."

Jason's mind spun. He looked at the children around him; all were on the verge of fearful crying as they heard Zakharov's voice—they easily sensed the danger they were all in. Richter was no better. He was edgy and disconnected from the drugs still coursing through his body, but the sickness was quickly being replaced by pure mind-numbing fear. He wasn't afraid to die, but he was afraid of others coming across his body and those of the children and blaming him for not protecting them.

There was an entire superpower's military and law enforcement standing ready to protect whatever Zakharov's newest target was—but right now, there was only one man ready to protect these children. His choice was clear.

The van slowed, and Jason heard the crunch of gravel and felt the bumps of a tractor-worn dirt road. "Well, Major?" Zakharov asked casually. "What is your answer?"

He took a deep breath, then said, "I'll do it, you sick bastard."

"Excellent choice, Richter." The van stopped, and the side and rear panel doors opened. "I never doubted you for a second. You may be a genius, but you are not a heartless berserker."

They were in a dark field about a hundred yards off the paved road. Jason could see the glow of a town off on the horizon, perhaps three or four miles away, but he couldn't tell in which direction. In the opposite direction was another, larger town, about equal distance away. A second van full of Zakharov's commandos had pulled up behind them. Two men with assault rifles took up security positions, while the others assembled in the rear of the van, pulling the folded CID unit out of the back and setting it down on the ground.

"Work your magic, Major," Zakharov said.

Jason gathered the children around him, gave Zakharov a glare, then spoke. "CID One, activate." The children gave out a quiet combination of fear and delight as they watched the dark shape seemingly grow out of the field and appear before them.

"Truly amazing technology, Major," Zakharov said. "I commend you. Allow me." He cleared his throat and dramatically said, "CID One, pilot *up*." One of Zakharov's men had to jump out of the way as the CID unit obediently crouched down, extended one leg behind itself, leveled its arms along each side of its back to act as handrails, and the entry hatch popped open in the middle of its back. "How delightful. I wish I was of the proper size to give it a ride, but unfortunately I will have to leave that honor to someone else."

Zakharov barked an order, and one of his men jumped up and slid inside the robot, with the Russian terrorist issuing instructions as he did so. A few moments later, the hatch closed, and the Cybernetic Infantry Device came to life. They watched in fascination as the commando experimentally made the robot jump, dodge, and dart around the field, finishing off with triumphantly upraised arms, like a superheavyweight boxer who had just won a world title.

"It works! Excellent." They tried their handheld radios—the man inside the robot had no trouble adjusting the radio scanner to pick up the handhelds' frequency and making the connection. "It appears my missile attack had no ill effects. I am satisfied." He pulled a pistol out of its holster. Jason felt a roaring in his ears as he realized that Zakharov had everything he wanted, and that sealed his fate. "And now, Major, as for you and the children . . . you are free to go."

"Wh . . . what . . . ?"

Zakharov grasped Richter by the shoulders, and, with Jason still protectively clutching the children, turned him around. "Walk in this direction, Major. Do not turn around, and do not try to head for the road—if my men or I see you on the road, we will gun you down. Stay together and do not allow the children to leave your side—if you do, our deal is off. Keep walking toward those lights. In about an hour, you should reach a farmhouse; if you miss it, in another hour or less you should reach the town. By then, my men and I should be long gone." He issued more orders in Russian, and in an instant the CID unit ran off into the night and the commandos boarded the vans and drove away. Within moments, Richter and the children were alone.

"*¿Dónde iremos ahora, señor?*" one of the children asked.

Jason recognized the words "where" and "sir"—he guessed the rest. "Don't worry, kids," he said. "*No problema*. Help is on the way."

He led the children toward the lights of the town, carefully leading them across the furrows and ditches crisscrossing the fields. Soon his eyes had fully adjusted to the darkness, and he could make out stars. He found Polaris, the North Star, and realized he was walking east. He began to feel better—he didn't know where he was at all, but at least he knew which way he was going.

Although he remembered Zakharov's warning, he needed to find help as quickly as possible, so as soon as he saw a truck on the highway, he decided to risk it and started angling toward it. About fifteen minutes later, he reached the edge of the field adjacent to the paved road. He instructed the children as best he could to stay in hiding, then crawled through the dirt until he reached the road. He couldn't see anything nearby, but several yards away he spotted a road sign, and he decided to risk trying to pinpoint his location. Half-crawling, half-crouched, he dashed through the edge of the fields until he reached the sign. It was very dark, and the sign was weathered and hard to read; it was riddled with bullet holes, commonly found in rural signage, but soon he read . . .

. . . and instantly, he knew what Zakharov's *real* objective was.

He had no choice: when he saw the next vehicle, a pickup truck, coming down the road, he flagged it down, forcing it to stop by practically throwing himself in front of it. Thankfully it was a farmer and not a terrorist. He talked fast, convinced the driver to help him, then gathered the children together and helped them into the cargo bed. He breathlessly used the farmer's cell phone to call for help . . .

PECOS EAST TRAINING AREA,
CANNON AIR FORCE BASE, NEW MEXICO
THAT SAME TIME

Ariadna Vega threw open the office door and flipped on the light. "We got it!" she shouted.

FBI Deputy Director Bruno Watts, asleep on the sofa in Jason Richter's office at the Task Force TALON headquarters complex, blinked at the light but was instantly on his feet. The task force's new commanding officer did not look like your typical "snake-eater" ex–Navy SEAL—he was shorter than average, wiry, and rather soft-spoken around others. As his hair thinned and grayed he decided to shave his head, so he could still intimidate even in an office or social setting, but otherwise no one would ever recognize him as one of the world's most highly skilled and experienced experts in unconventional warfare and counterterrorist operations. "What is it?"

"CID One's locator beacon just went off," Ariadna said breathlessly. "The unit's been activated."

"Where?"

"About twenty miles northeast of Amarillo, Texas."

"Amarillo . . ." Watts tried to think of the significance of that city, but nothing came immediately to mind. "What about Richter?"

"No word from him, but he's the only one who could have activated the CID unit."

"But it doesn't mean he's controlling it, right?" Since taking command of the unit, Watts had been taking a crash course in the Cybernetic Infantry Device—and the more he learned the more excited he got about employing this incredible high-tech weapon system.

"He's alive, I know it."

"If he is, he's got some explaining to do," Watts said. "Are we . . . ?"

"We're getting ready to launch right now," Ariadna said. "We're only about a hundred miles away—less than fifteen minutes in the air."

"Good. You stay here and man the command post. Give me any updates you receive." He pulled on a leather jacket and hurried out to a waiting helicopter that would take them to Cannon Air Force Base, where a jet was waiting to fly him to Amarillo.

Just before touching down on the parking ramp, Watts suddenly slapped his hands together. "Shit!" he shouted, and he fumbled for the intercom control panel inside the helicopter. He dialed his microphone to "COM 2" and keyed the mike button: "Talon, this is Alpha."

"Go ahead, Alpha," Ariadna responded from the task force command center.

"Send an urgent message immediately to the FBI office in Amarillo and the Department of Energy. Whoever's got the robot, I know what their target will be."

On FM Road 293 four miles west of where Richter and the hostages had been dropped off, the two vans encountered the first roving patrol, an armored Suburban belonging to a private security company. The men inside the Suburban radioed the two vans' license plate numbers to their headquarters inside the plant; they in turn contacted the Texas Department of Public Safety. The response came back a few moments later: vans rented in Amarillo, not reported stolen or missing, rented to private individuals.

A second request went out for the IDs of the renters. The data came back moments later: both vans rented to individuals from Mexico, no local address, no local destination. That got a lot of folks' attention. The Carson County Sheriff's Department was called and a request made to do a traffic stop and an ID and citizenship check, with the Potter and Armstrong County Sheriff's Departments, alerted because the vehicles were so close to their jurisdictions. Although FM 293 was a public road, the Department of Energy had agreed to use the full force of the U.S. government to defend and indemnify the state, county, and local law enforcement agencies from any liability in conducting investigations requested by plant security.

There was no question that whatever plant security wanted, they would get, for this was the Pantex Plant, America's only facility dedicated to the assembly, disassembly, and disposal of nuclear weapons. Administered by the Department of Energy's National Nuclear Security Administration (Defense Programs) and operated by a conglomerate of three nuclear engineering companies, Pantex's mission was to assemble, disassemble, inspect, and store nuclear warheads.

After contacting the sheriff's department and requesting a traffic stop, the security patrol returned to its rounds and continued to monitor the perimeter security while long-range telescopic low-light TV cameras continued to track the vans. FM 293 was actually separated from the plant itself by over two and a half miles. In between the road and the plant were two explosive incineration pits where the high explosive parts of nuclear weapons were destroyed or where testing of new explosive materials could take place, and also by a one-mile-square storage facility, mostly abandoned. At one time nuclear warheads awaiting distribution to military facilities were stored there, but no new warheads had been produced for decades. The plant itself was one mile south of the storage facility.

The vans were observed traveling west on FM 293 until it intersected Highway 136, where remote monitoring from the Pantex facility was terminated. The Potter County Sheriff's Department was notified that the vans were now in their jurisdiction, and dispatchers put out a message on their units' data terminals to be on the lookout for the vans and do a traffic stop and search if possible. But as soon as the request was handed off to multiple agencies, concern over the vans quickly waned. The vans hadn't stopped or done anything suspicious; no laws had been broken. If Carson County hadn't had probable cause to stop and search the vehicle, Potter County certainly didn't. The request to stop the vans was relayed but largely ignored by the graveyard shift on patrol.

But the assault was already underway.

It took less than seventy seconds for the Cybernetic Infantry Device to carry two of Yegor Zakharov's commandos and their

backpacks full of weapons and gear the six tenths of a mile between FM 293 and the access road to Sheridan Drive west of the
north end of the Pantex facility. The land was cleared and fur-
rowed dirt, a simple buffer zone between the explosive incineration pits and the public road that looked like normal
farmland—but the area was covered by a network of laser
"fences," covering everything from one to ten feet aboveground,
that would alert plant security if any of the beams were broken.
But it was easy enough for the CID unit's infrared sensor to see the
laser beams, and even easier for the robot to jump over the fences,
even loaded up with all of its "passengers" and their gear. The
robot dropped off the men and their equipment at the intersection
of Sheridan Drive and North Eleventh Street and ran off into the
darkness.

North Eleventh Street between the incineration pits and the
weapon storage area was unlighted. They proceeded quickly
down the road about a half-mile until they came to a single
twelve-foot-high fence running eastward, with a security vehicle
access road just outside the fence. At the end of the fence was a dirt
and stone berm twenty feet high and a hundred and twenty feet
thick, topped with another twelve-foot-high fence. There was a
five-story guard tower at the corner of the berm. Floodlights
erected every five hundred feet illuminated the top of the berm
and the entire area beyond as brightly as daytime.

Called Technical Zone Delta, or TZ-D, this was the weapons
storage area. TZ-D had two main purposes: storage of plutonium
"pits"—the hollow sphere of nuclear material that was the heart of
a nuclear device, for eventual reuse or destruction—and storage of
nuclear warheads, from the United States military as well as Russia and other nuclear nations, awaiting dismantling. TZ-D was divided into four Technical Areas, or TAs. TA-1 was the security,
inspection, and classification area at the single entrance to the storage facility; TA-2 was the eleven igloos, or storage bunkers, set
aside for nuclear weapon electronic components and triggers; TA-

3 was the forty-two-pit storage igloos, each housing anywhere from two to four hundred pits; and TA-4 was the eight igloos set aside for storing warheads awaiting dismantling.

TA-4 was the target.

The two vans seen earlier on FM 293 were now spotted by Pantex security monitors heading east on Farm to Market Road 245. They had apparently left Highway 136 and were now approaching the weapons storage area at high speed. The tall guillotine gate at the entrance was closed, and the security detail on duty around the entire facility was placed on its highest state of alert.

Both vans swung off FM 245 onto the access road to the weapons storage area. Two commandos got out of the first van, carrying shoulder-fired rockets, and they made quick work of the relatively weak antitrespassing guillotine gate. Two hundred feet beyond the first gate was the outer entrapment area gate. The security detail had already deployed a massive solid steel barrier just in front of the outer entrapment gate that rose up from the ground and completely blocked the entrance. But the commandos didn't even try to blast away the barrier. After discarding the spent missile canisters and retrieving fresh ones along with automatic assault rifles and satchel charges, the van veered off the road, crashed into the fence to the right of the barrier . . .

. . . and a thousand pounds of high explosives detonated, completely demolishing the fence and destroying the pass and ID guard shack inside.

At that moment, the Cybernetic Infantry Device emerged from the second van, rushed at the breach in the outer gate, and cleared away the flaming, twisted debris enough for four commandos to get inside. Two commandos rushed inside the TA-1 security building, blasting the doors open and throwing flash-bang grenades inside to disable any security personnel inside without damaging or destroying any records. They then retracted the steel vehicle barrier, opened the gates, brought the second van inside the compound, and then closed and secured the entryway. The

CID unit picked up two commandos and their equipment and rushed inside the weapons storage area.

When the assault on the front gate commenced, the two commandos in the northwest corner of the facility prepared for their attack. A single shot from a Dragunov sniper rifle dispatched the security guard that had come out of the tower to take up his sniper position, and moments later a TOW antitank missile round destroyed the tower. Two satchel charges destroyed the fence at the top of the berm, and several more shots took out the few remaining security patrols inside the compound.

"Two, report," Yegor Zakharov ordered on his portable transceiver.

"Moving inside," the leader of the commando team that had performed the frontal assault radioed back. "No resistance."

"I will need the igloo number immediately, Three."

"Three copies." The two commandos inside the TA-1 building were hurriedly looking through the office, searching charts and records on the contents of the dozens of igloos inside the weapons storage area. Finally they found what they were looking for in the fire marshal's office: a wall chart with symbology written in grease pencil over each igloo in the compound. "One, this is Three," the leader radioed, "according to the fire hazard chart I found, Igloos Alpha Four-Four and Four-Five contain weapons that each have thirty-seven kilos of insensitive high explosives."

"Keep looking for more specific records, Three," Zakharov responded. "Two, meet me at those igloos."

"Two."

While two commandos took up security positions at the entrance to the weapons storage area, the CID unit carrying several satchels and backpacks ran through TZ-Delta directly to the igloos where the warheads awaiting disassembly were stored. He set the equipment down . . . and as he did, the head of the commando traveling with Zakharov exploded. The CID unit immediately turned to the east. "Sniper on the northeast tower!" he radioed.

"Shield me," Zakharov said. As heavy-caliber bullets pinged off the CID's composite armor behind him, the Russian picked up a backpack and began placing shaped explosive charges on the steel doors to the first igloo. The entire front of each igloo was a thick steel plate wall, with a single man-sized steel entry door secured with a heavy steel bar with two palm-sized padlocks locking it in place. It was easy to blow the locks apart with plastic explosives and enter the igloo.

Zakharov found what he was looking for within moments. He recognized them immediately—because he had once commanded Russian Red Army units that employed similar weapons. These were 15A18A warheads from active R-36M2 intercontinental ballistic missiles. The R-36M2, appropriately called "Satan" by the West, was Russia's biggest, longest-range, and most accurate ballistic missile, capable of raining 10 independently targeted warheads on targets more than eleven thousand kilometers away with unprecedented accuracy. The missile was so accurate that the warheads could be made smaller, so the R-36M2 carried 10 of these warheads, each with a yield of over seven hundred and fifty thousand *tons* of TNT.

The igloo contained an entire ballistic missile squadron's worth of warheads—one hundred and twenty warheads, packed in aluminum and carbon fiber coffins for shipment. After ensuring that there were indeed warheads in the coffins, and they were the real thing and mostly intact, the CID unit dragged two coffins out of the igloo.

A commando had driven the second van over to the igloo. The sniper apparently realized he wasn't going to kill the robot and wasn't going to get a clear shot at Zakharov, so he started targeting the van—luckily they got the vehicle behind an igloo before the sniper could shoot out the tires or put a hole in the radiator or engine block. "Time to take care of that sniper," Zakharov told the commando piloting the CID unit.

With the sniper's location pinpointed on his electronic display—

every time he fired, he drew a line right back to his own position, thanks to the robot's on-board millimeter-wave targeting radar—the CID unit grabbed an antitank missile and sped off. He located the sniper easily, still atop the northeast guard tower; with the CID unit's radar helping him to aim, he could not miss. He then hurried back and loaded the warhead coffins on the van and, with the robot carrying an antitank missile and running in front of the van, they headed for the exit.

Two security vehicles were just pulling up to the entrance to the weapons storage area—both were put out of commission when the CID unit simply lifted them up and flipped them over, with the officers still inside.

The van and its two-legged escort traveled east on FM 245, north on North Fifteenth Street, east again on County Highway 11, north on County Road L, and then east on FM 293 until reaching the outskirts of the town of Panhandle. "Slow your driving, damn you, and do it *now*," he spat at the commando driving the vehicle. "We did not make it all this way to be pulled over by a country bumpkin policeman." On his walkie-talkie, he said, "Proceed as directed."

"*Da, polkovnik,*" the commando piloting the CID unit responded, and dashed off back to the west along FM 293. Being ultracareful to obey all stop signs and traffic signs, the van made its way through the quiet tree-lined streets of Panhandle, finally reaching Sixth Street, which took them right to Carson County Airport. Thankfully, the airport looked completely quiet. He did notice a Civil Air Patrol unit building and a Cessna 182 parked outside, but it too appeared closed.

Zakharov pulled out his transceiver and keyed the mike button: "Five, report." No response. He tried a few more times—still no response.

"Sir, what do we do?" the commando driving the van asked worriedly.

"Relax, Lieutenant," Zakharov said, trying to sound upbeat.

"We are early, and our plane may be running late. We will try to make contact with one another on the planned schedule."

"Should we recall the robot?"

"Negative," Zakharov snapped. "The farther it gets from this place, and the sooner it is spotted somewhere else, the better off we will be."

The CID unit ran at full speed directly west on FM 293. At the intersection of FM 293 and FM 2373, just northeast of the weapons storage facility, the pilot had to jump over a single security vehicle that had just set up a roadblock, and he sped off before the startled officer could fire a shot.

Resistance was stiffer the farther west he went. The entire intersection of FM 293 and Highway 136 was blocked off in all directions, and he decided to use his last antitank missile to destroy the biggest security vehicle before speeding south on Highway 136. He hopped onto North Lakeside Drive and continued south. Soon there was a police helicopter trying to follow him. Although he made a show of dodging here and there as if he was trying to evade the chopper, he was careful not to let the helicopter lose him. He got off Lakeside Drive at Triangle Drive and soon found himself at his destination: Amarillo International Airport.

He hopped a security fence on the northwest corner of the airport not far from the control tower, then sprinted across a field in front of the tower and across the northeast end of the main runway. He used the radio frequency scanner in the CID unit to check for any indication that he'd been spotted. It didn't take long: on a UHF frequency he heard: "Attention all aircraft, this is Amarillo Ground, hold short of all runways and hold your positions, unidentified person on Taxiway Kilo near Foxtrot. Break. Airport security, we see him, he's heading southeast on Kilo about halfway between Foxtrot and Lima, and he's *haulin' ass*." At the same time, on a different frequency: "Attention all aircraft inbound to Amarillo International, be advised, the airport is closed due to police action. Repeat, Amarillo Airport is closed due to police action. Stand by for divert instructions."

"Jason! Thank God you're alive!" Ariadna cried over the phone. "Where are you?"

"I'm in Panhandle, Texas," Jason replied. The farmer had just dropped him and the children off at the Carson County Sheriff's office. "You've got to get TALON out here right away. I think Zakharov is going after . . ."

"Pantex," Ari interjected. "Watts guessed that too when the CID unit was activated out there. We're already airborne with two CID units. We should be arriving in less than two minutes. We . . . stand by, Jason . . . J, we've just been told that Amarillo Airport is closed due to 'police action.' We're trying to contact airport security."

Jason turned to the deputy beside him, who was scrolling through lines of text appearing on a computer terminal. "Deputy, can you tell me what's going on at Amarillo International?"

"Some guy on the runways," the deputy replied, reading through the messages in growing disbelief. "We think he's on a motorcycle or somethin', because he's goin' pretty damned fast. They closed down the airport 'til they can catch 'im."

"Deputy, listen to me," Jason said. "That's a hijacked Cybernetic Infantry Device on that airport—a manned robot." The deputy looked at Richter as if he had grown another head. "Task Force TALON is coming in to capture him. I need you to get permission for their plane to land, *right now*."

"That's Potter County—I don't got no jurisdiction out there . . ."

"Call *someone* and tell them to let that plane land!" Jason shouted. He gave the deputy the plane's tail number and call sign, then turned to the phone again: "Ari, I'm trying down here to get you permission to land, but if you don't get a call from the tower in about sixty seconds, land anyway."

"Got it, J," Ariadna said. "Are you all right?"

"Zakharov kidnapped me and a bunch of kids and forced me to activate the CID unit . . ."

"Mister, did you just say *Zakharov?*" the astonished deputy asked, his mouth dropping open in shock. "You mean, the guy that blew up Houston? *He's* out there?" He turned to the phone and yelled, "Dammit, Dispatch, screw the airport police and put me through to the control tower at Amarillo. Yegor Zakharov the Russian terrorist is on the airport, and those Talon guys want to land so they can go get him. Do it, *now!*" The seconds ticked by mercilessly. Finally TALON was on the ground, and the CID units were being dispatched.

It did not take long: "J, we found CID One," Ari radioed a couple minutes later. "It was abandoned. The guy piloting it is gone."

"You've got to find him," Jason said. "The sheriff's department says some weapons are missing out of Pantex. They won't say how many, but they did say 'weapons,' plural."

"We'll get him, J, don't worry," Ariadna said. "Watts is scouring every inch of the airport. Nothing is going in or out of that place until we're done."

Jason got to his feet and said to the deputy, "I need to get out to Amarillo International right away."

"I can take you. Let's go."

As they hurried out of the office, Jason's attention was drawn to a large wall map of Carson County—and he froze. "Deputy," he called, "change in plan . . ."

"One, this is Five. Authenticate Yankee-Papa."

"One authenticates 'seven,' " Zakharov replied. He initiated a challenge-and-response code himself, using an improvised code sheet he had made up just for this mission. The reply was correct. "We are ready to load. What is your status?"

"In the green and ready," the pilot of the Pilatus PC-12 cargo aircraft responded. Minutes later they heard a faint turbine engine sound. They couldn't see it, and the pilot did not report his position as any pilot flying into an uncontrolled airport would normally do, but moments later he heard the distinctive "squeak squeak" of tires hitting the runway, and the sound of the turbine engine in ground idle got louder and louder. A few minutes later, the big single-engine turboprop cargo plane taxied to a stop about fifty yards away, and the large cargo door on the left side of the fuselage opened up.

"*Go!*" Zakharov ordered, and the driver pulled onto the ramp from their hiding place. Two commandos with automatic weapons jumped out of the PC-12 to take up security positions, while two more men jumped out, ready to help load the warhead coffins. The van's driver blinked his headlights in response when one of the security men flashed a signal, then dimmed them as he drove closer to the open . . .

Suddenly there were two brilliant flashes of light from somewhere across the dark runway, and two streaks of red-orange fire sliced across the still night sky and plowed directly into the right side of the cargo plane, causing it to explode in a massive ball of fire.

"*Holy shit! What in hell was that?*" the sheriff's deputy exclaimed. They had just pulled onto the airport property when the cargo plane exploded, less than a half-mile in front of them. He immediately hit the cruiser's lights and sirens.

"No!" Jason yelled. "Turn them off!" But the deputy wasn't listening. He got on his car's radio and called for help. "Don't go in there! Something's happening . . ."

"Just shut up and stay put," the deputy said. He raced across the empty parking lot up to the airport security fence, pulled out a white plastic passcard, and touched it to a magnetic card reader. Just as the gate started to open, an alarm bell rang in Jason's brain, and he suddenly bolted out of the squad car. "Hey, where in hell do you think you're goin'?" Jason didn't reply—he just ran faster.

By then the gate had opened far enough, and the deputy gunned the engine and zoomed inside . . .

. . . and no sooner had he advanced a few car lengths when a volley of automatic gunfire erupted, peppering the car and its driver in a deadly barrage of bullets. The smoking, unguided car started moving in a slow left circle, eventually crashing into a parked airplane.

Frozen with confusion and fear, Jason hid behind the terminal building until he was as sure as he could be that he wasn't being followed, then sneaked through the open gate and up to the shattered squad car. Thankful that no interior lights came on when he opened the passenger side door, he tried unsuccessfully to pull the shotgun out of the dashboard mount, then went around to the driver's side. The body of the dead deputy slid onto the ground when he opened the door—ironically, that made it easier to pull the Glock semiautomatic pistol from the deputy's holster on his right hip. He remembered to take the magazine from the officer's utility belt before sneaking toward the burning cargo plane.

Zakharov was stunned into speechlessness. What in hell happened here? He couldn't even imagine that his own men could turn against him and try to hijack these stolen nuclear warheads, but that was the only logical explanation.

The driver had immediately raced away from the stricken plane, and now they were in a different hiding spot, between two hangars on the southwest side of the airport grounds. He had his Dragunov sniper rifle at the ready across his chest on its sling; his pistol was in his right hand and the last antitank missile launcher was slung over his shoulder; the commando had an assault rifle ready.

"Who is out there, sir?" the commando asked.

"I was going to ask you the same thing," Zakharov growled.

"Sir! I would never betray you!"

"No one else knew of our plans!"

"I would die before even thinking about turning on you, Colonel!"

He thought about killing the guy just to be certain, but he needed him to help him escape. "All right, Lieutenant, all right. There is only one entrance and exit to this place, and that is bound to be guarded. But there has got to be another emergency exit on the north side of the airport. We will find it and get out that way."

"Yes, sir." He put the van in gear, pulled away from the hangars, and drove north between the rows of airplane hangars. When they ran out of paved parking area, they went across the dry grass. Using their parking lights, they found the airport security fence.

"I will drive," Zakharov said. "Use your flashlight and find the gate." The commando got out, pistol in one hand, flashlight in the other. The commando wisely covered most of the lens with his hand in order to shed as little light as necessary. Moments later they came across a dirt road, and moments after that they found the gate, with a rusty chain loosely holding it closed. The commando fetched a pair of bolt cutters from the van, placed the jaws on the chain . . .

. . . and suddenly flew over sideways violently as a bullet pierced the left side of his skull, killing him instantly. Zakharov took time to let out a weak gasp of shock before reaching for the shifter . . .

"Freeze, Colonel. Hands where I can see them." The voice . . . had a Spanish accent, not a Russian one! He slowly lifted his hands and turned. He couldn't see the face of the man in the open driver's side window, but he could smell the cordite coming from the muzzle of the sound-suppressed pistol he aimed at him. "Both hands, out the window. Reach for the handle outside the vehicle and let yourself out."

Zakharov complied. "Who are you?"

"A loyal employee of a friend of yours, Colonel," the man said. Zakharov heard the van's cargo doors open, and excited voices in Spanish reported that there were two warheads inside. "Congrat-

ulations, Colonel. There have been many security breaches at the
Pantex Plant over the past fifty years, but I believe you are the first
to actually steal a weapon from there, let alone two. The Comandante will be very pleased."

"The Coman—" And then Zakharov understood everything.
"You mean, this is . . . this is the work of *Felix Díaz?*"

"He surmised your objective and your plans and set up this ambush for you," the man said. "Now we will take the warheads.
Your body will be found here, along with the body of a local sheriff's deputy—I would not be surprised if they deduce that it was a
collaboration between you and yet another corrupt cop. Meanwhile the warheads will be on their way to Mexico." Zakharov
heard the rustle of leather as the man raised his pistol up to head
level. "The legend of Yegor Zakharov will end right . . ."

Suddenly several shots rang out, and Díaz's henchman fell over
backward. Zakharov dropped to the ground and pulled his pistol.
He saw a muzzle flash ahead of him on the other side of the fence,
fired at it, then dodged around the front of the van to the passenger side. He opened the door and reached between the front seats,
looking for his sniper rifle but only finally finding the last antitank
missile launcher. He grabbed it and turned . . .

 . . . and ran headlong into a fist aimed squarely at his one remaining eye. "Not so fast, Colonel," he heard a familiar voice say.
His pistol was pulled out of his hand.

"Richter!" Zakharov retorted. "Give me my gun back and help
me get this vehicle away from here, or we are both dead!"

"I'm not helping you do *shit,* Colonel!" Jason said through
clenched teeth, muting his voice. "Tell your men to drop their
weapons or I swear to God I'll kill you."

"They are not my men, you idiot!" Zakharov said. "Would my
men blow up our only escape? They are Felix Díaz's men!"

"Felix Díaz . . . the Minister of Internal Affairs of Mexico?"

"His men followed me here to steal these weapons."

"You lying sack of shit . . . !"

"Call me names if you want to, Richter, but I am getting out of here!" The big Russian, sensing rather than seeing where Richter was, swung both arms as if he were chopping a tree, and his fists landed squarely in Jason's gut. He stepped over the American Army officer and ran toward the runway.

Jason had to struggle for several long seconds before he could catch a full breath. Just as he was able to get up on one knee, he felt a man running past him, shouting something in Spanish. A burst of automatic gunfire opened up, aimed in the direction of where Zakharov had run off to. Jason raised the dead deputy's Glock, aiming just past where he saw the muzzle flash, and fired. The Spanish gunman screamed in pain and fell.

"Zakharov, *stop!*" Jason yelled, and he took off after the Russian. He hadn't run more than a few yards when he heard gunshots behind him and felt bullets whizzing past his head and snapping at his heels, so he ran faster and began dodging back and forth. He heard more voices in Spanish behind him—they were coming for him, and they were getting closer. Other Spanish voices seemed to be yelling in celebration . . .

. . . and he realized they were celebrating because they were about to get away with the warheads. Two nuclear warheads . . . in the hands of a crazed politician like Felix Díaz?

Just before he reached the edge of the runway, he heard a voice with a Russian accent yell, "Get down, Richter!" In the darkness he saw a man appear on the opposite edge of the runway, a weapon raised, aimed at him. He screamed something, then dove for the ground. Just as he hit the ground, a blinding flash of light erupted right over his head. A split-second later, there was an immense explosion. A balloon of fire roiled over him, briefly illuminating the entire airport grounds and the high plains of the panhandle of Texas for miles around.

"May I suggest, Major," he heard Zakharov yell from the relatively dark side of the runway, "that you get your stupid ass up and run as far away from here as you can? There was at least thirty kilos of plutonium in those warheads."

Jason turned. Zakharov had fired that antitank missile at the van and destroyed it, and the warheads along with it. Nuclear debris was going to be scattered around this area for miles . . . and he was right in the middle of it.

All thoughts of capturing Yegor Zakharov disappeared as Jason Richter got up and started to run. The fence on the eastern side of the airport property was no barrier at all—he had enough adrenaline coursing through his veins to practically clear the ten-foot fence without touching it. He didn't stop running until he had crossed three roads and came upon a farmhouse. He had just enough energy left in him to pound on the front door with his fist, then tell the person who came to the door that they had to leave immediately, before collapsing from sheer exhaustion.

CHAPTER 11

"Welcome back. I'm Bob O'Rourke, back behind the platinum microphone, here in the *Bottom Line* studios in east Sin City in the greatest state in the great United States of America, Nevada," he began. "It has been one harrowing encounter after another since I was last on the air, not to mention all of the calamities that have occurred in that same time span, and I'll bring all my loyal listeners up to speed:

"First of all, let me talk about the incident here at the studio a couple days ago. It is true: during the melee that ensued after I tried to go from my truck to the studio, caused solely by the illegal trespassing rioters and their irresponsible organizers, I pulled out my legal, licensed concealed weapon and fired it straight up into the air. No one was hurt by my action, a fact I am extremely proud of. I must tell you that my concealed weapons permit instructors tell us in the strictest terms *never* to fire a warning shot: they say never pull your weapon unless you intend to use it, but if you do pull it, use it, or you may lose it. I violated that instruction. This time, the shots scared the rioters enough to allow me to get away, and even encouraged the dangerous crowd to disperse, so more violence and injury was thankfully averted.

"It is also true that I was dog-piled, handcuffed, had a couple fingers broken, arrested, and held in custody by the Clark County Sheriff's Department for most of that day. But as you can tell, I am today a free man. The District Attorney has said he is not sure if he intends to charge me with a misdemeanor for carrying a concealed weapon in a 'cocked and locked' condition, which is not permitted in Clark County. I cannot comment on that. The only thing I will say is I'm glad no one was hurt by my actions, I am thankful for the assistance and bravery of the Clark County Sheriff's deputies who were on duty that morning, despite what they've done to my hand, and I will vigorously defend my rights under the Second Amendment to the Constitution and Nevada law if the District Attorney insists on pressing charges.

"But now let's talk about the real issue of the day—the real meaning of the sudden upsurge in violence against America by the illegal immigrant community:

"The violence and chaos in the illegal immigrant population and border security realm is growing by the day. Two days ago, as you well know by now, nine Americans and three Mexicans were killed, thirty were injured, and the American embassy in Mexico City was severely damaged by an explosives-laden bus. The bus had been carrying members of the Federal District Police, who were there to escort the U.S. ambassador to Mexico, Leon Poindexter, to a meeting with Mexican president Carmen Maravilloso and Minister of Foreign Affairs Hector Sotelo in the Presidential Palace.

"This proves without a doubt, my friends, one of two things: either the Mexican government is directly responsible for these attacks, or the Mexican government is unable or unwilling to stop these murderous attacks, which are probably being carried out by followers of the terrorist Comandante Veracruz. It is imperative that the U.S. embassy and all U.S. consulate offices in Mexico be closed immediately and our representatives returned to Washington before there are any more terrorist activities targeting Americans. I encourage all Americans living and working in Mexico to get out as soon as you can as well.

"The morning's news alerts have been focusing on another horrific crime that occurred in southern California earlier that morning, this time perpetrated by none other than the Mexican Army—yes, you heard me, the *Mexican Army,*" O'Rourke went on. "Two infantry squads, about fifty men, of Mexican Army regulars and paramilitary border security soldiers attacked an encampment of the American Watchdog Project, which was set up several miles east of the U.S. military border security base near Boulevard, California, called Rampart One. Five men were killed, including one medical doctor from the California Army National Guard. No, I take that back. Five American citizens were *slaughtered* by the Mexican Army, shot at close range with automatic weapons.

"As I've reported many times on this broadcast, the White House has sharply reduced the number of National Guard troops in this area recently in a vain attempt to lessen tensions between the United States and Mexico. The American Watchdog Project, who as you know lost their leader Herman Geitz recently to an unknown assassin while your humble correspondent was on patrol with his team, had set up a camp between Rampart One and the western edge of the Calexico border fence to watch out for illegal immigrants crossing the border here to make up for the loss of National Guard troops deployed there.

"It is true that the Watchdogs had taken a number of illegals into custody, including a pregnant woman. The Mexican government says the attack was in response to this illegal arrest; they say that they had eyewitness evidence that the Mexicans in captivity were being tortured and sexually abused, and they point to the recent disputed incident with the National Guard troops as further evidence of increased violence against migrants. The Mexican government says it did not order the Mexican troops to initiate the attack, but the local commander took it on his own authority to organize and conduct the raid.

"But in all the squawking from the Mexican government and the Hispanic human rights groups about the Watchdogs, complaining that the United States is unlawfully committing acts of atrocity against Mexicans, here's something you haven't heard on the news yet about this incident. I spoke with the Imperial County sheriff this morning, and he confirms that the American Watchdog Project members had intercepted a group of illegals crossing the border a few miles west of the Calexico fence. When I asked why *they* had intercepted the group instead of calling in the National Guard or Border Patrol, as they always do, the sheriff explained that the pregnant woman they had found was in the later stages of labor and was ready to deliver a child. The sheriff's department had been notified, and a doctor, Army National Guard Captain William Abrams, had been summoned to the scene by the Watchdogs to help deliver the infant. In fact, I have in my possession the recordings from the Imperial County 911 Emergency Call Center and the recordings from the police radio transmissions, giving precise descriptions of the woman and her medical condition, her identity, and the identities of several of the men traveling with her, and I'll play those recordings for you at the top of the hour, so stayed tuned.

"Bottom line, my friends: the Watchdogs were trying to help this woman, not hurt her. The woman was assisted across the border obviously so she could have her baby born on U.S. soil, which is a very common practice as illegals attempt to circumvent the law and take advantage of our Constitution. But the Mexican Army staged a so-called 'rescue mission' and ended up killing five Americans in cold blood. The woman and her child are missing; there has been no word from the Mexican Army or the Mexican government except to condemn the Watchdogs for their actions.

"This falls precisely in line with the highly suspect episode recently where a California National Guard soldier stands accused of raping a female illegal immigrant. Even though the woman's story about how she came to be in that area and if she was traveling alone or with others has been totally inconsistent and unsupported by any evidence, it is the American government that is being vilified around the world, even before any facts are in. It is

frighteningly obvious to me, my friends, that the Mexican government is fabricating these lies in order to incite the Hispanic community to violence against America on both sides of the border,
turn world opinion in its favor, and provoke outright war with the
United States.

"Yes, folks, I said 'war,' and I am not exaggerating here. Prus-
sian General Carl von Clausewitz said in the early nineteenth century that 'War is the continuation of policy by other means,' and
that is exactly what is happening here today. The Mexican government knows it has absolutely no hope of influencing Congress,
the White House, or the American people that illegal immigration
is good and should be encouraged, expanded, or at least tolerated,
so they have decided to switch tactics and attempt to force America's lawmakers and policy makers to drive the debate back to the
fore by committing acts of devastation, mayhem, and murder
against us. This is nothing short of state-sponsored terrorism, my
friends, the scourge we have been fighting since the first U.S. air-
liner was hijacked in 1961, and last year actually declared war
against.

"So if this is war being waged against the United States, where
is our defense? Where is the vaunted but horrendously expensive
Task Force TALON, the high-tech combined FBI and military
unit charged with hunting down terrorists wherever they may be
found anywhere in the world? We've sent TALON to Brazil,
Russia, Great Britain, Egypt, and even right here in America—
but where are they now?

"Unsubstantiated reports are that one of TALON's robots had
actually been hijacked and used to terrorize the area around
Amarillo, Texas just a couple days ago. The government is not
commenting at all, but there was some sort of security breach at
Amarillo International Airport and possibly another at a government facility I will not mention here because of national security. But all I see is confusion, a lack of leadership, and chaos
happening here, folks. It is all very disturbing—very, very disturbing indeed."

O'Rourke withdrew a slim folder of e-mails, photocopied forms, and notes. He paused for a moment, as if perhaps reconsidering his next move; then, popping more chocolate-covered espresso beans in his mouth, went on: "Let me give you an example of how really screwed up the government's immigration and border security programs are, ladies and gentlemen. Yesterday my staff received an anonymous e-mail from an individual that was so outrageous, but so factual-sounding, that we thought we'd investigate. Normally I wouldn't waste my time or my staff's with such nonsense, but this anonymous message actually had relevant and believable evidence attached to it. It turns out it was *not* so outrageous, my friends.

"I'm sure you recall the deputy commander of Task Force TALON, Dr. Ariadna Vega, the young woman who helped design and build the incredible manned military robots involved in the hunt for terrorist mastermind Colonel Yegor Zakharov and also involved in setting up the first military security bases along the border. Prompted by this anonymous correspondent, we checked on Dr. Vega's background, and we have reason to believe that she and her parents are here in the United States illegally. Yes, folks, *illegally*. Dr. Vega's father attended the University of Southern California on an educational visa, where he obtained a doctorate degree, but he never left the country when his visa expired. Instead, he apparently sent for his family back in Ensenada, Mexico, where they were smuggled across the border sometime in the mid-1980s.

"But that was not the worst part, my friends, not by a long shot. Now although the Vegas were productive and apparently law-abiding visitors to the United States, they were still here illegally. Miss Ariadna Vega attended USC and several other American universities, obtaining her doctorate degree in engineering, like her father. She was then hired by the U.S. Army Research Laboratory as a computer and electrical engineer, eventually joining the Infantry Transformational BattleLab, one of the government's most highly classified offices, working on very advanced weapons for future infantry combat soldiers.

"But how, you might ask, does an illegal immigrant get a top-secret security clearance and become the number-two person in a major border security unit? The answer: she falsified her documentation, folks. She took great pains to cover her tracks, all the way from junior high school through college and university. Of course, the state of California does not keep very good records of the citizenship status of its students, arguing that it's a violation of their constitutional rights and California law, so the government investigators charged with checking background information obviously ran into plenty of stone walls and dead ends when they looked into her past. But those were stone walls partially erected by Miss Vega and her family.

"We have obtained copies of Miss Vega's Mexican and American birth records through third-hand sources, but have not been able to validate either set of documents' authenticity, so we have no direct evidence as of yet. Of course, the U.S. Army will not turn over any fingerprint records to us so we can verify this information. But a professional's examination of the footprints on both sets of birth records conclude that they appear to be *identical*. The baby's footprints of course could be faked. But the compounding of circumstantial evidence tells us here at *The Bottom Line* that Dr. Ariadna Vega, deputy commander of Task Force TALON, is indeed an illegal alien—and, it appears, has violated several federal laws in order to obtain a highly classified government position that is normally not open to foreign nationals because of trust, loyalty, and security concerns.

"Now I'm not saying that Miss Vega is a dangerous spy out to destroy America. There is no question that she is a hero after her actions in hunting down and defeating the Consortium terrorist group that attacked America last year. In my opinion, she doesn't deserve prison time. The question is, however: does she deserve to still have access to classified government programs and still be in charge of our nation's border security? I don't think so. And it begs the wider question: does her immigration and citizenship status have anything to do with TALON's ineffectiveness in securing

our borders? *The Bottom Line* wants to know, and we *will* find
out, I promise you."

PECOS EAST TRAINING RANGE,
CANNON AIR FORCE BASE, NEW MEXICO
THAT SAME TIME

It was called a "30-30"—dropping a lightly armed and equipped
commando from thirty feet in the air into the water, from a helicopter traveling thirty nautical miles per hour. The tactic allowed
the fastest possible forward flight through hostile airspace without
injuring the nonparachute-equipped landing soldiers.

But this "30-30" was different. First, the commandos weren't
dropping from a helicopter, but a different type of rotorcraft: a
CV-22 Osprey tilt-rotor aircraft, the special operations version of
the world's first active military tilt-rotor transport. Able to take off
and land similar to a helicopter but then fly at fixed-wing turboprop speeds, the V-22-series aircraft were the newest aircraft in the
active U.S. military arsenal, pressed into service for utility, transport, cargo, and search and rescue as well as inserting special ops
forces well behind enemy lines. All V-22 aircraft were equipped
with forward-looking infrared scanners and inflight refueling
probes; the special operations version was also equipped with a
highly precise satellite navigation suite, terrain-avoidance radar
and millimeter-wave obstacle detection radar, state-of-the-art
electronic countermeasures systems, a twenty-millimeter Chain
Gun in a chin turret steered by the pilot or copilot using head-
mounted remote aiming displays, and long-range fuel tanks.

The second difference with this "30-30" was that it was not over
water, but over the hard sun-baked high desert of east-central
New Mexico. The third difference: the soldiers involved were not
ordinary commandos, but Cybernetic Infantry Devices from Task
Force TALON.

Using a steel handrail on the upper fuselage as a handhold, Major Jason Richter stepped aft along the CV-22's cargo bay toward the open cargo ramp. "CID One is in position," he radioed.

"You sure you want to do this, Major?" FBI Deputy Director Bruno Watts, the new commander of Task Force TALON, asked. He was secured in the front of the cargo bay of the CV-22, watching the exercise. "You won't impress me at all if you break your fool neck."

"Thirty seconds," the copilot radioed back, and the red "READY" light came on in the cargo bay.

"I already told you a dozen times, Watts—I'm doing it."

"You sure you feel up to it?"

"The doc cleared me . . ."

"You did one blood test and a bone marrow test, then went back to the base and started putting on a CID unit. You don't look good, and you're not acting very right in the head."

"Get out of my face, Watts."

Bruno Watts grasped Jason's CID unit by the base of the helmet. "I'm telling you, Richter, you're not ready to go back into the field yet. I'm grounding you as of right now."

"Who's going to run this drop test, Bruno—*you?*" Jason responded. "You haven't even made it through one briefing on CID. So unless you want to climb inside this unit, get the hell out of my face." He turned and faced the open cargo door again.

Watts scowled at the robot's back, unaccustomed to subordinates he hardly knew calling him by his first name. But that appeared typical of Richter and others in this task force: they had been doing their own thing for so long that they had absolutely no regard for rank or common organizational structure. "The job of the commander is to command, Richter. You think you're being a leader by skipping out of the hospital and doing this training mission, but all I see is a guy with a chip on his shoulder, out for some payback."

"You sound like Kelsey . . . I mean, Director DeLaine," Jason remarked. "Why do all of you FBI agents sound alike?"

"Makes you wonder, doesn't it, Major?" Watts said.

"Ten seconds. Stand by."

Jason turned around and gave a thumbs-up to the two other CID units standing behind him, piloted by Harry Dodd of the U.S. Army and Mike Tesch, formerly of the Drug Enforcement Agency. He then stepped back to the edge of the cargo ramp at the rear of the CV-22 and turned around so he was facing forward, still holding on to the overhead handrail. Tesch and Dodd waited closely in front of him. When he saw the red light in the cargo bay turn to green, he stepped back and off the ramp.

The idea was to land on his feet, absorb the shock of the drop, and simply continue running, but like most plans his didn't survive impact. He landed squarely on his feet in a running stance, but immediately face-planted forward and ended up cartwheeling across the desert for almost a hundred feet before crashing into a cactus. Mike Tesch's landing wasn't much better. His plan was to land on his butt, cushioning his impact with his arms, and let his momentum carry him up to his feet. But as soon as he hit he bounced several feet in the air, and he landed headfirst on the ground.

Harry Dodd's landing was almost perfect, but only because he didn't try to run right out of the landing. Instead, he performed a picture-perfect parachute landing fall, hitting the ground with the balls of his feet, twisting to the right, letting his left calf, thigh, lat muscles, and shoulder take the brunt of the impact in a smooth rolling action, then letting his legs flip up and over his body until they were pointing down along the flight path. When his feet reached the ground, he simply let his momentum lift his entire body up and off the ground, and he was instantly on his feet and running. By the time the dust and sand settled, he had run back and was checking on Tesch and Richter. "You okay, sir?" he asked Richter who had just picked himself up off the ground.

"Almost had it there until that stupid cactus got in my way," Jason complained. "Where'd you learn to do that roll? It looks like you hardly got dusty."

"Army Airborne school, Fort Benning, Georgia, sir," Dodd said. "Looks like I'll be teaching TALON how to do a correct PLF."

"Buster, this is Stronghold, looks like everyone is still in the green," Ariadna Vega radioed from TALON headquarters after checking CID unit's satellite datalink status readouts. She was able to see each unit's landing via optical target scoring cameras located throughout the Pecos East range and had to force her voice back to normal after laughing so hard at Richter's and Tesch's attempts. "Proceed to maneuver positions."

Following computerized navigation prompts visible on their electronic visors, the three CID units split up and proceeded to preplanned locations, about a mile from a large plywood building erected on the Pecos East range. Once they were all in position, Jason launched a GUOS, or grenade-launched unmanned observation system, drone from his backpack launcher. The bowling-pin-sized device unfolded its wings and started a small turbojet engine seconds after launch, and the little drone whizzed away with a low, rasping noise and just a hint of smoke.

"Good downlink back here," Ariadna reported as she watched the streamed digital images being broadcast via satellite from the tiny drones. "Report in if you're bent." The sensor on the GUOS drone was not a visual camera, but a millimeter-wave radar designed to detect metal, even tiny bits of it buried as far as twelve inches underground. On their electronic visors, metallic objects big enough to pose a threat to the CID units appeared as blinking blue dots against the combined visual and digital imagery.

"I've got a good downlink," Jason said. The terrain up ahead was littered with blue dots—in this case, sensors and booby traps planted by the "defenders." Judging by the pattern, the objects appeared to be put in place randomly, as if seeded by aircraft. "Numerous surface devices up ahead, guys."

"I must be bent, One—Three's got nothing," Tesch radioed.

"Okay, Three, hang back as briefed and wait for the signal."

"Roger."

"One, this is Two, I can circumnavigate the cluster in front of me," Harry Dodd reported after studying his visor display. "I need to move a little more in your direction. On the way. Cover me."

Immediately when Dodd said that, the warning bells in Jason's head went off. "Negative, Two, hold your pos . . ."

And at that exact moment, Jason's threat warning system blared. The GUOS drone had picked up the presence of a large vehicle not previously detected from farther away. "Heads-up, guys, we've got company up ahead."

The disguising job was a work of art, Jason had to admit. The Air Force special operations guys had flown in a Humvee loaded with TOW antitank missiles, covered it with a heat-absorbing blanket to shield it from infrared sensors, and then expertly camouflaged the whole area so from the air it appeared to be nothing more than a slight rise in the desert floor. If they had only used infrared sensors on this approach instead of the millimeter-wave radar scanners, they might have never detected the Humvee until it was too late.

Jason and the two other CID units made short work of their target. They fired volleys of smoke canisters at it with their backpack launchers, simulating grenade attacks, then assaulted the plywood "headquarters building" from different directions. Within minutes, the operation was a success.

Not expecting to be called back so soon for an extraction, the CV-22 Osprey was still on the ground at Cannon Air Force Base refueling, so the CID units had a few minutes to wait. While they waited, the three TALON commandos recalled the GUOS drones back to their garrison area before their fuel ran out, and discussed their techniques on this practice operation. Ten minutes later the Osprey was back, and the CID units could practice their exfiltration technique—a recent modification to the old Fulton Recovery System used for decades by Air Force special operations teams to retrieve men and equipment on the ground without landing.

Dangling from the back of the CV-22's open cargo bay were three "trapezes"—carbon composite rods about five feet long, suspended from composite cables, resembling circus high-wire trapezes. As the Osprey flew overhead, each CID unit raised his arms and, positioning himself perfectly, hooked his arms onto the trapeze bar as it passed overhead. As the first CID unit was pulled up, the second and third CIDs were retrieved in the same manner. Within minutes, all three CID units were reeled inside the Osprey's cargo bay.

"That was a *blast!*" Harry Dodd exclaimed. "I thought that damned bar was going to slice my head off, but hooking your arms on it like you said worked perfectly!"

"It might work better if the bar snagged us on our chests instead of our arms and hands," Jason surmised. "We just need to lower the bar down a couple feet. Make a note of that, will you, Ari?" No response. "Stronghold, this is One. How copy?" Still no response. "TALON, this is One. How copy?"

"Loud and clear, One," Bruno Watts responded. He had dismounted from the CV-22 as it was being refueled on the ramp at Cannon Air Force Base and was now driving back to the task force's headquarters east of the base. "Let me try to raise Stronghold. Break. Stronghold, this is TALON."

"TALON, this is Delta," U.S. Marine Corps First Lieutenant Jennifer McCracken, TALON's deputy commander for operations, responded. "I'm here at the mobile ops center. The place is empty. I was listening in on the exercise and came out here when I didn't hear Charlie reply."

"Find her, Delta," Watts ordered. "I'll be there in fifteen."

"We'll be there in ten," Jason said.

Jennifer was waiting for them out on the short airstrip outside TALON's headquarters buildings when the CV-22 touched down a short time later. "She took a CID unit, a grenade launcher backpack, two pilots, and the C-21, sir," she said as soon as Jason stepped off the cargo ramp. The C-21, the military version of the Learjet 20 bizjet, was Task Force TALON's rapid airlift aircraft. McCracken handed Richter a note. "Here's the message she left with the crew chief."

Jason read the note. "Jennifer, find out what airlift we have available the quickest for three CID units and get it out to Cannon. We're taking these three CID units airborne. Load up weapon backpacks. Go." She hurried off, her secure cell phone already in her hands. Jason had his own phone open seconds later. "Sergeant Major, I've got a situation . . ."

"I just heard it myself, Jason. Jesus, I'm sorry. No one here got any heads-up at all from him at all."

"What in hell is going on, Sergeant Major? Heads-up from whom?"

"Bob O'Rourke," Jefferson said. "Apparently the guy 'outed' Ariadna as an illegal alien on his radio show less than an hour ago."

"He did *what?*" Jason exploded. "*An illegal alien?* That's crazy! I've known her for years! She has a top-secret clearance, same as mine . . ."

"We don't have any hard facts yet, Major, but O'Rourke says he has documentation, including a Mexican birth certificate and apparently falsified American birth records. We're checking with Los Angeles County and the State Department to get her records from Mexico, but I need Ariadna secure before the press descends on her. I suggest you confine her to quarters before ICE or the FBI . . ."

"She grabbed a jet and a CID unit and headed to southern California," Jason said.

"Oh, Jesus," Jefferson exclaimed. "Where is she headed?"

"Northridge, Thousand Oaks . . . southern California, somewhere," Jason said. "Her dad's a college professor; her mother works with him, I think. I'll have to check the records." He paused for a moment, then interjected, "If Zakharov is still alive and still in southern California, he may try to kidnap the parents to get to Ariadna. I'm on my way . . ."

"I'll get the Los Angeles FBI office over there right away and bring in her parents. They may need to bring their Hostage Rescue Team. Send me whatever docs you have on her and her family."

"What do you mean, docs on 'her?' " Jason asked. "Why do you need docs on Ari? You have everything you need on her."

"Apparently not."

"Don't give me that shit, Sergeant Major!" Jason exploded. "Don't even *think* about making Ari a target just because of what that flakeoid O'Rourke has to say!"

"Sir, the White House has already called for an investigation," Jefferson said. "The FBI and Army Criminal Investigation Command have already been directed to bring Ari in and do a complete background . . ."

"She is *not* going to be arrested, Sergeant Major—I *guarantee* that!" Jason cried. "I'll bust the head of any federal agent who tries to lay a hand on her! She's a *hero,* for God's sake! She's been injured and almost *killed* in the line of duty!"

"Jason, the best place for her is with the FBI. Director DeLaine knows her—I'm sure she'll handle her case personally."

"No way! She's not a criminal! Tell the FBI to back off, Sergeant Major!"

"I'm not going to do that, sir," Jefferson said. "If she broke the law, she has to come in. The longer she stays out, the more she'll be suspected of being a spy. She'll have to—"

"*A spy?*" Jason retorted. "Are you *insane?* No way in *hell* is she going to go down as a spy! I'll kill anyone who tries to charge her with that, I swear to God . . . !"

"Major Richter, shut up, sir, *now,*" Ray Jefferson said. "Listen to me, sir: Dr. Vega will get all the protection and legal help we can offer her . . . but *not* if you or she tries something crazy. Get her back on base and keep her there."

"Sergeant Major, under my authority as deputy commander of this unit—"

"You've been relieved as deputy commander of TALON, Major. Director Watts is in charge—"

"—I am directing elements of Task Force TALON to immediately deploy to southern California to set up surveillance on Dr. Vega's family, who I believe will be the target of an assassination or kidnapping attempt by the Consortium," Jason said. "I am requesting that you notify the FBI and Justice Department of my orders and have them contact me through my headquarters so we can coordinate our efforts, but you can advise them that I am fully prepared to take whatever steps I feel necessary to accomplish my mission. Unless I receive valid countermanding orders, my unit is in target pursuit mode. TALON out."

Jason saw a truck pull up to the CV-22 Osprey, and crews started loading Cybernetic Infantry Unit backpacks and weapon canisters aboard the tilt-rotor aircraft. At the same time an Air Force Suburban roared up the taxiway and screeched to a halt in front of him, and Bruno Watts jumped out. "I just got a call from the National Security Adviser, ordering me to keep you on the ground!" he shouted over the roar of the Osprey's massive turboshaft engines. "What is going on? Where the hell do you think you're going?"

"I'll submit my ops plan in the air," Jason shouted back.

"Like hell you will, Major!" Watts snapped. "This equipment is not your personal property! I am in command of this unit! Until I get clearance from Washington, I'm ordering you . . ."

"Excuse me, sir," Jennifer McCracken said, stepping up to Watts. "I'd like a word with you."

"Not now, Lieutenant." Then, with surprising speed, Watts grabbed Jason's left wrist with his left hand and lifted his sleeve with his other hand, revealing the remote control wrist keypad for the CID units. "And don't even *think* of trying to summon one of your robots to grab me, Major," he growled. "Sergeant Major Jefferson warned me about you. He said you're not above doing anything to get your . . ."

With equally surprising speed, Jennifer McCracken swatted away Watts's grasp on Jason, twisted his arm upward and backward, rotated her hips, and flipped Watts back over her right leg and down onto the tarmac. With one leg on his left arm and his other arm twisted behind him in a come-along hold, Watts was immediately immobilized. *"What in hell do you think you're doing?"* Watts shouted. "Let me up, McCracken, *now!*"

"Sir?"

"Hold him there until we're airborne, Jennifer."

"Yes, sir."

"*Are you two crazy?*" Watts retorted. He tried to struggle free, but it was quickly and painfully obvious that the somewhat nerdy, quiet, and very businesslike young Marine knew exactly what she was doing. "I'll have you all court-martialed!"

"You're messing with a member of Task Force TALON, sir," McCracken said. "You can court-martial us after Dr. Vega has been brought to safety."

HENDERSON, NEVADA
A SHORT TIME LATER

"We suffered almost a half-million dollars' worth of damage that our insurance probably won't cover," the station manager moaned, checking reports filed by the police and the insurance adjusters. "The ambulance company sent us a bill for transport of seventeen persons to the hospital for a variety of injuries; and every one of our Latino maintenance workers have left."

"But the show had the highest ratings in the history of talk radio," Bob O'Rourke's agent chimed in immediately, "and all but a couple of our sponsors have asked for multiyear advertising contract extensions. I'm expecting a call from the syndication folks, asking for the same—they might even be interested in doing a TV show. Congratulations, Bob."

"Thanks, Ken, thanks very much for the news," Bob O'Rourke said, ignoring the station manager. As he usually did after a show, Bob O'Rourke relaxed in his office with his producer, Fand Kent, and the show's other staff members; he would have one beer, discuss upcoming topics and research assignments, and then O'Rourke would move on to the half-dozen other promotional functions he had scheduled most afternoons, usually golf games with sponsors, speaking engagements, personal appearances, or commercial tapings. He clinked glasses and bottles with his staff, took a deep pull on his beer, then looked at his heavily bandaged right hand. "If I had known just a few broken fingers would get me all that, I would've done it long ago." The laughter was a little strained, but no one in that room ever failed to laugh at one of Bob O'Rourke's jokes, no matter how lame or unfunny—they all valued their jobs too much.

"Bob, the district attorney, the FCC, the mayor, the sheriff's department, the state Department of Public Safety, the FBI, and even the White House are screaming mad at you," the station manager said. "They want to talk with you right away, especially about this Vega thing."

"I have nothing to say to any of them except I stand by my information and will refuse all requests to reveal my sources," O'Rourke said.

"That's all you need to say, Bob—I'll get your attorney on those calls right away," the agent said. "Don't worry about a thing. All those people don't do a damned thing whenever some nut job like Comandante Veracruz wants to speak, but when a proud American wants to talk, they all want to squash him like a bug." O'Rourke tipped his bottle in thanks. "I've got a car waiting outside to take you to the CNN affiliate, and then we'll come back here for a few more satellite pieces with Fox News and the BBC. Then . . ."

"Can't. I have that match with Jason Gore at two at the country club."

"Jason said he'd be glad to slip it to tomorrow if you'll autograph a bunch of visors for him."

"Deal." He looked worriedly at his agent. "About the car . . ."

"Don't worry about your Excursion. The insurance company will total it, I'm sure, and I've already put out feelers to a few charities to auction it off on eBay."

O'Rourke gave his agent a shake of his head, and he bent down closer so he could whisper, "No, Ken, I mean the car for this afternoon."

"No worries, Bob. I found a company with armored limos. They're comping the car for the week as long as they can put their signage in the back window and at the parking areas at your events. All your sponsors and venues said no problem."

"An armored car, you say?"

"This company has a fleet of armored Suburbans that were rejected by a very wealthy real estate developer from Bahrain because they were *too* heavy—they wouldn't fit on their jets," the agent explained. "These things are like friggin' tanks, Bob. It's a good deal."

"I like my regular service . . ."

"They don't have armored limos, Bob, and besides they hesitated to help you after yesterday's broadcast. Frankly, Bob, they ran like frightened chickens. Screw 'em."

"But is this a good company . . . you know, are they trustworthy?"

"Don't worry about a thing. I checked 'em out. They're new, but I spoke with the owner and he seems okay. Young, a real gogetter, anxious to make a name for himself." He read O'Rourke's eyes and added, "And yes, he's an Anglo, and all his drivers are Anglos. I said don't worry. I have a bodyguard assigned to you, recommended by one of your sponsors, and I'll be along every step of the way to keep an eye on things." O'Rourke looked worried but said nothing as he reached for another beer.

More TV and media crews were outside the studios when Bob O'Rourke emerged about a half hour later after his staff meeting. The bodyguard took up a position on the other side of the car, facing the crowds being kept away by a greatly expanded police presence. O'Rourke made a few comments for the reporters, waved to the crowd with his left hand, raised his bandaged right hand defiantly to the delighted cheers of his supporters who easily drowned out the protesters on the other side of the street, and entered the massive armored Suburban limousine, making a pleased mental note of the inch-thick steel and Kevlar in the armored doors and three-inch-thick bulletproof glass.

His agent was already inside. "I told you, Bob—first class all the way," he said, checking out the very high-tech electronics and devices inside. "This is probably what the President's limo looks like." He handed O'Rourke the remote to the twenty-four-inch plasma TV inside. "Here—you might be able to catch the news piece on yourself."

O'Rourke took the remote and turned the TV on. "Get me another beer, will you?"

"Better take it easy, Bob—you have a full afternoon."

"Just get me another beer and shut up, will you?"

The agent shook his head, silently determined that this would be the last one until dinnertime. He opened the ice cabinet section of the limo . . . and his mouth dropped open in absolute horror.

At the same time, the bodyguard had got into the front passenger seat, and the limo driver trotted around from holding O'Rourke's door open to get in the driver's side . . . but instead of getting in, he dashed off down the driveway, past the media crews, and disappeared into the crowds on the street.

"Get out! Get out!" the bodyguard's muffled voice shouted through the closed blast-proof privacy window. "Get out of the car, *now!*"

"What the hell . . . ?" The agent's eyes widened in surprise, then fear, then abject panic. "Holy shit, this thing's full of . . . !"

O'Rourke tried the door handle. "The door's locked!" He tried the other handle. "This one's . . ."

At that instant, the one hundred pounds of C4 explosives planted in the liquor and ice cabinets inside the SUV exploded. The armored body and windows of the SUV contained the explosion for a fraction of a second until, like an overfilled balloon, the powerful explosives first blew the windows out, then ripped the rest of the vehicle into a thousand pieces. Huge tongues of fire leaped out horizontally through the limo's shattered windows, and then the area for an entire block was showered with flying shards of metal, a wave of fire, and a tremendous concussion, knocking over every person, vehicle, and any other standing object within one hundred yards and shattering every window for another hundred yards.

CALIFORNIA STATE UNIVERSITY,
NORTHRIDGE, CALIFORNIA
A SHORT TIME LATER

The white panel truck exited northbound Highway 101 at Reseda Boulevard and headed north, not speeding but zipping through many stoplights that had just turned red. It turned right on Vincennes Street, past Darby Avenue and onto the California State University–Northridge campus. West University Drive deadended at Jacaranda Walk, but the truck squeezed through a narrow brick campus entryway and continued eastbound onto the wide tree-lined sidewalk down two blocks until reaching Jacaranda Hall Engineering Building, the driver beeping its horn occasionally to warn students.

The scene on and off campus was one of absolute confusion. There were several antimilitary, antiadministration, and anti-immigrant protest groups up and down West University Drive. The streets were littered with garbage, discarded signs and banners, and projectiles. The acidy smell of tear gas could barely be detected, wafting in from many directions. Long lines of Hispanic men, women, and children were walking down both sides of the street in both directions, with cars following them, honking horns at them, or simply unable to move because of the chaos. Media crews were everywhere, adding to the confusion.

Cal State–Northridge's campus security was already out in force trying to keep most of the protesters and displaced Mexicans from swarming onto the campus, but they focused their attention squarely on the white panel truck as it drove up over the curb and onto the sidewalk on campus. The situation stopped being serious and had suddenly gotten potentially deadly.

The truck took a left onto East University Drive, then an immediate left into the handicapped parking area outside Jacaranda Hall. Just as campus security patrols arrived, they saw the driver get out of the truck's cab and step inside the back of the truck. Three patrol cars, lights flashing, blocked the truck. "Driver of the white panel truck," one of the officers said, using the loudspeaker on his patrol car, "this is the campus police. Come out of the vehicle immediately." There was no response from the vehicle, even after several repeated calls both in English and Spanish.

After the duty sergeant arrived and assessed the situation with his officers, it was quickly decided to evacuate Jacaranda, Sequoia, Sagebrush, and Redwood Halls and Oviatt Library, and call in the Highway Patrol and the Los Angeles County Sheriff's Department. The recent bombings in Las Vegas and Mexico City, plus the considerable unrest among the Hispanic population all across California, put everyone on hair-trigger alert.

Within ten minutes the sheriff's department's bomb squad arrived, and ten minutes after that a remote-controlled tracked robot was dispatched, carrying a bag with a cellular phone inside, plus microphones that could be attached to the outside of the truck with remote manipulator arms to listen to what was happening inside. By that time the buildings surrounding the truck had been evacuated and a one-hundred-yard perimeter established. The robot motored to the closed and locked double cargo doors in the back of the truck, just far enough away for one door to be opened.

A loudspeaker on the bomb squad's robot crackled to life: "Attention, any persons inside the truck. This is Sergeant Louis Cortez of the Los Angeles County Sheriff's Department. We would like to speak with whoever is inside. We will not harm you. A remote-controlled unarmed robot is behind the truck. It is carrying a bag containing a telephone. You may open the right-side cargo door, reach out, and take the bag containing the phone. We assure you, we will not trick you. The bag contains only a phone, and we will not attempt to arrest or attack you. We wish to speak with whoever is in charge. Please take the phone."

The deputy began repeating the message in Spanish when those outside the truck could see the right cargo door handle move, and moments later open. The robot was positioned perfectly—all the person inside had to do was open the door less than six inches, reach out less than half an arm's length, and grab the . . .

Suddenly both cargo doors burst apart and completely flew off their hinges when some sort of tremendous burst of energy erupted from inside the truck. The police instinctively ducked down behind vehicles and barricades, expecting the shock wave of a huge bomb blast to crash into them—but there was nothing. When they looked up, all they saw . . .

. . . was a large ten-foot-tall two-legged cyborg that had just jumped from the back of the truck. As the astonished police officers watched, Ariadna Vega, piloting the Cybernetic Infantry Device, dashed around the truck and into the main entrance of Jacaranda Hall—she was out of sight even before most of them realized what they had just seen.

The entryway and hallways inside the building were empty—Ariadna was able to monitor the campus police radio frequencies from on board the CID unit, so she knew that everyone had been evacuated. Running on all fours—the approved CID technique for assaulting a building, learned the hard way from Task Force TALON's assault into an oil refinery office building in Cairo—she headed upstairs to the third floor of the engineering building. She briefly considered how she would do her final approach to the target, but quickly decided there was only one way to do it

Staying low so she wouldn't hit the ceiling, running on all fours, she galloped around a corner, down a hallway . . . and crashed directly through the door at the end of the hall. It took her just two heartbeats to see that the outer office was empty, so she turned and bulldozed herself directly through another door to her left, then immediately rose up on her left knee, turned toward the windows, raised her mechanical arms in order to grab anyone within reach, and deployed the twenty-millimeter cannon in her backpack, all in one smooth motion. She heard a woman and a man scream, and the lights flickered. *"Freeze!"* she shouted. *"No one move!"*

She then heard the sound of clapping. Ari turned and saw none other than Colonel Yegor Zakharov himself, seated on her father's comfortable armchair at the head of an informal meeting area in front of her father's desk, applauding her entrance! The coffee table in front of him had a tray with coffee cups and saucers on it—the ones *she* had given to her father when he became the chairman of the school of engineering at Northridge!—and even a plate of cookies. She aimed her cannon directly at Zakharov's smirking face and . . .

"No le mate, niño," Ariadna's mother Ernestina said. Ariadna looked up in complete surprise and saw her father seated behind his desk in the corner behind Zakharov, with her mother right beside him. They were clutching each other, but in surprise, not fear. "Is that you, Ariadna?"

Ariadna immediately reached out, and in the blink of an eye had Zakharov by the throat, holding him up high enough so his toes just barely touched the carpet. *"¿Es usted el daño dos?"* she asked.

"We are fine, dear," Ernestina said. "Yegor has been a complete gentleman."

"Yegor . . . gentleman . . . ?"

"Let him explain, Ari," her father Dominic said. "You can make up your own mind, but we believe what he has told us."

"You . . . *believe* . . . *him?*" Ariadna asked incredulously. "This man is an international terrorist and a mass murderer! He has masterminded the most deadly attacks in the entire *world!* What has he told you? Has he drugged you? Has he . . . ?"

"He has not done anything except make an appointment to talk to us. He said . . ."

"He made an *appointment?*"

"Perhaps you should let the man breathe so he can tell you himself, Ari," her father said with a hint of a smile on his face. "He looks like he is beginning to turn blue."

"I should kill him just for coming near you!" Ari turned back to Zakharov who indeed was starting to look like he was in some distress—he gasped like a fish out of water for several moments after she finally lowered him to the floor and loosened, but did not release, her grip on his neck. "You came here to kill my mother and father, didn't you, *hijoputa?*"

"*Ariadna!*" her mother admonished her. "Watch your language!" It was comical to watch the robot shake its head in disbelief.

"I came here . . . to give you . . . information," Zakharov said, his voice strained and croaking as he caught his breath. "Kill me if you want, but hear me out. I may even be able to help you."

"*Your* help? You want to help *me?*"

"I have been double-crossed, Dr. Vega, and I lack the resources to exact my revenge," Zakharov said. "Listen to me for two minutes, and I will tell you who is behind this Mexican immigration madness."

THE WHITE HOUSE,
WASHINGTON, D.C.
A SHORT TIME LATER

"I apologize for the confusion, Mr. President," Felix Díaz said when he took the call from the President of the United States in the president of Mexico's office. "I am somewhat at a loss to explain what has happened. All I know for certain is that President Maravilloso, the vice president, the Minister of Defense, and several other Council of Government ministers are missing or incommunicado. As fifth in line of presidential succession, I have temporarily assumed the role of president until a thorough investigation can be conducted."

"Do you think this is related to the embassy bombing in the Federal District, Minister Díaz?" the President of the United States asked. "Is there a coup underway? Is all this being engineered by that right-wing fanatic Comandante Veracruz?"

"Again, sir, I do not have that information at this time," Díaz said. "The situation here is confusing and fluid."

"I want to know just one thing, Minister Díaz: are all these announcements and threats from this Comandante Veracruz guy sanctioned and endorsed by the Mexican government? I require only a simple yes or no answer."

"I assure you, Mr. President, that this Comandante Veracruz character does not speak for Mexico," Minister of Internal Affairs Felix Díaz replied. "However, Ernesto Fuerza is a private citizen of Mexico; he has not been charged with any crimes here in Mexico, and therefore has the constitutional freedom to move and speak wherever he chooses; and if the private media outlets in my country wish to give him airtime to voice his opinions, that is their decision."

"Minister Díaz, his remarks are inflammatory, counterproductive, and obviously dangerous," Conrad said. "Cities and counties all over the United States are complaining of traffic gridlock, acts of vandalism and violence, theft, assaults—all because of this man's announcements. Since your Internal Affairs Ministry controls the communications outlets in your country, I want to know if his remarks are officially—"

"I have told you my government's official position many times, Mr. President," Díaz interrupted. "Mexico wishes to participate in formulating a just, fair, and equitable immigration and border security program with your government."

"And that is?"

"Very simple, sir: all military forces on the U.S.-Mexico border must be removed; all Mexican citizens being held in detention facilities must be released immediately; an in-place guest worker program should be initiated immediately, with Mexican citizens wishing to work being allowed to register with their employers or directly through your Citizenship and Immigration Services bureau without requiring them to return to Mexico; all Mexican workers in the United States are to be guaranteed the federal or state minimum wage, whichever is higher; and all Mexican citizens living and working in the United States for more than two years should receive a Social Security identification card, not just a useless taxpayer ID number."

"What you want is being debated in Congress as we speak, Minister."

"It has been debated for far too long—and as it is being debated, our citizens are dying in your deserts, being cheated out of fair wages, being denied workers benefits, and are not allowed to even open a bank account or see a doctor in some areas," Díaz said. "That must stop immediately, Mr. President. Otherwise I think our people should do exactly what Mr. Fuerza recommends: for their own safety, they should get out of the United States and not return until things change."

"Minister Díaz, millions of your people will suffer if they just leave like this," Conrad said. "Already thousands of innocent persons, mostly Mexicans, have been injured by assaults, traffic accidents, bombings, fighting, and looting. Several hundred have been killed. In the meantime they have no jobs, no income, and have only succeeded in creating chaos, fear, and confusion. Many of your people have been accused of hate crimes, racial attacks, sabotage, vandalism, and even murder. Is this what you want?"

"Mexico wants only justice, equality, and freedom, Mr. President," Díaz said. "What happens in the streets of your city and in your halls of Congress is entirely up to you. I suggest you control the hatemongers and racists in your *own* country first, like Bob O'Rourke, before accusing the poor displaced persons from Mexico!"

"Bob O'Rourke was killed early this afternoon, Minister Díaz, by a powerful bomb planted in his car," the President said. "I assumed you were aware of this."

Díaz was silent for a long moment, then: "If you expected me to be sorry O'Rourke is dead, Mr. President, I will no doubt disappoint you," he said in a quieter tone. "It matters not. He was not a spokesman for your government, anymore than Comandante Veracruz is of ours. Prod your Congress into passing some real immigration reform legislation, and sign it into law immediately, or the blood of many more innocent hardworking people will be on *your* hands."

President Conrad was silent for a few moments, then: "I understand that things are difficult there now, Minister Díaz," he said. "I called to ask if the United States can do anything to help. President Maravilloso gave her permission for us to send the FBI and military investigators to your country to—"

"I'm afraid that will be impossible now, Mr. President," Díaz said. "As director of internal investigations in Mexico, I cannot spare the manpower to lend to American investigators while attempting to conduct our *own* investigation. The Council of Government, the legislature, and the people will not permit an American investigation to override our own."

"You don't understand, Minister," the President said. "The El Centro incident occurred on U.S. soil, involving American military and civilian personnel. The U.S. embassy is considered American soil. You have treaty obligations that permit us to bring in our own investigators in cases such as this. I demand your government's full—"

"Excuse me, sir?" Díaz interrupted, his voice fairly shaking with anger. "Did you just tell me that you 'demand' something? How dare you speak to me like this? You would never dare to tell even a pizza deliveryman in your country that you 'demand' something—I think you would be polite and *ask* instead. How dare you make demands of this government?"

"Sir, a horrible crime has been committed on our territory," President Conrad said. "The FBI is our chief federal investigation organization. Because the incident involved a U.S. Marine Corps helicopter, the Department of Defense and the Navy are also going to be involved, along with other agencies. The aircraft that attacked near El Centro came from Mexico—you admitted as much yourself. Now I expect . . . no, Minister, I *demand* that your government cooperate with the FBI and the Navy Judge Advocate General's investigation. You will also—"

"Mr. Conrad, Mexico has its own investigation to conduct," Díaz retorted. "As I recall, no Mexican investigators were allowed on U.S. soil to look into the deaths of Mexican citizens at the hands of your military at Rampart One for several days, until your so-called investigators had a chance to sanitize the crime scenes so no useful evidence could be collected by our Border Affairs investigators . . ."

"Are you accusing the United States of destroying evidence in a criminal investigation?"

"I am telling you, Mr. Conrad, that Mexico does not, nor probably ever will, know the true reason for the deaths of our citizens at the hands of the robot working on behalf of Operation Rampart, and that is because of the unreasonable and illegal demands you placed on us," Díaz responded bitterly. "We were not allowed to investigate or question witnesses for almost three days after the incident occurred. Now you expect Mexico to not only allow your FBI and Navy to accompany our investigators, but you *demand* that they *take over our* investigation, dismissing all Mexican law enforcement agencies like some third-rate circus-clown act? I think not!"

"Minister Díaz, I certainly did not—"

"Mr. Conrad, the Foreign Ministry here has requested permission from your Department of State to allow me free diplomatic travel within the United States, specifically to address the United Nations Security Council to air my country's grievances concerning your arming of the border, illegal detainment of Mexican citizens, and acts of violence against Mexican citizens," Díaz said. "I have not received the courtesy of a reply, which I find very disturbing. Is it your intention to deny me entrance into your country and full diplomatic privileges?"

"Of course not—not at this time," the President replied. "Mexico is not on our list of sponsors of terrorism—although if the situation worsens or if we receive additional information concerning your government's involvement in terrorist acts in the United States, that could change."

"That sounds like a threat, Conrad," Díaz said. "Are you threatening me, Mr. Conrad? Are you trying to bully me into actions contrary to my government's policies and laws?"

"I'm stating facts, Minister Díaz," the President said. "I will confer with the Secretary of State and inquire on your application, and I see no reason at this time for there to be any undue delays. But the United States does not allow heads of governments that sponsor terrorism to enter the United States."

"I hope you are prepared for substantial international condemnation if you refuse to allow me to address the United Nations in New York," Díaz said angrily. "I hope your surprising lack of judgment and consideration is caused by grief and confusion over the recent violence, Mr. Conrad, and not by some new confrontational and racist policy toward the United Mexican States. Think carefully before you act on these hateful impulses or faulty paranoid advice from your neoconservative, warmongering advisers."

"I will take your advice under careful advisement, Minister," President Conrad said. "In the meantime, I have a possible solution for all those Mexican citizens who might wish to return to the United States."

"Oh?"

"We have developed an identification technology that is simple, unobtrusive, accurate, and reliable," the President said. "Within a matter of weeks it can be ready for mass implementation. It will provide thousands of citizens with an identification code that can be used by immigration and law enforcement personnel to determine any person's identity."

"We already have identification cards, Mr. Conrad."

"This is not a card—it is a pill that a person swallows. The pill . . ."

"Did you say, a *pill?*"

". . . releases thousands of tiny nanotransceivers in the body that transmit a coded signal when interrogated. The coded signal can be matched with official identification documents to—"

"Are you suggesting that our people *swallow a radio beacon* that reports their location to authorities twenty-four hours a day?" Díaz asked incredulously. "This is the most insane and intrusive idea that I have ever heard!"

"It sounds radical, I know," the President said, "but the devices are completely harmless—"

"You are crazy, Mr. Conrad! I could never recommend that the citizens of my country ever participate in such an outlandish—!"

"Minister Díaz, I am proposing that each Mexican citizen who wishes to return to the United States may be allowed to simply walk back into this country and return to his or her job and home simply by providing a Mexican identity card and swallowing a NIS pill—"

" 'Nice?' That is what you call this . . . this Big Brother eavesdropping monstrosity?"

"The presence of the identification code proves that the individual has chosen to obey the law and respect our borders and security obligations," the President said. "The NIS system will reduce the time it will take to identify individuals eligible for guest worker status: anyone with the code can stay and participate in a guest worker program; anyone not having such a code will be detained. It is a fair, unobtrusive, and easy solution . . ."

"This is no solution at all—it is a gross marginalization of a human being's basic right to freedom and privacy!" Felix Díaz retorted. "Do you actually expect that this so-called 'Nice' program will replace serious and equitable negotiations between our nations for a resolution to this crisis, or do you expect to just dictate that this otherworldly, Draconian abomination be implemented?" He did not give President Conrad a chance to respond. "You may call me when you have a *serious* solution to discuss, sir. Good day to you." And the connection was terminated with a loud *Crraack*!

The President returned the handset to its cradle and sat back in his chair, looking out the window. "Well, the NIS idea went over like a lead balloon," he said morosely. "But as I was explaining it to Díaz, it started to sound better and better to *me*."

"It will never fly, sir," Chief of Staff Thomas Kinsly said. "It's a crazy idea anyway—I would be surprised if anyone in Mexico was even the least bit interested in the idea. But what about Díaz, sir? Did it sound like he's in charge now?"

"Absolutely," the President said. "Felix Díaz definitely sounds like he's taken over—he hardly mentioned Maravilloso and anyone else in the government, as if they never even existed. Jeez, I thought Maravilloso was a bomb thrower—Díaz has got her beat ten ways to Sunday." He turned to Kinsly and asked, "What do we know about Díaz, Tom?"

"Felix Díaz is a major player—very wealthy, very popular, very politically connected, hawkish, an obvious front-runner for president in their next elections," Kinsly said. "The rumors are that he and Maravilloso have been carrying on with each other for a few months—right in the presidential palace too, I hear.

"The Internal Affairs Ministry is one of the most important and far-reaching in the Mexican government, and Felix Díaz is a hands-on, knowledgeable administrator," Kinsly went on. "He controls the intelligence apparatus, the border patrols, the antidrug bureaus, the federal police, and all domestic investigations—almost everything except foreign affairs, the courts, and the military, and he probably has a big hand in those as well. The Ministry of Internal Affairs is almost as well-equipped as the military, especially along the border."

"I need information on the situation out there," the President demanded. "I need to find out if Díaz has staged a coup and what we're up against."

"We don't have a functioning embassy in Mexico City that can help us go find out information for us, sir," National Security Adviser Ray Jefferson said, "so we're going to have to rely on technical and human intelligence to get information, which will take time. But if these attacks by Mexican émigrés are being supported or even *organized* by Felix Díaz, and he's now in charge of the government, we could be looking at a long, protracted, and deadly ongoing insurgency against the United States—perhaps even a guerrilla war."

The President's head shot up as if a gun had been fired in the Oval Office, but the Chief of Staff was the first to retort: "Sergeant Major, as usual, you're overreacting to recent developments. What could his motive possibly be?"

"Exactly what's happening, Mr. Kinsly: chaos, pandemonium, hatred, distrust, confusion, fear, and violence," Jefferson said. "An insurgency forces the issue of immigration reform—more accurately, immigration *liberalization*—onto the front burner."

"How? What's he hoping to gain?"

"Do you think, Mr. Kinsly, that Congress is likely to enact any legislation that will *curb* immigration now, with thousands of Mexican workers leaving the country every day?" Jefferson asked. "Folks won't focus on the violence—in fact, I would think more folks would likely blame the U.S. government for *causing* the violence with our 'radical' border security measures. Proimmigration reform measures will be seen as the way to stop the violence and get everyone's lives back to normal. The more restrictive or onerous the rules and requirements for establishing the right to work, deportation, pay, benefits, and citizenship, the more the people and Congress will oppose it. All attempts at meaningful border security and illegal immigration control will be pushed aside."

"That's crazy," Kinsly said. "You can't possibly believe that Mexico is *purposely* encouraging people to attack the United States in order to force a resolution to the illegal immigration situation?"

"No, Mr. Kinsly—I'm suggesting that forces within the Mexican government, possibly aided by the Consortium and also by radical leaders like Ernesto Fuerza, are staging violent attacks against the United States in order to incite their people to react against the United States, whether by violence or simply by leaving their jobs and heading south," Jefferson responded. "There could be other reasons as well—political, financial, criminal, even public relations—but by doing what they're doing, they are forcing the United States to expend a lot of political, financial, and military resources on this issue. I don't know if the Mexican government is assisting the insurgents, but they don't have to—all they need do is play along. Whatever they're doing, Mr. Kinsly, it's *working*."

"I'm still not buying it, Sergeant Major," Kinsly said. At that moment the phone rang. Kinsly picked it up, listened . . . and groaned audibly. "A suspected terrorist attack at a university north of Los Angeles," he said after he replaced the receiver. "Possibly a truck bomb outside an engineering building. L.A. County sheriffs and California Highway Patrol bomb squads are on it." The President said nothing, the National Security Adviser noticed, as if suspected terrorist truck bombs were as common as traffic accidents nowadays. But that's what the world had come to, he thought ruefully: if it wasn't bigger than Nine-Eleven, the Consortium attacks on Houston, or the floods in New Orleans, it hardly registered on the White House's radarscope anymore.

At that moment Ray Jefferson's wireless PDA beeped. Knowing that only an extremely urgent message would have gotten through to him while in a meeting at the Oval Office, he pulled the device from his jacket pocket and activated it. He read quickly, his face falling; moments later, a look of astonishment swept across his face. "I have an update on that situation at the university, Mr. President," he said, shaking his head in amazement, "and you are *not* going to believe it."

CHAPTER 12

The target was more than eleven hundred miles ahead—almost six hours of one-way flying.

The aircraft made their last refueling over U.S. territory from an MC-130P Combat Shadow aerial refueling tanker low over the Sulphur Springs Valley area of south-central Arizona just before going across the border around 9 P.M. local time. Flying at less than five hundred feet aboveground, the aircraft were still spotted by U.S. Homeland Security antismuggling radar arrays and balloons, but the word had already been passed along, and no radio contact with the aircraft was ever made or even attempted.

After refueling, the two aircraft flew in close formation, with the pilots using night vision goggles to see each other at night. Each aircraft was fitted with special infrared position lights that were only visible to those wearing NVGs, so from the pilots' point of view it was very much like flying in hazy daytime weather conditions. The pilots of each aircraft would trade positions occasionally to avoid fatigue, with the copilot of one aircraft taking over and then moving over to the other aircraft's opposite wing. The two propeller-driven aircraft were fairly well matched in performance, with the smaller aircraft having a slight disadvantage over its four-engined leader but still able to keep up easily enough. Throughout all the position and pilot changes, and no matter the outside conditions, the aircraft never strayed farther than a wingspan's distance from each other and never flew higher than eight hundred feet aboveground.

Mexican surveillance radar at Ciudad Juárez spotted the aircraft briefly near the town of Janos as it made its way southeast, and one attempt was made to contact it by radio, but there was no response so the radar operators ignored it. The Mexican military was tasked primarily with counterinsurgency operations and secondarily with narcotics interdiction—and even that mission ranked a *very* distant second—but those forces were primarily arrayed along the southern border and coastlines: in northern Mexico near the U.S. border, there was virtually no military presence at all. Certainly if a low-flying plane was spotted going *south,* it was no cause for alarm. A routine report was sent up the line to Mexican air defense headquarters in Mexico City, and the contact immediately forgotten.

From Janos the aircraft headed south over the northern portion of the Sierra Madre Occidental Mountains. The aircraft flew higher, now a thousand feet aboveground, but in the mountains it was effectively invisible to radar sweeps from Hermosillo, Chihuahua, and Ciudad Obregón. Over the mining town of Urique, the aircraft veered southeast, staying in the "military crest" of the mountain range to completely lose itself in the radar ground clutter. This two-hour leg was the quietest—central Mexico was almost devoid of any population centers at all, and had virtually no military presence. They received the briefest squeak from their radar warning receivers when passing within a hundred miles of Mazatlán's approach radar, but they were well out of range and undetectable at their altitude.

The aircraft performed another low-altitude aerial refueling on this leg of the journey, ensuring that the smaller aircraft was completely topped off before continuing further. The MC-130P had a

combat range of almost four thousand miles and could have made
two complete round trips with ease; the smaller aircraft had only
half the range and needed the extra fuel to maintain its already-
slim margin of safety. Once topped off, the MC-130P orbited at
one thousand feet above the ground about sixty miles northwest of
the city of Durango, over the most isolated portion of the central
Sierra Madre Occidental Mountain range and directly in the
"dead spot" of several surveillance and air traffic control radar systems. The electronic warfare officer on board the Combat Shadow
was on the lookout for any sign of detection, but the electromagnetic spectrum remained quiet as the two aircraft split up.

Just north of the city of Zacatecas the smaller aircraft jogged
farther east to avoid Guadalajara's powerful air traffic and air defense radar system. Now the aircraft was no longer over the
mountains but flying in Mexico's central valley, so it was back
down to five hundred feet or less aboveground, using terrain-
avoidance radar, precise satellite-guided navigation, night vision
devices that made it easy to see the ground and large obstacles, and
photo-quality digital terrain and obstruction charts, with computerized audio and visual warnings of nearby radio towers and
transmission lines. Northeast of the city of San Luis Potosí, the aircraft made a hard turn south to avoid Tampico's coastal surveillance radar.

Now the aircraft was flying in the heart of Mexico's population
centers, with 80 percent of the country's population within one
hundred miles of their present position—and most of the country's air defense, surveillance, and air traffic radars as well. Plus,
they had very little terrain to hide in now. Staying far away from
towns and highways, relying mostly on darkness to hide their
presence, the aircraft's crew prepared for the most dangerous part
of the mission. After over five hours of relative peace and quiet,
the last twelve minutes was going to be very busy indeed. The
crew performed their "Before Enemy Defended Area Penetra-
tion" checklist, making sure all lights were off, radios were con-
figured to avoid any accidental transmissions, the cabin was

depressurized and secure, and the crew members waiting in the cargo area were alerted to prepare for evasive maneuvers and possible hostile action.

Somehow, after the events that had transpired in the past several days, it was not hard to imagine they were flying over enemy territory—even though they were flying over Mexico.

Immediately prior to the last turning point over the town of Ciudad Hidalgo, eighty miles northwest of Mexico City, came the first radio message on "GUARD," the international emergency frequency, in English: "Unidentified aircraft at the two-niner-zero degree radial of Mexico City VOR, seventy-three DME, this is Mexico City Center, squawk Mode Three five-seven-one-seven; ident, and contact center on one-two-eight point three two, UHF three-two-seven point zero. Acknowledge immediately." It was repeated several times in both English and Spanish, even after the radar return completely dropped off the scope.

The message was never answered, of course—which only served to alert the *Fuerza Aerea Mexicana,* the Mexican Air Force, and the Interior Defense Forces of the Ministry of Internal Affairs. The Mexican Air Force had one airbase northeast of Mexico City dedicated to air defense, with nine F-5E Tiger II fighters assigned there; two were on twenty-four-hour alert. By the time the aircraft was twenty miles west of Mexico City, the fighters were airborne. But the pilots had had very little actual night low-altitude air defense training, and the radars on the American-made Tiger IIs were not designed to detect low-flying aircraft against a heavily industrialized and populated background, so the fighters could do nothing else but fly a medium-altitude patrol pattern, away from the commercial airline arrival and departure paths and surrounding high terrain, and hope that Mexican air traffic control could spot the unidentified aircraft again and vector them in close enough for visual contact.

But the Internal Affairs Ministry's response was far different. Primarily charged with identifying, tracking, and stopping insurgents and revolutionaries that might threaten the republic, the

ministry responded to every such alert, no matter how small, as if
it was an impending coup or attack on the capital.

The Political Police, which commanded a larger helicopter
force than the army and air force combined, immediately
launched several dozen helicopters of mixed varieties over the
capital, mostly American- and Brazilian-made patrol helicopters
that carried a flight crew of two, an observer/sniper in the rear,
along with searchlights; a few were equipped with infrared cameras. The helicopters flew preplanned patrol routes over the capital, concentrating on scanning government buildings, embassies,
and residences for any sign of trouble. Another dozen helicopters
were placed on standby alert, ready to respond immediately if necessary; the Internal Affairs Ministry also could commandeer as
many aircraft of any kind as it wanted, including helicopter and
fixed-wing gunships and large transports. A small fleet of VIP
helicopters was also placed in standby or prepositioned to various
places around the capital, ready to whisk away high-ranking
members of the government to secure locations.

At the same time, the twenty-five thousand members of the
Federal District Police were put on full alert and ordered to report
to their duty stations or emergency assignments. Within the Federal District, the Federal District Police had ultimate control, even
over the military; they were just as well equipped as the armed
forces, including armored personnel carriers, antitank weapons,
attack helicopters, and even light tanks. These ground and air
forces were deployed throughout the Federal District and immediately began closing off side streets, shutting down bars and
restaurants, restricting citizens to their homes, and establishing
strict movement control throughout the capital. The highest concentration of Federal District Police were at the Palacio Nacional,
Zocalo, Embassy Row along the Paseo de la Reforma between the
Mexican Stock Exchange and the Chapultepec Polanco district,
the major hotels near the Independence Monument and Lincoln
Park, and the Internal Affairs Ministry itself.

Mixed in with all these protective forces were the Political Police, whose primary job was to maintain surveillance on all of the important and high-ranking Mexican politicians, their families, and major associates—including their staffs, bank accounts, telephones, e-mails, and postal correspondence, unofficial as well as official; and the *Sombras,* the Special Investigations Squad, assigned to keep an eye on the highest-level persons in the Mexican government and report any suspicious activities directly to Felix Díaz. During these emergencies, every member of the Political Police was brought into the ministry headquarters at the Bosque de Chapultepec and ordered to update their contact files and begin careful monitoring of their assigned targets to discover any clues of possible conspiracies against the government.

Located in the south-central edge of Chapultepec Park just south of the zoo and west of Castillo de Chapultepec, the Ministry of Internal Affairs complex was in effect a walled fortress—unlike most government buildings in Mexico City, citizens were not permitted to freely come and go, and there were no tours. A series of Napoleonic-style office buildings surrounded the complex, creating the outer wall of the complex, with Federal District Police armed with automatic weapons stationed on the rooftops. On each side, the buildings were connected by Spanish-style arches with ornate iron gates. The gates looked decorative, but they had been stressed to stop a five-ton truck from crashing through them, and the width of the opening had been purposely reduced to less than that of an armored personnel carrier.

Inside the outer walls formed by the older office buildings were the ministry's operations buildings—the investigator's offices, communications, arsenal, and barracks, housed in three plain-looking rectangular boxlike buildings arrayed in a triangular shape radiating out from the center of the complex. In the center of the triangle was the main ministry building, a Stalinist-era-looking eight-story tower, resembling simple blocks progressively smaller in size stacked atop one another, topped with a tall antenna housing structure that supported hundreds of antennas of all sizes and kinds. The building not only housed the minister's offices and those of his extensive bureaucratic staff but also the electronic eavesdropping and computer centers, the intelligence analyst's offices, the extensive prison complex, the offices of the Political Police and *Sombras,* and a so-called special medical center in the subfloor areas—the interrogation center.

Unlike most of the beautiful, graceful architecture of the Bosque de Chapultepec or the Zocalo, the Internal Affairs Ministry was a dark, uninspiring, foreboding, and ominous place—and that was just the feeling from the outside. Very few persons ever spoke about the facility openly, especially about the activities in the center building—what the people of Mexico City called the *"lugar de la oscuridad"*—the "place of darkness." It was meant as a message to the people of Mexico City: we are watching you, and if you dare cross us, this is where you will be taken.

"Why the hell did we come back here, Elvarez?" Minister of Internal Affairs Felix Díaz snapped as they headed through the security blast doors to the command center conference room. "If we're under attack, I should be heading to the airport to evacuate."

"The safest place for you until we get a report on the evacuation route is here in the ministry building—it can withstand anything except a direct aerial bombardment," deputy minister José Elvarez said. "As soon as I can verify the security of the Métro and the airport, we will depart. In the meantime, you can get a firsthand report on the situation."

"Bullshit, Elvarez. Let's head to the airport in a ministry armored vehicle right away and . . ."

"Sir, I cannot plan an evacuation route without a report from our agents throughout the city, even if we took a main battle tank," Elvarez said emphatically. "And if you do not personally direct your staff to secure the records, gather information, and handle the emergency, they will all flee the building and leave it wide open for whoever caused this alert."

"I will personally cut out the eyeballs of any man or woman who runs out on me," Díaz growled. Obviously he wasn't happy about this situation, but he quickly followed along. The rest of the

senior staff of the Internal Affairs Ministry was already in place
when Felix Díaz entered the conference room. "Take seats," he ordered. "Report."

"Mexico City Air Route Traffic Control Center notified the
Minister of Defense that an unidentified low-flying aircraft was
spotted briefly on radar about seventy miles outside the city," the
command center duty officer responded. "Defense notified us immediately, and we issued an emergency situation action order to
all Internal Affairs departments immediately."

"Any sign of the aircraft?" Díaz asked. "Identification?"

"No, sir," he replied. "As you know, Minister, there is only one
major threat to the government or the Federal District from the
air, and that is a special operations commando insertion mission,
most likely from the United States. This aircraft was traveling at
over three hundred kilometers an hour, which means it was not a
helicopter."

"What, then?"

"Most likely a reconnaissance flight, a probe of some kind, or a
warning to us," the duty officer said. "Too slow for an attack jet—
possibly a turboprop plane such as a C-130."

"A warning?"

"A simple message, sir: we can fly over your capital any time we
like, and there is nothing you can do about it," Elvarez said. "The
Americans made many of these warning flights in the past over
Nicaragua, Haiti, and Panama prior to the start of hostilities
against them—it is a common scare tactic."

"Contact the Foreign and Defense Ministries and ask if the
Americans requested to perform such a flyover—a test of their
radar systems, perhaps, or an embassy rescue exercise, or other
such reason that was not communicated to us." Elvarez relayed
the order immediately. Díaz thought for a moment, then
shrugged. "A probe seems unnecessary—the Americans have
been spying on us for decades and have many of our people on
their payroll," he said, thinking aloud. "A warning message
sounds more likely . . ." He stopped, his eyes widening in fear.

"But we can't count on this just being a warning—we must assume we are under attack unless proven otherwise. Status of our force deployments?"

"All units reporting force deployments fully underway," Elvarez said. "I have personally received visual staus reports from my staff on the most important locations—those spots will be fully manned within the hour."

"The Internal Affairs Ministry complex?"

"All defensive systems fully manned and operational, sir. All defense and security sectors reporting fully manned and ready."

"And the Defense Ministry?"

"Under full surveillance and secure," Elvarez replied. Although the Ministry of National Defense was located at the Palacio Nacional, the chiefs of staff, the bulk of the defense bureaucracy, and the headquarters of the First Military Zone, the actual military forces assigned to defend the capital, were located at a large base in the extreme western edge of the Federal District, just three miles northwest of the Internal Affairs Ministry complex, known simply as the Campo Militar. The First Military Zone was the largest of Mexico's thirty-five zones, with just over fifteen thousand infantry, marines, and airmen assigned to a dozen bases in the area; two battalions, about six thousand infantry and marines, were assigned to the Campo Militar itself. "They do not seem to have placed the Campo Militar garrison on alert or deployed any forces anywhere in the Federal District. They responded immediately with a security and status report and gave us a fairly complete equipment list, as required. It has not yet been visually verified that this equipment is indeed available to us but that report will be in shortly."

"Where is General Rojas? Have you succeeded in locating him yet?"

"It now appears that General Rojas was in the Campo Militar garrison all along," Elvarez reported, after a quick scan of his notes. "After the alert, one of the command post officers let it slip that the general was en route to the battle staff area; this was later verified by several cellular telephone traces."

"But not visually verified?"

"No, sir."

"Then we should assume that Rojas's whereabouts are un-known," Díaz said. "I want his exact location pinpointed and vi-sually verified, and I want it done immediately."

"Yes, sir." Elvarez relayed the order, then referred to a notebook in front of him, checking off items on a checklist. "Alert plus thirty minutes items appear to be completed, sir," he said. "Next action items are at alert plus one hour. I shall notify the Palacio Nacional and the Senate and Chamber of Deputies that . . ."

At that moment they could hear the deep rapid-fire staccato of a heavy machine gun, and seconds later an alarm bell sounded and telephones on the conference table began to ring. *"What is it?"* Díaz demanded.

"Air defense gun emplacements in the Internal Affairs Ministry complex engaged an unidentified helicopter," Elvarez said after getting the telephone report. The armed forces of the United Mex-ican States had a grand total of fifty air defense pieces: forty M-55 quad 12.7-millimeter antiaircraft gun units mounted on an M-16 half-track vehicle, most over sixty years old and in various states of functionality; and ten RBS-70 laser-guided antiaircraft missile launchers mounted on Humvees. Of these fifty pieces, eight of the antiaircraft guns and two RBS-70 SAMs protected the Internal Affairs Ministry—the rest were assigned to military bases.

"What's happening?" Díaz shouted.

"One aircraft hit, sir!" Elvarez shouted. "Very large rotorcraft, type unknown but believed to be American . . ."

"Of course it's American—who else would be invading Mexico now?" Díaz asked sarcastically. The lights flickered briefly in the conference room seconds before they heard a loud *booom*! echo through the walls. "Where did it go down?"

"No visual contact yet, sir."

"The American commandos will already be on the ground—they may have been here days ago," Díaz said. "Special ops teams usually come in groups of twenty-four." The former air force officer had received many briefings over the years on procedures for both American and Russian special ops forces. "Tell all security units that we are under air assault. Shut down the complex and order all personnel to repel any unidentified persons at all costs!" He turned to Elvarez and said in a low voice, "Start document destruction procedures immediately—and for God's sake, get rid of that *evidence* down in the medical center! *Now!*"

Every person not strapped in on board the CV-22 Osprey special ops tilt-rotor aircraft was thrown off his feet by the sudden shock and explosion off the left wing—except for the four Cybernetic Infantry Devices standing hunched over near the open ramp in the back of the cargo bay. "Hang on, guys," the pilot said on the intercom, "we just lost the left engine. I turned us right into a triple-A truck. Check the auto crossover."

"Crossover indicating green, but I'm still not getting full RPMs on the left," the copilot shouted. "Check hydraulics . . ."

"Got it!" the flight engineer chimed in. "I'm initiating manual emergency hydraulic pressurization—the auto system didn't activate."

"Hurry it up—we're going to hit real hard if we don't get power . . ." But even as the pilot spoke, the crew could feel the Osprey starting to pick up speed and altitude. "I think I got it. Stand by, guys, I'm going to bring it around and try for DZ Bravo again—it looks like that triple-A is sitting right on the edge of Alpha. We'll be facing southwest instead of northeast so your target will be behind you. Gunners, keep an eye out to the southeast—we might have more triple-A or missile trucks inbound. Here we go."

The digital maps playing in the CID units' electronic visors told them what the pilot just reported: the initial plan was to drop to the northeast so their target, the central Internal Affairs Ministry building, would be right in front of them, but that was not going to happen now. The Osprey executed an impossibly steep-banked right turn, the good right engine now screaming at full power. The CV-22 Osprey had an automatic crossover transmission that allowed both tilt-rotors to be powered off one engine—it was generally thought that the system would only deliver enough power to do a controlled crash. The pilot obviously thought otherwise.

Everyone felt their bodies go a little weightless again as they executed the tight turn, but moments later they experienced some extra g-forces as the turn stopped—and then they felt a little weightless again as the Osprey dipped suddenly, then felt the g-forces push down on them again as the flight crew arrested the rapid descent and slowed to drop airspeed. The crew in the cargo bay had never heard screeching noises like that coming from any aircraft before—it sounded as if the tilt-rotor was going to burst apart into a million pieces at any moment.

"Stand by to release recon drones . . . ready . . . now." The assistant flight engineer pulled a lever on the right side of the cargo bay, and a rectangular box containing four grenade-launched unmanned observation system drones shot out through the open cargo bay and disappeared into the darkness.

"Goose One and Two in the green . . . nothing from Goose Three . . . Goose Four . . . nope, lost that one too," Jason said. "We lost the two southernmost drones, guys. Keep that in mind—coverage to our south might be poor." He turned to the twelve commandos in the forward part of the cargo bay, then pointed an armored finger at a man handcuffed to them. "I want him with me as soon as we get in that building," he said. "If he tries to run, shoot him."

"Yes, sir," the team leader responded.

"Five seconds."

Another severe rumble and scream of metal split the air. "Is this thing going to hold together for that long?" Mike Tesch in CID Three asked.

The pilot didn't dare try to answer that one. Instead, he shouted, *"Green light! Go!"*

Jason Richter and Jennifer McCracken in CID One and CID

Two jumped first. There was no time to practice a good parachute landing fall—students in the U.S. Army Airborne School practiced them for five full days before being allowed to jump from anything higher than a three-foot platform—so Jason's landing didn't look much better than the first time he jumped from the Osprey. But Jennifer's landing looked like she had been jumping from special ops planes all her life. "Good job, Lieutenant," Jason told her after he picked himself up off the ground. "Done this before, I see."

"Army Airborne School, class zero-four dash eleven, and Marine Corps Mobile Airborne Training Team certified same year, sir," she replied. Even in the CID unit, Jason could see the look of confusion in her "body" language. "Are you telling me you've never attended jump school, sir? You've jumped out of planes twice now and never learned how to land? I'm surprised you haven't broken every bone in your body, sir."

"I'll take that as a compliment, Lieutenant," Jason said as he checked his systems. "Let's go." He and McCracken had jumped on the very outside of the easternmost spoke of the outer buildings surrounding the central Internal Affairs building. Tesch and Dodd had been dropped off on the other side of the complex. As soon as Tesch and Dodd reported they were on the ground and ready, they headed in.

Automatic gunfire from above erupted almost immediately as machine gunners opened fire from atop the administrative buildings. The GUOS drones picked up activity on the far side of the buildings, and the CID units were able to accurately target their backpack grenade launchers and machine guns on those positions—they had no choice but to run away from the gunfire.

As Harry Dodd reached the end of the southwestern admin building, a Humvee with a large missile launcher unit suddenly appeared. "SAM unit!" Dodd shouted. Just as he set his aiming reticle on the vehicle, it launched a missile skyward. "Poppa Bear, *missile launch, missile launch!*" he shouted, seconds before ordering his grenade launcher to open fire. Just before his two grenades hit, the Bofors RBS-70 missile streaked away.

But as he watched, several dozen streaks of light and blobs of white-hot energy fanned out across the sky less than a mile away, bright enough to light up the Bosque de Chapultepec for miles around—the CV-22 Osprey ejecting decoy flares. Dodd knew that all of the CV-22's other countermeasures were active as well—an active missile-tracking laser that blinded an enemy missile's seeker head, decoy chaff, and electronic radar and laser jammers as well. The RBS-70 missile stayed dead on course, but just for an instant. Moments later Dodd could see the motor exhaust flame wobble, slightly at first and then greater and greater. Seconds later it exploded—and there was no secondary explosion.

"Thanks for the heads-up, Talon," the assistant flight engineer radioed. "I saw that missile coming up at us and thought it was heading right for the blank spot between my eyes. Good hunting down there."

The CID units spread out once they reached the central head-quarters building, with each CID unit taking a cardinal position. On Jason's order, Mike Tesch sent two grenade bursts into the front entranceway from forty yards away, blowing the doors open. Seconds later came a murderous burst of heavy machine gun fire, followed by several grenade detonations.

That was the signal to begin the real assault. The other three CID units on the other sides of the building began climbing the outside of the Internal Affairs Ministry. Each CID unit would simply leap up to the windowsill above, pull itself up to the window, jump up to the next window, and continue. When it reached its preplanned floor, it climbed inside. Jennifer McCracken continued up to the roof of the building, where she planted explosives around the base of the antenna tower and blew it apart moments later.

"We lost the microwave datalink and all radio contact, sir," Deputy Minister Elvarez said. "They probably destroyed the antenna tower on the roof. The secure hardwire lines and circuits are still operational." He leaned toward Felix Díaz. "The roof of this building is the most vulnerable spot, sir. If they have troops on the roof, it is only a matter of time before they get inside."

"What is the status of the document destruction?"

"Just started, sir. Magnetic records can be erased in minutes, but the paper documents and any records stored on other than the mainframes and servers will take much longer." The lights flickered and went out, and this time only the battery-powered standby lights stayed on. "Sir, you will have to evacuate to a secure location, and do it quickly," Elvarez said urgently. "We may have only moments before this building is overrun."

Díaz nodded. "All right. The information officers will have to ensure that the data destruction is completed."

"Yes, sir." Elvarez picked up a phone and punched in an extension number. "Report . . . very well, we are on our way." He hung up the receiver. "We will have to take the stairs because the elevators are out," he said, "but the tunnel to the Metro system is open and guarded. We have already closed down the number seven and nine lines, and a train is available immediately to take us to the airport. A plane is waiting to get us out of . . ."

At that moment they heard a loud *crash!* and the very walls of the command center started to shake. "What in hell . . . ?"

Elvarez studied the readouts on his computer screen, but he didn't need a computer to tell him that the outer doors to the command center had been blown in. "This way, sir—there's no time!" he said. "The emergency chute." He unlocked a cabinet in a corner of the room, moved a hidden lever, then swung the cabinet aside, revealing a hidden doorway. There was a dark hole in the floor, surrounded by what appeared to be a thin, gauzy white material. "This is the emergency fire escape tunnel, sir," Elvarez said. "The material is fireproof and is designed to slow your body as you slide down. Simply extend your arms slightly to slow yourself down if you feel it necessary, but allow yourself to go all the way down without delay."

"Where does it lead?"

"It leads to a fire valve inspection room in the underground parking area in the first subfloor," Elvarez said. "I will go first and secure it." Elvarez drew a sidearm, removed his shoes, and stuffed them into his pockets, then stepped into the fabric tube and disappeared. "It is safe, sir," he called from several feet below. "Take off your shoes and follow me."

The tube was snug but not constricting. All Díaz had to do was to think about making his body narrower and he slid faster, and when he thought he was going too fast, his elbows would unconsciously protrude and slow him down. He heard Elvarez say something, but he was at least a couple floors below him now and it was hard to hear inside the tube.

"I'm down, sir," Elvarez said a few moments later. "It's clear. I can see you now. Keep moving." Díaz slid faster. "The way is clear to the tunnel to the Métro station, and the train is waiting to take us. Slow down a little, sir, just a few feet more . . ."

He felt like a turd passing through the colon when he popped free of the fabric fire tube and landed on the gray painted concrete floor. The plain concrete block room was lit by a single lightbulb overhead and was filled with pipes of all sizes. Díaz took a few moments to put his shoes back on, then followed Elvarez outside. "How far is it to the Métro station, José?" he asked. "Are we going to walk, or . . . ?"

He stopped . . . because his path was blocked by four soldiers in black fatigues, Kevlar helmets, and automatic rifles—American rifles! "Freeze, asshole!" one of the soldiers shouted in English, then in Spanish. "*¡Consiga en sus rodillas! ¡Manos en su cabeza!*"

Díaz complied immediately, lowering himself to the concrete floor and locking the fingers of both hands atop his head. "I am Minister of Internal Affairs Díaz!" he shouted. "Who are you and what are you doing in my building?"

"Task force TALON, United States of America," the soldier said. He covered Díaz and Elvarez while two others searched them and took their weapons, radios, telephones, and identification. "You are under arrest."

"Under whose authority?"

"I have a warrant for your arrest, Felix Díaz," the soldier said.

"A warrant? An *American* arrest warrant? Signed by whom—Mickey Mouse?"

"A federal judge in San Diego," the commando replied. "We'll take you to see him shortly."

"On what charge?"

"Murder of federal officers, conspiracy to commit murder, attempted murder, and destruction of . . ."

"*¡Cada uno para inmediatamente!*" someone else shouted. Suddenly about a dozen Mexican army soldiers ran from the tunnel leading to the Métro station, quickly entered the garage area, and surrounded the American soldiers with rifles raised. "This is the army of the United Mexican States! No one move!"

"Thank God you showed up!" Díaz exclaimed happily, rising to his feet.

"*El ministro Díaz, es usted lastimó?*"

"No, I'm fine," Diaz said. He pointed to the TALON commandos. "I want these four men bound and gagged and taken away—and *no one* is to have any contact with them, understand?"

"*Entiendo, señor,*" the Mexican soldier responded . . . and then two of his men spun Díaz around, slammed him up against the concrete wall, and stripped his jacket down over his arms.

"*What in hell do you think you're doing?*" Díaz screamed. "I am the Minister of Internal Affairs and the acting president of Mexico! Do as I ordered you or I will have you all *shot!*"

"Or drugged . . . like you did to Carmen, you rancid piece of shit?" Díaz gasped and turned around . . . and saw none other than the Minister of National Defense, General Alberto Rojas, standing before him.

"*Rojas!*" Díaz exclaimed, forcing himself to choke down his surprise and panic. "Where in hell have you been? I have had the entire ministry out looking for you!"

"Hiding from you and your *Sombras,* Díaz," Rojas said. "Making a few phone calls as well—to my new friends in Clovis, New Mexico."

"You are helping the Americans? You will hang for that, Rojas!"

"I am not afraid of facing a court-martial for what I have done, Díaz—but I cannot say the same about your own prospects in a courtroom," Rojas said confidently, "especially with the evidence we've discovered here." He turned and watched as a gurney carrying a body under a white sheet was rolled out of the garage to be carried upstairs. "You didn't even have the brains to dispose of the body, Díaz."

"Me? Why would I dispose of the president's body?" Díaz asked incredulously. "The president was being kept here, secure, until an investigation could be concluded. But I think I know who killed the president: Ernesto Fuerza."

"Fuerza? Comandante Veracruz?" Rojas exclaimed. "How do you know this?"

"I made the mistake of bringing him and the Russian terrorist Yegor Zakharov to meet the president, as she requested," Díaz said. "I was told to leave them alone, and I complied with her wishes. The next thing I know, Fuerza and Zakharov were gone, and the president was dead."

"Why did you not report this immediately, Minister?"

"I initiated an immediate investigation and sent agents out across the country to track down Fuerza and Zakharov. But the government was in disarray, and I took it upon myself to preserve the president's body and continue the investigation in secret. I dared not reveal any of this to the Council of Government, in case one of them was involved in . . ."

At that moment one of the Cybernetic Infantry Device robots entered the parking garage, carrying a man by his arms in its armored fists . . . none other than Yegor Zakharov! "You caught him!" he exclaimed. "Where did you find him?"

"Our friends in the United States had him in custody," Rojas said. "He told us a very interesting story about you and your alter ego—Comandante Veracruz. If you are lucky, Felix, the judges of the Supreme Court will only sentence you to a *single* death sentence, instead of dozens."

"*What?* You are not going to believe *this* man, are you, Rojas? He is an international terrorist, a mass murderer, and the most wanted man in the world! He would do or say anything to save his skin! He will lie, cheat . . ."

Díaz stopped . . . when he saw the Mexican soldiers help José Elvarez up. His eyes bulged in horrible realization. "What is going on here?"

"Just helping a key witness to his feet, Felix," Rojas said. "You are correct, Felix: no judge on earth would believe Yegor Zakharov even if he swore on a roomful of Bibles that the sky is blue. But they *might* believe your own deputy minister."

Díaz gulped deeply, his mouth dropping open in sheer numbness. He looked at the faces around him and could not recognize one man who might help him at all. His gaze finally rested on Alberto Rojas. "You win, General," he said. "But you know that I did all this for one reason: to help our people. Our citizens were dying and being exploited by the United States by the *millions*. Someone had to do something. Only I had the guts to take the fight to the Americans. I provided the inspiration for freedom and justice that the rest of the government could not." Rojas said nothing. Díaz took one step toward him and said in a low voice, "You may not like what I did, Rojas, but you know I did it all on behalf of the Mexican people. Yes, I failed, but not for lacking the courage to try."

Rojas averted his eyes, and Díaz knew he had hit a nerve. "I have the courage for one more thing, General. Give me a gun and put me back in that room and I will save all of you the time and trouble of putting me on trial."

The defense minister looked at Díaz, put his hand to his holster . . . then shook his head. "At one time I might have granted your request, Felix—but then I had to walk into your torture chamber and identify the body of my dear friend, President Carmen Maravilloso, lying on a slab in your house of horrors down there," he said. "You are not a patriot or a revolutionary, Felix Díaz—you are nothing but a murderous piece of human shit.

"You will be taken to the United States and put on trial first, and then if you are not sentenced to death you will be sent back to Mexico to face murder and conspiracy charges here. Get him out of my sight."

Jason carried Yegor Zakharov outside to the waiting CV-22 Osprey tilt-rotor aircraft, surrounded by both Task Force TALON commandos and Mexican army soldiers. Internal Affairs agents and employees were being escorted out of the ministry buildings at gunpoint, and boxes of records were being carried out and loaded into trucks. "So, Major Richter," Zakharov said casually, "I have done what you have asked. You should let me go now. That was part of our deal, was it not?"

"It was not," the robot's electronic voice replied.

"Then you intend to kill me, after all I have done for you?"

In the blink of an eye, the robot spun Zakharov around so he was now facing the robot, still suspended in the robot's grasp; then, Richter deployed the twenty-millimeter cannon in his weapon backpack. The huge muzzle of the weapon was now pointed forward over the robot's right shoulder, inches away from Zakharov's face.

"I could do it now, Zakharov," Jason said, the robotic voice slow and measured, "and no one would say a damned thing about it."

"I could have slaughtered Vega's entire family . . . !"

"Everyone expected you to do it. We were prepared for it, believe me."

"But I did not do it, Major. I spared them, turned myself in, and helped you get Díaz."

"You think you're a big hero now?"

"There is so much more I could tell you, Richter," Zakharov said. "I could give you information that would put you within reach of thousands of the world's greatest criminals. Your task force could capture them, and then you would be the hero. All I am asking for is my freedom. I will give you my information. You check it out and verify its credibility. Then you fly me to a *wadi* in the Sahara or a deserted island in Indonesia, and we both live out the rest of our lives free from ever having to deal with one another again."

The robot suddenly turned away from the CV-22 and ran quickly out of the Internal Affairs Ministry compound, heading east until it came on an open area of the Bosque de Chapultepec. Then, to Zakharov's complete amazement, the robot dropped him. Zakharov was on his feet in an instant, looking around in the darkness. The brilliant lights of Mexico City illuminated the horizon in all directions except to the west; the light surrounding the Castillo de Chapultepec, the now-vacant Mexican president's residence, could be seen a short distance away.

"What are you doing, Richter?" Zakharov asked.

Jason said nothing for several long moments; then, Zakharov heard him say: "Run."

"What?"

"Run, Colonel," Richter said. "I'll give you five minutes. You might be able to make it to the Castillo, probably to Constitution Avenue, and once you cross there you'll be in the heart of that residential neighborhood. Run."

Zakharov took several steps backward and looked around himself again. Yes, he thought, he could easily make it to Constitution Avenue, and immediately he'd be in the San Miguel Chapultepec neighborhood, a mixture of wealthy homes and upscale businesses—perhaps even sympathetic Russian expatriates or oil company executives that he once did business with. The robot was good out in the open but bad in narrow alleyways and terrible indoors . . . yes, he might just make it. Go, he told himself, *go, now . . .* !

But as he stepped back, he saw the muzzle of that twenty-millimeter cannon tracking his head, aimed right between his eyes, and he knew that Richter had no intention of letting him go. He would let him run a short distance, then open fire. Like he said, no one in Mexico, the United States, or most anywhere in the world would blink an eye over his death.

Zakharov turned, dropped to his knees, and raised his arms to his side. The robot grasped his arms and pulled him effortlessly off his feet.

"Smart choice, Colonel," Jason Richter said, as they headed back toward the Internal Affairs Ministry complex. "Smart choice."

EPILOGUE

The speeches and proclamations were finally concluded. Underneath an arch of balloons and flags of Mexico and the United States fluttering in the cool breeze, the new president of the United Mexican States, Alberto Rojas, and the President of the United States, Samuel Conrad, stepped off the dais and into a new building erected just outside the Tijuana-San Diego border crossing and up to a special kiosk.

While TV cameras and dozens of reporters recorded everything, Rojas stepped up to the person behind the counter—Director of U.S. Customs and Border Protection James A. Abernathy himself—shook hands, and gave him his Mexican identification card and birth certificate. Abernathy handed the documents to a technician, who scanned the documents into a computer and gave them back. Rojas then stepped onto a designated spot on the floor, smiled as a digital photograph was taken, then pressed the thumbs from each hand onto a digital fingerprint reader. Finally he took a white capsule from a dispenser, held it up for all the reporters to see, swallowed it, and downed it with a glass of champagne.

Following Rojas, the President of the United States did the

very same procedure, including downing an NIS capsule. He then raised his own glass of champagne to Alberto Rojas and took a sip. Immediately afterward, the new Mexican Minister of Internal Affairs, Minister of Justice, and Minister of Foreign Affairs repeated the procedure, followed immediately by their American counterparts, and they toasted one another for all to see. Then the dignitaries watched as thousands of Mexican migrants started to follow the identification procedure. After a few minutes of photos, the dignitaries moved on, letting the Customs and Border Protection officers get to work processing the thousands of Mexican citizens returning to their lives and jobs in the United States.

"It doesn't solve a damned thing, does it?" Mike Tesch asked over the command channel as he watched a televised image of the proceedings on his electronic visor. He and several other members of Task Force TALON were piloting Cybernetic Infantry Devices just a short distance away, out of range of the TV cameras but ready to respond in case of a terrorist incident during the ceremonies. "Those who want to sneak into the United States illegally will still do so; those who hire illegals will still do it; smugglers who help them sneak in will still help them. Stuff like the Nano-transponder Identification System just punishes the law-abiding persons."

"It doesn't punish anyone, Mike," Jennifer McCracken radioed back. "NIS is just a twenty-first-century ID card, that's all. ID cards aren't meant to solve anything." She paused, then added, "It's a start. There's still so much to discuss, still so much legislation to write, still so many compromises to make. But it's a start." Just then, there was a beep in her headset. "Go ahead, TALON," she replied.

"Condor has spotted a situation about seven hundred meters northeast of your position," Ariadna Vega, in the control center for the Condor unmanned aerial reconnaissance airship, which was orbiting over the border area during the ceremonies. "Might be a demonstration on a street corner—I see some garbage on fire and about twenty individuals. Move a few blocks from the target on the west side of Route Nine-Oh-Five and stand by to assist the sheriffs department if necessary."

"Copy, TALON," Jennifer responded, and she started running alongside Interstate 5 north to her staging area.

Something made Ariadna look up from her console in the Condor monitoring and control center at the Pecos East headquarters of Task Force TALON at Cannon Air Force Base in New Mexico. She turned and saw Jason Richter watching her. "How long have you been there, J?" she asked.

"A few."

No one said anything for a few long moments; then: "Looks like the ceremony is almost over," Ari said. "No problems. I'm having Jennifer check out a minor disturbance—she'll be backup for the San Diego County Sheriff's."

"Good work."

Silence again; then: "You got my resignation, didn't you?"

"You can't leave, Ari."

"The Justice Department already said they'd drop the false statement charges if I resign."

"Screw 'em. You can fight it. We'll back you up all the way."

"No, I can't, J. It was wrong what I did. I love the United States, and I love all the opportunities I have . . ."

"You've earned them, Ari, and more. A *lot* more."

". . . but I got them by lying and cheating. I've slapped the faces of millions that follow the law and immigrate to this country legally."

"That was over twenty years ago, Ari. You were a kid . . ."

"Doesn't matter," she said. "I love this country . . . but I'm not an American. I don't have any right to pretend I am. I'm no better than all those poor migrants who pay coyotes thousands of dollars to sneak them in. I don't deserve special treatment. I don't deserve to be here."

Her words bit into Jason's brain like a punch to the head hard enough to create a lump in his throat. "So what are you going to do?"

"What all those thousands of people are doing," Ariadna said, nodding toward her monitors. "My folks and I are going to cross the border back into Mexico, get at the back of that line, and go through the NIS registration process. Then we'll go home and wait for whatever the government is going to do with us."

"That means you'll be back here, doesn't it?"

Ariadna shook her head. "No, J. I've had enough of this. I chickened out on you and on TALON, Jason. I had a job to do when we started Operation Rampart, and I didn't do it, for nothing but my own selfish reasons."

"But we all know why you . . ."

"That makes it even more humiliating for me!" she cried. "I let you down, I let everyone down. It's horrible to think I could have even stopped all this by doing my job back when we started. I will never live it down. I will never forgive myself."

Jason fell silent, then stepped over to her and put his hands on her shoulders. "So what will you do?"

"I volunteered for a migrant outreach program being started in southern California," Ariadna said. "A private Hispanic group wants to encourage migrants to come out of the shadows and register with the NIS program, so they're setting up a service to bring them in, help them bring the proper ID, take them to the border, facilitate getting them registered, then drive them back home. Once that's done . . . I don't know. Maybe go into teaching. Cal State Northridge looks like a nice school—maybe I'll apply there, if the regents aren't too mad at me for busting the place up."

"You'd make a good teacher," Jason said. "But . . . I think you'd make a better security consultant."

"A what? Security consultant? Sounds bogus to me." She turned and looked quizzically at her longtime friend. "You're not talking about Kelsey DeLaine's consulting firm, are you?"

"I heard she handed in her resignation to the President."

"Her and me, in the same outfit? I think that would be hilarious if it wasn't so scary." Her eyes narrowed as she looked at him carefully, then asked, "*You're* not thinking seriously about joining her, are you, J?"

"I don't know," Jason admitted. "I'm already out of TALON as of today—Bruno made sure of that. I suppose I could go back to the Infantry Transformational BattleLab at Fort Polk; Army Special Operations Command wants to talk with me about using CIDs in special ops . . ." He shrugged. "But Kelsey's group will be right there in San Diego, and it'd mean big bucks. I might be promoted to lieutenant colonel someday, but it's unlikely I'll go any higher than that. Maybe I'll take her up on her offer—get started with the rest of my life now, while I'm young and hopefully not so stupid."

"Work for Kelsey DeLaine?" Ariadna turned back to her monitors. "Sounds like a plan, J," she said stonily.

"Or . . ."

"Or what?"

"Sergeant Major Jefferson told me that he's forming a training corps to give the National Guard some high-tech surveillance and infantry systems, leading up to integrating the Guard completely into the Homeland Security role and eventually merging them completely into the Department of Homeland Security." She half-turned to him. "This group is being set up at Los Alamitos Joint Reserve Forces Training Center, which I learned just happens to be . . ."

"A couple hours' drive from San Diego."

"True." He felt her shoulders slump, and he reached down and wrapped his arms around her. "But . . . it's just about a half hour from Cal State–Northridge, if the traffic's not too bad on the 405. Right?" He felt her entire body tense up, and he thought, You idiot, you just blew it—but moments later he felt her hands touch his, then she reached around and squeezed her arms tighter around him. "I'll stay in for my twenty and maybe shake things up a little bit in the National Guard. Sounds like fun, huh?"

"But what about . . . about you and Kelsey?"

"Ari, it's always been you, and only you," Jason Richter said. "But we worked together, *closely* together, and dating you or becoming your lover would've complicated everything—our careers, our lives, our relationship. I didn't want to risk losing you."

"But now . . . ?"

"Now . . . I realize that if I don't tell you how I feel, I'll *definitely* lose you," Jason said. "Besides, I suddenly find myself without a job and with my career and reputation pretty much down the crapper. I'm a good catch, huh?"

She laughed and pulled him closer. "I'm still going to go down and register, Jason," Ariadna said softly. "I think I owe it to . . . to all the ones who didn't make it across . . . you know, to do the right thing."

"Then I'll go and stand in line with you and your folks," Jason said. "It'll give me a chance to get to know them, no?"

Ariadna rose to her feet, embraced him, and gave him a long, deep kiss. He could feel her softly weeping in his shoulder as she held him closely.

"So, Dr. Vega," Jason asked, "does this mean that maybe I'm not the last man on earth anymore?" Another hot, passionate kiss gave him all the answers he needed.

UXO MANAGEMENT AREA, TWENTYNINE PALMS
MARINE CORPS DEPOT, CALIFORNIA
THAT SAME TIME

In a remote corner of the sprawling one-thousand-square-mile Marine Corps Air Ground Combat Center at Twentynine Palms Marine Depot in the Mojave Desert of southern California was a maze of hundreds of low concrete bunkers, surrounded by twenty-foot-high razor-wire chain-link fences, guard towers, lights, and K-9 patrol areas. Formerly a weapons storage area for nuclear weapons, the area had been converted for use as the Marine Corps' primary unexploded ordnance disposal site in the western United States. Using a sophisticated computer-coded tracking system, every bullet, shell, bomb, or explosive charge ever used by the United States Marine Corps since 1997 could be accurately tracked from creation to detonation. And if it wasn't used in training or on the battlefield, it ended up here: the UXO Management Area not only cataloged and tracked munitions and explosives, but also disposed of unused ordnance in an environmentally friendly manner.

The one-thousand-acre UXO Management Area was highly automated and needed only a very small staff to run it, mostly civilian contractors with a Marine first lieutenant or captain overseeing a company-sized cadre of administrative staff and guards. The civilians monitored the equipment and computers and provided support services such as facilities maintenance and prepared meals for the small Marine force.

But in one of the three hundred and seventy weapon storage bunkers scattered across the barren desert landscape was one bunker that had its own chain-link fence enclosure and its own guard post. Although all of the bunkers were air-conditioned to keep the explosives stored inside stable, a thermograph of this bunker would have showed it several degrees cooler than most of the rest. Inside, the bunker was divided in half by steel bars. On one side of the bars was a simple desk and storage cabinets for the guards posted outside . . .

. . . and on the other side of the bars was a stainless steel cot, bedstand, washbasin, and toilet. This was the secret prison cell for terrorist mastermind Colonel Yegor Zakharov, his holding cell set up for him while he awaited trial in federal court.

Zakharov's schedule since his arrest and detention at Twenty-nine Palms was pretty much the same every day: six guard shift changes per day, where the Marine guards would check in on him, then handcuff him and search his cell; and three meals per day. Once a week he was taken outside to a portable shower to bathe.

As a federal prisoner awaiting trial he was allowed to have law-books and documents, but they were closely cataloged and taken away from him at night. He was allowed no TV, no radio, no books.

The evening meal and shift change occurred at the same time, so the oncoming Marine guard and the contractors with the meal would arrive at the same time. While the contractors waited out-side in a pickup truck, the oncoming Marine guard would inven-tory and log in his weapons, ammo, and equipment in the bunker, receive the prisoner status briefing from the offgoing guard, check in with the security headquarters via radio to assume responsibil-ity for the post, take the keys and passcodes from the offgoing guard, and then the offgoing guard would formally relinquish his post and depart. The new guard would then handcuff the pris-oner, conduct a search of the cell and the prisoner, take away all of his books and papers and lock them in a cabinet, and then go out-side to get the meals for himself and the prisoner.

"Hold on, comma es-tay you-stead hot, Maria?" the Marine guard said in pidgeon Spanish as he walked over to the pickup truck. "Boners tarheels."

"It's '¿Cómo está usted hoy, Maria? and 'buonas noches,' Sergeant: 'good evening,' not 'good afternoon,' and your pronunciation is terrible as always," Maria Arevalo said with an amused smile. "When will you ever learn Spanish?"

"I said it the way it was *meant* to be said, Maria," the Marine ser-geant said with a smile. "C'mon in out of the heat."

"I must go."

"O-kay, darlin'," the Marine said. "I'll see you later. Ay-dos!" Maria rolled her eyes in mock frustration at the Marine's clumsy attempt at Spanish and headed back to her pickup truck.

The Marine reported by radio that the meals had arrived, the contractor was heading back to the admin area, and he was about to open the bunker door. He rang the outer buzzer, then looked through the viewfinder in the door to be sure the prisoner was up against the back wall as he was supposed to do whenever he heard the bell, punched in the code to unlock the door, and went inside with the meal. "Chow time," he said. He put the cardboard meal container on the small metal table, then turned to close the bunker door . . .

. . . and he never saw the baseball bat hit him on the side of his head.

Zakharov scrambled to the steel bars of his cell and looked on in astonishment as he saw the Marine guard hit the ground and a woman rush inside to check him. *"¡Usted es un ángel!"* he said happily. "I hope you brought explosives, my dear, because to use his key code to unlock this cell you have to call the security office first, so unless you can do a deep man's voice you will need a . . ."

"I wouldn't worry about any of that, Colonel Zakharov," a man's voice said in English—and U.S. Border Patrol agent Paul Purdy entered the bunker. He looked at Maria. "Is he okay?"

"He is unconscious." She checked his pupils. "No concussion— I think he will be okay. His head is bleeding but not badly."

"One lump on the noggin and maybe a slight career setback— a small price to pay to rid the world of you, Colonel," Purdy said casually. He walked to the cell, withdrew an automatic pistol, and began screwing a sound suppressor to the muzzle. "Remember me, Colonel?"

"Agent Paul Purdy. I remember now," Zakharov said. "You intend to kill me while I am locked in this cell? Is that how an American kills, Agent Purdy—from inside a robotic shell, or when his victim is behind bars?"

"I'll give you as much as you gave Victor Flores, Colonel—and you don't deserve none of it." Purdy dropped into a shooter's crouch, extended the gun, and aimed.

"I'll see you in hell, Agent Purdy."

"Don't wait up," Purdy said, and he fired a bullet into Zakharov's one remaining good eye. Blood, brains, and bone splattered across the far side of the cell, and the almost headless corpse hit the concrete floor with a sickening thud.

Purdy casually unscrewed the suppressor from his gun, turned, and looked into Maria's horrified face. "Sorry you had to see that, darlin'," he said.

Maria tore her eyes off the grisly scene in the cell, looked at the Border Patrol agent, then stood on her tiptoes and gave him a kiss on the corner of his mouth. "Victor would have wanted me to give you that," she said.

"Oh, I think Victor would have wanted you to give me a *lot* more'n that, darlin'."

"Stop it, you old letch. By the way—this means I will probably need a new job somewhere, Purdy."

"I told you, I got you covered," Purdy said. "I found a nice business for you up in Stockton, good schools for your kids—trust me, darlin'." He put an arm around her waist. "Now how about you and me head on over to the Joshua Tree Saloon and celebrate with a couple of tequilas? Then maybe take a drive out into the desert and celebrate the new spirit of peace and happiness between America and Mexico?"

"Shall I invite my husband to join us too, Purdy?" Maria asked with an alluring, mischievous smile on her face.

"Ouch. You did it to me again, darlin'—you went and mentioned the 'H' word," Purdy said, putting a hand on his heart as he escorted Maria out of the bunker. "You done broke my heart again."

ACKNOWLEDGMENTS

Thanks to my friends Gene and Alison Pretti for their generosity.

Special thanks always to my wife, Diane, and to my editor, Henry Ferris. Writing a novel on a difficult topic is never an easy task, but these two caring persons made the task much less challenging for me.